# REFINE

HOUSE OF OAK BOOK FOUR

## NICHOLE VAN

Fiorenza Publishing

Refine © 2015 by Nichole Van Valkenburgh
Cover design © Nichole Van Valkenburgh
Interior design © Nichole Van Valkenburgh

Published by Fiorenza Publishing
Print Edition v1.0

ISBN: 978-0-9916391-8-2

To Norma,
for loving all things Jane Austen-ish
and teaching me to do the same.

And to Dave,
for always supporting my late night pastry runs.
I love your enabling heart.

# Prologue

Timothy Linwood laughed.

Had he known it would be the last time he would laugh, he would have savored the moment more. Reveled in the joy bursting in his chest like so many champagne bubbles.

Instead, he merely cringed when his voice cracked between childish giggle and manly guffaw.

Such was life for a fourteen-year-old.

"Again, again, again!" His four-year-old sister, Marianne, jumped up and down, bouncing her dark curls. Pudgy hands clapping.

Smiling indulgently, Timothy placed the metal boat into a long basin of water set on the stone landing. He twisted the metal flywheel that was the ship's steering wheel, sending the boat churning through the water.

Marianne's high-pitched laughter rang down the curved stairs and across the garden. But, most disconcertingly, through the open french doors at Timothy's back.

"Hush, Marianne. You will wake Mama." He tried for stern, but a wide grin belied his words.

He darted a glance through the doors into the drawing room. Their mother was still asleep on the long chaise, an empty bottle of laudanum resting sideways on the small table beside her. She had already taken two full doses, though it was barely early afternoon.

"Again." Marianne nudged him and then giggled, stifling the sound behind her little hands.

It had all been worth it. The hours constructing the ship, secreting away the materials, working by candlelight, breaking at least twenty-one different rules . . . all to see Marianne's face wreathed in smiles, banishing that pinched, too-old look a child should never wear.

Fortunately, their father wouldn't return from London until next week. And, heaven knew, Mama probably wouldn't be conscious before then. A few more days of precious freedom.

He wound the boat. Marianne laughed, leaning forward with clasped hands, anticipation palpable. He released the mechanism and the toy sprang to life.

Her excited squeals filled the air before she caught herself, covering her mouth again. Timothy lounged back on his heels, smiling broadly. The merriment felt good. Lifting him from the inside out. Hydrogen in his veins, just like those newly-invented hot air balloons he had read about. Quicksilver.

But it was far too short-lived.

"What is this, boy?" A deep voice came from the doorway behind him, the sound skittering down Timothy's spine. The boat gave a final sputter, bobbing to a stop.

Timothy staggered to his feet and whirled around, unconsciously placing a protective hand on Marianne's tiny shoulders. And then looked up, up, up into his father's impassive gaze.

Lean and dark-haired, Charles, Viscount Linwood, still towered over his only son despite the inches Timothy had grown in recent months.

Lord Linwood tugged stiffly on his silver-threaded waistcoat, gaze moving side-to-side, taking in the listing boat, Marianne's wide expression, surely cataloging each of the twenty-one broken rules.

Silence.

Charles Linwood locked eyes with him. Timothy had no confusion as to what would happen next.

"Marianne, you will return to the nursery." Words said without taking his gaze from Timothy's face.

Marianne whimpered. Grimly, Timothy unclasped his sister's hands from his leg and gently pushed her toward the door. Her soulful eyes lifted to his, bottom lip trembling.

"All will be well, sister," he said. "Go now."

Without a glance at their father, she ran into the house.

Timothy studied his sire. As usual, his father's face was as expressive as granite. No trace of emotion flickered, anger or otherwise.

A textbook example of Rule #37: *A gentleman is always in control of himself and his situation.*

And its corollaries:

*Rule #23: A gentleman suppresses emotion, whether of disappointment, of mortification, of laughter, of anger, etc.*

*Rule #59: A gentleman never allows his thoughts to be evident upon his visage.*

"You will recite rules three hundred and three through three hundred and nine for me." His father clasped his hands behind his back. "Now, boy."

Timothy swallowed, forcing his face into an impassive mask, mimicking his father's expression. Took a deep breath. Recited.

*Rule #303: A gentleman does not engage in trade.*

*Rule #304: Mathematics should remain in a theoretical sphere.*

*Rule #305: A gentleman does not toil with his hands like a common laborer.*

*Rule #306: A gentleman does not indulge in the vulgarity of practical mathematics.*

*Rule #307: A gentleman does not manufacture machines, either with his own hands or with the help of others.*

*Rule #308: A gentleman does not design or use machines to bring a good to market.*

As Timothy recited, Charles Linwood walked to the stone balustrade overlooking the back gardens, rigid back to his son.

"You are my heir." His father did not turn around. Did not raise his voice. "Rule number three: At all times, a gentleman should maintain behavior and a demeanor which honors the illustrious heritage and sacrifices of his ancestors." His father straightened his shoulders. "To engage in trade is a disgrace to the family name. Your actions reflect on us all."

Eyes staring sightlessly ahead, Timothy absorbed each word as a blow. He knew. He *knew* how he should behave. It was spelled out. Literally.

"Why?" His father's words barely a question. "Despite all my endeavors to impress upon you the importance of your duty, why do you persist in this lowering pursuit?"

Timothy swallowed and then locked his spine.

"'Twas for Marianne's sake, sir. I wished to see my sister smile." It was, at least, a partial truth. "Rule number nine."

*A gentleman always cares for the needs of his family.*

His father turned back to him, mouth tensed, eyes narrowed the smallest bit. An eyebrow rose slowly upward.

For Charles Linwood, it was a catastrophic display of disappointment.

"That is a lie you tell yourself, boy." His voice deathly quiet. Cutting. "You made the toy because you wished to. Your sister was merely an excuse. The rules shall never be placed in contradiction with each other."

That was Rule #301.

"If you truly care for Marianne, you will tame this . . . *proclivity*," Charles Linwood continued. "If you sully the Linwood name with such low habits, you will damage her prospects. Would you allow this silly infatuation to be the cause of her ruin?"

Timothy's heart pounded. Machines were his very breath. Ideas constantly assaulted him, flitting through his brain, restless. Numbers, gears, springs, levers . . .

Even as his father continued to lecture, Timothy noted his father's shadow on the flagstones and, almost unwillingly, mentally triangulated the man's height, the numbers practically visible before his eyes.

"It grieves me greatly to see you thus," Charles was saying. "I will stamp out this stain. I will mold you into a man worthy to bear the title of Lord Linwood. Do you understand?"

*Rule #1: A gentleman will ensure that the next generation is raised in a manner worthy of the Linwood name.*

There was only one answer to such a question. "Yes, sir."

"Bring that here, boy." His father gestured toward the boat, bobbing on its side in the basin.

Dutifully, Timothy picked up the toy, its metal cold against his skin. It had taken him nearly six months of long nights and cut hands to build. An obsession which had distracted him while he memorized Latin declensions and deciphered Homer in ancient Greek.

Solemnly, he set it into his father's outstretched hand. Charles turned the toy around, studying the curved edges Timothy had carefully formed and filed down. Not a single emotion flickered across the man's impassive face.

Turning, he gestured for Timothy to follow him. With deliberate precision, Charles walked down the curving rear staircase, across the large flagstones, through an arch and onto the back lawn, stopping in front of a small reflecting pond. Once there, his father set the boat adrift in the pool of water. And then with studied casualness, the man pulled a pistol from his frock coat and handed the weapon to Timothy.

"Now, you will dispatch this monstrosity. You will take this action as a metaphor for yourself, blasting away this unworthy part of you." Charles gestured toward the toy.

Timothy swallowed, hard and fast. He would not cry. He never cried. He could do this. It was the barest minimum he had expected if caught.

Images flooded through him. Equations and metal . . . cause and effect . . . even the mechanics of the pistol he now held. As he aimed and then squeezed the trigger, his mind saw the chain of events. The flint descending, scraping along the metal frizzen, creating a spark which landed in the flashpan, igniting the primed gunpowder in a flash of sparks which traveled through the touchhole, lighting the main charge which sent the lead bullet flying from the barrel—

The boat disappeared in a shower of smoke and metal fragments, some sinking into the pond, others landing on the ground around him. Timothy bit his quivering lip, focusing on the pain, the taste of blood in his mouth.

*Rule #23: A gentleman suppresses emotion . . .*

A solitary gear—the boat's flywheel—rolled across the ground, coming to a stop against Timothy's boot. He stared as the steering wheel wobbled and toppled over. Which meant he didn't see his father's hand coming.

The blow snapped Timothy's head back, causing him to stagger. He was proud he didn't fall over. Or even flinch, for that matter. And his tears stayed firmly locked away.

Thank the heavens for small miracles.

His sire *had* taught him well.

"That blow is for breaking rule number twenty-nine." *A gentleman will refrain from all displays of levity.* "Remember, this is all for your own good, Timothy. I do not enjoy having to discipline you thus." *Rule #77: A gentleman takes no joy in the righteous administration of just punishment.* "In time, you will thank me for this day, for saving you from this baser part of your nature before it destroys everything you value, including your sister."

Timothy tracked his father's dark head as the man strode back to the house. For nearly the thousandth time, Timothy wondered *why?* Why had God seen fit to give him the gift of mathematics but then doom him to love mechanics as well?

He needed to give it up. For good. Pack it away. He would not risk Marianne. She was the brightest part of his life. With their mother constantly enveloped in an opium haze and their stern father distant and absent, she was all he had. He was all *she* had.

He would see to Marianne's future. Ensure her bright smile remained undimmed.

Timothy looked back down, eyes resting on the solitary gear which had landed near his boot, its spokes perfectly cut and filed. That piece alone had taken nearly two weeks to make.

What did the Bible say? *When I was a child, . . . I thought as a child: but when I became a man, I put away childish things . . .*

Yes.

He would become the man his father wanted.

In a sense, he was no more than that gear, lying on the ground. A cog in the machine of history. A mindless automaton who would preserve the Linwood heritage and honor.

He picked up the gear, slipping it into his coat pocket. This he would keep. A *souvenir*, to use the French word. A remembrance of everything he needed to stamp out of himself.

There was no other way.

# Chapter 1

Prince Charming. That was all Jasmine Fleury wanted.

A dashing man to gallop into her life with a delectable smile and a good knack for dragon-slaying . . . er . . . problem solving. Namely hers.

Was that too much to ask?

Apparently, yes. Yes, it was.

Particularly as every knight-in-shining-armor she had come across ended up being a jerk wrapped in tinfoil.

Exhibit A: Her current phone conversation.

"Can you please state your full name and place of birth?" Mike's gravelly voice filled her ears.

"You already know all of that, Mike. Or you did." Once upon a time.

Silence.

"Look, Jas, I don't want this to be any more difficult than it has to be. I'm trying to be a professional here."

More silence of the fraught variety.

Fine. She could do this. She could be calm and collected. Professional.

Jasmine's pen *tap, tap, tapped* as she blinked and swallowed. Let out a slow breath.

"How could you?!"

Okay, so maybe not so much with the calm and collected.

Or, quite frankly, the professional.

She heard a shuffle over the phone, something beeping off. And then a long sigh.

*Tap, tap, tap.*

Mike drew a deep breath. "Babe, we've been over this—"

"Two years, three months and five days. *That's* how much of my life I gave you."

"Jas—"

"I'm not ready, you said. Commitment just isn't my *style.*" She drawled the word just as he would. "But, oh no. Come to find out commitment is *totally* your style. Audrey is *totally* your style. Turns out it was just *me* who wasn't your style."

"C'mon, Jas, you gotta move on—"

"Move on?! As in *your* definition of move on? No, thank you. Did you even wait two weeks after we broke up to go out with her? And now you're engaged . . . after what? Three months of dating?"

"Calling you was a mistake. Audrey warned me."

Unconsciously, Jasmine moved her pen over the large pad of sticky notes in front of her, doodling, her throat tightening.

"We were good together." She sniffed, pen still drawing. Curlicues and calligraphic letters.

"What?! No, we weren't. We fought all the time. We were terrible . . . awful."

"We could have made it work. We just needed to try harder—"

"Jas, Jas, Jas."

She could practically see him shaking his head.

"If something is right, you don't have to *make* it work. Love isn't difficult. I know that now. Things with Audrey are effortless."

"But—"

"You can't fix everything and everyone. No matter how much you may want to."

Jasmine swallowed and wiped her wet cheeks with her free hand.

She didn't even bother trying to stem the tears. She had been known to cry over a diaper commercial. Ya know, the one where the baby crawled around with a puppy licking its face—seriously, you had to be heartless to *not* cry. But Mike hadn't even *sniffled* over it. How could she have missed the signs?

Stupid man. Stupid, stupid—

She made an emphatic swirl with her pen.

It's not like she wanted Mike back anyway. Not really.

They *were* awful together. Gah! The misunderstandings, the stone-walling . . . her tears, his *lack* of them.

It had just been the challenge of him. He had been so broken. Humpty-Dumpty to her King's Men.

She had been convinced she could put him together again. Mother him back to emotional health.

Classic Fixer-Upper Syndrome.

Why hadn't she seen the break-up coming?

Granted, most normal people couldn't see into the future. And it wasn't as if she had visions or anything.

But when her best friend, Emme Wilde, left to conduct research in Herefordshire, Jasmine had just *known* that Emme would bring a husband home with her.

It came to her as everything else did. A whispering sense pulsing through the ground beneath her feet. A rippling of the ocean of the universe. Jasmine could generally sense the life force of everyone to some degree. Others' lives lapped against her, wrapped around her, tugged her into the web of humanity. But with those close to her, like Emme, the sense extended from mere awareness to something akin to vision.

She had seen Emme's life circle reaching out to intertwine with another, slipping through the cracks of time itself.

And sure enough, Emme had shown up three months later with James Knight in tow. The two had been married for nearly three years now and had a darling five-month-old boy, Arthur.

Granted, there was the small matter of James having been born a nineteenth century aristocrat at nearby Haldon Manor. And that little something in the cellar of Duir Cottage which had made Emme and James' love match possible.

Emme's brother, Marc, had found his soulmate the same way, whisked away and returning with Kit at his side. Jasmine had attended his wedding to Kit Ashton over the holidays and, as Kit had walked up the aisle to Marc, both looking so radiant and happy, Jasmine had felt the relentless destiny of the moment. The tendrils of life twirling around them, as if Marc and Kit being together had been decreed eons before.

Why could she never see the course of her own life so clearly?

Despite their differences, Jasmine had really thought Mike was The One.

Wow. Had she been wrong.

So here she was. Thirty-two years old and starting all over . . . trying to meet guys, being set up on blind dates, her life full of all sorts of junior-high-like awkwardness.

Her own happily-ever-after just as far out of reach.

And no sense that it would ever happen—

"Uh, Jasmine. I really don't need to hear this—"

"What?"

"You're doing that ranting thing of yours. Ya know, where you talk out your internal monologue. Humpty-Dumpty? Really? And what is this about lives intertwined and James being a nineteenth century aristocrat?"

Wait—no! She had been *thinking* that, not talking . . .

"Nope. You were talking. I got all of it . . . And for the record, I don't think I was ever The One . . ."

Jasmine groaned, feeling the tell-tale burn on her cheeks.

Why did mortification have to actually *hurt?* And when would she ever learn—

"Still talking, babe."

*Argh!*

"I'm so sorry, Mike. You know how I am—"

"Trust me. I do. Still working on those filters, eh?"

He had no idea.

Jasmine set down her pen and purposefully pinched her lips, holding them between her fingers.

Her grandma, Marmi, had made Jasmine do that as a child when Jasmine couldn't seem to separate her thoughts from her voice. She had gradually outgrown the bad habit, but stressful situations brought it roaring back.

And given how everything had gone down with Mike . . . Jasmine had not been her best self in recent months.

In fact, it had been Emme who had suggested her current stay in Duir Cottage. After 'The Break-up,' Jasmine had wanted to get as far away from Mike as possible. Bless Emme's sweet heart. She knew that when bad things happened, Jasmine needed space. A getaway. The quaint cottage that James owned in rural Herefordshire had called to her.

The house always had, though this was her first time visiting. English-countryside picturesque with a gabled roof and honey-stone half covered in wisteria, the cottage pulsed with energy. The building had sighed in welcome when she arrived, the sinuous oak branches carved into the front door mimicked the swirling strands of energy she sensed encircling the cottage. As if the time portal thrumming in the cellar imbued the structure with a palpable energy, a rippling circle of awareness that felt nearly sentient.

Tendrils wrapping through and around each soul . . . drawing lives together.

Still holding her lips, Jasmine glanced up from her drawing and looked at the open-concept kitchen/dining/sitting room. Age-darkened beams cut across the white-washed ceiling, lit in sharp relief by a bank of paned windows to the right. The marble countertop was cool under her hand, the stainless steel appliances a quiet hum. She looked down the room toward the looming fireplace at the opposite end, so tall she could practically stand up in it. Though at only five foot two, she was short enough to stand upright inside most things.

Between the kitchen island and the fireplace, there was an expanse of rough-hewn dining table, overstuffed sofa and matching wingback chairs. All cluttered with dirty dishes, doodled sticky notes, graphite pencils, books, unfolded laundry, the remains of takeaway tikka masala and a bag of vintage clothing finds from Oxfam in Hereford.

Yeah. It was probably time to straighten up. Funny. She had no problem tolerating physical messiness.

But emotional upheaval? Not so much.

She knew what she needed to do. Man up. Put on her big-girl pants. Let the situation with Mike go.

She looked down at her sticky pad and then froze, studying what she had written.

*Wow.* Talk about karma. Just when she needed it most, the universe sent her a sign.

Bless the universe. It was always doing things like this.

The words drawn in scrolling calligraphy, surrounded by paisley swirls—

*Trust the process.*

Marmi's voice drifted through her mind. A fleeting whiff of lavender. The hushed sense of a hand touching her hair.

And then it was gone.

Jasmine took in a deep breath, sending up silent thanks for the small gift, eyes pooling again.

"Jas? You still there?"

Yeah.

Wait . . . lips!

"Yeah," she said breathlessly, wiggling her mouth to bring feeling back.

Mike cleared his throat. "Look, if this is too hard, I can try to find another way." She could hear the pleading in his voice. He *really* didn't want to find another way. "But we started down this path a year ago, and my dissertation committee is excited about the research. They're already talking publication. Our personal history aside, this research is fascinating. Would you be willing to give it a try? Please?"

He knew right where to strike. Knew she couldn't resist the plea for help. She was *such* a bleeding heart.

*Trust the process.*

She still stared at the words. Could she? Like exercise and teeth flossing, *knowing* you needed to do something didn't automatically make it happen.

Deep breath. More wiping of her face.

*Whew.* Still not talking out loud.

See. Progress.

They were over and done. Jasmine and Mike . . . never to be. She wasn't getting him back. Didn't really want him back.

It was going to be okay. She could do this again. Meet someone, move through the initial awkwardness, build a relationship, find that right man who wanted to build a life together.

*Trust the process.*

With a determined lift of her chin, she picked up the sticky note and strode around to the fridge, slapping the paper onto its surface, right next to another sticky note which read:

*Crying over a guy? Pick your head up, Princess. Your tiara is slipping.*

Exactly.

Positive thinking. Karma. Let the universe bring back to her what she gave to it.

Mike had dumped her, but she could be gracious. Forgiving. Kind.

"Sure," she heard herself say around the lump in her throat. One more sniffle. "You're right. I want to know too."

"Good." His relief was palpable even through the long distance connection. She heard a shuffle and another beep. "Okay, I have the recorder turned back on. I am just documenting this for research reference. Could you clearly state your name and place of birth?"

Right. Clinical. Professional. Just the facts, ma'am.

"Jasmine Aurelie Fleury. Born in Boston, Massachusetts on June 21, 1983."

"Thank you. Could you tell me a little about your family?"

Jas took in a steadying breath. "Sure. My parents were John and Aurelie Fleury. I am—or was, I suppose—the youngest of three children—"

"You use past tense. What happened?"

She closed her eyes. Mike knew all of this, of course. But for the research . . .

"My family was killed in a car accident in January of 1990 just outside Gainesville, Florida, when I was seven-years-old. We were living in Florida at the time and had just spent the day at Disney World. It was one of those foggy nights and forty-three cars plowed into each other. I was thrown from the vehicle. An oil tanker overturned and spilled its load and then somehow ignited. The rest of my family was trapped in our car." Her mother and father, two older sisters. "Twenty-seven other people died in the crash, but I survived with just cuts and bruises. It was one of the worst accidents in Florida history."

Vague memories of that night surfaced.

Sensing the horror lying up the road, the world itself rippling with *significance.*

*"Stop! You've got to stop!" Fumbling for the door handle.*

*Falling. Fire flaring. Figures coming at her through the mist. Screaming. Endless screaming.*

"And then after that?" Mike prompted.

"Uh . . . Marmi—my paternal grandmother—flew out from Seattle and took me home. She raised me until her death when I was fifteen. After that, I lived with my aunt, Rita—" And then an uncle and then a newlywed cousin in a hippie commune and then back to Rita. No one had wanted her for long. Everyone too busy with their lives to worry overmuch about an orphaned niece, but why go into it? "—until I turned eighteen and came into the inheritance Marmi left me. I've been on my own ever since."

And wasn't that the truth? Always alone. Marmi had been the closest thing she had ever known to *home.*

Unconsciously, she reached for the pendant around her neck, fingers tracing the intricate Celtic design. A dara knot nestled inside a quatrefoil shield knot.

The gold pendant had been a gift from Marmi when she was very small—a charm of protection, strength and wisdom. Her grandmother's legacy to her—that and a small trust fund.

Marmi's estate had been divided equally between her four children at her death. As the only living survivor of Marmi's middle son, Jasmine had inherited her father's portion. The amount wasn't mind-boggling, but it was enough to supplement Jasmine's meager earnings as an artist.

"Thank you for that information." Mike was in the zone. Totally professional. "To the best of your knowledge, what is your family's history?"

"My grandparents immigrated from France in the 1950s. That's my mother's family. My father's family is more of typical American mongrel mix, despite our French surname . . . a dash of Irish, some English. I am not sure when they came to the United States."

"Excellent. As you know, we have found your genetics to be unusual, and we appreciate your help with this research." *Blah, blah, blah.*

As a Ph.D. candidate in Genome Sciences at the University of Washington, Mike had initially drawn her blood for a sequencing class, just intending to use her genome for practice, isolating her genetic haplogroups. Neither of them had expected to find anything interesting.

But he had hit pay dirt. Despite her apparently varied, typically-American background, Jasmine's DNA had pulled up some unusual results. She had unique genetic markers tied to the Breton people of northwest France. In fact, the entirety of her genome had baffled Mike and his adviser, getting everyone on-board to study her family for his dissertation.

Though they were still researching her mother's ancestry, it seemed like she did have some Breton heritage. But what were the chances her bloodline had been passed down that cleanly?

Mike was still talking. "You belong to a Breton haplogroup that is rarely seen outside of Bretagne. Less than fifteen percent of modern Bretons carry this gene, and it's the only place it's found in the entire world. For my research, I want to understand how these specific genes have remained so pure within your family tree. We have taken blood samples from twelve of your other relatives, mostly aunts and uncles.

My goal has been to use all of your genetics together to get a clearer snapshot of your history."

They had been through all of this months ago. Jasmine had watched Mike personally swab the cheeks of her family members over Thanksgiving. Things had been rough with her family in recent years, and Jasmine felt the distance keenly. Like they didn't have time for her or each other. But everyone had been really enthusiastic about the testing. Super supportive, actually. It had been nice to see her uncles joking about the cheek swabs. Hopefully, this whole testing thing would bring everyone back together.

She had been waiting to hear the results.

Mike had gone silent. Had she missed something?

"Jasmine, did you hear me? I said, we've hit a snag."

"A snag?"

"Yeah. I'm not sure how to explain this, but I've run all of the tests twice just to verify everything. The results have been the same each time."

Jasmine's heart started to pound.

"Your results consistently give the same unique Breton markers. But your family shows the expected mixture of haplogroups common among northern European immigrant families without any trace of Breton heritage."

"Excuse me?" she choked.

"Look, Jasmine, I'm really sorry. But there's no easy way to say this."

Mike paused. And then let the bomb drop—

"You're not related to your family."

# Chapter 2

Lord Linwood's study
Linwood House
London, England
March 8, 1815

"Pardon me?" Timothy, Viscount Linwood, turned his head away from the rain drip, drip, dripping down the window to stare at the man standing behind him. "I could not *possibly* have heard you correctly just now."

Daniel Ashton, his new Man of Affairs, cleared his throat and repeated himself. "You are on the verge of bankruptcy, my lord."

Timothy blinked. Opened his mouth and then shut it again. Frowned. Impossible.

It was simply . . . unfathomable.

Timothy took three measured steps over to the bookcase to his right, using the movement to force his racing heart to slow. Reaching out, he adjusted a book, ensuring it was perfectly aligned with its brethren. His hand shook.

That was . . . not good.

He tried to swallow, but his neckcloth was suddenly too tight. Nigh upon strangling, really.

Where had all the air in the room gone?

He turned back to Daniel. The young man stood motionless on the other side of Timothy's enormous oak desk, two ledgers and a stack of papers in his arms.

The tall case clock in the corner ticked emphatically. Rain drummed against the window. The sound of London traffic drifted into the room, muted but ever present.

Timothy finally managed to swallow, the sound painfully audible.

"How?" His voice more of a growl.

Daniel instantly took a step back, eyes flaring.

Timothy caught a glimpse of himself in the mirror above the fireplace mantle: dark hair, gray eyes, stern face . . . all normal.

But the emotion . . . eyebrows drawn down, lips curled in a snarl, forehead wrinkled.

*Rule #37: A gentleman is always in control of himself and his situation.*

Even if the world came tumbling down around his ears.

Case in point.

Emotions were pointless, useless things. They merely clouded judgment.

Timothy lowered his head and took in a slow, measured breath . . . ran a hand over his coat pockets, feeling the familiar shape of his talisman gear tucked inside. Tugged down the sleeves of his coat. Patted his waistcoat. Ensuring all was neat and precise.

*Rule #23: A gentleman suppresses undue emotion, whether of disappointment, of mortification, of laughter, of anger, etc.*

He was a fortress. Impenetrable.

*Rule #6: A gentleman will always act with honor and courage, even when faced with a daunting situation.*

Contained. Feeling nothing.

*Rule #4: A gentleman's primary duty is to see to the health and care of his family.*

A machine. A cog in the enormous ship of history, as the subtle weight of the gear in his pocket ever reminded him. He would overcome this setback. History demanded no less.

*Rule #21: A gentleman of solid worth is reticent.*

His heart stopped its frantic beating. His throat relaxed.

Done. Mask back in place.

He raised his head. Daniel was only the messenger. The man was not the problem. Anger and frustration would not provide a solution. They would only make the situation messy and uncomfortable.

"Please be seated, Mr. Ashton." Timothy gestured toward the chair in front of his desk, hand steady now. "I would hear how you arrived at this conclusion."

Timothy took a seat behind the desk, as Daniel spread out some papers and then retreated to a chair, sitting down. Timothy dragged the papers to him, aligning them together. The familiar columns and rows of figures neatly summed calmed him. Numbers, calculations . . . mathematics.

Coolly rational and objective at all times.

Just like himself.

"The pages on your left are Mr. Brown's numbers, organized by year, starting in 1801." Daniel gestured, indicating his predecessor's work. "The pages on the right are my own calculations of those same years."

Timothy looked over the numbers, quickly adding the long columns in his head. The discrepancy was immediately obvious.

Someone had been methodically skimming profits from the estate. Mr. Brown's numbers showed a healthy estate. Daniel's numbers told a different story. He was, indeed, on the brink of bankruptcy.

Timothy lifted his head, a question mark clearly showing on his face.

"Mr. Brown skillfully embezzled from the Linwood estate over a period of fifteen years, starting with your late father."

Timothy nodded carefully. A rogue blast of anger punched through his defenses.

*Rule #19: A gentleman never loses his temper.*

He straightened the papers again. Lifted a minuscule bit of fluff off the desktop.

*Rule #104: Cleanliness is next to Godliness.*

It was not quite enough.

Timothy raised his head and studied the room, pondering the soothing symmetry of the study in his London townhouse. An homage to Classical aesthetics with its marble, pedimented door frames, coffered ceiling and herringbone wood floor. Everything washed in colors of white and soft green, excepting the dark bookcases lining the walls.

A space that exemplified his refined world.

The room hung with blue gloom, rain still pattering against the matching floor-to-ceiling windows with their wide panes of glass.

One more breath. Another comforting touch of the gear in his pocket.

Everything shut back away.

"My father trusted Mr. Brown implicitly." His voice calm. Steady. Even if it did sound like it was coming from far away. "He appeared to be the very epitome of a respected, upright steward and handled the reins of the viscountcy with aplomb and dignity for well over two decades. There was never a need to check his numbers. Besides which, the vast holdings of my estates would have made such an endeavor impractical given the time I dedicate to my position in the House of Lords—"

Timothy stopped mid-sentence.

Babbling. He was babbling.

He locked eyes with Daniel. Despised himself even more for what he saw there.

Pity. Daniel's soft blue eyes exuded sympathy . . .

*Rule #51: A gentleman is never an object of pity.*

"I am terribly sorry to be the bearer of such bad news, my lord." Daniel spoke carefully. Laying the words down tentatively, as if they were fragile things Timothy might tear apart.

Wise man.

*Rule #68: A gentleman never takes out his frustrations on a servant.*

Three weeks ago, Timothy had called the young man to London, promoting him from being merely the steward of Kinningsley, his seat in Herefordshire, to managing all of his estates and holdings. Daniel had proved his worth over and over during the past year, becoming one of Timothy's most trusted advisers despite being nearly a decade younger than Timothy's own thirty-three years. In fact, Daniel had been instrumental in resolving a delicate situation regarding some missing documents and a French covert agent. Daniels' sister, Miss Katharine Ashton, had disappeared with that scoundrel Marcus Wilde, but Daniel had remained behind.

Fortunately, as here Daniel was again . . . saving him.

"Mr. Brown was skilled in his deception. The best charlatans always are," Daniel continued. "It appears the money was going toward gambling debts and other unsavory activities. In speaking with his widow, his finances are in disarray. There is nothing to be recovered."

Again, Timothy's throat tightened. His stomach clenched. He lurched from his chair, banging a knee into the desktop and scrambling papers in the process. Even worse, he didn't pause to straighten everything as he walked over to the window.

*Rule #5: A gentleman will ensure that all estates and properties, real or otherwise, are passed on to the next generation in better condition than he received them.*

He stared sightlessly out over the dripping landscape, the small back garden hinting at the green of spring. Servants moving in and out of the mews behind the house. His coachman clicking Timothy's town carriage into motion, pulling it around to the street.

What was to be done? How was this battle to be fought?

Before he could respond, the door to his study burst open in a flurry of activity.

"Brother." Marianne greeted him with a smile as she breezed into the room.

As usual, his sister was the only bright spot in his day. She was safely and happily married to Arthur Knight, a wealthy gentleman who owned Haldon Manor, a grand estate near to Kinningsley in Herefordshire. Timothy's financial woes would not affect her, thank goodness.

Her warm smile lit up the room as she strode over to him at the window and kissed his cheek. In her arms, she held her little daughter, Isabel. The child's nurse stood discreetly in the doorway.

"We have come to say our quick goodbyes." Marianne offered an apologetic smile to Daniel. "Arthur waits for us in the carriage. We are off to Lady Rutland's country party."

Marianne, Arthur and their toddler, Isabel, had been living with Timothy for the past year while planning to rebuild their own home, Haldon Manor, which had been destroyed by fire. They had come with Timothy to London in February, amusing themselves in town while Timothy saw to his duties in the House of Lords. Though Marianne and Isabel would be gone only five days visiting Lady Rutland, Timothy would feel their absence keenly. He always did.

Isabel regarded Timothy with her huge gray eyes, dark hair falling across her forehead. Looking so much like Marianne at the same age. It was no wonder he loved her to distraction.

*Rule #4: A gentleman's primary duty is to see to the health and care of his family.*

Timothy nodded in greeting and then took Isabel from his sister's arms, her plump body warm and soft.

As usual, he had no idea what to do with his small niece. His instinct was to hug her close, let her know that he would always care for her. But he had learned long ago that instincts of this sort were to be ignored.

*Rule #42: A gentleman refrains from overt displays of affection.*

"Go on," Marianne urged with a laugh. "You can kiss her. She will not bite. At least, she seems to have put that particular phase behind her."

Surely a kiss did not qualify as an overt display of affection.

Swallowing, Timothy forced his arms to relax, to hold Isabel a little closer. He planted a sober kiss on her forehead.

And that was all he was allowed.

"Down." Isabel instantly twisted in his arms.

At fifteen months, his niece was a bundle of constant energy. She had recently learned how to run and practiced her new-found skill at every possible moment.

"Downdowndowndown," she repeated, squirming.

Marianne shook her head, still smiling. "You are an incorrigible little love. Off you go. Nurse will see you safe."

Timothy dutifully set Isabel onto her sturdy feet and watched as she giggled gleefully, running across the room to the arms of her nurse in the doorway.

Marianne popped on her tiptoes and planted another kiss on his cheek. "Take care, Timothy. We shall return before you know it. Try not to mope."

Flashing a wry grin, she was gone. Moments later, her departing carriage sounded outside.

Taking vital warmth and life with her.

The case clock chimed the quarter hour.

The townhouse felt like a mausoleum. Haunted by his ancestor's expectations and devoid of his sister's life-affirming presence.

And now this final blow with his finances . . .

"Shall we continue, my lord?" Daniel tentatively gestured toward the ledgers he held.

"Of course," Timothy nodded, remaining standing. "I will retrench. Make economies and concessions."

"This is beyond mere retrenchment, my lord. This is the white flag of surrender. Your current financial obligations far outstrip your income. Even with the strictest economy, the two numbers will not meet. Your holdings are too agrarian—"

"The Viscounts Linwood have ever relied upon the land for their income. Anything else is beneath our dignity—"

"Perhaps, my lord. But many lords speculate in industry with great success. The world has changed in the last thirty years and will continue to change—"

"We, however, do not change, Mr. Ashton. Anything that stinks of trade is anathema to the Linwood name."

"With all due respect, my lord, Napoleon has recently escaped from Elba and is again on the march. England will most likely face difficult economic times in the near future. I do not know that you have the luxury—"

"As a lord of the peerage, my life is not my own, Mr. Ashton. The entire point of my existence is to maintain the honor and respectability of our family name. To ensure that my title and heritage pass on, untainted and intact, to the next generation. It is my life's purpose. I will not see the family honor polluted." They were his father's words, but true nonetheless. Timothy held up a staying hand as Daniel opened his mouth in protest. "That is all I will say on the subject."

Silence.

Timothy's fingers drummed against his thigh. And then he consciously forced them to still, spreading them flat against his leg.

Daniel cleared his throat and stood, placing the stack of ledgers he held on the desk.

"Perhaps we could review your current expenditures, my lord, and find a way to buy you a little more time."

"Proceed." Timothy gestured toward the ledgers.

Daniel opened one to a page of tallied numbers.

"I fear, my lord, that you will need to make some difficult decisions. In reviewing your expenses, it appears that you pay £300 per annum to a Mrs. Drake of Manchester—"

"Yes, yes." Timothy waved a dismissive hand. "My father's youngest sister, Margaret. Her husband drank himself into the grave, leaving her destitute. My stipend ensures a roof over her head."

"And the large sum of £2000 paid to Mr. Frederick Linwood?"

"My cousin . . . a commission in the Ninth Light Dragoons. Frederick wishes to marry, and the officer salary ensures him of an income."

"And Lady Farrest? You have sent her £25 each month for the last seven years. Such expenses—"

"—ensure that Lady Farrest can pay for the care of her invalid daughter. I fail to see the point of all these questions, Mr. Ashton. As Lord Linwood, I am the *paterfamilias*." *Rule #63: The* paterfamilias *must see to the care and comfort of all family members who cannot or are unable to care for themselves.* "If a widowed great-aunt needs a roof repaired, I see that it is done. If a maiden cousin wishes to wed and her father is deceased, her suitor comes to me for permission. The financial health of the Linwood viscountcy stretches far beyond my mere comfort. It impacts the lives of my extended family, as well as the thousands of tenants who rely upon my land for their sustenance. In short, a solution to this crisis must be found. And found soon."

Timothy's fingers were twitching to drum against his thigh.

*Rule #91: A gentleman never fidgets.*

To control the impulse, he retrieved the gear from his coat pocket, clenching it tightly in his fist, the spokes cutting into his skin. He focused on the pain.

But Timothy knew the solution. It stared him baldly in the face. He just didn't want to acknowledge it. Even as Daniel said the words:

"Well then, my lord, you have no choice. You will have to marry an heiress. The sooner, the better."

Timothy turned back to the window. "Heiresses within the aristocracy are few and far between. Is there even a good candidate?"

"Not . . . precisely, my lord. Your financial needs are large . . ."

"Meaning?"

"You will most likely need to look beyond the peerage for your bride."

Timothy turned back to stare out the window, barely repressing a shudder.

"Are you suggesting I marry a woman whose family is in . . . *trade?*" He said the word scathingly. As if it were a filthy, infectious thing. "How is marrying into trade any better than participating in it myself? That is hardly a solution, Mr. Ashton—"

"Of course, I am not recommending such a course, my lord." Daniel held out a placating hand. "I am merely pointing out the reality of your situation. There is one candidate who is perhaps acceptable—Miss Arabella Heartstone."

Timothy paused, half turned his body back to Daniel. Slowly nodded his head.

"I have heard of Miss Heartstone. She was a topic of conversation at White's yesterday afternoon. They say she is pretty, and her connections are not entirely unsuitable—"

"Indeed not, my lord. She is the great-granddaughter of an earl, and her mother is a cousin to Sir Henry Stylles, your neighbor in Herefordshire. Her father was a respected banker—so not the lowest levels of trade—and all his assets were sold upon his death, leaving the bulk of his wealth to his only child, Miss Heartstone. His widow was quite put out, apparently, as I believe she wanted the money for herself."

"And the girl's dowry?"

"Sixty thousand pounds, all in the five percents."

"Pardon? How much did you say?" Voice hoarse. "*Surely* I did not hear that right."

"Sixty thousand pounds. It is the largest dowry of any genteel unmarried lady in England. Enough to solve your financial woes."

Timothy fought to catch his breath. The sum was . . . staggering.

Daniel gave an amused grin. "Though as you might imagine, with such a spectacular carrot dangling in front of her, Miss Heartstone is the catch of this Season. They say her mother will settle for nothing less than a duchess' crown for her daughter."

A pause.

"You will need to woo her, my lord. The mother too. Convince them both that settling for a handsome, charming viscount will be sufficient. It will not be an easy task."

Timothy stared out the window.

In his mind's eye, he built a scale. A fulcrum with balancing weights on either side. On the right, he placed his heritage, his responsibilities . . . his familial duty.

On the left, he placed Miss Heartstone and her sixty thousand pounds.

There was no contest. A solution to his problem had been found. He merely needed to enact it.

"Shall I open a dialogue with the girl's uncle and guardian?" Daniel's voice quiet behind him.

Timothy half-turned his head. There was only one answer. "Yes. See it done."

Timothy gripped the gear more tightly. Had it drawn blood yet?

And wasn't that the perfect metaphor for his current life? A hand dripping with blood shed to save the family.

Cut by the cog that he was.

# Chapter 3

I still can't believe you're trying to make a go of this whole painting thing. Shouldn't you have a grown-up job by now?"

Jasmine rolled her eyes at her aunt Rita's statement. Mostly because she was on the phone, and Rita couldn't see her face.

Some things . . . some *people* never changed.

*This* was why it had taken her four days to call Rita. After her conversation with Mike, she needed answers.

Now if Rita could only be pleasant . . .

Jasmine slouched into the couch, staring at the fire roaring in the enormous hearth. English rain pitter-pattered against the windows.

She sighed and then said, "Despite what you may think, Rita, my painting pays the bills—"

"I thought Marmi's *trust fund* paid your bills."

Well, that too.

Jasmine worked as an illustrator and painter. Freelance graphic design jobs and her small inheritance from Marmi made ends meet, but old-fashioned oil painting was her first love.

Pity there was no money in it.

Or rather, there *was* money in it. You just had to be willing to part with your art.

But, for Jasmine, selling a painting felt like bartering away a child. And who would do that? How could she sell such a vital part of herself?

Though trust Rita to instantly twist the conversation to money-matters.

"I have been doing better with the painting, Rita," Jasmine said. "My job in Herefordshire right now is a private commission piece—"

"I thought you were just wanting to escape after your boyfriend dumped you, and some old friend invited you to paint their baby's bedroom?"

Okay, so that was (sort of) technically true. But trust Rita to make it sound so . . . unglamorous.

Jasmine preferred to think of it as 'enjoying a personal journey of self-healing while creating a privately commissioned piece of art for an estate in rural England.'

See? That sounded much better.

Why did Rita always have to be such a glass-half-empty kill-joy? And how could Marmi have had a daughter so fundamentally different from herself?

Jasmine stopped, her throat choking.

Marmi who, turns out, was her grandmother in name only. Because, according to Mike's oh-so-meticulous research, they didn't share a drop of genetic blood.

"I'm not sure how painting rainbows and puppy dogs on some kid's wall makes you an artist," Rita continued.

Yep. Total kill-joy.

"Rita,"—deep breath—"this project is hardly just tacky illustration. It's a highly-artistic, Pre-Raphaelite inspired homage to King Arthur. Like those Victorian paintings of knights and ladies Marmi loved."

A pause.

"Why would you paint something like that in a baby's bedroom?"

"The baby's name is Arthur James *Knight*. What else could I paint?"

Rita's dismissive snort summed up her opinion.

*This* was why she hated chatting with Rita. Her aunt had a talent for drama-creation. Rita could fabricate it out of absolutely nothing.

The painting *did* make perfect sense. Arthur was a traditional Knight family name—James' brother and grandfather being Arthurs among others. How could she *not* paint scenes of Camelot for his nursery? A mural of ladies and knights talking and flirting against a backdrop of the city.

Emme and James had thought the idea was brilliant and had been particularly excited for Jasmine to incorporate actual landscape elements from Wales, one of the possible locations for Camelot.

She had just hit one teeny, tiny snag.

None of the sites she needed to visit were on a train or bus route. Which meant getting behind the wheel of an automobile. A wheel which sat on the British right, not the American left, side of the car.

James' shiny BMW, in fact, parked in the old stables behind the house.

But seriously. She was an average driver, at best. When at home. On the right side of the road. In her well-worn Volkswagen.

But you take the opposite of all of those things . . .

And she already mentioned the shiny BMW part, right? All that shine so very scratchable.

Jasmine had been relying on buses and Emme's bicycle to fetch groceries. But at some point—

"Well, I can't even imagine how ashamed I would be if *my* own daughter didn't have a real job at your age," Rita said.

Man, it was comments like that which explained why it had taken Jasmine so long to get up the courage to call her aunt . . . ehr, ex-aunt? Psuedo-aunt? Psycho-aunt?

Why did Rita have to be Jasmine's best source of family information?

"Have you heard Breanne's latest news?" Rita asked.

Of course . . . perfect cousin Breanne. Jasmine vaguely registered words like *made a partner* and *new house* and then she tuned out, letting Rita ramble on.

Jasmine shivered and reached for a velvet blanket, pulling it over her. The fire was warm enough but didn't quite compensate for the loose summery blouse and high-waisted culottes she wore. Classically vintage and comfortable (both characteristics Jasmine valued in clothing), the outfit also offered much-needed comfort, a closeness with her past.

Jasmine looked at the photo she held in her hand.

Marmi in the same loose blouse and culottes, gray hair a mass of shoulder-length curls with sunglasses sitting on top. Jasmine could practically smell the scent of lavender that always clung to Marmi.

Young Jasmine held Marmi's hand tightly, dark hair long and wild, dressed in scruffy blue jeans and a pink *Little Mermaid* t-shirt.

Man, she had loved that shirt. Loved it literally to pieces.

Jasmine hadn't changed that much over the years. Hair still dark, long and unmanageable. Eyes the same shocking blue. Though now a bit taller, she retained that child-like, elfin look. A woman perpetually trapped in a teenage body. Everyone assumed she was at least a full decade younger than she was.

Make that fifteen years. What had that woman at Oxfam asked?

*Does your mother know where you are?*

Ironic. Just so very, very, very ironic, all things considered.

She touched a finger to her younger self in the photograph, tracing her small body. Young Jasmine wore that same pendant—a Celtic knot nestled inside a quatrefoil—around her neck on a leather cord. When had Marmi given it to her? She tried to remember, but nothing came. Marmi worked as a shrink by day, but her first and lasting love had always been mysticism. Hence all the talismans and rituals and stuff.

She traced the glowing happiness on her childhood face.

Those had been good years with Marmi. Despite having lost her family, her grandmother had ensured that Jasmine never lacked for love. For that sense of home.

Had they all been duped? Had Marmi known?

And how do you casually ask your aunt if she really is your aunt?

There was only one way . . .

When Rita came up for air from her Breanne-tastic monologuing, Jasmine jumped in.

"So, Rita, remember how Mike took those cheek swab samples over Thanksgiving?"

Rita gave a non-committal grunt.

"Uhmm, the results came back . . ." Jasmine's voice trailed off.

"And let me guess—you're not related to us?" Rita registered a complete lack of surprise.

Well . . . didn't that explain a lot.

Silence.

Jasmine couldn't speak. She swallowed. Once, twice . . . and then gave up. She just moved the photograph away from the tears dripping off her cheeks.

"Look, Jasmine, I've wondered for a long time." A long-suffering sigh. "Why do you think we all went along so easily with the testing?"

*Ouch.*

"So . . . so was I adopted? Like . . . how did this . . . happen?"

"We think it was the accident. The one in Florida."

"The accident? How could that—"

"We got word John's family had been killed, and Mom freaked out. She just lost it and hopped on the first plane to Florida alone. She went to the hospital, hoping maybe one of her grandchildren had survived and found you. She insisted you were her little Jasmine, and the authorities released you into her care. I guess no one else came forward to claim you. The accident scene was such a mess. Forensics couldn't clearly identify which car you had been in.

"You looked like Jasmine, I suppose. But because John lived in Florida and we were in Seattle, none of us had seen the family in years. Except Marmi, of course. She visited at least once a year, so we just agreed with her when she claimed you were Jasmine. But there were differences too."

"Like what?" Jasmine whispered.

"You definitely were close in looks and age to our Jasmine, though no one remembered you being so tiny. And then there were your eyes. In the photos we *did* have of the real Jasmine, her eyes were smaller and more hazel. No one ever remembered Jasmine's eyes being like yours."

Jasmine swallowed. The *real* Jasmine. She had always known that no one else in her family had her eyes. While her hair was nearly black and impossibly curly, her eyes were a startlingly vivid, robin's-egg blue.

But blue eyes could be recessive, skipping generations. Jasmine had always chalked it up to genetic chance.

Jasmine closed her eyes, letting the tears fall, muffling her sobs with the velvet blanket.

Memories washed over her from that terrible night.

*"Minna . . . Minna." A firm hand shook her awake.*

*She opened her eyes. A girl. Her sister? She had the impression of desperate eyes and long, dark hair.*

*A woman screamed. Jagged terror filled with pain.*

*"Quickly," her sister said. "Open the door and run. It will save you."*

*Someone pushed her. She stumbled and curls of mist snatched at her, pulling her upright, tugging her forward.*

*And then she was moving, through fire and fog, brush grabbing at her bare feet.*

*Away, away . . . she had to get away . . .*

But, as usual, the memory caused confusion.

Why tell her to run away? Why hadn't her family gone with her?

And why was she Minna in her memories? Marmi had never called her that, but Jasmine had always assumed it was a family pet name. But if that wasn't the case, was Minna her real name?

Of all the nights of her life, why couldn't her memory of *that* one be clear?

"Why did you never say anything?" Jasmine asked. "There is probably a family out there who has been missing me—"

Rita sighed. It was her signature why-are-you-making-my-life-miserable sigh. Jasmine had heard it a lot as a teenager.

"No one came forward, Jasmine. After a few months, I contacted the police department in Florida, just in case, but none of the other victims matched your description. They considered the case closed. Mom was out of her mind with grief over losing John and the other children. She was fiercely adamant you were her grandchild. She felt you were her gift in this terrible trial."

*You are the child of my heart.* How many times had Marmi said those words to Jasmine?

"Why would I take that from her without a good reason?" Rita continued. "We just accepted Mom's version of everything and cared for you the best we could after she passed."

It explained so much. Why Jasmine had drifted from family to family like an unwanted stray. Staying until she wore out her welcome and then escaping to the next relative.

Everyone had known. Or at least suspected she was an outsider, not one of their own.

"I know Marmi left you great-grandma's china." A pause. The sounds of Rita shifting something. "It's been in the family for three generations now, and I would hate to see it leave with you. Would you be willing to part with it so Breanne can have a piece of her heritage? Especially seeing how it's not *actually* your birthright?"

Jasmine's breath snagged.

Yep. That comment was Rita at her best. Or was it worst?

"Uhmmm, I'm going to have to think about it. Marmi was pretty insistent that the set go to me—"

"Yes, but don't you think she might have seen things differently had she known?"

*No.* Jasmine instinctively rebelled at the thought. *I was the child of her heart, remember?*

"I'll think about it, Rita," was the only answer Jasmine gave.

"I'd appreciate it. It's the least you can do for us."

And with that parting shot, Rita hung up.

Gah! Why did talking with Rita *always* go like this?

Jasmine chewed on her cheek, staring sightlessly into the popping fire, its warmth doing little to help.

An errant draft flickered the flames, rustling the sticky note she had slapped onto the flat screen television to the right of the fireplace.

One of her doodles:

*You know my name. Not my story.*

Ironic. Just so terribly ironic. Jasmine knew her story—but her real name? Not so much.

And, right next to it, another maxim:

*Don't confuse your path with your destination. Just because it's stormy now, doesn't mean you aren't headed for sunshine.*

Marmi *would* have loved her anyway.

They were two old souls, lives tangled together by ties that were even stronger than blood.

*"Look at how the trees droop this Fall. Can you feel their wariness?" Marmi stood at the back door, hands on hips, staring into the Washington forest.*

*Jasmine turned toward the trees and closed her eyes. Felt wind whisper through her. Heard branches rustle. A heaviness threading through it all, the sense of a silver ribbon lacing the ground. Not quite grief or melancholy . . . more the anticipation of pain. Of hardship.*

*"Winter will be harsh this year. Mark my words."*

Jasmine reached for her sticky notes and pen. As usual, drawing soothed.

Her hand sketched, almost of its own volition. She always kept a sticky pad close at hand . . . one of those larger sizes of soft, off-white paper. The adhesive back ensured that she could instantly display her art anywhere. Practical for someone who was far too scattered to keep track of things like tacks or tape or, heaven forbid, a frame.

How many hours had she and Marmi sat side-by-side in companionable silence, her grandmother reading while Jasmine sketched? Marmi loved posting Jasmine's work all over the house. Sometimes there had been hardly an inch of wall space in their old bungalow for another drawing, but Marmi always found room.

It was Marmi who had taught her that eternity stretched, not as a river, but as a vast ocean. The life of each human being was dropped into the ocean by the hand of the Maker—the impact causing expanding rippling circles. If the rings of one life intersected with those of another, they formed a link. A supernatural bond. A pathway powerful enough to traverse time itself.

These bonds formed the time portal's power. Jasmine felt their presence here, a swirling mass of lives tied between past and future, stretching through the portal. The pathways allowing a chosen few to travel through the portal and hence through time. It was somehow . . . comforting. Familiar. A huge cosmic web that encompassed as many people as possible.

Something Jasmine ached to be caught up in.

She continued her doodling. As usual, barely paying attention to what she was doing, the motions muscle-memory.

When a friend was having a bad day, who brought him or her the right essential oils to perk up their day? She did. When someone needed life advice or their horoscope read, who was there with incense and a star chart? She was.

She was always the group Mother. (Not to be confused with the group *Smother* . . . which was a totally different thing, despite what that mean roommate had claimed back in her sorority days . . . Jasmine wasn't being controlling—merely offering persistent, unsolicited advice.)

But it didn't seem to matter. The more Jasmine reached out to others, the more Fate pulled people away from her.

Mike had been small potatoes . . . but her entire family?

It was almost too much to comprehend.

*No one came forward . . .*

The pain ached.

Jasmine looked down at what she had drawn.

*Does your mother know where you are?*

Wasn't that the question of her life?

# Chapter 4

*You must marry.*

The words hung like a millstone around Timothy's neck as he watched the dancers move through the quadrille forms.

Despite the gloomy March weather, the ballroom was full to bursting.

Timothy had come to the ball with one goal:

Be introduced to Miss Heartstone and determine if he could accept—more like tolerate—her as a wife. And, if yes, begin his campaign to convince her of the same.

Marianne and Arthur had joined him this evening, having returned from Lady Rutland's entertainments. Even better, Miss Heartstone and her mother had attended the same house party, allowing Marianne to form an acquaintance with the heiress, who she declared to be a perfectly amiable young lady.

Marianne had drifted off as soon as they arrived at the ball, promising to find Miss Heartstone and facilitate an introduction.

It was the perfect opening gambit.

Timothy positioned himself so he could see the entire ballroom at a glance. Bright silk skirts swirled around gentlemen dressed in dark tailcoats, the strains of the orchestra soaring above the hum of conversation and clink of wine glasses.

This was Timothy's milieu. His place.

He nodded polite greetings to other lords who drifted past him and then spent a pleasant thirty minutes discussing a recent mathematical paper with a Scottish earl. Timothy published papers himself on occasion, keeping the mathematics theoretical, of course, as was most proper.

"Nephew, a pleasure to see you this evening." A cool voice drawled at his elbow.

Timothy turned as his uncle, Mr. John Linwood, came to stop beside him.

Timothy nodded in greeting. "Uncle, what a delight." His tone indicated otherwise.

Encountering his uncle was akin to seeing his father's ghost. Tall. Thin. Silver-haired. Regal. Immaculately dressed. Eyes the same clear gray. The man ensured Timothy had never missed his sire's presence. His father's younger brother smoothly filled the void.

Without sons of his own, Mr. John Linwood focused all his fatherly attention on his brother's only son. Attention Timothy barely tolerated.

Uncle Linwood surveyed the room, a quizzing glass in hand adding to his air of disdain. "I have been given to understand that you are in sudden need of cash." His uncle *always* knew the happenings of Timothy's life. "I expect you will do your duty."

It was his father's script. The one Linwood men never deviated from. Duty. Honor. Family. Above all else.

"How fares Cousin Emilia?" Timothy asked, deftly changing the subject.

"Events are progressing most satisfactorily."

Uncle Linwood's concern for Timothy was second only to his drive to secure suitable husbands for his four daughters. It was a never-ending challenge. His eldest daughter, Emilia, was on the verge of betrothing herself to the second son of a duke. The alliance would further their family connections within the upper echelons of the peerage.

"I trust your current financial crisis will be solved quickly and without much undue attention," Uncle Linwood continued. "You owe the family no less. No whiff of scandal can touch us during this particularly . . . *delicate* time."

Hence Uncle Linwood's concern over Timothy's finances and marital status.

*Rule #11: The disgrace of the* paterfamilias *is the disgrace of all.*

How many times had Timothy's father said that?

His uncle eyed him speculatively. "I hear there is a splendidly eligible heiress in attendance this evening. A Miss Heartstone, I believe."

"Indeed," was Timothy's cool reply.

"This Miss Heartstone's dowry could not come at a more needed moment. It is time you did something about filling the nursery at Kinningsley."

At thirty-three, Timothy most certainly should have married by now.

It was his biggest failure. The one area of his life in which he did not live up to the expectations of his heritage.

*Rule #2: A gentleman will marry early and provide an heir and a spare to ensure the bloodline continues.*

Starting at the age of twenty-one until his death when Timothy was twenty-five, his father had discussed—and then lectured, badgered and, finally, threatened—Timothy to secure a bride.

*All for naught*, his father would repeat.

Timothy was not unilaterally opposed to marriage. He just had yet to find suitable inducement.

Heaven knew he would never marry for love. Linwood men, as a general rule, seemed immune to the emotion.

"I am actually well acquainted with Miss Heartstone's uncle and guardian. He is a man much like us. Would you like me to open a dialogue with him concerning the chit?" his uncle asked.

Timothy shifted his weight. Not a trace of emotion touching his face.

"I have already instructed Daniel to do so, Uncle. At this point, I should like to actually meet the lady before taking things any further."

"Does it matter, boy? You will have her even if she is wall-eyed and pock-marked. The family is depending upon you right now to preserve our honor. You are the *paterfamilias*. Do not fool yourself into thinking you have a choice in this matter. You *will* secure her."

Uncle Linwood's biting tone did not go unnoticed.

Timothy clasped his hands behind his back, back ramrod straight. No agitated foot-tapping. Forcing the cool anger of his muscles to stay at bay.

*Rule #37: A gentleman is always in control of himself and his situation. He* was the master.

Out of the corner of his eye, Timothy noted Marianne approaching.

"Thank you for the reminder, Uncle."

Timothy clicked his heels in a sharp bow and turned away, striding to greet his sister, dismissing his uncle while walking a razor thin line between politeness and outright contempt.

A line he masterfully maintained.

Marianne arrived with both arms interlinked—a young woman on one elbow and a middle-aged lady on the other.

As usual, his sister was lovely in a blue silk gown with tiny puffed sleeves and white lace trim, her dark hair arranged in delicate curls around her face.

And as for her companions . . .

"Good evening, brother," Marianne said as the trio stopped in front of him. "Allow me to introduce Mrs. Heartstone and her daughter, Miss Arabella Heartstone. Both of whom I met last week at Lady Rutland's house party." The ladies curtsied. "Mrs. Heartstone, Miss Heartstone, may I present my brother, Lord Linwood?"

As required, Timothy bowed to Miss Heartstone and her mother.

"Lord Linwood, delighted I am sure to make your acquaintance." Mrs. Heartstone favored him with what could only be described as a tolerant smile. As if *she* were the one bestowing a favor. "Your sister quite dotes upon you."

Mrs. Heartstone resembled a mushroom. Literally and figuratively. A poofy brown turban sat upon her head, held up by a stocky body draped in a dress of the same color silk.

A grasping fungus trying to push herself and her daughter into the laps of those above their station. With sixty thousand pounds on offer, she would succeed.

Mrs. Heartstone simpered. "In fact, I was telling my darling Arabella just yesterday that if Lord Linwood is as fine a gentleman as his sister makes him out to be, well then, any woman in England would be proud to stand at his side."

The words prettily said, but a calculating gleam negated their sincerity.

"Timothy is the kindest of brothers, I assure you." Marianne smiled warmly.

"I am sure of it." Mrs. Heartstone touched a hand to her turban. "Though I was speaking with the Marquess of Hartington just yesterday— you know, the Duke of Devonshire's heir"—Timothy knew *precisely* who Hart was. He had gone riding with him two days before.— "and he declared my Arabella to be this season's reigning beauty. Add her fine looks to her stupendous dowry and Arabella can have her pick of men."

"Mama, please!" Miss Heartstone whispered, a hint of distressed color touching her cheeks.

Miss Heartstone was perfectly . . . unremarkable.

Her fashionable white muslin gown revealed a figure which was neither too tall, nor too short, too plump, nor too thin. Her hair and eyes were a simple brown. Her round face was not unpleasing but, again, not distinct either. She kept her gaze turned toward the floor, the image of maidenly decorum.

In other words . . . utterly forgettable. A shy debutante just like his mother had most certainly been. A girl like the hundreds he had been introduced to before her.

She had probably never had a single original thought. No spark of life or vitality.

And why did that thought depress him?

*Honor, duty and sixty thousand pounds*, he reminded himself. Sixty thousand pounds that he desperately needed. And though it galled him to admit, his uncle was right. Whether he liked her or not, Timothy had no choice.

No better time than the present to make his intentions clear.

"Miss Heartstone, may I have the honor of this dance?" Timothy held out a gloved hand to the still blushing lady.

She murmured something indistinct and placed her gloved hand in his. He supposed this meant she accepted his offer.

Head held high, he led her onto the dance floor and into the familiar one-two-three steps of the waltz. They twirled in silence once. Twice. At least, Miss Heartstone had not inherited her mother's forward ways.

"Are you enjoying your time in London?" he asked, looking down at the top of her brown curls.

"Indeed." She did not lift her eyes to his, but instead kept them fixed on his cravat.

Now what to say?

"I am glad of it. Have you had a chance to attend the opera?"

"Yes." Still without lifting her eyes. "Mama and I were kindly invited to join Lord Winston and his son in their box." Another earl hungry for his son to marry an heiress.

Silence hung between them, awkward and heavy.

Miss Heartstone held her body stiff and unyielding. Out of the corner of his eye, Timothy saw Marianne chatting with Mrs. Heartstone. The girl's mother studied them with a calculating gaze. Obviously weighing the sight they made on the dance floor against his less-than-a-duke title.

Which was just absurd. He was a respected viscount and one of the most sought after matrimonial prizes on the marriage mart. To have to bow and scrape and *court* a woman like Miss Heartstone and her mother, practically beg for their condescension . . .

The entire scene reminded him powerfully of *why* he had never married.

His parent's marriage had been dynastically arranged, the union of two important families with little love lost between its principal parties.

Timothy could not remember a time when his mother had not been a slave to laudanum, spending her days in an opium-induced lethargy. Her way of dealing with his father's cold, and often cruel, behavior.

Twirling with the quiet, spineless girl in his arms, Timothy clearly saw that an alliance with Miss Heartstone could easily end the same way. Heaven knew he was hardly a warm man.

But marriages among the upper aristocracy were always thus. More business partnerships than anything else. And even if he had believed in love, there still remained the problem of his own personal preferences . . .

Timothy had always been attracted to, well . . . the wrong sort of woman. Women who bounced with life and energy, heedless of the dictates of society, rendering them unfit to play the part of his viscountess.

Women who were his absolute opposite.

He knew nothing about wooing such women. His few forays into that sphere had been unmitigated disasters. Fine words and easy affection were the arena of others. Like his deceased friend, James Knight, Arthur's older brother.

As usual, the thought of James caused something painful to burn in Timothy's chest. Something that felt suspiciously like grief and . . . regret.

Due to his father's strict code of behavior, Timothy had not been allowed to mingle with others as a child. But as the son of a wealthy landowner with an illustrious family name, James had been deemed worthy enough to be a friend.

Practically the only friend Timothy could ever remember having.

How many hours had they passed together as children? Listening to James go on and on about the adventures he would have someday. Watching James charm everyone with his easy-going nature and silver tongue. Including Miss Emry Wilde . . .

Timothy clenched his jaw, his hands convulsively tightening. Miss Heartstone stumbled. He held her upright and then forced his breathing to slow.

Emry Wilde.

Now *there* had been a woman who could command a man's heart. Pretty with her dark hair and unusual eyes. Clever. Witty. Never at a loss for words. An American of no particular breeding or wealth, as it turned out. Completely unsuitable to be his viscountess.

And yet . . .

She had captivated him. He admitted it. And he had pursued her, determined to make her his in the way his father had taught him.

*Rule #119: A gentleman's mistress must be kept secret from his wife and family.*

He had seen no other path . . . no other way to have her that allowed him to stay true to the obligations of his birth. He knew his father had kept several mistresses over the years. And so Timothy had offered to make Emry his wife in everything but name . . .

It had gone terribly wrong . . .

*Rule #80: A gentleman should never do anything for which he must apologize.*

And she had run into James' outstretched arms. Rumors said they had even married. Which made their deaths in a tragic carriage accident even harder to bear.

He winced at the memory. Regret was not a familiar emotion. A true gentleman did not live in such a way as to invite regret.

But he *regretted* his actions toward Miss Emry Wilde.

She was a woman of polite breeding and deserved better than his tawdry offer. But his attraction and the unsettled nature of her situation had blinded him.

So when Miss Emry's brother had appeared last year, Timothy had welcomed Mr. Marcus Wilde's trouncing him at fisticuffs. A small way of rectifying his wrong.

Timothy knew his personal weaknesses.

Machines, manufacturing, emotions which surfaced far-too-readily, a deep-satisfaction from work, an attraction to unsuitable women . . .

Common. Vulgar. Pathetically middle class. His father's voice sounded clearly.

All too true.

The music ended and Timothy delivered Miss Heartstone back to her waiting mother and Marianne. Miss Heartstone was instantly surrounded by other young men, each determined to press his suit.

Mrs. Heartstone watched with eagle-eyes as a young lord led her daughter on to the floor.

Marianne cocked an eyebrow at Timothy. Obviously encouraging him to speak to Mrs. Heartstone.

"Your daughter is lovely. I hope to spend more time with her." He clasped his hands behind his back again.

Mrs. Heartstone said nothing for a moment. "Your seat is in Herefordshire, I believe, my lord. Near to that of my cousin, Sir Henry Stylles."

"Indeed it is."

"I am quite fond of my cousin and enjoy visiting him when time permits."

A strong opening. "You must make time to visit him, then. I am sure the entire countryside would welcome your stay."

"Your estate, Kinningsley, it is newer?"

"Yes. Only a mere fifty years old. A beautiful homage to neoclassical style, if I may say so."

"Excellent, my lord. And you live there by yourself, I understand? You have no other sisters and your own mother is deceased?"

"Yes." Translation: *There are no other women in my life to cause you trouble, should your daughter decide to marry me.*

Mrs. Heartstone pursed her lips. "I have a fascination with dowager cottages. I find them darling and comfortable. Does Kinningsley have such a house?"

*Ah.* The question seemed innocuous enough, but Mrs. Heartstone was clever. He would give her that much. Her husband had left his money to their daughter, not to his wife. Ensuring that his widow would need to stay close to her daughter in order to have a roof over her head.

Clearly, Mrs. Heartstone wasn't interested in actually sharing a roof with her daughter, no matter how unencumbered.

"Kinningsley does not currently have a dowager house." He had to answer truthfully.

"What a pity." Mrs. Heartstone turned to Marianne. "Mrs. Knight, you have spoken so highly of the darling dower cottage attached to Haldon Manor. It is the height of modern convenience?"

"Yes," Marianne chimed in. "Duir Cottage is most comfortable."

"You should consider building such a house on Kinningsley's

grounds, my lord." Mrs. Heartstone turned back to Timothy. "Combined with your other charms, a prospective mother-in-law would find it a most attractive . . . incentive."

Duly noted.

"Your advice is most welcome, Mrs. Heartstone." Timothy managed to spit out the words without a hint of sarcasm. "A dower house modeled after Duir Cottage would be a welcome addition to my holdings."

"Excellent." Mrs. Heartstone repeated, her eyes sharp. "I shall inquire of my cousin, Sir Henry. We are off to Shropshire in May to visit old friends. A stay with Sir Henry around the middle of the month would be pleasurable. Assuming we could count on your most delightful company, as well?" Her look turned speculative.

"Naturally, Mrs. Heartstone. I would not miss any chance to enjoy your presence or that of your lovely daughter."

"I am glad we understand each other, Lord Linwood. I will be anxious to hear how the plans for your dower cottage are coming along. Such a lovely home would be welcome to any mother-in-law's heart."

Subtle.

She curtsied and made her way toward the other mamas gathered in an alcove.

"Well," Marianne said, turning to him, "it seems you may soon be building a dower cottage at Kinningsley."

Timothy nodded. Apparently that seemed a condition of Miss Heartstone's acceptance of any offer of marriage. Though where the money would come from, he had no idea.

He offered Marianne his arm and took his sister on a stroll around the ballroom.

"Miss Heartstone is a lovely young lady," Marianne observed, her voice carefully neutral.

"Indeed. She is politely well-bred."

"And . . ." Marianne prompted.

"And what, sister dear?"

"You appear interested in Miss Heartstone, despite finding her somewhat . . . dull."

He would have used the word *tedious*, but *dull* would suffice.

He turned his head, only to realize his sister had been studying him rather than the room. Something sad and knowing lingered in her eyes.

"Have you decided to marry then?"

Pity. *That's* what he was seeing on her face.

It seemed a catching disease around him.

*Rule #51: A gentleman is never an object of pity.*

Unable to bear the scrutiny, Timothy looked back toward the milling crowd of people, teeth grinding together.

Marianne adjusted her hold on his arm. "Timothy, you need not marry where you do not love."

Ah, but he did. That had *always* been his destiny.

Timothy's hand sought out the gear in his coat pocket. Reassuring himself. He could do this. He could be a cog, a gear.

He had yet to tell Marianne of his financial predicament. It would only worry her needlessly.

"You do not need to become *him*." Her voice was soft, yet insistent. There was no need to define *who* she referred to.

Timothy managed to unhinge his jaw. "There is no shame in being the man my father was."

"Father was a bitterly unhappy person, forced to live in a cage of his own making—"

"I am not unhappy, Marianne. I may not have deliberately chosen my life's path, but it is hardly a cage, as you say. I will do my best to preserve our heritage and family honor. You all rely upon me."

"Nonsense. It is not your job to guide our way. Heritage is merely an emotion. It is nothing tangible in the end. A good heritage is merely a compilation of happy memories passed along to the next generation. It is most definitely *not* a pretty house full of dust-collecting things or the approval of a group of arrogant people."

Timothy let out a slow breath, stopping mid-stride, turning his gaze to his sister.

Her eyes positively dripped with pity.

Marianne sighed, no doubt correctly reading the stubborn set of his jaw.

"I know you, brother mine. You have a huge heart and an enormous capacity to love. You just need to let go—"

"Do not concern yourself over me, Marianne. I know what I am about."

Two days later, a note was delivered to Linwood House. One paragraph stood out:

*Arabella and I look forward to visiting our cousin, Sir Henry, and waiting upon you at Kinningsley around the fifteenth of May. Mrs. Knight mentioned that you plan on building a dower house. Hopefully, you have chosen a fair prospect for it. I look forward to seeing your plans for the cottage.*

Timothy set the paper down on his desk. Daniel, again seated across from him, raised an eyebrow. He had clearly seen Mrs. Heartstone's signature.

"Miss Heartstone's uncle and guardian is amenable to the idea of an alliance with the Linwood viscountcy." Daniel glanced toward the note. "Will you offer for Miss Heartstone?"

"Do I have a choice?"

Daniel's silence spoke volumes.

"Do I have funds to build a dower house? It would seem to be a condition of Mrs. Heartstone's cooperation in the match," Timothy said instead.

If the question caught Daniel off guard, he didn't show it.

"You could begin the process and complete it after the marriage. Building a house takes time, of course." There was a wink hidden in Daniel's tone.

Timothy sat back in his chair. "There is possibly a space beyond the back lawn that will be nice. Far enough away from the main house so as to not be seen. I will look at it. I am off to Kinningsley tomorrow, as events there require my presence. 'Twill be a brief visit. With so many hangers-on, Miss Heartstone is at risk, and Uncle Linwood is increasingly anxious that I secure her hand. If not for my sake, then for Cousin Emilia's. Uncle is determined to bring the Duke's son up to scratch."

"I will await your return, my lord."

"Excellent. I believe I will stop by Duir Cottage on my way and sketch its floor plan. If Mrs. Heartstone wants a building like it, she shall have one."

Daniel paused and then shifted in his chair, as if concerned. "Do you think that wise, my lord? Arthur has guards stationed there, I believe."

Duir Cottage had been built on the site of an ancient oak tree which had been incinerated by lightning several years previously. Though the house seemed innocuous enough, last year Arthur had placed a round-the-clock guard on the cottage. He had claimed it was to protect the house from a spate of robberies which had plagued the area.

"I am Linwood. There is not a man in all of Herefordshire who would gainsay my authority." Linwood shot Daniel a stern look. "I will explore Duir Cottage at my leisure."

# Chapter 5

Jasmine slowly drizzled honey into a small pitcher of milk, the early morning light catching the pouring stream, turning it into fire-licked amber.

The earth smelled musty and new under her knees, heavy with spring rainfall. The morning had dawned clear and cheerily bright. Miraculous, given the perpetually gloomy March weather.

But the sun was fitting. A symbol of the spring equinox. The day when earth sloughed off the death of winter and embraced new life. A chance for rebirth. For hope.

The honey running out, she whisked the milk with a fork, blending the two together.

Marmi's tutoring flitting through her mind.

*Honey for the darkness of winter left behind, sweetening the future.*

*Milk for the light of summer that was to come. The nourishment rebirth required.*

*Light and dark in equal amounts. That moment of balance in the year when all things become possible.*

This was the fifteenth time Jasmine had celebrated the equinox without her grandmother, planting bulbs in the back garden as a symbol of rebirth.

Jasmine swallowed back the raw burning in her throat.

Not going to think about it.

"Damn and blast. Is there any more milk?" James Knight fumbled next to her, righting his now empty pitcher. "I've gone and spilled mine."

Opposite her husband, Emme patted his hand. "Here, darling, you can have some of mine." She poured a little of her milk into his glass. "I've even already mixed the honey into it for you."

James winked at her.

"So now what?" Marc Wilde sat back on his haunches, tamping the damp earth in front of him with one hand, a well-mixed jar of milk and honey held in the other. "And please tell me it will be quick, because there is a shower and some bacon calling my name inside."

"You water your bulb with the milk and honey mixture." Jasmine demonstrated by pouring her pitcher over the packed earth, pale milk sinking into black soil.

Solar feast days were always particularly hard for Jasmine. The company of good friends made it all more bearable.

Emme and James were passing through on their way home. Emme had just finished presenting at an academic conference in Edinburgh which explained why they had left little Arthur with Emme's mother in Seattle. Normally, the cheerful baby traveled with them. Marc and Kit were on their way to Indonesia for a press junket about Marc's latest movie.

"You do this every year?" Kit Ashton-Wilde asked, still whisking her milk and honey together. The diamond of her large wedding ring flashed in the golden sunlight.

Jasmine nodded. "Marmi was fanatical about celebrating the ancient feast days. You should have seen her summer solstice preparations."

Now her eyes joined her throat, doing the whole burning/stinging thing.

Jasmine took a deep breath and brushed her hair back, surreptitiously wiping her eyes in the process.

Marmi *was* her grandmother. Maybe not by blood but their hearts were forged of the same fire. Souls twined together regardless of how they came to find each other.

She had seen it clearly in her dreams the night before.

*Fog swirling. The shape of trees around her. So alone.*

*Home. She needed to get home. But how?*

*A ribbon of gold suddenly appeared. A liquid tendril arching through the mist.*

*It curled around her, welcoming. Tugging her forward. First at a walk. Then, a gentle run.*

*The smell of lavender seeped in, growing until it filled her senses.*

*A figure emerged from the mist. Bright-eyed. Welcoming.*

*A smile she knew so well.*

*And then they were embracing. Home.*

Jasmine had awoken with wet cheeks.

Rita had become more vocal about Jasmine returning the china, insisting it needed to stay with those who shared DNA with Marmi. After some soul-searching, Jasmine had texted Rita, telling her she could have the dishes. It was only stuff, after all. And she believed firmly in sending out good karma, padding her life with potential sweetness.

Like this equinox ceremony. Another drop in her good-karma bucket.

Using her spade, Jasmine patted the ground one more time, smoothing the damp dirt over the bulb she had just planted and watered.

She could feel the pulsing energy under her fingers, the thrum of power and welcome. Some of it came from the house, the ever-present time portal amping the natural hum of living things. Caressing, soothing, tangibly familiar somehow.

"Did you ever meet Marmi?" James asked Emme.

"No." Emme poured her jar over her planted bulb. "Jas and I didn't meet until college. Folk dancing class."

"Man, you two got waaaaay too into that." Marc chuckled.

Emme lifted her head, fixing him with her best sisterly you-are-so-annoying stare. "Folk dancing is a long lost art, I'll have you know—"

"Exactly. How else can we stay connected to the past if we don't cherish traditions like that? Or continue things like this?" Jasmine nodded toward the fresh mounds of dirt in front of each of them. "It's a way of understanding our own ancestors."

Particularly if you suddenly found yourself without any.

Ancestors, that is.

Well . . . at least any that you knew.

*Blink, blink, blink.*

Not going to think about it.

Rebirth. Renewal.

Starting over. Literally.

*Trust the process.*

Deep breath.

Marc opened his mouth, intent on saying more, but Kit nudged him with her shoulder. "I think it's a fabulous tradition. My father and brother would have loved it," she said, something sad touching her eyes.

Marc kissed her forehead.

Kit shrugged. "Being separated from Daniel by two hundred years does hurt sometimes."

Marc tucked Kit into his arms, holding her and murmuring something indistinct in her ear which seemed to banish her gloom.

Everyone finished pouring their milk and honey mixture over their planted bulb.

"You know, this reminds me a little of mealtime when I was at Eton as a lad," James said. "We would be served porridge for breakfast but the headmaster at the time was so frugal, he denied us honey to sweeten it. Linwood built this ingenious little tube with a stoppered mechanism that you could hide up your sleeve. You slid the tube down into your hand and pressed a trigger which poured honey surreptitiously into your oatmeal. It was sheer genius."

"Now why are you ruining a perfectly good morning by bringing someone like Linwood into it?" Mark asked.

"Here, here." Kit chimed in with a grimace.

James sighed and tamped the earth over his bulb one last time. "Who knows? I must be getting nostalgic. Linwood is an ass at the best of times. But he, very rarely, *can* be a decent human being. He made those little honey tubes for anyone who asked. Must have taken him forever."

Jasmine had heard *all* about Lord Linwood over the years. Particularly that one incident with Emme where Linwood had made a decidedly indecent proposal—

"So have you heard back from the police department in Florida?" Emme asked, collecting a couple of pitchers. Marc, Kit and James instantly bent over to gather the rest, Marc muttering something that sounded suspiciously like, "Bacon . . . at last."

"Yes." Jasmine gathered the leftover bulbs and garden spades. "They left a message late last night, time zone differences being what they are. Apparently, the Freedom of Information Act requires that I fill out an absurd amount of paperwork before they can tell me anything."

"Ouch," James said, placing a glass jar on a kitchen tray. "Sounds like it could be months before you learn anything at all. Particularly as you're here in the U.K."

Jasmine gave a resigned nod. She had realized that pretty quickly.

"James has people in the States, you know." Emme said over her shoulder, hands full of crockery as she headed for the back door.

Jasmine glanced at James, who gave her his signature wide smile. "That is true. I do have people."

"Sleuthing people?"

"Sherlock Holmes-esque people." James nodded. "My man Cobra could get to the bottom of just about anything."

"Cobra? He seriously goes by Cobra?" Kit shook her head. "Please tell me he wears a superhero cape—"

"Cobra rocks." Marc picked up a spade, knocking the dirt off it with his shoe. "He could tell you what the President had for breakfast just by looking at the flag over the White House."

"He could find your real parents for you." James placed all the tools into a bucket and headed for the house, as well. "Just say the word."

Wow. It was tempting . . .

"But you've already done so much, James." Jasmine hurried after him, brushing dirt off of her circa-1975 overalls. Another of Marmi's hand-me-downs. "I *am* staying rent free in your house."

James held the back door open for her. "No one else needs the house right now, so that hardly signifies. You are actually doing us a favor by keeping an eye on everything."

Jasmine seriously doubted that was true, but whatever.

She stepped out of her muddy rubber boots, leaving them on the back porch as she walked into the kitchen.

Man, some help navigating all the paperwork would be *so* nice. But she hated feeling like even more of a mooch and, in the end, she could be patient. Really, she could. She just needed to trust karma and realize that sunshine really was along her path somewhere. Things wouldn't always be this dark . . .

"Talking out loud again, Jas," Marc said from behind her.

*Drat.* Jasmine pressed her lips together.

"You *could* use the help." Emme nudged her shoulder. "And you *are* painting that mural for baby Arthur's room, right?"

"Exactly." Jasmine nodded with more enthusiasm than she felt.

Any day now . . . she just needed to get behind the wheel of James' BMW . . . sketch that visual inspiration—

Tomorrow she would do it. Buckle down and force through her fear and worry. Put on her big girl pants. Drive a car. She could do it. Tomorrow.

Or . . . maybe the next day . . . definitely before the weekend.

*Wait* . . . she paused, assessing everyone's reaction.

Nothing.

*Whew.* That had stayed inside her head.

"Emme's right," James said. "You have been refusing money for the mural, so how about we trade? You paint Camelot scenes for little Arthur, and we'll pay you in shady investigators?"

Well . . .

"I love it." Emme beamed at her husband. And then moved closer, giving him a lingering kiss before turning back to Jasmine. "It's all settled then. Cobra is on the case."

Two hours later, everyone was showered, packed and running back and forth through the kitchen. James and Emme had a plane to Seattle to catch, anxious to see little Arthur. Emme had said five times in as many minutes how much she missed him. Marc and Kit needed to be in Jakarta by the next day as Marc's publicist had lined up a series of interviews.

Assuming, of course, they all made their flights.

Jasmine intended to paint, paint, paint. She was in the land of King Arthur, for heaven's sake, visual richness all around her . . .

It was a gift. She needed to stop procrastinating and get started.

She had changed into a vintage baby doll dress. It was the same blue color as her eyes with a white scalloped collar and long tight sleeves. She had found the dress last week at Oxfam for only three pounds. Total score. Thick black tights, her favorite Doc Marten boots and a sheer paisley-printed scarf in her hair. (Also Oxfam, only a pound fifty . . . Britain had the *best* vintage shopping, and it had only taken her three bus transfers to get to the store . . . extra bonus that she didn't have to drive . . .)

Jasmine stood at the kitchen sink, nursing a cup of coffee, staring out the window as Marc and James maneuvered luggage into the trunk of the hired car which would take them to the Bristol airport. They kept taking bags out, rearranging, trying to fit everything together like a giant 3-D puzzle. Kit and Emme stood back offering helpful suggestions.

Or were they just laughing at their men?

She couldn't tell.

The sun had risen well into the sky, and the glare made it hard to see clearly. Jasmine stood on her tiptoes, trying to get a better angle. Being five foot two was a pain. Wait. Where had that step-stool with the missing leg gone?

Thirty seconds later, she had dragged the stool out of the broom closet and was teetering on its unbalanced three legs, giving her a much better vantage of the goings on in the backyard.

Laughing. Kit and Emme were definitely laughing.

Which Jasmine *should* have found funny.

The situation most definitely was *not* tear-inducing.

But . . .

It was just soooooo sweet. Emme, her best friend for . . . like, forever . . . had finally found The One in James. And Marc (who *no one* had thought would settle down) used every up and down of a suitcase as an excuse to kiss Kit.

It was all so lovey-dovey, happy-sappy that Jasmine couldn't do anything *but* cry. The question was only if it was going to stay a subtle polite cry or turn into something messier . . .

Which made the loud throat clearing and deep-voice sounding behind her all the more startling.

"Pardon me, girl, but where the *hell* did you come from, and what have you done to this cottage?"

Jasmine was quite sure she squealed (loudly) as she tumbled off the stool, sending it flying with a crash.

She hit the wood floor between the sink and the kitchen island. Hard.

Knocking every last bit of breath out of her body.

What—? Who—?!

Jasmine coughed and rolled onto her back, trying desperately to suck in air.

The sunlight above her suddenly dimmed. She opened her eyes and stared up, up, up into a pair of gun-metal gray eyes.

Upside-down gray eyes set into a chiseled upside-down male face which featured a decidedly grim upside-down scowl. Which didn't quite make it a smile, despite what some might think.

*Oh no* . . . surely this couldn't be. Arthur had set guards on Duir Cottage. No one was going to inadvertently travel through the portal on their combined watch.

Right?

She closed her eyes. Opened them again.

He was still there. And his frown had deepened. Though it did actually look more like a smile, now that she thought about it . . .

*Blink.*

Still there. His expression becoming more of a glower. All framed by dark hair and an immaculately tied cravat.

*Damn and blast.* To use the 1815 vernacular.

"I repeat. Who are you and what have you done to this cottage?" His bass voice vibrated through the room. Accent posh even to Jasmine's untrained American ear.

Coughing, Jasmine rolled to her knees and pushed herself upright. Not as if Mr. Frowny-Face were offering to help her.

With one last cough, Jasmine lifted her head. And kept right on lifting it. Even standing at her fullest height, the man still towered over her.

Scratch that. He *loomed*.

And dressed like something straight out of central casting for Masterpiece Classic. Cravat, coat, waistcoat topped by a rippling greatcoat which hung to the heels of his glossy knee-high boots.

His eyebrows narrowed, as he swept a gaze over her ensemble with its decidedly *not* Regency-period short dress and chunky boots. And then fixed his eyes firmly on her face.

He slapped his beaver top hat against tan breeches which appeared to be . . . why, yes, made of sewn leather. Mmmm . . . interesting.

How could leather fit that tightly? It seemed to defy the laws of physics. And were the breeches comfortable because it wasn't like leather really breathed and given the English humidity and skin-tight fit, wouldn't they chafe something fierce—

"Chafe?! Pardon?!" Mr. Frowny Face became even frownier. "I am the one asking questions here, girl."

*Right.*

Jasmine pinched her lips together and swiped her damp cheeks clean. Who was he?

*Snap, snap, snap.* The beaver hat was taking a beating. But, hat aside, the man held the rest of himself almost unnaturally motionless. And then, as if realizing what was going on with his hat, he stopped that too.

"Are you capable of speaking coherent English, girl?" There went that posh accent again. Scathingly condescending. "And if not, please find someone who does."

Up went her eyebrows. Yeah, he wasn't winning any brownie points here.

"And you are . . . ?" She crossed her arms with a toss of her head.

"A man who does not tolerate impossibly insolent chits." His eyes narrowed. "I can hear from your accent you are an American and, therefore, a foreigner in these parts. A word of advice. If you wish to avoid spending time in the local gaol, I suggest you start answering my questions."

*Wow.* Talk about arrogant, pompous, rude . . .

*Oh no!*

Her eyes flared wide. He could be anyone, really.

But based on the stories she had heard, she had an awful, terrible, sinking suspicion . . .

"Please tell me you are *not* Lord Linwood?"

# Chapter 6

The girl continued to stare at Timothy with her impossibly beautiful face and impossibly huge blue eyes with traces of tears still clinging to impossibly long lashes—

"Well? *Are* you Lord Linwood?"

Impossibly insolent, as well.

When he had first seen her teetering precariously on that decrepit stool leaning toward the window and apparently crying, he had assumed her to be a child. With her hair down her back and her skirts so short— not to mention her loud sniffles—she surely was no more than eleven years of age.

But his perusal of her revealed curves no child's body would have.

And as she spoke, her voice was the alto of true womanhood with a strong American twang, forcing him to revise his estimation of her age upward.

He refused to look downward again. Her attire . . .

Timothy swallowed.

He could see every aspect of her shapely legs. No imagination required. Even the loosest Covent Garden opera dancer would blush to wear so little.

How old was she really?

Aaaaand he was tapping his hat again.

*Rule #91: A gentleman never fidgets.*

He was a fortress. Contained.

Slow breath.

His hand stilled.

He turned away from her.

Better not to contemplate her clothing. Or the lack thereof. His spine tingled from the heat of her gaze on his shoulders.

He surveyed the room. Again. Nothing was as it had been.

He had stopped at Duir Cottage, as he had promised, determined to copy the basic structure of the house in building a dower house for Kinningsley. If Mrs. Heartstone wanted a house, then she should have one.

The guards Arthur had set were easily sent away with threats of legal action. Noting the size of the front parlor and study as well as the four bedrooms upstairs, he had drawn a quick mental map of the house, already contemplating ways to make the large kitchen and scullery more useful.

The lack of general storage had been puzzling until he found the trapdoor and stairs down to the empty cellar. There had been a carved slab of stone opposite the stairs and the air had felt alive . . . almost as if it were electrified somehow. Touching the slab had caused a jolt to course through him, followed by a falling sensation. Odd really.

Shaking off the feeling, he had retreated up the stairway . . .

. . . to find everything changed.

The kitchen and scullery were gone. The enormous fireplace still dominated the space in front of him, but that was the only recognizable feature. Instead of work baskets and cook pots, high wingback chairs now flanked the fireplace, facing an overstuffed sofa. A large, rough-hewn table with chairs stood between him and the sofa. The entire back half of the house sported large windows that opened onto an overgrown back garden, flooding the room in light.

But, beyond that, he was at a loss.

Behind him, the kitchen gleamed in marble and steel. A large pale marble-topped cabinet sat in the center of the space, and there seemed to be some sort of spigot over a sunken basin, but everything else was unknown and baffling. Large metal cabinets and strange objects.

What had happened?

His ever-logical brain could not come up with a suitable explanation. Surely the strange tiny woman knew.

She stirred behind him.

"Yoo-hoo." A small hand waved in his peripheral vision. "Still waiting for an answer here. Are you Lord Linwood?" He heard her tapping a foot, impatiently.

Definitely an insolent little piece of baggage.

He turned his head toward her, his eyes automatically wandering south toward her bared legs and oversized boots, one bouncing, before he caught himself.

No looking down—

"Of course, I am Lord Linwood." He carefully set his hat on the large table in front of him, studiously averting his gaze from the woman. "Would you care to explain your presence here?"

"Nonononono. I so didn't sign up for this," was her baffling reply. The foot tapping stopped, and she moved toward the window. "*Please* tell me they haven't left yet. I can handle all the lovey-dovey stuff and deal with my family, but I don't have a license to babysit aristocrats and have no intention of getting one anytime soon . . ."

She was clearly addled in the head. Pity. As she was a pretty little thing, despite her attire. Perhaps she had been set upon by thieves who had torn her dress . . .

. . . and changed the entirety of the house in the process . . .

The door off the kitchen opened with a sharp crack.

"We're off," another loud, decidedly-American voice announced.

Timothy twirled just in time to see Mr. Marcus Wilde walk into the room.

At least . . . the man *appeared* to be Mr. Marcus Wilde, as he sported the same dark hair and green eyes Linwood remembered.

But there the similarities ended.

This man was dressed most oddly in dark blue pantaloons with a white collared shirt under a leather coat. But the coat was worse for wear, scratched and battered. Furthermore, the man lacked a neckcloth of any sort, his shirt merely being unbuttoned at the throat.

It was a most ungentlemanly display of dishabille, particularly with a lady . . . ehr, young woman? . . . present.

"Whoa." Mr. Wilde froze, his eyes darting between Timothy and the small woman.

"Mr. Wilde, I presume?" When faced with a baffling situation of unknown proportions, good manners were always a gentleman's best friend.

"This is sooooo . . . not good." Marcus' eyes went wide.

"Would you care to explain what has happened here?" Timothy swung his arm, encompassing the odd room, fighting to keep his voice calm.

*Rule #37: A gentleman is always in control of himself and his situation.*

Marcus Wilde's presence at Duir Cottage was . . . unexpected, as he had last been seen in the area nearly a year ago. Arthur claimed Marcus and Miss Katherine Ashton—Daniel's older sister, in fact—had immigrated to America. Which perhaps explained Marcus' accent. But how could one travel to the Americas and return in only a year? And with a new accent, no less?

Timothy found his patience wearing decidedly thin.

"Marc, are you coming? Traffic might be bad and—"

Miss Katherine Ashton now appeared in the doorway. Her face immediately mimicking Marcus' frozen surprise.

Yes. The woman was definitely Miss Ashton, but with her hair loose and—

"Miss Ashton, I wonder what your brother would say if he discovered you wearing trousers?" *And a loose satin bodice,* Timothy mentally added.

Had the whole world gone mad?

Miss Ashton shook her long mane of auburn hair. Blinked. "Lord Linwood . . . uh . . . what a—"

"Surprise?" Marcus finished for her, raising an eyebrow. And then, a huge smile broke across his face. "This is gonna be so good."

Marcus rubbed his hands together—as if in glee?—and stepped around Miss Ashton to the open door.

"Hey guys, you gotta come check this out," he called to someone out in the garden, beckoning with his hand. The guards Timothy had sent away, perhaps?

Or, even better, Arthur's steward himself, who would assist Timothy in bringing some sanity to this entire farce.

"We managed to get the lot of it in, but it's a tight squeeze." A voice sounded just outside the door, coming closer.

Something cold and sharp chased Timothy's spine.

He knew that voice as well as his own.

No. It couldn't be—

A painfully familiar blond head appeared in the doorway.

"Marc, Kit . . . you coming?" The man froze, just as the others had done.

*Whoosh.* The air rushed from Timothy's lungs so quickly he had to grab onto the marble counter to keep from losing his balance.

Because the figure standing in the doorway, morning sun turning his hair into a halo of fire, could *not* be.

James Knight.

But that was . . .

Impossible. Just utterly—

James had *died* . . . buried in the parish churchyard with a headstone firmly lodged above ground. Timothy had donned all black, walked behind his coffin, mourned at his graveside. He had *grieved.*

How—?!

"Timothy." James paused. And then nodded his head in greeting. "This is unexpected—"

"And I thought beating up the guy was fun." Marcus laughed, still rubbing his hands together.

Miss Ashton nudged his shoulder. "Hush, Marc. Be nice. Poor Linwood is white. If he faints, I expect you to catch him . . ."

Timothy's mind fought to find some logical explanation, but there was really only one conclusion to be drawn.

If he and James were both here, facing each other and talking—

Then that meant—

He clutched the marble counter more tightly, forcing himself to stay upright through sheer will alone. "Did I die? Is this . . . is this heaven?"

And if so, why did he have no memory of dying? Was that how it worked?

Even more, why was heaven so odd? He would have expected more white and better-fitted clothing . . . or at the very least, *more* of it—

"Heaven!" Marc, chuckling, shot James a broad wink. "Cause you look like an angel, my brother." He wiggled his eyebrows.

James rolled his eyes.

Timothy frowned.

His hand sought out the gear hidden in his coat pocket. Still there. How could such a thing follow him to heaven?

It made no sense. Just . . . none.

James ran a ragged hand through his hair, shaking his head.

"Look, uh, Linwood"—James placed his hands on his hips—"you're not dead and this isn't . . . well, it's not quite heaven—"

"But you died." Timothy pointed out the obvious. "Arthur retrieved your body from that carriage accident—"

"Yeah . . . that's not *quite* how everything played out."

"Are you saying Arthur lied?"

"Well, a little . . ." James rubbed the back of his neck. "Sooooo don't have time for this right now," he muttered.

Timothy cleared his throat. Something tight and hot clenching his chest. An emotion that felt like elation. Joy at knowing his friend still lived.

*Rule #23: A gentleman suppresses undue emotion, whether of disappointment, of mortification, of laughter, of anger, etc.*

Why was it suddenly so hard to breathe? He tugged on his coat sleeve. Forced himself to think logically. James returning from the grave would *not* be a good thing.

If James were still alive . . . the implications for Arthur and Marianne were dire. Arthur would lose everything, have no way to support Marianne, no inheritance for Isabel.

And with Timothy's own finances in ruins, he would be in no position to help—

"Marc, *please* tell me you aren't looking for more bacon? Cause the driver is anxious about traffic and so help me, if I miss this flight and have to wait even longer to see little Arthur—" A dark head poked around the door frame.

And then, predictably, froze as every eye in the room swung her way.

Timothy should have expected *her* to be here too.

"Miss Wilde." He gave a polite bow.

Miss Wilde cocked an eyebrow at him, eyes instantly guarded. She strolled over to James, wrapping both hands through his arm. Possessively. "I do believe you meant Mrs. Emry Knight," she said, voice so very cool.

*Ah.* So James and Miss Emry had, indeed, married.

But none of this explained anything . . .

James Knight was *alive.* Well and truly alive.

His oldest friend . . .

Timothy could see James' chest rising and falling. The faint shadow of unshaven whiskers on his cheek. Blue eyes slightly blood-shot, as if he were tired.

And why was everyone dressed so oddly? The women in far-too-revealing trousers. The men looking more like day laborers than gentleman. The house so changed—

"Look, Jas, I am so sorry, but we have to go." James was talking to the small woman. Her lovely eyes flared wide with alarm as she clutched James' arm.

"No . . . no, you can't leave me with him." Her voice a low hiss. "You know how he is. You guys have told me *all* the stories—"

"Linwood's a gentleman. Really, he is. He won't harm you." James patted her arm.

To Timothy's dismay, everyone else in the room looked skeptical.

Of all the—

"Of course, I am a gentleman. How could the matter ever be in question?"

James lifted his head, fixing Timothy with his blue eyes.

"Linwood, may I present Miss Jasmine Fleury?" James tugged the woman by the elbow, turning her to face Timothy.

"Miss Fleury." Timothy bowed, giving all and sundry a textbook-perfect example of his *gentleman-like* manners.

Miss Fleury of the scanty clothing and summer-sky eyes gave no reply. Not even a nod of her head or a curtsy.

Instead, she turned back to James, as if Timothy weren't even in the room.

And *he* was the one being accused of poor conduct?

"What am I supposed to do with him? You can't just leave—"

*Beep, beep.*

A loud noise sounded from the yard.

"Jas, we *have* to go." Emme hugged the smaller woman and turned toward the door. "We can't miss our flight. My mom has to go back to work tomorrow, and we need to be there to get Arthur. You can deal with this. It won't be too bad—"

"Yeah, Jas. Who better to deal with this situation than you? Trust the process." Marc snatched Miss Fleury into a quick embrace and then laughed as she groaned and pushed him away. He winked at her and slipped past his sister, stepping out the door, a hand wrapped around Miss Ashton's.

"We'll call once we land in Seattle." Emme touched James' arm. "I'll be in the car."

James pulled a leather purse of sorts from his pocket and removed a rigid, gold card. He tucked it into Miss Fleury's hand.

"Take this. I authorize any and all Linwood-related expenses."

"James, that's not exactly my concern here—"

"And as for *you*"—James turned to Timothy—"I expect you to treat Jasmine as if she were your sister."

"I fail to see how Miss Fleury should be of any concern to me."

The woman in question gasped.

What did she expect him to say? She was not a blood relation nor even a gently-bred lady, it seemed.

Though with all that black hair tumbling everywhere and dainty fey face, she probably had whole legions of farmers and day laborers vying for her hand.

"Some people never change."

Was that sarcasm in James' voice?

"You *will* care for her, Linwood," James continued, "or Marc and I will shred you to ribbons—"

"How dare you, Knight!"

James chuckled, an odd light in his eye. "You know, it is strangely *really* good to see you, Timothy."

And then the unexpected happened.

James Knight took two steps forward and clasped his arms around Timothy's shoulders. Giving him what seemed to be a . . . hug.

*No one* embraced him. Ever.

Timothy couldn't remember the last time someone had touched him in such a manner.

Particularly not another man . . .

That odd thing happened with his breathing again. Something hot burning in his chest. Was he actually *happy* to see James?

Shocked, Timothy held himself intensely rigid, arms clenched at his side.

James chuckled and slapped his back.

And then he turned to Miss Fleury. "Cobra will be in touch. Can't wait to hear what comes of this."

Of all the baffling things—

With a final pat of Miss Fleury's shoulder, James strode out the door.

Leaving a dreadful silence in his wake.

# Chapter 7

That. Did. *Not.* Just. Happen.

Surely, her friends had not just up and left her . . . with the most arrogant, boorish, stuck-up, jerk of a lord to ever inhabit the nineteenth century?

And now, it seemed, the twenty-first as well.

Jasmine stood frozen, James' credit card clutched in her hand.

Like *that* was going to help.

Lord Linwood held himself almost unnaturally still, eyes focused on the doorway where James had just exited. One hand pressed against his coat pocket, as if feeling for something.

He was exactly . . . and yet not-at-all what she had expected him to be.

The expected—rude, cold, arrogant. Icily contained.

The unexpected—handsome . . . startlingly so. Why had no one ever mentioned that? All that thick dark hair with those gray, nearly transparent eyes set into a chiseled, masculine face. Had she ever seen eyes *that* colorless? And tall. Taller than either James or Marc. Easily . . . what? Six two? Six three?

Granted, the pristine cravat, tight (leather) breeches and long nineteenth century overcoat didn't hurt either.

She tilted her head. Yep. Total costume-drama eye candy.

Not that it really mattered. For her, a man's personality so completely influenced his attractiveness, it was nearly impossible to separate the two. And based on that reasoning, Lord Linwood would never be truly good-looking, would he?

Though an energy pulsed through him. As if underneath all that rigid hauteur, something volcanic seethed.

What would it be like to break through his reserve? To find the man underneath?

And wasn't that idea strangely . . . fascinating?

She frowned.

No, surely she had *not* just thought that. There was *nothing* attractive about Lord Linwood.

She was just going to run with that.

Not. Attractive.

Cause anything else would just be . . . *ehww*, right?

Jasmine cleared her throat.

So . . . now what?

How did one deal with a nineteenth century lord?

And why, why, *why*, was he here? What did Fate and the portal mean for him?

Linwood shifted, now gazing at a point about six inches above her head. As if he were stubbornly refusing to look at her.

Yeah, not attractive at all. What had she been thinking? Such an arrogant, impossible—

"Miss Fleury, any explanation which would illuminate this odd sequence of events would be appreciated. I am a busy man with pressing business to attend to and do not have the luxury of frittering my morning away." He tapped a gloved hand against his thigh.

Where to start?

Jasmine sagged against the counter, setting the credit card down and resting her head in her hands. She massaged her temples and then raised her head.

"Look, your lordship . . . Linwood . . . Timothy . . . however you prefer to be addressed—"

"*My lord* will suffice."

"Right." Jasmine paused. "So, *my lord*, there's no easy way to say this. You are *not* dead. This is *not* heaven. You have, however, traveled precisely two hundred years into the future."

Linwood jerked his head down, instantly locking eyes with her. Though his body didn't move per se, shock blazed from him.

Yep. Something definitely seethed underneath that aristocratic disdain.

"Pardon?"

"You are currently in the year 2015, not 1815. The stone slab in the cellar actually covers an ancient time portal."

Linwood turned slowly, taking in the room. Looked back at her. Blinked. And then reeled every last bit of emotion or shock or . . . whatever back inside.

Really . . . interesting.

"Though I am sure you find this humorous, Miss Fleury, I do not appreciate such games. But perhaps you are somewhat lack-witted and do not mean to trifle with me."

Wait, wait . . . what? Did he just imply—

"Excuse me? What did you call me?"

"Lack-witted. Is your hearing affected too?" His face was utterly devoid of emotion now. As if *feeling* were something he did not permit himself to do. "James cannot have traveled far, and he will hopefully have a more lucid explanation of these events. I will merely retrieve my horse and be on my way." Linwood picked up his hat, setting it firmly on his head. "Good day, madam."

He touched the brim of his hat and, turning on his heel, walked out of the kitchen, down the central hallway and out the front door, closing it firmly behind him.

Ooooooookay.

Good luck with that.

And wow. Lack-witted? He truly was a perfectly odious person.

How long would he look for his horse?

Jasmine shook her head.

*Crack.* The front door opened.

"Madam, what have you done with my horse?"

Jasmine stared at the viscount, scowling at her from the doorway into the central hall. The closet door, which led down to the cellar, stood open beside him.

She sighed. "I am sure your horse is happily standing right where you left him in the nineteenth century. But as you are now in the twenty-first century—"

"Bah!" He sliced the air with his gloved hand. "You must cease with this ridiculous nonsense."

As if realizing he was showing emotion—cause, ya know, heaven *forbid*—he forced his face to relax, retreating behind that impassive mask. Again.

Well, at least the man would never have to worry about wrinkles.

Did he yo-yo like this all the time? Or was finding out you had time-traveled two hundred years into the future a special occasion?

She was placing her money on the latter.

Jasmine sank her head into her hands again. She *so* didn't sign up for this. Babysitting an arrogant nineteenth century viscount was not how she envisioned spending her time at Duir Cottage.

"You must go back through the portal, if you wish to return to your own time." She raised her head, gesturing toward the open door in the hallway.

He stared at her for a moment. And then shook his head and turned toward the steps down to the cellar. He stood, confusion flitting across his face.

"I clearly must be fevered or dreaming or have hit my head in some way," he muttered, pulling his hat off his head. He rolled his shoulders and then rubbed his fingers through his hair. "Though nothing is sore. Most curious."

The mother part of Jasmine knew she should do something. Say something nice. Offer him some coffee or tea. Reassure him that every-thing would be alright.

But . . . why? Neither of them wanted him to be here.

And he *had* just called her lack-witted.

He looked back over at her. "So . . . to return, I . . ."

"Just go back into the cellar and touch the stone slab. That should do the trick."

Fingers-crossed. Hope and pray.

He nodded and snapped his hat against his leg. And then disap-peared down the steps.

Only to come back up fifteen seconds later.

"You are still here."

"Aaaaand so are you."

They regarded each other for a moment. Well . . . she stared at him while he focused on a point to the right of her head.

Whatever.

Silence.

"Madam, this game grows tiresome." Voice low and decidedly growl-ish.

"Neither of us wants you here." She rounded the kitchen island. "Let's just get you through that portal, shall we?"

She swung an arm, motioning him back down the stairs. Following him down the steep stairs, she had a clear view of his wide, wide shoul-ders. Well, that and his jerk of surprise when she flipped on the cellar light. The lonely light bulb shone weakly from the ceiling.

He took the few steps across to the slab of granite standing guard over a simple dark depression in the earth.

Jasmine held back, at the base of the stairs. This was the first time she had really studied the portal, oddly enough.

No. It wasn't odd.

She had deliberately *avoided* coming down here. The potency of the portal overwhelmed her. She constantly felt its pulsing electricity thrum-ming through the ground at her feet, tendrils of power drifting into the outside world. Being in the enclosed space amplified the feeling.

It was like an old friend who knew all your secrets and had *expectations* of you. She could feel its energy swirling around her, as if in greeting. Welcoming but daunting at the same time.

Linwood pressed both hands against the granite slab, standing in the dark depression. Nothing changed.

*Drat.*

She couldn't be stuck with him. Just . . . no way. Not happening.

*C'mon, stupid portal. Let him through*, she mentally pleaded.

The energy in the tiny room swirled and then, honest-to-goodness, it shrugged.

As if to say, *I'd love to help but I can't. Deal.*

Was *everyone* abandoning her today?

And why would the portal let him through in the first place? *She* didn't want him to be here. *He* didn't want to be here . . . so why?

Linwood turned around, frowning when he saw her, shaking his head. "This is obviously some sort of odd dream or hallucination." Confused. Bewildered. "Mayhap I just need to return home and lie down."

She shouldn't have found that tiny symbol of his agitation so fascinating, and yet . . .

It was a glimpse of the man housed inside that aristocratic armor. A small boy peeking out. Hurt and alone. Desperate for someone to understand, to soothe his troubles—

*Gah!* Enough!

*This* was how she ended up with lackluster boyfriends. She was such a sucker for a romantic hard-luck story, trying to see good where it didn't exist—

A loud buzzing sounded from upstairs. And then Idina Menzel's voice followed. Tinny and muffled.

*Let it go. Let it go. Can't hold it back anymore . . .*

Her phone.

Linwood deepened his scowl.

Ignoring him, Jasmine scrambled up the stairs, skidded around the large kitchen table and dove for her phone on the sofa before the call went to voice mail.

"Hello." Breathless.

"This Jasmine?" A gravelly, American voice greeted her.

"Yes." Still breathless.

"Cobra."

She shot a glance toward Linwood who had followed her up the stairs and was now prowling around the kitchen.

James wasted no time, didn't he? Figured. James couldn't be bothered to help her with the arrogant nineteenth century viscount currently poking his nose into the fridge, but the second she needed some sleuthing done . . . *bam*, Cobra was on the line—

"You need something done with a nineteenth century viscount too, ma'am? Cause I know people—"

*Oh, right.* Jasmine rubbed her forehead and took a deep breath. She needed to get a handle on her lack-of-internal-monologue issue—

"You're still talking, ma'am. And the first thing you need to do is tell that viscount to pull his head out—"

"Mr. Cobra—"

"It's just Cobra. No mister."

"Yeah. Uh, okay . . . Cobra—"

How did one end up with a name like Cobra, anyway?

Wait, had she said that—

"Do you really want to know, ma'am? It's not a pretty story."

*Focus, Jasmine.*

She shot a glance back at Linwood. He had shut the fridge and was now glaring in her direction. He instantly turned his head, looking away.

Had he been staring at her?

His hat still beat against his thigh. But that was the only motion in his body. His profile was utterly impassive, eyes gazing straight ahead. Every last trace of that vulnerable boy gone. She mentally traced a line from his forehead, down the length of his straight, aristocratic nose, over the bump of surprisingly soft-looking lips—

"Ma'am, you still there? James said something about your needing help tracking down your lost family?"

Jasmine cleared her throat and turned away from Linwood, sitting down on the couch.

She had enough problems of her own without adding a handsome, arrogant viscount into the mix.

The hairs on her neck prickled. Linwood was staring at her again, wasn't he?

The sensation left, followed by the sound of the front door opening. Probably still trying to locate his horse. Stupid man.

"Ma'am?"

Linwood was *not* her problem.

"Why, yes, Cobra. I could use some help."

# Chapter 8

His horse was gone.

Timothy stood on the stoop, hat still pounding against his leg.

Granted, the entire front garden of Duir Cottage was gone . . . or at least drastically changed.

Ivy now covered the low stone wall surrounding the house and a giant oak tree planted to the left stretched over the roof. Had the oak been there as a sapling when he entered the house?

He couldn't remember.

Damn.

The entire situation was disconcerting.

That feeling rose again. The one where his heart pounded beneath his breast with such force it quickened his breathing and made it seem as if the very air itself were a heavy weight intent on suffocating the life—

He closed his eyes.

He would almost label that feeling *panic* . . . but then everyone knew a Linwood never panicked.

When the French broke ranks and charged King Henry V during the Battle of Agincourt in 1415, it was Sir Robert Linwood who beat them back. Fighting with lethal focus when everyone else bolted. He had been made a baron for his bravery; the man's armor and chain mail proudly stood in the corner of Timothy's study at Kinningsley. A constant reminder.

*Rule #6: A gentleman will always act with honor and courage, even when faced with a daunting situation.*

*That* rule was said to have come down from Sir Robert himself.

Sir Robert had not panicked. And neither would Timothy. He felt for the gear in his pocket, clutching it tightly.

This was not real. This was a dream. A weird hallucination. He just needed to return to Kinningsley, lay down, rest. Decide how he was going to convince Miss Heartstone of the Sixty Thousand Pounds to accept his offer.

He tried to call up her face. Had she been blond? No . . . brown? He had waltzed with her . . .

But the more he tried to dredge up Miss Heartstone, the more fugitive she proved.

All he saw in his mind's eye were a pair of wide blue eyes staring from a heart-shaped face framed by hair so very dark and tumbled. And a skirt . . . so short it left little to the imagination—

Timothy stopped himself right there.

Miss Jasmine Fleury was not his problem. Besides, she probably wasn't even real. And, even if she were, she was obviously mad. Wearing the clothing of a child, talking to herself, acting as if she were having a conversation with that silver box she held to her ear.

Twenty-first century? Bah. What utter nonsense.

And as for the strange sight of James Knight and Miss Emry Wilde?

Perhaps the kippers he had for breakfast were spoiled. Had he drank too much wine last night? Or worse, had someone slipped opium into his morning tea?

Unbidden, a memory of his mother surfaced. Dressed in a loose white gown, standing on a chaise in the drawing room, arms thrashing, screaming at the butler to gather all the snakes and lock them away.

There had never been a snake at Kinningsley.

Timothy had stood inside the doorway, watching as the butler and two footmen pantomimed gathering phantom snakes from the floor and furniture, putting them into a bag. His mother watching from her perch, hands clasped to her heaving chest, eyes darting around the room, tracking things no one else could see.

One of many, many such episodes. Opium ate at the mind. She had once mistaken the vicar for King George and spent the entirety of the poor man's visit murmuring 'Your Majesty' over and over while curtsying.

Fortunately, his father had been a year dead by that time. The embarrassment . . .

A Linwood never behaved in such a fashion.

As for Timothy, this odd episode just underscored the strain of his current situation. With Napoleon again on the march, his estate on the brink of ruin and the prospect of a loveless marriage looming, it was no wonder his mind struggled.

It was as if his firmly repressed baser self . . . the side that loved machines and labor . . . were determined to break free.

But he was Linwood. This too he would conquer.

Just as his ancestors had beaten back invaders and fought usurpers.

*Rule #3: At all times, a gentleman should maintain behavior and a demeanor which honors the illustrious heritage and sacrifices of his ancestors.*

He would persevere.

Stuff all those undesirable parts of himself back into that walled-off portion of his soul where they belonged. Maintain the way of life his forebears had fought for. Safeguard the reputation of his family. Restore the family coffers, ensure that his estate went forth whole and intact into the future.

Duty. Responsibility. Honor. Patronage.

It was his burden and, yet, formed the bedrock of his purpose in life.

He would entertain no other options.

There. That was settled then.

Unable to locate his horse, he would merely return to Kinningsley on foot, rest for the remainder of the day, force this unpleasant side of himself away.

With one last glance at the changed cottage, Timothy donned his hat and strode up the gravel lane.

As expected, after a few minutes of walking, the lane intersected the larger road which led to Haldon Manor. Or, at least, the burned out remains of Haldon Manor.

But when Timothy reached the road, it too was different. Instead of the typical packed earth rutted by carriage wheels, the road was now a dark, solid surface. Frowning, he bent down to examine it. It appeared to be gravel embedded into a type of black pitch and then compacted in some manner.

As a road surface it was certainly . . . ingenuous. Unbidden, his mind cranked on the possibilities. A carriage would roll most smoothly over it and at a much higher rate of speed, ensuring that commerce reached faraway markets in record time—

Such a road was hardly practical. The labor to construct it, not to mention the cost, would surely offset any economic gains . . .

*Rule #306: A gentleman does not indulge in the vulgarity of practical mathematics.*

He wasn't going to think about such things. Well . . . not too much. Perhaps he could write a theoretical paper about it. Nothing applicable, of course, just theorems and ideas.

Though, he had to give his imagination credit for sheer ingenuity.

He paused at the juncture of the road, considering turning left toward Haldon Manor.

But no. Arthur wouldn't be there and, with the house gutted, there would be no where for him to rest regardless. Kinningsley would be preferable.

He would follow the road into Marfield and procure a horse from the ostler at the Old Boar Inn. He could be home before luncheon.

Turning to his right, he started walking down the middle of the odd pavement.

Green tinged the trees and birds chirped wildly, darting in and out of branches. A gentle breeze rustled through the forest, seeming to draw nearer.

Timothy paused, studying the trees. Actually, the branches weren't moving, and he felt no wind upon his face.

And yet the rushing sound grew louder and louder by the second until the sound isolated itself behind him.

Whirling around, Timothy stared as the oddest . . . carriage, he supposed . . . bore down on him. He caught a general impression of gleaming silver metal, smoky windows and black wheels.

The strange carriage barreled toward him. Fast. With no signs of slowing.

Wait—was there a person in the vehicle?

Self-preservation set in.

Darting to the side of the road, Timothy stared as the vehicle zoomed by with a roar.

Puzzled, he walked back into the center of the road, staring. The conveyance disappeared in the distance.

What *was* that? Where were the horses? Had the carriage . . . or wagon . . . or whatever broken free from its traces? But how was it hurtling along at such a fast pace, as the ground was level?

He looked back and forth, seeing nothing else and hearing no shouts of alarm.

Was the vehicle self-propelling? He had read all about the exploits of Richard Trevithick and his 'puffing devil' steam locomotive engine and had even managed to visit one of the machines at the mining works near Merthyr Tydfil in Wales when he found himself in the area. The visit nothing more than theoretical curiosity, naturally. The fact that it had sent his head spinning into a web of design possibilities had merely been an unwelcome side-effect. Fortunately, he had been able to channel the ideas into mathematical theorems and a well-received paper in a respected journal.

But machines such as Trevithick's were deafening, unwieldy and put out excessive amounts of smoke and steam.

Things this carriage had not . . .

Though the odd carriage had rolled smoothly along the hard road surface. So, clearly, his mind had prepared for the appearance of the vehicle.

Was that how hallucinations worked?

He should have never indulged his fascination with steam engines. This strange episode was nothing more than a punishment for his inability to focus on those things that he should.

*Rule #308: A gentleman does not design or use machines to bring a good for market.*

If he were a less logical man, he might start to doubt his own sanity.

Timothy shook his head.

The sooner he returned to Kinningsley, the better.

Adjusting his hat atop his head, Timothy continued up the road.

An hour later, panic had set in with a vengeance. When Sir Robert Linwood had fought the Frenchies at Agincourt, he had *known* what he faced.

Timothy on the other hand . . .

He had reached the main road and walked toward Marfield. Well . . . at least what he supposed to be the main road and Marfield. There were just enough landmarks and similarities for him to get his bearings.

But beyond that, everything had changed.

It turned out those odd carriages were everywhere. Parked stationary and empty along the roadside and next to red brick houses. Moving along the streets with people driving them using small wheels. Several vehicles had passed him with what sounded like music playing.

He had finally stopped and peered into one, cupping his hands to the glass. The inside featured seats separated by levers and knobs. More knobs dotted a panel where the wheel sat.

It all definitely looked . . . futuristic . . . to coin a term.

Was this what his overworked brain thought the future would be like?

He approached the center of town, those vehicles still passing at regular intervals.

A woman walked toward him, dressed like Miss Ashton and Miss Emry . . . ehr, Mrs. Emme Knight . . . in tight-fitting, dark blue trousers and a tight short coat, somehow balancing and walking on shoes with a high, thin heel. Her hair hung straight to her shoulders and her eyes, cheeks and lips were covered in a thick layer of cosmetics. She had one of those rectangular boxes pressed to her ear and was talking into it, just as Miss Fleury had done, paying little attention to her surroundings.

She raised her head as they neared and then froze, staring at him with a raised eyebrow. Determined not to be put off by such rude behavior, Timothy touched his hat in the barest of greetings, permitting the slight nod of his head to communicate his elegant breeding.

Her head swiveled as he passed, and he was quite sure she said something like, "Hey Jen, is there a Jane Austen festival going on right now?"

Which made not one iota of sense on any level.

Perhaps he was finally losing his mind.

But as he moved farther into town, such reactions and people became more commonplace. People whirling to stare at him pass.

Men, women and children all dressed similarly in those dark blue trousers with various types of coats and . . . tunics, for lack of a word to describe them. There seemed no consistency in hair length between the sexes . . . or, quite frankly, hair color. He had seen a woman with blue (blue!) hair step out of one of those carriages, waving to the person inside.

There was also no clear distinction between classes. Where were the gentlemen and ladies in their finery? No where did he see a single horse or cart of any sort.

The Old Boar Inn drew into sight. Or, at least, he recognized the building with its white-washed plaster exterior and dark crossing beams. But gone was the wagon yard and bustling ostler. And instead of the head of a grizzled boar, the sign over the entrance stated:

*The Shining Dog*

*Dog Grooming and Tearoom*

*'Grab a cuppa with your puppa'*

Timothy stood transfixed. Surely his mind had finally cracked.

Bewildered, he turned, taking in the rest of the street. Next to The Shining Dog, a window front with the words 'Hopping Holidays' above it advertised a four-day weekend in Boston starting at only three hundred pounds, exclusive of airport taxes and fees. All departing from Heathrow.

Which, if Timothy's memory served him right, was a tiny hamlet west of London.

Why would one start in Heathrow when going to Boston? And why travel for months to only stay four days at a cost of three hundred pounds? Such a journey would surely be only a tenth of that amount.

The window next to Hopping Holidays was equally confusing. It sported images of children's faces with the words 'Have You Seen Us?' written above. The text written in the middle was baffling.

> *Thousands of fostering children wait for suitable adoptive families. If families aren't found, children can be lost in the system. It is estimated that over two hundred children have vanished without a trace—*

Jabbering voices erupted from The Shining Dog. Timothy whirled back to see three slim women walk out. They were dressed much like Miss Fleury had been with severely shortened skirts and hair hanging loose. All three sported those precarious-looking shoes and cosmetics on their faces. Most interesting, the women were foreigners, clearly from the Far East. China, perhaps?

One of them looked in his direction and then froze, squealing with delight and clutching the arm of her companion. She pointed excitedly, talking quickly. All three women staring at him now, grinning widely.

Timothy looked behind him. Surely they weren't this excited to see him?

But apparently, they were.

Within seconds, the women surrounded him. They held those odd rectangular things in their hands and were talking in a language he didn't understand. One of them waved her hand and called to someone else across the street. Two more similar women turned toward them and then excitedly crossed the street.

Two minutes later, Timothy was surrounded by seven (or was it eight?) petite dark-haired women. The first girl (woman?) who had seen him kept saying something that sounded like 'Mr. Darcy. Photo?'

When Timothy did not respond (which how was he supposed to know how to respond to such a phrase, assuming he had even heard her correctly?), she finally gave an uncaring shrug, snatched his arm uninvited and stared at her companion with a wide smile. The companion nodded and held up her rectangular box and touched it, giggling excitedly.

Bewildered, Timothy watched as the women eagerly traded places. The first one now holding up her own thin box while the other woman clung to his arm.

The next five minutes proved more of the same. People grabbing his arms, turning him this way and that, everyone holding up those ridiculous rectangular boxes. He was quite sure at least one of them had pinched his . . .

A blush rose in his cheeks.

The entire group dispersed once everyone had a chance to stand next to him and smile at a box. Perhaps this was some sort of odd Chinese ritual? And if so, why did one of the women stuff a piece of paper into his waistcoat pocket before they all hurried off?

Frowning, he pulled the paper out. The face of an unfamiliar woman peered back at him. A woman with a crown atop her head and the words twenty pounds next to her head.

A twenty pound note?

And a queen?

Timothy took more steadying breaths. Swallowing. Trying to fight back that choking feeling. He stuffed the note back into his waistcoat pocket, if only to spare himself the sight of his shaking hands.

It only partially helped.

Finally, he loosened his neckcloth. A horrid breach of etiquette, but it seemed the only way to get air into his lungs.

Focus. He could focus.

He just needed to get to Kinningsley.

He started walking up the street again.

Around the corner, the parish church stood exactly where it always had with its simple Norman-era body and gothic-inspired steeple.

Looking comfortingly unaltered, though perhaps more careworn around the edges. The same stone fence encircled the graveyard. So not everything was different in this dream . . . or whatever this was.

Perhaps Kinningsley would be exactly as he had left it.

Turning away from the church, he continued up the road. Two more buildings down, Timothy froze in front of what appeared to be a bank.

A board of sorts hung in the window beside the door, gleaming with red numbers which fluctuated every few minutes. The top number was in pounds sterling. That was easy enough. The next number appeared to be United States dollars . . . was this currency conversion? Like a currency exchange?

And if so, what was a euro?

Raising his head, Timothy read the top of the board, that sense of suffocating returning with a vengeance.

*Exchange for March 20, 2015*

The numbers practically shouted at him.

Two hundred years. That's what Miss Fleury had said.

Trying to slow his breathing, Timothy slowly pivoted, taking in the street one more time.

Time travel? The very thought was . . . just . . .

Inconceivable.

And, yet . . .

The logical side of his brain asserted itself. Powerfully.

If this were a hallucination, it was frighteningly consistent. He had yet to see anything which would contradict the hypothesis that he had indeed traveled two hundred years into the future.

Everything, though outlandish and wildly different, conformed to known physical laws and norms.

He hadn't seen any fish swimming through the air. Nor spotted people walking upside down from ceilings.

Even though every part of him howled at the thought, he was a scientist in the end. And when faced with an enormous contradiction, he applied the idea of Occam's Razor.

The simplest solution was probably the correct one.

And based on that, he was in the future. Having traveled from 1815 to 2015.

But how? And why?

And what did this mean for himself, Kinningsley and the viscounts Linwood? What about Miss Heartstone and his financial crisis?

He needed to return to his estate, to see his fine house with its pedimented columns and cream-colored stone, a wide expanse of lawn in front . . .

Timothy continued up the street nearly at a run.

Kinningsley was located three miles outside of Marfield. Timothy knew this. But, according to his pocket watch, nearly two hours had passed, and he had yet to find the turnoff to his estate.

Granted, everything had changed. In 1815, the road was a pastoral pathway through woodlands and the occasional tenant field.

In 2015, the street was a busy thoroughfare lined with low red brick houses. Enormous vehicles passed him, rumbling the ground underneath his feet with their weight. Most of the large carriages sported the words 'Helm Enterprises' on their sides with a picture of a clipper ship underneath.

He paused in front of a walled garden, trying to get his bearings. Through the house opposite the road, he could make out the top of the hill which rose beyond the long drive, leading to the front doors of Kinningsley. But surely, even now, he should be on Linwood land . . .

Shaking his head, Timothy crossed the street and continued on, passing three more houses. Another loud roar sounded behind him and he turned his head . . . just in time to see a large carriage barrel through a deep, water-filled hole. Drenching Timothy from head to foot.

The cold water shocked the breath out of him.

Too angry to speak, he stood in stunned silence, arms held out from his body, water running off the brim of his hat, dripping from his great coat, mud splattered over his waistcoat and buckskins. His tasseled Hoby boots surely ruined.

He wiped the dirty water from his face with a soaking gloved hand.

And then he saw it. The gates leading to Kinningsley. Directly across the road. Stone pillars with carved lions in front and an arched gate with the Linwood coat of arms hanging above.

But it was all wrong . . . the pillars were worn and overgrown with ivy and moss, barely recognizable. And though his coat of arms still hung from the top of the gate, the metal had lost its luster and sat in weathered dinginess. The gate looked like it hadn't been used in years.

Even worse was the white sign affixed to the gate with damning words written in bold lettering:

*Helm Enterprises*
*Headquarters*
*Transportation and Logistics*
*Main entrance 100 yards*

The bottom of the sign had an arrow pointing to the right.

Timothy wasn't sure how long he stood staring at the sign.

It just . . . couldn't be.

No. No. No.

He refused to accept this.

He turned and strode the requisite hundred yards to the 'main entrance,' feet squishing in his boots with every step.

One hundred and *three* yards later, he stopped in front of a more obviously used gate. Wide with thick metal horizontal bars attached to a high stone fence on either side, the gate completely blocked access to the land beyond. Peering through the opening, he saw low utilitarian buildings and a paved road curving off. Beyond the buildings, several tall industrial chimneys rose, belching smoke and steam.

He couldn't see the main house. Should he have been able to see it from here?

He couldn't remember.

The terrible shaking/choking sensation returned. Timothy tried to swallow against the tight vise around his chest. Pressed his shaking hands against his thighs. But to no avail.

A few minutes later, he found himself crouching on his heels, still sopping wet, doubled-over, hat on the ground, hands threaded around his head, gasping in long, loud breaths.

It was his worst nightmare come to life. His lands turned into a factory, the Linwood name polluted and gone.

No legacy. No heritage.

*Rule #1: A gentleman will ensure that the next generation is raised in a manner worthy of the Linwood name.*

Ah . . . the irony.

*This* was why lords did not dabble in trade. *This* was why his father had been so fiercely adamant that Timothy squelch that part of him.

Because *this* was where a love of machinery led . . . to shattered honor and no inheritance to pass along.

Choking and gulping in convulsive breaths, the devastation washed through him. He could practically hear his ancestors howling in their graves.

How had this come about? Did he, Timothy, end up stuck in 2015, leaving his estate in 1815 rudderless and vulnerable to such exploitation?

Without Miss Heartstone and her sixty thousand pounds, was this what his heirs were reduced to?

The panic swamped him again at that thought.

Gasp. Swallow. Breathe.

Or just hold on and pant through the emotion. Which seemed to be what his body insisted on doing.

But his next thought was even worse—

What if he *did* return home, married Miss Heartstone, sacrificed his every hope and dream and desire on the altar of the viscountcy, and this was the result anyway?

Was his entire existence for naught?

# Chapter 9

DUIR COTTAGE
AFTERNOON ON SPRING EQUINOX
MARCH 20, 2015

Cobra had been thorough in his questioning—Jasmine gave him that much. He had plumbed her mind for every last morsel of information, dredging up a long forgotten memory in the process.

*Water chimed, falling gently from the marble fountain into a shallow pool below. "Papa! You're home!"*

*She lifted her head to watch a rugged man with brown hair cropped short gather her dark-haired sister into his arms. Jasmine squealed and ran to join them.*

*Joy. Happiness.*

A fragmented memory, but something new, nonetheless.

Cobra had found the courtyard to be interesting, as it implied she might be from Florida. And the name, Minna, gave him something to go on. He promised to be in touch in a couple days.

So basically . . . wait and see.

After hanging up with Cobra, Jasmine did the breakfast dishes, straightened up her art supplies, threw in a load of laundry, pondered sketching some general ideas but ended up doodling a cute saying she had found on Pinterest (*When in doubt, wear red.* It turned out super darling with the words nestled inside a couture red dress . . .) and then decided it was probably time to clean the cottage's two bathrooms . . .

As she finished scrubbing the second vanity, she admitted to herself she was in full-on avoidance mode.

Voluntary cleaning of bathrooms was usually an obvious tell.

Linwood had vanished.

And the only place he surely hadn't gone was back home to 1815. *That* she would have noticed.

But since he had walked out the door while she chatted with Cobra, she hadn't seen a single sign of him.

Soooooo . . . what?

Why should she care?

He was a grown adult who, despite his snooty personality, did not seem lacking in the smarts department. He knew where she was. And probably could find Duir Cottage again. He was familiar with the area, after all. Granted, the area of two hundred years past, but . . . whatever.

So he had decided to leave?

Great. Good riddance.

Not her problem.

She repeated the phrase approximately fifty-two thousand times as she doodled words and scrubbed bacon grease and shined chrome.

Not. Her. Problem.

But . . .

What if he were hurt? Struck by a car or something?

She pondered the possibilities as she stomped out back to the old stables. She contemplated driving the (sleek, gleaming, please-don't-dent-me) BMW for about two seconds and then rejected the thought.

Better to just use Emme's bike.

Why was she doing this? Linwood didn't deserve her concern. Most definitely didn't want it.

Gah! She was sooooooo done with the whole must-mother-everyone thing. Someone somewhere had to have an addict recovery program for it.

Like 'Twelve Steps to Mother Addiction Rehabilitation.' It would be a support group. Where they all took turns making brownies for each other and asking (cautiously, solicitously) if everyone was keeping up with the program, staying on task, needed any help . . .

See. This just outlined her very problem. She should turn around, go back inside, let Linwood solve his own problems . . .

But . . .

What if he had been arrested? The man didn't even know what a telephone looked like. They would probably haul him off to a mental hospital, and *then* how would she find him?

That was her line of thinking as she pedaled onto the main road into Marfield and belatedly realized she really should have put on a coat instead of the too-thin sweater she sported. (Which was darling, by the way, with its mother-of-pearl buttons and lace cuffs which offset perfectly the scalloped collar of her dress . . . She was heading off to find a *cough* handsome *cough* viscount, for heaven's sake. She hadn't thought about the weather. C'mon, a girl had to do what she had to do.)

The wind picked up, cutting easily through her clothing. Clouds gathered ominously.

Just what the day needed.

Her cheeks were surely red and wind-blown as she wound her way through town, looking left and right.

Nothing.

Had he been mugged?

For what, though? His fancy hat? His scathing wit?

Jasmine smirked.

Not likely.

Probably, Linwood had insulted some innocuous woman who was just walking by and accidentally bumped him with one of those cloth, eco-friendly, Food Co-op bags. Some sweet old lady named Ethel who had just nipped into town to purchase shortbread biscuits and some Earl

Grey for her afternoon tea and had picked up a few grapefruit on a whim because they were in season and on sale (well, last week, anyway . . . maybe they still were) but now her bag was super heavy walking home and Ethel hadn't brought her roller-cart-basket-thingy—because, hello, biscuits and tea were not rolling basket purchases and how was she supposed to know that grapefruit would still be on offer?—then Ethel bumps into his high-and-mighty-ness Lord Linwood who lets loose a whole cartload of nineteenth century snobbery on the poor woman, reducing her to tears and then her grandson, Freddy, happened by and . . .

———————

In the end, Jasmine only had to ask five different people.

Her question: "Excuse me, but have you seen a man dressed up like Mr. Darcy from *Pride and Prejudice*? Ya know, tall, cravat, coat, dark-haired . . . brooding?"

Answers:

"No."

"Hell, no."

"No, but if you find him, love, send him my way."

"Pleeeeeease tell me he's wearing a top hat and extra tight breeches too? Because anything less will kill this story for me."

"Why, yes, dearie. Did you check the churchyard?"

And that was that.

Jasmine found Linwood sitting against the ancient wooden door of the parish church.

Sopping wet with mud spattered over his waistcoat, breeches and boots. Hat resting on the ground beside him. Hair plastered to his forehead. Cravat untied and hanging loose around his neck, shirt opened at the throat and soaking wet.

Head back. Eyes closed. Wrists resting loosely on his pulled up knees.

Basically, beautifully mussed.

"I can't believe you did that to Ethel's grapefruit."

His eyes snapped open. "Pardon?"

*Drat.* She hadn't meant for that to come out—

"I cannot say I am entirely certain what, precisely, a grapefruit *is*, much less who Ethel could be or why she would have one." His look turned quizzical.

Trust Linwood to not let something politely go.

"Just . . . nevermind." She changed the subject. "I found you."

"Indeed. You did." A calculated pause. "Miss Fleury." His tone dripped condescension. Pointedly reminding her that he was to be addressed as 'my lord.'

The. Nerve.

She had gotten off her *cozy* couch and put on her *cutest* sweater and then had biked *miles* in the cold only wearing the aforementioned not-terribly-warm (though, remember, cute) sweater, and had uttered the phrase 'cravat, coat, dark-haired and brooding" *five* times to complete strangers, two of whom had made it very clear they thought her a nutcase—

She was an *American,* for crying out loud. Americans 'my lorded,' like, no one. Wasn't it against The Constitution?

Life, liberty and the pursuit of happiness of not having to call people lords?

It was definitely something like that . . .

Reading the ire on her face, he raised a cool eyebrow, flicked his eyes up and down her person, clearly dismissing her darling sweater (lace cuffs and pearl buttons!), and then closed his eyes, resting his head back on the door. Again.

Completely ignoring her.

*Oh!*

She totally should have said *all* that out loud.

"Well, *Timothy* . . ." She lingered nice and long on his name, causing his head to jerk back to attention. That was better. "Given that I have just spent the better part of two hours searching for you, I would expect perhaps a teensy bit of gratitude."

Or even a casual 'jolly well done' or whatever it was British lords said to each other in Parliament—

"Jolly well done?"

Damn. *Now* she stopped filtering—

"I am terribly sorry, *Miss* Fleury,"—the Miss a sibilant hiss—"but as I know the precise location of Duir Cottage relative to my current position, I was unaware that I was, in fact, lost—"

"Please! Look at yourself. You are the absolute *definition* of 'lost.'"

"I beg your pardon?"

Jasmine gestured her hand up and down, indicating his clothing.

Which, to be honest, was a complete mess. Wet, muddy, disheveled.

*He* was a complete mess.

His pale eyes gave her another similar perusal. No doubt noting her knees knocking a little from the cold. Though did he linger just a tiny bit on her cute sweater?

And why, why, *why* would she care even if he had?

"What happened?" she asked, folding her arms across said darling sweater as the March chill seeped in. Why hadn't she grabbed her coat? Stupid vanity.

Silence.

"You are cold." It was not a question.

She looked at his drawn lips, noting the bluish tinge. "So are you," she replied.

He shrugged and then pushed himself to his feet.

Make that up, up, *up* to his feet. She craned her neck to see into his face.

Did his body *have* to be as big as his ego?

With purposeful calm, he pulled off his long, drenched overcoat, resting it carefully over the top of a nearby gravestone. Underneath, he wore a dark blue wool coat, tightly tailored to his broad shoulders. His greatcoat had spared his blue coat from mud and ruin. Which, given how lovely it looked, wasn't a bad thing.

With purposeful tugs, he stripped off the blue coat, leaving himself in an untied cravat, waistcoat and shirtsleeves. All three of which were soaked to the skin in a strip running from his chin to his waist.

And, no. She had *not* just stolen a glance at the wet white shirt glued to the front of his chest.

Nope.

She raised her eyes up to his, determined not to look down again. Which was a bit of a mistake. As his eyes were baleful and direct, at present.

"You are cold," he repeated, shoving the blue coat into her hands.

Jasmine startled and reflexively grabbed the coat. Opened her mouth to give a resounding retort. Shut it. And then frowned.

Without waiting to see if she put the coat on, he turned, picked up his overcoat and, taking several steps away from her, shook off the excess water.

Jasmine stood very still. Painfully aware of the coat in her hands, still warm from the heat of his body.

Deliciously warm, in fact.

She tentatively moved her hand. The wool was incredibly soft, feeling almost like cashmere. And it was lined with . . . silk? A gorgeous, nubby silk. Hand-dyed with natural colors, surely. And all definitely hand-sewn with precise stitches. The hours of workmanship in such a garment—

Why would he do something so chivalrous?

Talk about taking the wind out of her sails.

She should refuse to wear it. Sheerly on principle.

But he was right. She was cold. And she would hate to be rude.

Especially given that he had done something vaguely . . . decent. Nice, even.

With a grudging sigh, she slid her arms into the still-warm coat, shivering as the heat of it hit her chilled back. Feeling just a little too much like he had wrapped her up in his arms.

The coat drowned her, as was to be expected, but she pushed her hands down through the silk-lined sleeves and then pulled the bulk around her, burying her nose into it for added warmth.

What was the English saying? In for a penny, in for a pound?

Something like that.

And then she got a noseful of the coat. Or, rather, a noseful of *him*.

Wool and sandalwood with subtle hints of fresh hay and wood smoke.

Was this what the nineteenth century smelled like?

A far cry from the cigarette smoke and carbon monoxide of twenty-first century cities.

Or was the smell his own? Eau d'Linwood?

That didn't actually sound too bad.

She took another deep breath. Fine. It smelled rather divine too.

How could such a nasty person smell so good?

Though, given that he had just relinquished his coat to her, he couldn't be all bad . . .

Linwood gave his long overcoat one last good shake, surprisingly muscular shoulders rippling underneath his white shirt—not that she noticed . . . well . . . not too much—and then shrugged into it.

Seeing his hat still sitting next to the church door, Jasmine stooped and picked it up.

"You almost forgot your hat."

Linwood turned around, and she extended the hat toward him.

"Thank you." He reached for it. Their gazes tangled.

She froze, hand still clutching the hat brim.

His eyes . . .

So pale. Bloodshot.

Gutted. Shell-shocked.

Lost.

His cheeks clearly stubbled with a five o'clock shadow and speckled with dabs of mud.

He flinched at her gaze. As if he disliked what he saw there.

Clearing his throat, he instantly turned away, tugging his hat free of her grasp in the process.

He slapped his hat against his thigh, back half to her. An errant breeze ruffled his hair.

What had she done?

And did she care to make it right?

"Thank you for your coat," she said after a moment. "You were right. I was cold."

Silence. *Tap, tap, tap* went the hat.

"I do not need, or even desire, your *pity*, Miss Fleury," was his cool reply. His deep bass ringing through the churchyard.

*Ah.*

Well, then.

"I did not desire or need your coat . . . but you gave it to me anyway, *Timothy*. And I, at least, had the decency to say thank you—"

He whipped around, eyes narrowed and angry. Brows drawn.

And then, paused. Reeled everything back inside. Face becoming instantly impassive.

Kinda eerie how he did that.

"I am a *lord*, Miss Fleury. A viscount of the realm. So spare me your bleeding heart—"

"Excuse me? Pity is hardly a weakness or even an unwelcome emotion. It simply means that I'm human and my *bleeding* heart empathizes with your difficult situation. That same heart which decided to get out the door and come find you before something bad happened—"

"I am a grown man. I have been taking care of myself for more years than—"

"Pahlease! Take care of yourself? You're a nineteenth century *viscount of the realm*." Jasmine was rather proud of how she captured his refined, aristocratic drawl. "From what I understand, men like you can't even dress, shave or, quite frankly, *bathe* themselves. Does your valet chew your food for you too? Pray, explain to me how that constitutes 'taking care of oneself'?"

Linwood's eyes were back to spitting anger. His jaw clenched. Something rippled on his cheeks, there and then gone between blinks.

Why did she get such a thrill from riling him? Why should she care to elicit some emotion from him, no matter how negative?

He was just such . . . a starched shirt.

And, let's face it, she was much more of a wet-plastered-to-the-chest-shirt kinda gal.

Though his shirt right now . . .

Jasmine shook her head. Not looking down, remember?

"I would not expect one such as *yourself*"—he spit the word like a curse—"to understand the refined ways of the aristocratic world."

"I understand your little aristocratic world, alright. So arrogant and full of itself. It's a wonder you can see past your bloated sense of pride."

"Pride, where it is warranted, is hardly a sin—"

"That pride keep you warm at night, your *worshipfulness*? Does it make you happy as you stroll around your big empty house with all its big empty rooms full of . . . of . . . stuff that can do nothing more than silently sit . . . all big and empty-like?"

Linwood blinked. "Pardon?"

Right. What was she trying to say? And why did he bring out the worst in her? What was she fighting here?

She crossed her arms, his heavy coat sleeves tangling her hands. Giving her another hefty whiff of Eau d'Linwood in the process.

"Do you realize how obsolete you are?" She tossed her head. "Every last aristocrat could vanish off the planet right now, and the world would keep on spinning without a blip."

His head reared back, as if her words had slapped him. Something that looked suspiciously like . . . like *pain* . . . danced across his face.

Lost. Forlorn.

And then, between one breath and the next, he shuttered it all away.

Wow. How many years did it take to master that level of self-control?

"You are entitled to your own opinion. Please forgive me if I choose not to share it with you." With a curt, stiff nod, Linwood jammed his hat on his head. "You are welcome to the use of my coat for as long you need. I bid you good afternoon, Miss Fleury. "

He gave a short, exquisitely polite bow and then turned, striding out of the churchyard.

He *would* say something about the coat. Talk about making her feel like a heel.

She wanted to peel it off her shoulders and throw it right back into his arrogant, stubborn, proud face—

Jasmine pinched her lips together, staring at his hyper-erect back as he swung open the gate and stepped onto the street. His head swiveled back and forth, obviously trying to determine where to go.

*Just walk away, Jasmine.*

This broken man clearly did not want her mothering help.

She did not need to be the damsel-in-shining-armor to his knight-in-distress.

And then, *it* happened.

The unthinkable.

His shoulders . . . *sagged.*

Not much. Just a faint inch or two of droop. But it was enough.

And in that motion, Jasmine understood the depth of his distress.

In the space of a few short hours, his world had been upended. A proud man used to always being in control. In command.

Stripped of everything he had ever thought important.

And what had she called him? Obsolete?

Yeah, that hadn't been too nice.

*You know my name. Not my story.*

Unbidden, the words drifted through her mind.

What *was* the story behind this man? He hadn't just been born this way, right?

*Ugh.* Why did compassion always get the better of her?

The least she could do was call a truce.

Sighing, Jasmine trudged through the gate, stopping beside him on the curb.

He glanced at her. And then turned his face back to the street. Cleared his throat.

And then . . . actually shuffled his feet.

She totally should *not* have found the motion endearing.

"If you would be so kind as to point the way to the nearest inn—"

"James would kill me if I sent you off to a hotel. The house is more than big enough for the two of us. Let me show you a modicum of hospitality."

"I do not wish to trespass upon your—"

"Look. We're both eager for you to return to your own century, and as the portal is in Duir Cottage, you need to stay close. Besides, someone needs to make sure you don't get plowed down by one of those huge lorries."

She emphasized the point by gesturing her chin at a Helm Enterprises truck thundering past.

"A bit late for that," he muttered.

Jasmine instantly bit her lips, knowing Linwood wouldn't appreciate her laughing at his disheveled state.

"Is that what happened to you?"

He ignored her question.

"What are those called again?" he asked instead, indicating the road where the truck had just disappeared.

"A lorry . . . well, that's what the British call them. Americans would call that a truck or a semi, I suppose."

"Ah. So all these vehicles are . . . lorries?"

"No, just the big ones. The smaller ones"—Jasmine nodded at a passing Ford Fiesta—"are formally called automobiles. But everyone just refers to them as cars."

"*Auto* from Greek meaning 'self.'" He nodded. Processing.

"And then *mobile*, from Latin meaning 'moving,'" Jasmine added without thinking.

He arched an eyebrow. "Ladies still study Latin, I take it?"

"No. Just me."

She had totally rocked AP Latin in high school. Cause she was only good at things if they were pointless and practically useless outside of a trivia game.

"Did you drive one into town?" He flicked a hand toward a passing car.

"Not . . . exactly. Let's get you home and, along the way, allow me to orient you to the basics of twenty-first century life."

# Chapter 10

THE ROAD TO DUIR COTTAGE
TWILIGHT ON SPRING EQUINOX
MARCH 20, 2015

Timothy found the walk home to be . . . illustrative.

It provided a welcome distraction from the weight which had set up solid residence about four inches left of his breastbone.

Kinningsley was no more. Or, at the very least, had been sold off, turned into a factory.

The very thought—

Staring unseeing at the road ahead, Timothy slowly breathed through the now-familiar sensations of chest-tightening, throat-choking, heart-beating, hands-tingling.

*Rule #37: A gentleman is always in control of himself and his situation.*

This too would pass.

Instead, he glanced down at Miss Fleury next to him, guiding that bicycle—completely Greek in origin, that one, *bi* meaning two and *cycle* meaning circle—fascinating how the twenty-first century just put words together . . .

Yes, the mental diversion was useful.

It provided a nice buttress between himself and those panicky sensations.

Of course, just looking at Miss Fleury proved the best distraction of all.

By Jove, she was utterly lovely.

Creamy skin and button nose. All that hair hanging loose, held back with a sheer bit of fabric. When she had come upon him at the church, still dressed in that impossibly short skirt, but now topped by a form-fitting tunic held together with a tiny row of pearl buttons—

Timothy swallowed and slowed down his breathing . . . for an entirely different reason.

He had shoved his coat into her hands as much to preserve his sanity as to provide her with warmth.

Unfortunately, the coat had not been entirely successful in its aim. It had swallowed her up, arms pushed through his long sleeves, delicate, small hands clutching the lapels, leaving her lovely eyes peeping out from the collar.

Making him wonder—with more curiosity than was wise—what it would be like to re-don the coat and, yet, still keep its arms around her like that. Hold her to his chest—

More forceful breathing ensued.

Best not to think of such things.

He would not trespass upon her hospitality long. Miss Fleury spared little love for him. And if she thought of him at all, it would be to wish him good riddance as she pushed him through the time portal, those tiny hands of hers pressed firmly into his spine. Sending him back to his nineteenth century existence. Never to be seen, heard or even thought of again. This strange interlude shortly forgotten.

And why did that thought feel oddly . . . dissatisfying?

*Rule #23: A gentleman suppresses undue emotion, whether of disappointment, of mortification, of laughter, of anger, etc.*

Ice. He would be ice. Contained. Impervious.

Numb.

They had finally turned off the main road and onto the drive which led to Haldon Manor. Thankfully this road was calmer and they walked down the middle of it.

Asphalt, she called the pavement.

Which was just one of many new words.

Thus far, he had learned:

Queen Elizabeth II reigned, but she had no real authority. Britain was fully a democracy now. Which meant the House of Lords and hereditary peers had little power, as well.

Miss Fleury took particular delight in pointing out *that* salient fact.

The United States and Britain were close allies. As were the French. His brain struggled to imagine a world where this happened.

Other interesting words.

Euro and European Union, of which Britain was sort of a part. She had been vague on the particulars.

The aforementioned automobile and its related car, truck, semi, bus, motorcycle, train and tractor. Surely he was forgetting some.

Airplane and airport. Still trying to grasp at that concept. Metal birds which flew through the sky? Miss Fleury insisted that an airplane's wings remained static and did not flap. But how was that possible if it flew? He had yet to see a bird fly without moving its wings. Which had led to more new words, namely—

Video, television, film, movie. Like a play only enacted in a location, not on a stage. And then projected onto, or into, a screen? And you could make your own?

Miss Fleury had promised to show him "a video of an airplane flying on my phone but cell reception is bad here, so it will have to wait."

At which point, she waggled that rectangular silver box at him.

That box, turns out, was the *phone* in question. Or, more aptly, a telephone. (Root words meaning 'voice at a distance'—Miss Fleury's grasp of Latin was nearly as good as his own.) The device allowed one to speak with another person instantly, even halfway around the globe. She had listed other things that a phone did, most made little sense, but which had led her to describe . . .

Computer and Internet. Quite frankly, he had given up trying to understand by that point. The concepts just seemed too . . . vast.

Or perhaps it was Miss Fleury's garbled description. Something about information being pushed through a 'pipeline' that crossed all geo-political boundaries?

So many words he did not know.

That feeling arose again—heart pounding, palms sweating—but he was able to more quickly tamp it down this time. That sense of numbness providing a welcome barrier between himself and the messy emotions the year 2015 elicited.

And James Knight had stayed here in this century? Voluntarily?

Miss Fleury had clarified that story.

"Emme was the first person to go through the portal that we know of. You know how she was found in 1812. She and James fell in love, and James liked the idea of this century, so he left his nineteenth century estate to Arthur and came through to this century to be with Emme. He's been here for almost three years now. He and Emme married about two years ago and have a darling baby boy."

Something sharp jabbed Timothy in the chest. James? A father? Why did that idea cause him to feel . . . jealous?

What was happening to him?

Timothy shook his head.

"But Marcus and Miss Ashton . . ." he said. "Daniel Ashton is my man of affairs. Does he know about the portal? And what about Arthur? Heavens, does Marianne know too?"

"Both Arthur and Daniel know about the portal. Marianne is your sister, right? I don't think she knows. Arthur is the portal's protector in the nineteenth century, setting guards to make sure no one inadvertently gains access. Though it seems to have failed, in this case."

Which brought up a lingering question about the third Knight sibling . . .

"And Miss Georgiana Knight? Was she involved with the portal too?"

Miss Fleury lit like a lamp. "How is Georgie? I miss her so much. She was here for about a year or so. Remind me to tell you about antibiotics sometime. Isn't Georgiana the best? And I was so happy to hear of her marriage to Sebastian. Emme really liked him when they met—"

"Pardon? Are you speaking of Sebastian Carew? The Earl of Stratton?"

"Exactly. You know him too?"

"Naturally. We have worked together in the House of Lords. He is a fine gentleman."

"Yeah, that's what James said. Sebastian was here for a couple of weeks with Georgiana."

Was Timothy the only person of consequence who did *not* know about the portal? How could Arthur, and then Sebastian and Daniel, have kept this information from him?

It was one more point of failure.

Close friends, and even family, keeping enormous secrets from him. Kinningsley on the brink of collapse in 1815 and turned into a *factory* in 2015. All he thought he knew, everything he had been raised to value . . . utterly upended.

Panic pounded on his chest. Again. The sensation was becoming such an unwelcome nuisance.

*No.* He would not give in. He was Linwood.

He fought it back. The numbness enveloped him. Blessedly freeing. Like floating in a fog, where nothing seemed real.

Though it was only fitting as they neared the turnoff to Duir Cottage that the skies opened up with an impressive English spring deluge.

Rendering his outsides just as damp and miserable as his insides.

Both he and Miss Fleury were shivering by the time she stowed her bicycle into the former stables. Timothy stood dripping wet just inside the door, staring accusingly at the glossy car parked snug and warm. The letters 640i blazoned on the back.

It looked . . . expensive. Like an apt conveyance for a gentleman.

Why hadn't she brought this? He had seen women, as well as men, driving the cars through town. Perhaps she didn't drive then? Or perhaps Americans didn't drive, only the English? America was a rude and backward country after all.

Sweeping back her drenched hair, she met his gaze. Noted his studied perusal of the car.

"Do you not drive?" he asked.

"I do."

He waited expectantly. She made a moue with her lips and then shrugged.

"It's a long story. And I'm freezing." She moved past him and then turned back. "Besides, modern plumbing just became your new best friend."

An hour later and Timothy had to mostly agree with Miss Fleury's assessment. Modern plumbing was *almost* his new best friend.

His first love was electricity, however. The house was not lit by candles nor warmed by fire.

No.

Everything ran on electricity. One only had to press a switch to instantly illuminate any room. Everywhere he turned, there was something new. Some machine or curiosity which Miss Fleury had deemed so far beneath her as to not warrant mention.

Things such as the clock at his bedside which displayed time numerically in bold illuminated red.

And then there was the washroom . . . a space gleaming with shining surfaces, mirrors and metal.

He had installed bathing rooms at Kinningsley several years prior, providing flowing water to four flushing water-closets. But in examining the water-closet in this wash room—things Miss Fleury had called a toilet and a bathroom, respectively—he realized the mechanisms were much more advanced. He had lifted the lid off the tank of the toilet and studied the series of valves inside.

Fascinating. So when one pressed on the lever, it opened the valve, allowing water to flush into the bowl, using gravity to displace—

No. Not going to obsess on the mechanics of this era.

He firmly replaced the heavy tank cover.

Shutting away all his curiosity.

Well, perhaps not all.

How did the hot water work here? Did electricity heat it too?

He had created a plunge pool off his chambers at Kinningsley with water heated by a boiler located in the cellars. But Duir Cottage wasn't large enough to boast such a boiler.

Granted, none of it compared to the marble-and-glass shower. He had heard descriptions of portable washing tents which sprayed their occupants with water. But this bathing device had a variety of nozzles and water could rain from the ceiling or massage your back from the side . . .

It was a thing of beauty.

He began calculating the water pressure needed to achieve the precise jets . . .

*Damn and blast!* This age was seductive as the most alluring siren.

Though Miss Fleury had been right about one thing. He *had* never shaved himself.

Why should admitting that fact to himself cause a flash of . . . embarrassment?

He was a viscount. A lord of the highest standing. There was no shame in adhering to the strictures of his station in life. Perhaps he could use one of those phone-things to contact James and discuss the hiring of a valet, if only for the day or two he might be here.

He most certainly would need the help of a valet to navigate modern apparel. Thus far, he had been decidedly unimpressed with what he had seen.

Timothy knew he had an impeccable sense of fashion.

*Rule #127: A gentleman embodies style and elegance of inner being and physical person.*

He required every minuscule part of his wardrobe to be precisely tailored, pressed and immaculately turned out.

The clothes Miss Fleury had provided met none of these requirements.

The dry undergarments were passable.

But he had stared for a while at the clothing she had laid out on his bed. She called it 'lounging clothing,' because they were 'in for the night.'

The items had apparently been purchased for Sebastian who was only slightly larger than Timothy, so Miss Fleury supposed the clothing would fit well enough.

Loose trousers with a dark-blue plaid pattern in what appeared to be a finely woven cotton with only a drawstring to hold them up.

They felt so . . . odd.

He would have preferred silk. And the trousers should have been more closely tailored.

As for the shirt . . . it was of a stretchy cotton and was pulled on over the head without using buttons of any sort. It seemed to take the form of whoever wore it, as it stretched to envelop his chest like a glove showing every curve and plane. Far too form-fitting for polite company. But, he admitted grudgingly, surprisingly comfortable.

The only saving grace for the entire outfit, if he could call such attire an *outfit*, was the banyan. Dark green and luxuriously soft, it wrapped around him. Like being enveloped in warm pudding.

Though it sadly lacked a belt.

Yes. He would definitely need to contact James and arrange for a tailor, as well. Even a short stay required proper apparel. In the meantime, he would have to suffer through as best he could.

Fortunately, as he bathed and dressed, that remarkable emptiness settled. Solid and unmoving. Blissfully numbing.

Proof that, even under the strain of this most unusual situation, his breeding as a gentleman was secure.

Pulling on a pair of stockings (again, made in that same soft, stretchy material), Timothy trudged downstairs to the cellar, flipping on a light as he went, instantly illuminating the space.

Electricity. What a marvel.

The air in the cellar pulsed with an almost palpable energy. The portal stood opposite the wooden stairs, odd carvings on its surface and a dark depression in the earth beneath it.

But as had been the case earlier in the day, he touched it to no avail. He could feel something pulse and vibrate under his hands. But nothing happened. His vision did not darken. No vertigo assaulted him.

Surely there was a mechanism which triggered the portal to open. But what?

A rogue blast of pain and fear broke through his reserve.

What if he was never allowed to return? What if Kinningsley was doomed to become everything he had been taught to despise?

*Rule # 11: The disgrace of the* paterfamilias *is shared by all.*

Surely there was a way to rectify this? Change the future?

Tugging on the tight shirt (it seemed to have a tendency to climb up his chest), he exited the cellar.

Miss Fleury was in that strange room where the kitchen had previously been, but it now seemed to provide the function of a kitchen, a dining room, as well as a sitting room. All in one.

She was in the sitting room portion, seated before a crackling fire in the large hearth, the room lit brighter than noonday despite the blackness outside. Light blazed from small holes in the ceiling, from pendants hanging over the central counter in the kitchen, from a chandelier over the large dining table, from sconces along the walls.

The room itself was decidedly untidy. Odd shiny packaging cluttered nearly every surface . . . refuse of some sort. Stacks of paper littered the kitchen table, covered in drawings. A loose jacket hung over the back of a dining table chair. A long shawl over another. Books tumbled here and there.

Pieces of paper fluttered on the walls, the cabinets, some even stuck to the fireplace mantel—all prettily decorated with swooping lettering.

*Trust the process*, one read.

*When in doubt, wear red*, said another.

What process? And why the color red?

More things which made no sense.

Miss Fleury herself was curled up on the sofa, back to him, feet tucked underneath her, wet hair in a loose braid over one shoulder. She had changed as well into a deep red baggy tunic and skin-tight black trousers that seemed to be made of the same material as his shirt.

She was drawing. Pencil moving confidently across white paper. He paused, staring over her shoulder at the figures taking shape.

A lady in medieval dress, standing atop a crenelated castle wall. An armored knight below her, seated on his horse, looking upward toward his lady. Miss Fleury was sketching in a young squire holding the reins of the horse when a thought occurred to Timothy. One which explained the sorry state of the housekeeping:

"I have not seen a single servant since I have been here."

Letting loose a decidedly un-ladylike screech, Miss Fleury nearly jumped off the sofa, whirling around, hand flying to her throat.

"I would expect a lord to announce his presence." She sent him a stern look. "Or, even better, have a butler do it." She resettled herself, sitting back atop her feet, shaking her head.

"If I could locate a butler, I assure you, my presence would be most thoroughly proclaimed." He came around the sofa and, shifting a shawl onto the hearth, sat in one of the pair of wingback chairs which flanked the fireplace.

Miss Fleury's head snapped back up. "Wait. Was that a joke?"

"I am not *entirely* devoid of humor, Miss Fleury." He lounged back in the chair, crossing his legs at the knee.

She studied him for a moment, firelight flickering in her blue eyes.

"I am going to say the jury is still out on that one." She cocked her head.

Timothy shrugged and then gestured up and down, indicating his loose trousers and too-tight shirt. "I donned this clothing, did I not?"

And then, the brightest light in the room came on.

Miss Fleury . . . smiled.

An expression of genuine delight which grew slowly and ended with a startled chuckle. Mischief gleaming in her eyes.

Timothy quite forgot how to breathe.

He could not remember if he had ever made a young lady smile. Or, rather, smile out of genuine delight over something he had intentionally said.

The sensation was . . . marvelous. Like champagne bubbles in his blood.

Though it had the unwanted side-effect of shattering his numbed state. Emotions crashed through him.

Silence.

Timothy could think of nothing else to say. She had effectively scattered every coherent thought from his brain.

<hr />

*Wow.* What just happened?

Jasmine slowly picked up her sketching pad, trying to ignore the palpable energy that had walked into the room with Linwood.

Was he always like this? So . . . larger-than-life?

It was those eyes of his. Nearly unnaturally pale . . . like looking into a silver mirror.

They pierced you straight through.

And, really, the man should *not* look that good in pajama bottoms and a tight t-shirt, a cashmere robe thrown casually over the top. Even his clothing would never be so gauche as to not be perfect on him.

Why had no one ever mentioned how forceful his presence could be?

Or . . . wait?

Was that the very thing which others automatically scourged him for? The sheer *power* of his decidedly intimidating personality?

Was he truly arrogant? Or just . . . misunderstood?

*You know my name. Not my story.*

He continued to regard her with those mirror eyes.

"I find it hard to believe that Knight does not employ, at minimum, a cook? Certainly you do not prepare your own meals?" His voice cut through the room.

Well . . . how about she called it a draw? Arrogant *and* misunderstood.

The doorbell rang. Linwood glanced about in alarm.

"What was that—"

"Dinner."

Jasmine chuckled as she paid the delivery person (with James' credit card, naturally) and carried the Indian takeaway back into the kitchen, setting it on the table. Linwood walked over, brow furrowed, studying the boxes as she opened them.

"Curry?" he asked.

"Yep. Though for the record, I can make a mean chicken enchilada."

His head swiveled up. "So you *do* cook?"

"Everyone cooks. Even the Queen of England could fry herself up some eggs, if needed." She threw the words over her shoulder as she grabbed plates and forks from the kitchen island.

Linwood just stood still. Or, at least, marginally more still than normal. Processing this, apparently, difficult thought.

Royalty caring for themselves.

*Mind-boggling.* She wanted to wiggle her fingers at him, as if casting a spell.

"C'mon, big guy," she said, handing him a plate and sweeping a pile of papers out of the way on the table. "Eat up. You have to be starving."

With a blink, he took the offered plate and sat down with a thud. Jasmine pursed her lips. Hard to say which specific thing had set him off.

The notion of the queen cooking? The idea of eating food from a box? Having to kick it in the twenty-first century with her for an undetermined amount of time? Low blood sugar?

They ate in silence for a few minutes. She pulled out her phone and reviewed her texts. Emme had messaged to say they arrived in New York and 'thanks, Jas, for taking care of things.' But the *sub*text was all wow-I-can't-believe-you're-stuck-with-that-loser-viscount-cause-he's-just-*ehw.*

Not helping.

Dinner was better, however. The chicken korma was delicious, creamy with just the right amount of sweet. It was heaven with the heat and tang of the tikka masala. All sopped up with naan still hot and dripping with ghee.

Linwood dug in with gusto. Jasmine couldn't fault his appetite.

"So why are you here, Miss Fleury?" he asked as he helped himself to another spoonful of korma. "Do you live here?"

That's right. Somewhere in the orient-the-viscount-to-the-twenty-first-century-thing, they had never talked about her.

Well, for starters, there was one thing they needed to get straight—

"We need to get something straight?" Linwood asked, pausing with his fork midway to his mouth.

*Drat.* Jasmine cleared her throat.

"Look, if we are staying here together, we should start calling each other by our first names." She pointed at herself. "Jasmine." She pointed at him. "Timothy."

He put down his fork and raised a haughty, *pardon-me?* eyebrow. Pure disdain.

She crossed her arms, matching his condescending eyebrow-ness. "It's the twenty-first century way. And I do believe there is this old saying, perhaps you've heard it. When in Rome . . ." She rolled her hand. *And so on.*

He studied her for a moment, smoothing his face back to its impassive mask.

"You do realize that goes against every ounce of breeding beaten into my body, correct?" He sat back in his chair.

She stiffened.

*. . . breeding beaten into my body . . .*

What an *interesting* choice of words.

What *was* his story?

"Other than my sister, I have never referred to any woman by her given name," he continued. "I shall probably not even refer to my wife—should I ever acquire one—by her given name. She would be 'Lady Linwood' or 'my lady' to me."

Now it was Jasmine's turn to sit back in her chair. Unsettled.

"That has to be about the saddest statement I have ever heard." she said. "No wonder you're so emotionally distant. You have this thick wall of protocol and manners which thoroughly bury all normal human interactions—"

"I beg your pardon?"

She leaned toward him, as if imparting a secret. "Look, we have this thing in the United States we call a *chill pill*—"

"A chill pill?"

"Exactly. It's not a literal pill, but instead something you metaphorically take in order to force yourself to relax. To let go of stressors in your life."

"Stressors?"

"Exactly. Things which cause stress. Or make you feel uptight."

"Uptight? Like this shirt I am wearing?" He plucked at the form-fitting t-shirt. "Really, Miss Fleury, you need to speak English—"

"And you need to call me Jasmine."

A pause.

"I . . . cannot do that."

"Yes, you can. Take the chill pill and call me Jasmine. It's not hard. Relax."

Another long pause.

Linwood . . . ehr . . . Timothy, that is, angled his body toward her and stretched an arm along the back of the upholstered dining chair. The other hand beat a steady tattoo on the tabletop.

"Let me be sure I clearly understand your reasoning, Miss Fleury—"

"Jasmine."

"*Miss Fleury*," he said with deliberate emphasis. "According to you, due to the presence of a mystic time portal in the cellar of my brother-in-law's dower house, I currently find myself two hundred years and several miles removed from my estate with no guarantee of returning any time in the near future. At this moment, my manners—the very behaviors which make up my breeding as a gentleman—are the only hope I have of maintaining my tenuous hold on sanity. So I ask you, *Miss Fleury*, to please allow me some modicum of self-preserving pride."

Well.

If that didn't just suck all the air out of the room.

Jasmine folded her arms and squirmed, tucking a foot underneath her.

Fine. Whatever.

"I still intend to call you Timothy," she finally said. "It's the *American* way."

Arms still outstretched, he coolly nodded his head.

"But you should think about it. Taking that chill pill. I think you could do with a little R and R," she said.

He raised a quizzical eyebrow.

"Rest and relaxation," she clarified.

Both eyebrows went up. *Ah.*

Though aside from the drumming of his fingers, he didn't look too stressed. Just sort of . . . vacant.

Like he was checked out.

She would expect him to be panicked or, at the very least, more visibly angry.

Everything he had ever known had been stripped from him. Surely there would be some sort of mental distress over it. A mourning of what he had always thought to be true.

But this tense . . . nothingness. It was not unlike . . .

*Uh-oh.*

What were the five stages of grief again? Marmi had always talked about them with one client or another—

Denial, Anger, Bargaining, Depression, Acceptance.

Though the denial phase could be more aptly named 'shock and awe.'

And given how coolly his most honorable lordship, Viscount Linwood, had been eating his basmati rice . . .

She was going to place her check mark firmly in the little box next to 'Denial.' Not that his emotional health was her problem or anything. She wasn't in charge of him. No mothering needed.

But . . .

"Soooo," she said with deliberate casualness, "how are you . . . feeling? Anxious? Panicked?"

He studied her for a moment, fingers still drumming. And then smoothed his hand flat on the table. Quieting even that small sign of agitation.

Rock still.

"My emotions are as they always are . . . imperturbable."

Imperturbable. Meaning . . . composed, calm, collected? Had she *ever* heard someone drop such a word into casual conversation?

And by imperturbable, did he mean numb? Anesthetized?

Wait—

"Anesthetized?" he asked, pondering the word. Probably breaking it into its respective parts. Did anyone else realize how freakishly smart he was? "That is an appropriate word, I suppose. You may describe me as such."

And then, with eerie imperturbable*ness*, he went back to eating his rice.

# Chapter 11

She was drawing again. Miss Fleury. Jasmine.

Jasmine Flower. It was an appropriate name.

Timothy stood in the doorway of the bedroom, staring at the large canvas stretched along one edge of the room. It was about four feet high and probably ten feet long. What were her intentions with it?

The crib in the corner proclaimed this to be the baby's room.

Arthur.

James had a son. Named after his brother and grandfather.

Why did seeing James' life here cause something *pained* to ripple through his chest? A longing. Almost like . . . envy.

That morning, Timothy had awakened to brief disorientation. No footman bringing in hot chocolate and a buttery scone, stirring the hearth fire to life.

No.

His bedroom was already suitably warm. And, given that Queen Elizabeth would fry her own eggs, it seemed unlikely anyone would cook breakfast for him.

He had availed himself of the shower again and had successfully limited his mathematical mind to innocuously calculating the trajectories of the water jets instead of fixating on the mechanics behind the shimmering overhead lights. He was determined to resist this era and its siren-like alluring machinery.

Though he rubbed his stubbled chin in regret. How did men shave in this age without the help of a valet? But there were no servants here. His entire way of life upended. Just as Kinningsley had become a factory.

And with that thought, the terrible chest-crushing panic returned. After a few tense moments of concentrated breathing, he forced it back, finding instead that wonderful sense of being *anesthetized*—lovely word that.

Thank goodness.

Miss Fleury had left dark trousers, a shirt and a jacket upon his bed while he was in the bathroom. All in the modern style he had seen James and Marc wearing, though perhaps a little more tailored.

The ensemble was not entirely lacking in merit. The shirt, a pale blue color, had a marvelous subtle sheen to it and the gray jacket molded suitably well to his shoulders.

It would suffice for now.

She had also returned his blue coat, dry and no worse for wear. Thankfully, his gear was still in the pocket. He had slipped it into the jacket he currently wore before tracking down Miss Fleury in baby Arthur's room.

The room was cheery and flooded with light and, blessedly, somewhat neater than the kitchen area. Though like downstairs, there were those same mysterious sheets of paper attached here and there on the walls, each featuring a different saying.

One stood out:

*Sometimes good things fall apart, so better things can fall together.*

Did she believe this drivel? What utter nonsense.

Miss Fleury had her back to him and not wanting to startle her, he rapped a knuckle on the door frame.

She turned around, greeting him with a wan smile.

Her hair was piled haphazardly on top of her head with curls escaping here and there, a wide sheer strip of fabric wrapped around her crown to hold most of the mass back from her face. Though she still sported trousers, they were thankfully loose and silken, their bright blue color matching her eyes.

No, her clothing had seemingly swapped places.

Now it was her white shirt which was skin tight with a low scooping neckline and sleeves extending to her wrists. Showing quite clearly *exactly* how much of a woman she truly was. Had she been wearing such a shirt yesterday, he would not have thought her a child for even a fraction of a second.

Honestly, did the woman have *any* pity on him?

She raked her eyes up and down his attire.

"You clean up good," was her cryptic remark.

Timothy ran a self-conscious hand over his chin. He *hated* having to admit he had never shaved himself. But if he were going to be presentable . . .

"Thank you . . . I think. Though I shall need to find myself a valet or, at the very least, a barber."

She paused. And then popped her hip to the right and cocked her head. A sly grin spreading.

"Riiiiight. Because you really *don't* know how to shave . . ."

He chose to ignore the comment and merely glanced about the room instead. Tried to control that damn panic which threatened again.

*Be numb. Anesthetized.*

She took pity on him.

"I'll consider getting you a razor, some shaving cream and a YouTube video. But I'm making no promises."

He turned his eyes back to her. Her words made no sense—

"A suitably trained valet should be sufficient, Miss Fleury."

A beat.

"Yeah, I'm not sure valets even exist anymore. Well, besides people who park cars for a living. And I know you don't mean *that* sort of valet. I could probably locate a stylist for you . . . I'll have to ask James. Though you might want to consider keeping the stubble. It's not a bad look on you."

"Sarcasm, Miss Fleury?"

She cocked a surprised eyebrow. Blinked. "No. Just . . . stating a fact."

She turned back to . . . whatever it was she was doing. There were sketches on the floor and taped to the far wall. More knights and ladies.

"You still have not told me why you are here," he said.

She shrugged and then stood, still facing away from him, hands on hips, foot tapping. Shaking her head, she started to mutter. It was something she did quite frequently.

"Well, you see, my boyfriend, Mike, dumped me over Christmas—which was as awful as it sounds—and then the man got engaged to some dumb floozy just three months later. Which is how I ended up here, because Emme knows I have this habit of running away when my emotional life is all whacked. It was all fine and dandy until Mike called with glee to tell me I'd lost my family too and hey-isn't-that-just-so-interesting?"

She wiggled her fingers in the air and then kept right on talking.

"Okay, so maybe it wasn't exactly with *glee*, but he could have been a teensy bit nicer about it all. I mean, we're talking my entire sense of self-identity here. And then James gets his man, Cobra, to track down my family—which is fine and all, but how far can you trust someone who willingly names themselves after a snake? It's this weird combo of too-precious and totally creepy—"

"Boyfriend?" What did that word mean? Not to mention— "How does one lose a family?"

She whirled back to him, lovely eyes so very, very wide. And then groaned, tipping her head into her hands, muttering words which sounded suspiciously like *not again*.

"What I meant to say is that I'm an artist." She lifted her head. "I am a painter and Emme and James hired me to create a work for little

Arthur." She spread a hand, indicating the long canvas and room, in general.

"Of knights and ladies?"

"Exactly. What else would I draw for a baby named Arthur Knight?" She shrugged. "It is to be a King Arthur inspired series of scenes, depicting the feats of the Knights of the Round Table. Herefordshire was part of the historical kingdom of the Britons, not to mention Caerleon and the castles of southern Wales which are only an hour away by car—so I plan to use visual references from the area."

"You do realize that Arthur was most likely more Roman than British in origin, right?

A pause. "Well . . . I suppose. I think I saw some History Channel special on it—"

"The true King Arthur probably looked nothing like all these sketches of medieval knights."

"Well, aren't you a Debbie Downer?"

"Pardon?"

"Never mind." She waved a careless hand. "The mural is meant to play on the baby's name and capture the romance of a bygone era—"

"The Middle Ages was hardly a romantic time period—"

"Are you deliberately trying to be a kill-joy?" She stopped, hand flying to her hip again. Eyebrow raised.

"Not at all. Merely pointing out inconsistencies. Have you visited Wales yet?"

"I'm . . . uh . . . putting together a plan." She sighed and pursed her lips. "So, what are *your* plans for the day?"

Before he could answer, she glanced down at the drawings at her feet and then bent to rearrange them, muttering again. "Have you checked the portal yet? Because, you *definitely* need to make it a point to check that portal every chance you get. Like three thousand times a day. At minimum. Actually, you probably should just camp out down there. I will toss you the occasional cheeseburger and fries. Cause you never know when the portal might let you through and, heaven knows, I plan on throwing a *huge* block party as soon as it does—"

"I have already checked the portal three times this morning."

Miss Fleury's head snapped back, eyes whirling toward him. She pinched her lips tightly together. Had she not realized she was talking aloud?

Silence.

"Right." She stood, brushing her hands down her loose trousers. "Uhmmm, so as I was saying, what were you planning on doing today?"

"I was considering utilizing the car—"

Up went her eyebrow. "The car? You do realize they're not terribly simple to drive, right?"

He matched her eyebrow with one of his own. "It is an inanimate machine, Miss Fleury. It is not like controlling a spirited horse—"

"There is no *way* I am going to be responsible for letting you get behind the wheel of that high-performance, manual transmission, insanely expensive, just-waiting-to-be-dinged vehicle parked out back. James would murder me. With a blunt knife. In cold blood." She emphasized her point by moving her pencil across her neck in a cutting motion.

Timothy blinked. Knight was hardly the type to be so concerned about a mere possession.

Reading his disbelief, she continued, "That car cost well over a hundred thousand pounds, Timothy. I'm terrified to so much as *breathe* on it."

A hundred thousand pounds? Timothy felt the world spin.

"Such a figure is breathtaking, Miss Fleury."

The sum was . . . staggering. For a mere method of conveyance? Surely, all those cars were not that expensive.

She froze, clearly startled by his reaction. "Well, I mean, I'm sure inflation has been a factor—"

"Inflation?" He fought the image of a car filling with gas like a hot air balloon. That was surely not what she meant—

"Like the value of money going down. Wait, let me check it for you." She pulled her telephone out of a pocket and then spoke to it. "Okay Google. How much is one hundred thousand pounds in eighteen fifteen money?"

Silence and then a tinny voice sounded from the box: "One hundred thousand pounds in twenty fifteen would be the equivalent of three thousand pounds in eighteen fifteen."

Miss Fleury shrugged as if to say, *There. You see.*

"Three thousand pounds? So roughly the cost of a lovely pair of matched bays and a high-perch phaeton?"

Now it was her turn to look confused. "Sure."

A beat.

And then they both spoke at once:

"You'll have to talk to James—"

"You ask your phone a question, and it tells you the answer? Does this Google person know everything?"

Miss Fleury broke off with a delighted laugh. It was a beautiful sound, clear and bell-like. Bringing to mind spring flowers and summer breezes.

"Yes. Google does know everything," she chuckled. "But it's not a person. It's a computer . . . or more like the aggregated repository of all human learning."

Well, that was certainly . . . useful, was it not? He sternly told himself that he did *not* find the concept endlessly fascinating. No. He did not.

He would focus on the task at hand.

"Could this Google tell me about the portal then? I need to understand the mechanism for triggering it."

Miss Fleury sighed and set down her pencil on a small table near the canvas.

"Google knows a lot of things, but it's not much help with the portal, unfortunately. Trust me. We've looked over the years . . ."

Timothy gestured. *Pray continue.*

And so she did. Timothy had to force his emotions down, down, down as she spun a tale about the universe as an ocean and bonds that could be created through time, allowing one to travel centuries in the blink of an eye.

"I really wish I had answers for you, Timothy." Her shoulders sagged. "But for others who have passed through the portal, there was a reason. Someone they needed to meet or something they needed to do or realize. Once you have done that, the portal will work, and you will return home."

"And until that point?"

She shrugged. "You need to figure out what you must do."

Timothy started to pace, back and forth, back and forth in front of the doorway. It was a frustrating lapse in control, but his feet needed to be moving. His hand sought the gear in his pocket.

Emotions kept surging against the wall of calm he had built around himself. Forceful, panicky things. He didn't know what would happen if they broke through. He needed to remain . . . anesthetized.

Kinningsley was a factory in this age. Some tragedy had forced his estate to make a degrading descent into trade. *That* was why he was here. He had to prevent this horror from ever occurring. Preserve his heritage.

The portal . . . the universe as a whole . . . had set this task for him.

Deep breath. He forced his feet to stand still. He turned back to face her, spine perfectly straight.

"Well, Miss Fleury, my path is clear. I will borrow the car and visit Kinningsley."


His words lingered in the small room. Jasmine cocked her head, trying to understand the non-sequitur.

At least he had stopped his pacing.

"Excuse me?" she asked.

He seemed energized. As if he had shaken free of his stage-one-grief-denial thing.

Which probably wasn't a good thing. Because he wasn't moving on to Anger, so this probably represented a regression of sorts.

And, on a completely unrelated topic, could she just get him a beard trimmer and convince him to keep the stubble? There was nothing sexier than a hot guy in expensive Italian threads with dark stubble on his cheeks.

You add in a pair of pale silver eyes and *boo-yah*—

"Kinningsley. My estate in 1815," he explained. "I tried to go there yesterday, but the gate was closed. There was a sign upon it—Helm Enterprises. Their headquarters are on the grounds of my estate."

Yeah, that stubble really had to stay. It so made his eyes pop. Uh—what had he just said?

"A company is headquartered at Kinningsley? And that's . . . bad?" Her head listed even farther to the side.

"Of course." Aaaaaand, he was pacing again. "How could this happen to my estate? It is a complete desecration of everything my ancestors fought and died to maintain."

He had a hand in his hair now. Man, he was definitely cuter when he was a little agitated. And if she had to hide every razor in this part of Britain to keep that stubble, she—

"Wait," she said as his last words caught up with her. "Your ancestors fought to *not* own a business? Cause owning a business which earns lots of money is . . . not good?"

He paused and then slowly removed his hand from his hair, staring at it. As if he were appalled his fingers had done something so gauche as to touch his head. He returned his hand to his side, again holding himself utterly still.

"Miss Fleury." His voice a model of restraint. "A finely bred gentleman, particularly a Linwood, does not dabble in *trade*."

"That makes . . . no sense. How could you be anti-money? Isn't that the definition of an aristocrat? Like if I said, *Okay Google, define aristocrat.* Google would come back with—*Aristocrat: Arrogant person who has cartloads of money earned from the blood and tears of serfs.* Or something like that."

He froze. Fixed her with that *look* of his. One part condescension mixed with two parts contempt and a dash of how-can-you-possibly-be-so-stupid.

"My family has never owned serfs. The nineteenth century is perfectly civilized—"

"My bad. Child factory workers then?"

Uhmm, okay. Make that *three* parts contempt.

And given how wide his eyes went, she had probably gone a teensy bit too far. But seriously, what was the problem here?

"The point, Miss Fleury, is that my legacy has been overtaken by merchants intent on trade. Merchants work. Gentlemen do not. That is what constitutes the difference between the classes."

"Work?"

"Precisely." There went The Look again. "If Kinningsley has become the headquarters for a large business, then my family must no longer be gentlemen. Can you not see the dire nature of this tragedy? Surely this is why the portal summoned me through. To cleanse this ghastly stain from my good family name. Someone, somewhere made a terrible decision and allowed Kinningsley to be raped in such a manner. That decision needs to be unmade."

*Whoa.* Had he really just used the word *raped?*

Ooookay.

"Fine, Timothy. We can try to go to Kinningsley. But let me just warn you. One of the facets of the portal is its determination to protect the space-time continuum."

He blinked. "The what?"

"Space-time continuum—the sequence of cause and effect which forms the basis of our reality. The portal—or rather, the universe in general—will not allow you to see or hear or learn information which might alter past events. At no point, in all of our dealings with the portal, has anyone changed the course of history. It's actually astonishing you were able to learn that Kinningsley had become the headquarters for some international conglomerate—"

"Are you stating there is nothing to be done about it? Even if I learn where, when and how the change occurred?"

"I'm saying it's extremely unlikely the universe will allow you to find that information. And if you *do* learn those things, you will not be able to affect the outcome. We can try to visit and learn what we can, but chances are, our efforts will be thwarted."

"What definitive evidence do you have which supports this hypothesis?"

Jasmine blinked. Man, this conversation had suddenly become way too technical.

"Well . . . no one has been able to yet, so—"

"Just because it has not happened up to this point, it does not signify that such a change is impossible."

Silence.

"True," Jasmine said reluctantly, though the idea felt wrong.

"As you admit, by permitting me to see the potential destruction of Kinningsley, Fate has already shown me more than others have been able to see. Why would it therefore follow that I cannot do more? It would make more logical sense that I have been sent here specifically to correct this situation."

"I'm not so sure . . ."

But Timothy seemed convinced. He nodded his head decisively. "Righting the wrong which has been done to Kinningsley is my purpose here. I am sure of it. We will leave now to visit my estate. I will drive the car—"

"No." Jasmine shook her head in exasperation. *This* she for sure knew the answer to. "No, you won't. *That* will not happen."

Did the man ever listen to anyone other than the delusional voices in his head? Besides, what were the chances James' car insurance covered snotty nineteenth century viscounts?

"If the automobile only cost three thousand pounds, James most certainly will not begrudge me its use."

"You're totally missing the point—"

"Miss Fleury, *you* clearly do not understand the seriousness of this situation." He stared at her with those steely gray eyes.

"You aren't driving." She lifted her chin, fixing him with her firmest look.

A beat.

"Very well," he said. "I will permit you to play coachman for me just this once. I will await your presence downstairs. You have three minutes."

And with a curt nod, Mr. Snotty Pants turned and left the room.

"I thought you said you knew how to drive one of these things."

"I do."

"Then why are you doing it so poorly?"

Jasmine resisted the urge to smack Timothy's sexy-stubbled arrogant cheek.

If only she could get a hand free . . .

"Careful. You are driving too close again."

"So help me, you touch my steering wheel one more time, I will personally cut off your finger."

Again, once she had a free hand . . .

Stupid clutch. James *had* to go and buy a stick shift. Cause having everything backwards wasn't already bad enough. She had to deal with manual, left-handed shifting too. She had reached to shift with her right hand over a hundred times by now, almost opening the car door more than once. Not to mention the windshield wipers and the signal indicator—also both on opposite sides. The windshield was exceptionally clean now—

Worst of all, the BMW was a stallion of a car. She could feel the power of the engine underneath the gas pedal. It *wanted* to go really fast. Was practically begging for it.

Timothy nudged the steering wheel, subtly correcting the car. *Again.*

"You nearly hit those stationary vehicles."

"I know what I'm doing."

"Are you sure?" Timothy asked. Jasmine could see his clenched jaw and wide eyes in her peripheral vision. That, and the death grip he had on his door handle. His knuckles as white as hers. This was probably *not* the best introduction ever to riding in a car.

"Look. As I explained to you, I learned to drive in the U.S. where everything is opposite. So cars drive along the right side of the road, not the left. And the steering wheel is where you are currently sitting, which means that my sense of distance is all off—"

"Why would Americans choose to drive on the opposite side of the road? Britains have always driven on the left. It makes sense because other vehicles pass to your right. How can this feel unnatural to you?"

Jasmine gritted her teeth. "Simple. It's opposite of everything I've ever known. Like trying to write correctly while looking in a mirror. Or like if you had to drive a carriage backwards with the horse behind you, sitting on the opposite side, but the reins were somehow in front of you and suddenly everything was reversed cause you were looking over your shoulder and trying to drive . . . ya know, like that . . ." She trailed off, biting her bottom lip.

A looooooooong pause and then—

"You do realize that, given the trajectories involved, what you describe is physically impossible? It makes no sense on any level."

"People take a whole year to learn how to drive one of these things. So I figure I got at least another three hundred and forty-seven days to master this. It's a process."

She swerved around a parked car, wheels squealing faintly, edging a little too close to an oncoming lorry. The trucker honked loudly.

Timothy tightened his grip on the door. "Assuming we live that long."

In the end, Jasmine successfully navigated the few miles between Duir Cottage and Kinningsley, Timothy pointing left and right, helping her remember which side of the road to stay on. His huge sigh of relief when she parked the car summed up his feelings about the experience.

But she had done it! She had driven in Britain for the first time. And the BMW was still shiny and scratch-free.

So far so good.

Getting out of the car, they crossed the street to a white metal gate, a sign blazoned with Helm Enterprises hanging from it. It only took a moment to realize the gate was locked. There was no call box.

After staring at it for a few minutes, Jasmine dug out her phone and googled the company's website.

What do you know? It was down.

So predictable.

She resisted the urge to give Timothy her most smug smile. This was what always happened when they went digging where Fate didn't want them to be. Seemingly simple tasks became impossible.

Another Google search and she found a company phone number.

Disconnected.

Again, predictable.

By this point, Timothy was seething. Pacing *and* with a hand in his hair.

Practically coming unglued. At least for Lord Linwood.

Well, she *had* tried to tell him this would happen.

Finally, one of those huge lorries chugged up the road, the gate slowly opening automatically. The driver pulled beside them and rolled down his window when Jasmine waved him down.

"Excuse me, sir," she said, pasting on her flirty smile. "We were wanting to speak with a manager, if we could."

The man scrubbed a hand over his bald head. "Oy, that's not gonna happen, miss. Been too much goings on with the corporate espionage case. No one is allowed to talk without speaking to lawyers first. Would be me job to talk to you, much less send you on to a manager. Terrible sorry."

And with a nod of his head, he drove through the gate which closed behind the lorry with clanging finality.

Yep. This was definitely the universe preventing them from seeing anything more.

"Was that man speaking English? I could barely understand him." Timothy stood beside her, hands on his hips, hair mussed from his fingers.

"Look, Timothy—"

"Lord Linwood," he growled, pale eyes snapping.

Uh-huh. Definitely coming unglued. The anger phase was going to be awful.

Or . . . spectacular. Kinda depended on your point of view.

"Look, *Timothy*, I told you." She *loved* a good I-told-you-so. Hah! "The universe won't allow you to see beyond this point. For some reason, you were to learn that Kinningsley has been turned into some company's base of operations. But beyond that, you won't be able to change anything. What's done is done. The path has already been determined."

He shook his head, hand going into his hair again. "No! I refuse to accept that answer. Why else would I be here but for this?" He waved a hand toward the estate in question.

"Don't look at me. I'm just telling you how things work—"

"Well, you obviously do not understand what is at stake."

He whirled away from her and stomped over to the gate, grasping the metal bars, hanging his head between his arms. Shoulders heaving, as if he had just run a marathon.

"I will not accept this!" He lifted his head and surveyed the tall gate. And then he pulled on his hands, lifting himself up, climbing the metal railings.

Jasmine gasped.

"No, Timothy, don't!"

This wasn't going to end well.

And sure enough, he had only gotten three rails up when a horrendous squall exploded out of the seemingly cloudless sky, pelting them both with blinding rain.

Lightning cracked. And then cracked again. Thunder boomed, vibrating the ground with its force.

"Get down, you idiot," Jasmine screamed. "You're going to get us both killed."

Another flash and loud bang.

Timothy clung to the gate. Stubborn fool.

Desperate, Jasmine ran to him and jumped up, grabbing his pant leg, tugging him downward.

*Crack. Boom.*

Another jump and tug.

Finally, he let go, dropping the few feet to the ground. Snatching his arm, Jasmine dragged him back to the BMW. Away from the gate. Away from temptation.

Before she even unlocked the car, the sun reappeared. Bright and shining. As if nothing had happened.

Timothy leaned his back into the car door, hands on his thighs, head bowed, panting.

"See." She gestured toward the gate. "Could the universe have *made* this any more clear? Kinningsley is a no-go-zone. We don't investigate. We don't ask questions."

"Like. Hell." He lifted his head, eyes full of steel. "This is my family you negate—my *honor*. The very blood which pumps through me."

"Timothy, there is some other reason—"

"No! This"—a finger pointed toward the dripping gate and estate beyond—"is why I am here. If only to understand what needs to change in the past." Jaw clenched, hair dripping wet.

"You're wrong, Timothy. The only question to ask is this: Why would the universe ensure you knew your estate had been turned into a hotbed of merchant activity? Ask yourself *that* question, *Lord* Linwood."

# Chapter 12

W hy *did* he need to know that Kinningsley had become the very thing he had been taught to despise?

Certainly, it was so he could correct the problem before it happened. That was the only logical explanation. Knowing this, he would return to 1815, marry Miss Heartstone and ensure that future generations could not betray the family name. Tie up the entail in such a way that his descendants would be unable to fracture the family heritage.

His path seemed self-evident. Except Miss Fleury insisted that was not the case.

Timothy stared at the ceiling. As he had been for the last three hours.

The bedside clock proclaimed it to be three twenty-three in the morning. The glowing red letters, searingly bright, left a ghostly impression when he looked away.

He had given up on sleep at precisely one fifty-one.

His talisman cog glittered in the low light, sitting in front of the clock. Reminding him of his exact place in the vastness of the universe. A gear. A small part of the whole.

If fixing the problem with Kinningsley wasn't his purpose here, as Miss Fleury insisted, then what other options were there? To know everything he valued would be gone within a generation or two?

His hopes. His dreams. His very . . . life . . .

Everything for naught.

*That* was the message he was supposed to receive?

*Your entire existence as a human being is moot, now be off with you.*

As a message, it seemed cruel and . . . pointless.

Even worse . . . he had spent the last ninety minutes listening to the damn hum of that clock with its damn bright *red* numbers—

Chest-tightening, palms sweating, heart pounding . . .

Breathe. He could breathe through this.

*Rule #19: A gentleman never loses his temper.*

Control. He just needed to regain control.

And still the clock hummed.

*That* was the price of electricity, he was coming to quickly realize.

An almost constant noise.

The lights buzzed, the refrigerator vibrated, the clock hummed—

He pinched the bridge of his nose. Breathe in. Breathe out.

A glance. Three twenty-six. The gear glowing.

He was *not* insignificant. He mattered. His existence *did* have meaning—

He was going . . . going . . .

Something violent wrenched free.

Exploded through his chest.

Roaring.

Acting almost of its own accord, his hand reached out and yanked the clock off its table, tearing it free from its socket. And threw it with every ounce of power in his body against the opposite wall.

It made a satisfyingly loud crash as it disintegrated.

He wasn't permitted a reprieve, however.

Seconds later, footsteps sounded in the hallway and his bedroom door was thrown open.

*Bam!*

Miss Fleury stood rimmed in light. The sconces in the hallway perfectly backlighting her slim form dressed in tight trousers *and* a tight shirt. The woman had no mercy.

Her head swiveled, surely taking in the broken clock.

Dimly, Timothy noted that he was sitting up in bed, lungs-heaving. Shirtless.

"Get out!" he shouted, twisting, looking for something to throw at her. "Just get the bloody hell out!"


Jasmine jumped back with a start, slamming the bedroom door shut.

Well.

Well, well, well.

That had certainly been . . . illustrative.

Muscles. Just lots and lots of . . .

She swallowed.

Were all lords built like that underneath their clothing? Because, if so, no wonder every romance heroine wanted to marry one.

The image of him sitting in that bed, bare-chested, hair rumpled, eyes fierce and snapping—

Yep. It was gonna linger. She wasn't going to lie.

And as for the shout and crash which had woken her . . .

Looked like the stay in the Duchy of Denial had been brief indeed. Onward and upward to the Empire of Anger.

The Island of Acceptance couldn't come soon enough.

Group text message. 12:09 P.M.

Jas:    mayday mayday mayday

James:    *Didn't we just celebrate the spring equinox, Jas? Mayday isn't for another 5 weeks.*

Emme:    *Are you planning the festivities already?*

Jas:    **face palm** international symbol of distress people

Emme:    *????*

Jas:    timothy linwood
I'm going to kill him
or he might kill me
it could go either way

James:    *You do realize that feeling is quite normal with Timothy, right?*

Jas:    the portal won't let him through but he has to go home or at least move on to bargaining as soon as possible

Emme:    *Bargaining?*

Jas:    five stages of grief . . . denial anger bargaining depression acceptance

James:    *Wait? Someone died?*

Jas:    only his 19th century sense of self
he's not coping well
there are bits of alarm clock all over his bedroom floor

James:    *Let me guess. Anger?*

Jas:    bingo

Jasmine stared as Timothy neatly lined up the salt and pepper shakers, labels facing toward him. Made a minute adjustment to his fork on its napkin. And then straightened the folded newspaper one more time, aligning it with the slats of the table.

For the fifty-second time.

She gave the eggs she was cooking a stir.

"I am only making you breakfast this one last time. You need to learn to take care of yourself."

Silence.

She was *such* a bleeding heart to even be doing this much for him.

Someone needed to cut every mothering tendency from her body.

It was just . . .

She still had yet to brave the British highway system (again) to gather visual references for the King Arthur mural.

Cobra hadn't come up with anything, though he claimed the police department in Florida was being cooperative. So she was no closer to finding her family.

And as for Rita . . . Jasmine should have anticipated her response to the china. Rita had texted earlier.

> *Thanks for the china. Breanne is excited.*

A pause. And then—

> *But Breanne was wondering about the old pillowcases you had. Didn't Great-Grandma Fleury embroider those?*

Jasmine had let out a long-suffering sigh. She should have seen this coming. You give an inch . . .

Why was karma playing with her like this? She refused to respond to Rita. Let the woman stew for a little bit.

All in all, her life was stuck in neutral.

And now she had an angry diva of a viscount storming around the house . . . well, more like a cross between angry diva and ice princess.

Generally cold but prone to outbreaks of fiery prima-donna-esque temper.

Timothy nudged the salt shaker infinitesimally to the left. Body hyper-erect. Every inch of him immaculately clean and brushed and pressed.

Except for that chin growth.

Somehow, Jasmine hadn't *quite* been able to find a razor for him yet. *Oops.*

Passive-aggressive, you say? Why, yes. Yes, she was.

How someone could be so arrogant and intimidating and yet so *pathetic* at the same time was beyond her.

And then there was the anger . . .

She dumped the eggs onto a plate and walked them over to him. Deliberately placing the plate lopsided and half on top of his fork.

He shot her The Look. Straightened the plate. Corrected the displaced fork. "As I have repeatedly told you, I prefer my eggs coddled."

"And as I have repeatedly replied, I don't *do* coddled."

Neither eggs nor viscounts.

"*That* is patently obvious, madam."

"You need to learn to take care of yourself—"

"I *can* take care of myself!" His eyes snapped. His chest heaved. "I have been taking care of myself and mine own for nearly my entire life, Miss Fleury."

"Really? Because what I'm seeing here is a grown man who can barely dress himself, much less cook food."

"My concerns are far greater than the mere cooking of a pair of damn eggs."

"Sounds like an excuse to me."

"I govern *thousands*, madam. People who rely upon me for their very life—"

"And where are these people?" She spread her arms, as if looking around. "Cause all I see here is an angry inconsiderate jerk who's upset that he has to lift a finger to provide for himself."

"Thank heavens I do not seek your bloody damn approval—"

"And what's up with all this swearing? You kiss your mother with that mouth?"

Man, if The Look could kill . . .

"Given that my mother was an opium addict who spent her days alternating between arguing with the Emperor of China and screaming at footmen to capture the flying snakes, we did not find much time to enjoy a cozy bloody damn relationship." His chest heaved.

Uhmmmm . . . *what?*

Was he finally losing it entirely?

*. . . my mother was an opium addict . . .*

She knew from Marmi's work as a counselor that the children of addicts usually lived in distorted realities. Either seeking out trouble, acting out, emotionally clingy.

Or the exact opposite. Cold, withdrawn, emotionally distant. Add in a generous helping of hyper-rigid societal structure and what was certainly a controlling, distant father . . .

Wow. The perfect recipe for a man like Timothy Linwood.

The blast of empathy shooting up her spine wasn't quite welcome. Her mothering-self didn't need any more reason to act out.

"Isn't a gentleman supposed to refrain from swearing in the presence of a lady?"

"If by *lady*, you refer to yourself, I have serious doubts as to that. You could not even qualify as a *servant* in my household." He flicked a dismissive hand over his breakfast.

Yep. He was still—

"And this, madam,"—he slid the eggs off the plate and onto the newspaper—"is what I think about your eggs!"

—an arrogant, inconsiderate jerk.

Timothy trudged downstairs, checked the portal, fetched the newspaper off the stoop, checked the portal, set the newspaper on the kitchen table, checked the portal, considered dismantling Miss Fleury's bicycle to study its mechanics, checked the portal, successfully resisted the bicycle temptation (again) and then checked the portal once more.

Nothing.

Which then necessitated him standing in the kitchen doorway for a good three minutes, pinching the bridge of his nose as he breathed through another chest-pounding, lung-tightening attack of panic.

Once he felt generally sure he could open his eyes without screaming, he glanced around the great room. Leftover dishes, clothing, books . . . and everywhere those ridiculous pieces of paper with their equally ridiculous perky sayings. Stuck to the walls, the cabinets, the refrigerator.

Why did James hesitate to hire a maid? A gentleman could not live in such squalor.

Though a space had been cleaned on the counter. If pushing back cups and stacking bowls on top of older newspapers counted as 'cleaned.'

A box with the word 'Nutri-Grain' on it stood in the cleared space. A note pasted to its surface, of course.

*Here is your breakfast. Enjoy. JF*

He stared at the paper, hand tapping. The woman was so—

Maddening? Infuriating? Homicide-inducing?

He lifted the note, tugging it free. There was some sort of mild glue on the back. He refused to find it interesting.

Miss Fleury had to have a supply of these somewhere. Glancing around the kitchen, he finally spotted what appeared to be a pad of the odd notes under a cup.

*Excellent.*

Jasmine strode into the kitchen two hours later, intent on a cup of tea and some biscuits. Through the open windows, she could see Timothy in the backyard pacing back and forth, hand in his hair, in full-on seething/brooding mode.

Good. Served him right for being such an egotistical, high-handed—

And then she saw the fridge.

*Yep.*

It was now official.

She was going to have to kill him.

A certain *lordly* someone had moved all of her sticky notes (the nerve!), neatly stacking them on top of each other in one corner. The rest of the fridge now sported what was basically a sticky note mural, each piece of paper containing a single swooping letter, all together creating the phrase:

*Cleanliness is next to Godliness.*

Arched in pretty calligraphy across the stainless steel surface.

She stood, hands on hips, foot bouncing up and down.

The man was *so* dead. Like sleep-with-the-fishes, never-find-the-body dead.

And then she realized every dish in the room also had a sticky note friend:

*Clean me.*

*Help me.*

*I am drowning in filth.*

The notes fluttered in the soft breeze flowing from the open windows. Mocking.

Yup. This was soooooooooo on.

She was doing it. Again.

That rhythmic noise which passed for twenty-first century music pounded through the house.

Breathe in. Breathe out.

Was it too soon to check the portal again? Had something truly changed in the last five minutes?

Unlikely.

Timothy focused on the newspaper article in front of him.

But sensations kept snapping inside his chest. Pounding around his heart. Kicking against his sternum.

Newspaper. Read. Focus.

The article blabbered on about things called cholesterol and heart health. And yet not one word about balancing bodily humors. Which is what everyone knew to be the actual problem. Had doctors in 2015 forgotten centuries of prior medical learning?

Just as gentlemen of this age had forgotten about the code of honor which made up the bedrock of being a gentleman? Namely, engaging in trade . . .

Why present him with knowledge about Kinningsley and then not allow him to act?

He felt like a sea captain, chained to a cliff face, forced to watch his mighty ship sink. A thousand tools at the ready to save her but unable to do a damned thing about it.

How could Fate be so cruel?

And why *was* he swearing?

*Rule #33: A gentleman should express his thoughts without needing to stoop to the language of a guttersnipe.*

A particularly loud chord rattled the windows.

So many problems to ponder, if only he could Hear. Himself. THINK.

He threw down the newspaper and took the stairs in a manner some-one else might have described as *stomping*.

But as a Linwood never stomped (*Rule #143*), that could hardly be the case.

Miss Fleury was in baby Arthur's bedroom, back to the door, sketch-ing figures on the long canvas. Music blaring from an apparatus set up in one corner. A chorus of male voices vibrating beneath his feet.

*. . . you don't know you're beautiful . . .*

She was bouncing her head and body around to the beat, swiveling hips clad in another impossibly short dress-ish . . . thing . . . with thick stockings underneath. Hair pulled up but in danger of falling down with each bop of her head.

So impossibly alluring and—

He swallowed.

The woman was a bloody menace to society. James should have her committed. Locked away.

A man should not have to look at her perfection day-after-day clad in such form-revealing clothing, and like the rest of his life, kept from doing anything about it—

"Miss Fleury!" he roared.

She paused. Turned around. Looked him up and down. Blue eyes snapping in challenge.

His face surely looked the same.

"I cannot speak to you with that infernal racket blaring!" A Linwood never shouted. And, yet, here he was—

"Exactly!" she yelled back. "That is *entirely* the point." She nodded her head toward the music machine.

And then she did it.

She. Turned. Her. Back.

Dismissing him.

As if he didn't matter. As if his existence were of no importance to her.

How dare she?!

Hands shaking, Timothy stalked over to the machine. He managed to corral his first impulse, which was to throw the blasted thing out the window. Instead, he pulled its wire out of the wall.

The instant silence was deafeningly glorious.

However, if he had expected a reaction from Miss Fleury, she did not deign to give him one.

She merely glanced in his direction and then went back to sketching.

"I didn't think you would take Zayn leaving the band so hard. I know I was pretty choked up this morning when I heard the news, but I didn't say anything because, well, you were busy shouting, yet again, that I needed to find you a valet—"

"Miss Fleury." He forced the words past his clenched teeth.

"—and you strike me as more a free-form jazz kinda guy anyway. Maybe some Philip Glass if you're feeling wild and crazy." She widened her eyes and wiggled her fingers as she spoke.

And then went back to sketching.

"Miss Fleury." He forcibly told his jaw to relax.

"Not a One Direction fan, I take it?"

His eyes narrowed. Deep breath. One more try.

"Miss Fleury. I feel my requirements are few. Yet vital." He ticked off his fingers. "Peace. Quiet. A valet. A cook. A maid. And, heaven forfend, people who speak coherent English."

She raised her head at that. Cocked him a decidedly challenging eyebrow.

And then suddenly frowned, patting down her (absurdly short) dress and hair as if looking for something.

"Nope. Not here." She looked into the pocket sewn into the front of her skirt. "Yeah. Looks like I'm fresh out of damns to give. Sorry. Maybe tomorrow."

She shrugged, tossing her dark head. Causing the entire mass of her hair to tumble down her back and curl around her heart-shaped face. Fierce and defiant.

"I would also appreciate a decrease in sharp-tongued, insolent, scantily-dressed *shrews*."

Her blue, blue, blue eyes widened at the insult. Pursed her soft, plump lips.

Folded her arms across her chest. Every line of her challenging him. Had he ever seen a woman so magnificent?

For some reason, the thought stoked his anger higher.

He stalked toward her, intent on doing something, anything, to wipe that mutinous look off her face.

She didn't back down an inch. Not even when he stopped a hair's breadth from her. She just craned back her neck, keeping her eyes firmly on his.

Stubborn, infuriating, recalcitrant—

"Anything else you would like to say, Timothy?" Her voice so very, very cool.

Her chest heaved under her folded arms. She was not as unaffected as she seemed.

And then it happened.

The worst possible thing.

All his rage and anger and fury transmuted into something much more hot-blooded.

Damn. She was beautiful. In every way.

Fiery and demanding. Unyielding. In all his years, had he ever met such a woman?

For the briefest of seconds, he allowed himself to imagine what a lush little armful she would be.

His eyes dipped to her mouth. A strand of hair curled across her cheek, a few threads clinging to her bottom lip. Unthinking, he raised a hand to brush the curl back.

The feel of her soft cheek under his finger shot through him. A bolt of lightning.

It was the first time he had touched her, he realized. How could a simple touch feel so . . . momentous? Like a jarring change in the entire physical chemistry of his body?

Three more fingers followed the first, helplessly brushing over her satin skin. The contact scrubbing every thought from his brain.

She gasped. And then instantly placed her palms on his chest, obviously intent on pushing him away.

But as soon as she made contact, it happened again.

A knee-weakening surge of electricity.

As if her touch had completed a circuit and now they were both caught in its sway. Helplessly held together. Unable to part.

Her fingers flexed and curled into his shirt. Undecided. Push him away or draw him closer?

With a mind of their own, his fingers curled around her cheek, cupping her face in his palm. Soft. Gentle.

Unbidden, his body dipped, bending down. The gravity of her mouth too powerful to resist.

Close. So close.

She tensed.

And then pushed. Hard. Forceful.

Shoving him away.

And then kept right on shoving, pushing him back, back, back until he stood in the hallway.

Gave an emphatic shake of her head.

And then *bam*, slammed the door shut.


Jasmine leaned against the closed door.

Had that just happened?

Like . . . really happened?

She mentally reviewed, ticking the items off on her fingers . . .

Loud music, shouting, insults, anger, arrogance . . . all normal.

And then, *wham*.

Timothy stalking toward her. Still all bristling jungle lion, but now with a prowling sexiness three shades past legal.

How could someone be so annoying and yet so *exciting* at the same time?

Her head was messed.

Though not regretting at all that he couldn't shave. Dark stubble with those quicksilver eyes . . .

And that sudden jolt. Jarring to life all those sparks and high wattage attraction that had been simmering for days.

Man, that was the *last* thing this situation needed.

But his touch . . . so careful. As if she were precious. Breakable. And his gaze . . . as she had looked up, up, up into his face . . .

She had caught a glimpse . . . a possibility . . . of *what if* . . .

So much seethed beneath that rigid exterior of his. So much intensity and emotion and passion.

Why *was* he here? Why had the portal let him through?

The portal's pattern so far had been fairly consistent. Nearly everyone who came in contact with it was led to their soul mate. But was that the case here? Because she couldn't see it happening . . .

Well, that wasn't entirely true. She *could* see herself (maybe, sorta) kissing him, once the worst of this anger phase passed.

Typical dysfunctional attraction to the dangerous bad boy who didn't play nice with the other kids.

C'mon. Who would turn down the chance to kiss a sexy real-life nineteenth century viscount? It was like the ultimate notch in one's kissing belt.

Forget captain of the football team (who, on a complete side note, had actually been a terrible kisser but a terrific guy-friend once they got past all the we-kissed-and-didn't-like-it awkwardness).

Where was she?

Timothy. Kissing. *Ehr* . . . or almost kissing . . .

Kissing him would be a bad idea. His head was already messed up enough, what with the 'destruction of his entire value system' and 'mourning of everything he had ever thought to be true' he had going on.

No need to add 'confusing infatuation with a completely unsuitable *shrew*' into the whole mix.

And, heaven knew, kissing and some wicked attraction was all that would ever happen between them, so why even go down that path in the first place?

She could only hope that the bargaining phase would bring more calm.

Or, at the very least, less shouting.

Jasmine woke to find a plethora of sticky notes attached to her bedroom door. All with a single word on them.

One note in the middle provided an explanation:

*Please accept this supply of* damns. *When you chose to give one, I require a valet, a cook and a maid. Naturally, you are welcome to provide these services yourself.*

If Jasmine had had her morning coffee and hadn't spent the last ten days living with the pompous jerk, she might have actually laughed. It was just pissy enough to be funny . . .

But it mostly just put the nail-in-the-coffin on the whole kissing idea. Total buzz kill.

She ripped one of the *damn* sticky notes off her door and strode off to find a certain Mr. Timothy Linwood.

There was only one damn she cared to give. And she intended to slap it in the middle of his high-and-mighty forehead.

Group text message. 10:45 A.M.

| Jas: | I'm pretty sure when this all goes down both of you will be considered accessories |
| --- | --- |
| *Emme:* | *James does look good in pink.* |
| Jas: | accessories to murder<br>your color will be orange |
| *James:* | *Duly noted. Linwood, I take it?* |

Jas:      he's entirely helpless and begging for a valet because he can't even shave himself what grown man can't shave himself

*Emme:*    *Punctuation, Jas. Try it. You might like it.*

Jas:      what grown man can't shave himself????!!!!!!!!

*Emme:*    *Uhmmmm, Linwood?*

Jas:      ding ding ding
          he's just sooooooooo angry and pissy all the time

*James:*   *I am sorry, Jas. I know Timothy can be a total ass most of the time.*

Jas:      he's asking for a cook and a maid but what he really needs is a babysitter and a punching bag
          or maybe some valium and a case of vodka
          HELP
          !!!!!!!!!!

*Emme:*    *Jas, we've got your back. Don't worry. James will come up with a solution.*

Jas:      literal tears
          bless you

*James:*   *I heard from Cobra. Still nothing concrete. Said he would call you today.*
          *And no more worrying about Timothy. I'm on it.*

# Chapter 13

This was soooooo not what she had in mind.

*Mayday,* she had said. *I need help.*

Babysitter. Punching bag. Valium. Vodka.

If not for Timothy, then for herself.

*I'm on it,* James had promised.

He was such a liar-liar-pants-on-fire.

How was *this* supposed to help?

She stared at the package she had just opened, its contents strewn on the kitchen counter.

Precisely three things:

A note written in James' swooping nineteenth century handwriting.

A yellow and black book: *How to Use a Smart Phone for Dummies.*

And a sparkling new top-of-the-line phone.

She lifted the box. Poked a finger through the packaging one more time.

Nope. That was it.

Aaaaaaand it was now official.

She was going to have to kill James too.

The bodies were starting to pile up.

How hard was this? She was stuck with Lord Hissy Fit—

*Mmmmm.* She could do better than that . . .

The Duke of Distemper?

The Earl of Umbrage?

The Count of Conniption?

The Viscount of Vexation . . .

Yeah. That was better.

*No, wait!* She had it—

She was trapped with *Lord Loser* and his whole anger mis-management thing. Good thing lords didn't go into business, because ol' LL would win the Worst Boss of the Year award right out of the gate—

"The Viscount of Vexation?" Timothy's smooth aristocratic drawl cut through the room. "I do believe there is a rather horrid penny novel by that name."

*Not again.*

Jasmine wanted to sink her head into her hands.

Or, better, throw LL's shiny new phone at his hard head.

From his seat in a wingback chair next to the fire, Timothy snapped the newspaper he was reading. The scene pretty much as it had been for the last several days. Him checking the portal, reading the newspaper, checking the portal, shooting pithy insults at her, checking the portal . . .

"You do realize, of course, you do not need to *say* aloud every word which crosses your mind, correct? People, as a general rule, edit their thoughts before speaking."

*Oooooooooh!*

"Yeah, well, most of us actually *understand* others have feelings too." She tapped her foot.

A flip of newspaper. "You are angry because I value honesty above flattering platitudes."

"Honesty? I think 'arrogance' is the correct word there."

"True superiority is hardly arrogance. It is knowledge—"

"Wow! You *define* the word delusional."

*Snap.* "You are merely unused to men who understand their worth."

*Oh!*

Of all the—!

Jasmine stood up, straightened her shoulders. Tucked the phone, book and note back into the box. Sashayed her sweet self across the room and dropped the box into LL's smart-mouthed lap.

Crushing his precious newspaper in the process.

He grabbed for the box before it could do any serious damage to his, *uh* . . . person.

She didn't wait to see his reaction.

"You're stuck here." She said as she grabbed her keys, purse and sketchbook off the kitchen table. "Deal."

James couldn't send real help. Fine.

She was suddenly a lot less worried about that BMW out back ending up with a scratch or a ding. And she did have some research to do.

Lord Loser could fend for himself.

And, yes.

She *did* slam the door nice and hard on her way out.


The room reverberated long after Miss Fleury stomped out the door.

Timothy clenched and unclenched his jaw. The woman was truly adept at dragging his emotions to the surface. Clearly something in the box on his lap had upset her.

Timothy lifted the box and pulled out three items.

A book, a phone and a note.

James' familiar handwriting shot a wave of a homesickness through him.

Though the words were terse.

*Timothy,*

*My old friend, I understand you are upset over finding yourself trapped in this century. Your concerns are duly noted. However, I will not be providing you with a valet, cook or maid. Modern technologies have made such jobs obsolete. I know you and, therefore, know how much you crave work, though you couch it in terms of serving in the House of Lords or seeing to your estate. Regardless, there is satisfaction in caring for yourself and your own. Such pride in accomplishments exists in 2015 as well, even if the means are different.*

*Though I have often faulted you for your boorish and condescending behavior, I have never doubted your intelligence or work ethic. Set down your newspaper and stop feeling sorry for yourself. You are capable of learning to navigate this century, and I am providing you with the tools to do so. Google is your best friend and will teach you all you need to know. Or to put it in a nineteenth century way: Loosen your cravat, give your ship full sail and enjoy the journey.*

*On another note, Jasmine is a particularly good friend of ours, and she is going through her own personal struggles. The last thing she needs is an arrogant lout harassing her. Stop it. And apologize while you're at it. I promise the words won't actually choke you.*

*If you return to 1815 before I see you again, I wish you a prosperous and long life.*

*Your friend,*

*James Knight*

*P. S. Marc keeps a punching bag, boxing gloves and other sporting items in a shed behind the old stables. Feel free to work out any aggression.*

Setting down the letter, Timothy studied the book and phone.

Did he want to learn to navigate this century? It seemed like capitulation. Accepting that he was going to be here for a while. Perhaps even forever.

He tightened his jaw and tilted his head back against the chair. Harsh breaths hissing in and out of his locked teeth. A persistent throbbing set up shop between his brows.

Two weeks. He had been here for over *two* entire weeks.

And nothing.

Besides learning of Kinningsley that first day, nothing more had been forthcoming.

He still remained convinced that the mere knowledge of what Kinningsley would become was sufficient. That he should be allowed to return to his own century. He could make the changes necessary from the past.

Yet the portal remained stubbornly closed, indicating his full purpose here was not complete.

But there had been no more clues as to what he was supposed to do or learn, aside from tolerate humiliation and navigate hopelessly confusing situations. And endure the presence of a certain headstrong, mercurial, enigmatic, captivating, alluring, spellbinding, bewitching . . .

At least she had been wearing a long skirt today. Granted, one that swirled and clung to her legs, but at least its length was a step in the right direction. Now if she would only wear an appropriate bodice—

Not that it mattered. She would never be anything to him. *Could* never be.

What was to become of Kinningsley? Without him at its helm (and, quite honestly, Miss Heartstone's much needed dowry), would the entire estate, in fact, sink? Be sold off, bit by bit, to pay creditors?

His chest tightened again. More hissing breaths. This damn panic would be the death of him.

When would these physical spasms end? He ran a shaking hand through his hair. And then that terrible thought hit. The one that had been haunting him for days:

Given what he now knew, what would he *do* if and when he returned home? How could he marry Miss Heartstone? Sacrifice. Bow to the conventions his birthright thrust upon him. Adhere to a gentleman's strict code of conduct. Stuff every last part of himself away . . .

For what? An obsolete future?

A scream stuck in his throat. Vise-like.

Lurching to his feet, Timothy staggered to the back door. Determined to reach that punching bag before he started throwing things.

An unnamed road west of Hereford
A few hours later
April 4, 2015

*Wow.* That had been close.

Jasmine clutched the steering wheel, knuckles white as chalk. Adrenaline pounding, dust settling around the car from her screeching stop.

How could a truck that big even *fit* down this road given the trees and overgrown hedgerows? Much less assume the narrow lane could accommodate her oncoming car as well? Fortunately, she had noticed the dirt pull off before hitting the semi head-on.

This little day trip had seemed like a good idea after her tiff with Timothy. Just a quick jaunt down to Caerleon in Wales, stopping to sketch along the way, cooling her temper. Sticking to back roads because they sounded . . . easier. Less trafficked. More space.

She gave a laugh just shy of maniacal.

Talk about naive.

The motorway would have been significantly simpler—

Even worse, how was she going to get this car back home and deal with Lord Loser?

She rested her head against the steering wheel for a second, swallowing her frustration. With only marginal success.

Between Rita's incessant texts about Marmi's stuff, Jasmine's own anxiety over the search for her real family, her inability to get a clear artistic direction for the mural in little Arthur's room, and a certain angry, rude, boorish, sexy, complicated, helpless, confused viscount . . . . Jasmine felt more than a little adrift.

Which probably explained why she was sitting on the side of the road, not sure how to continue forward but equally unable to return home.

Her dreams the night before merely added to the confusion.

*Golden ribbons snaked through the room and out the window. Marmi's house. The one she had grown up in. Lavender filled the air.*

*She reached out a hand and one of the bright tendrils wrapped around her wrist, the touch holding with velvet firmness. Tugging her forward.*

*The ribbon pulled her against the window, mashing her face to the glass, hands splayed against the panes.*

*And still it pulled, wanting her to move . . . somewhere.*

*The walls held her in. Trapped.*

*The tendrils swirled outside the window. Agitated. Concerned. Looping around themselves, a shape taking form.*

*Until a dara knot materialized . . . the same design nestled into the center of her necklace pendant . . . pulsing in the air—*

A noise jerked Jasmine upright.

*Let it go. Let it go. Can't hold it back anymore . . .*

She managed to get her phone to her ear after dropping it twice.

"Hello." She shook her head, clearing the fuzziness.

"This Jasmine?"

"Cobra?" Were his looks as grizzled as his voice?

"So here's where we're at."

The man just got down to business, didn't he?

"I got a copy of a birth certificate for one Jasmine Aurelie Fleury—AKA you-but-not-you. Born in Boston, Mass to John and Aurelie Fleury on June 21, 1983—"

"I believe I already told you that, Mr. Cobra—"

"It's just Cobra, ma'am."

Got it.

"And with an investigation like this, I start at the beginning. So just to be clear, Jasmine Aurelie Fleury was registered with the state and federal governments under that name from birth. She was never adopted and, her mother, Aurelie Fleury gave birth at home, so no chance this was a hospital mix-up."

A pause and the sound of papers shuffling. Jasmine stared out the windshield at the flowering shrubs lining the single-track road. When she wasn't moving, the byway was picturesque. Google Maps said she was still an hour away from Caerleon. How was she going to make the rest of the trip?

"So in chatting with that geneticist boyfriend of yours—"

"Not my boyfriend."

"Right." A pause. "Anyway, he says it's nearly statistically impossible for you to be genetically related to other members of your immediate family. Which means that your mother didn't muddy the water, so to speak, because you would still be biologically related to her."

What? *Oh!* She hadn't considered that but . . . good to know.

Cobra continued, "So it seems likely that a swapperoo happened at some point."

*Ding, ding, ding.* Wasn't this where they started?

And was *swapperoo* a word?

"Ding, ding, ding, *yes*. Swapperoo is most definitely a word. It's Native American for 'If you don't like my methods, you can kiss my—'"

*Filter, Jasmine!*

"Great, Cobra, I appreciate the info. So the car accident. Florida. January. 1990. That's the likely place a mix-up happened. When real-Jasmine got replaced with me-Jasmine."

"That's just it. The police wouldn't have released you to your grandma without being completely sure you were Jasmine Fleury."

Okay . . .

"Which means that no one else was missing a child."

"Didn't we already know all of this, Cobra?"

Silence. The kind that was all exasperated and wanted to hurt things. Silences like that happened a lot around her.

Did Cobra get cute when he was testy? Some men were like that—

"Cute? Hardly." He cleared his throat. "Forty-three cars were involved in the pile-up. Twenty-seven people died. As far as I can tell, none of the seventy-seven survivors match your age and description. I have followed up on all forty-three cars—"

"Impressive."

"Thank you. As I was saying, I've followed up on all the vehicles and none of them had a dark-haired girl between the ages of six and eight. Most certainly no one had the name Minna. Jasmine was the closest derivative name at the scene. None of the victims matched you either, though forensics is spotty on several cars, including the Fleury family. The fire incinerated nearly all the evidence. For example, another burned car belonged to a solicitor, his wife and young daughter on vacation from Gloucestershire. They were only able to identify that car through the spotty remains of the child's dental records."

"So . . ."

"I'm at a loss, to be honest. Given the state of the Fleury car, it is entirely possible that the body of real-Jasmine was in the wreckage and just missed. If the police already had a child who matched the age and general description of real-Jasmine, they wouldn't have continued to hunt for her. We know you were found at the scene of the accident. Your own memories, police photos and accident records place you there. The problem lies in the fact that no one else missed a child."

Which is what Rita had basically said at the beginning, wasn't it?

"Okay. So we have confirmed what we already thought to be true." Jasmine stared out the window. "I was there that night. I remember the fire and fog. The screams. Now what?"

"Well, I've run through an awful lot of hypothetical scenarios. I'll spare you my theories as they all boil down to this—either no one else knew you were in a car that night or, if someone did, they didn't care enough to ever ask about you."

Jasmine chewed on her cheek for a moment, trying to force back her stinging emotions.

With little success.

"I don't know how a little girl could be so unnoticed and forgotten. It's unusual." He just *had* to rub salt in the wound, didn't he?

Man, Cobra wasn't going to be taking home the crown for being Miss Tactful.

Jasmine swiped at her wet cheeks. Fortunately, she was extra-gifted at silent crying. When you cried so easily, you became expert at all sorts of crying: quiet, hiccuppy, sniffily, ugly, elegant . . .

Basically . . . she had a repertoire.

"You're crying, aren't you?"

Yep. No tiara for him.

She sniffled.

"Why would I want a tiara?" Cobra heaved a very long-suffering sigh. "Do you remember anything at all before that night?"

"No *sniff* not really *sniff*. I have vague memories of riding the teacups at Disney World—"

"I hate those things."

"That's okay. Not everyone likes a good spinny ride. But my next memory is my sister telling me to run and then being in the dark, trying to find someone to help me. I remember being afraid. Barefoot and cold. Branches scratching me. And then people coming at me through the mist. That's all." *Sniff*.

A pause and then, "Interesting. The police report states you were found within minutes of arriving on scene, fully clothed with minor bruising. No mention of any scratches. This case is just more complicated than I originally thought. I'll get answers. You had to come from somewhere."

Cobra hung up a minute later, promising to call if he had a breakthrough.

Jasmine rested her head against the driver's side window. Letting all the stress and worry and frustration and . . . hopelessness of the last two weeks rush over her.

*. . . how could a little girl be so unnoticed and forgotten . . .*

And knowing that bare fact, did she even want to learn the rest of her history?

She fought to pull out memories of the accident. Digging. Searching.

*Looking out the window. Fog rolling in. An enormous sense of unease.*

*A burst of revelation . . . there was an inferno up the road. Death.*

*But the fog . . . no one could see . . .*

*Golden tendrils swirling around her, tugging, urging. Escape!*

*She had to get out. Now. She had to be saved.*

*Fumbling for the door handle. Hands reaching for her.*

*"No, love. Don't open the door. You have to stay here."*

*But she had to get away. The tendrils pushed her forward, toward the door.*

*A child screamed. "Mummy, she opened the door!"*

*And then she was falling. Rolling. Safe from the danger ahead.*

Jasmine jerked her head upright, eyebrows drawn down.

How could that be? Why were her memories so contradictory?

She had always remembered her sister telling her to run.

Except maybe . . .

She hadn't.

# Chapter 14

The bleeding appeared to have stopped.

Though his left eye was only beginning the process of swelling shut.

Timothy dabbed at his cut knuckles and then wrapped his hand in a towel from the kitchen.

Next time, he would put *on* the boxing gloves. And not tire himself to the point that his reflexes seized. That punching bag had an unexpected right hook.

Though the aching tiredness of his muscles was a welcome reprieve. He could also write a treatise on the therapeutic effects of hot showers. And he had experienced only three of those soul-crushing panic attacks in the last hour, so he was making progress.

Perhaps.

His stomach growled. Forcibly reminding him that he had yet to eat today. He had seen Miss Fleury with packages of what appeared to be crackers or biscuits . . .

Opening a few cupboards, he found a can of something called Pringles and a bag labeled Haribo Extreme-Sour Gummies.

He opened the refrigerator, staring for a moment.

Surely, that wasn't—

His brows drew together. He carefully lifted the bottle with the words *Pepsi* scrawled across the side.

He stared at it far longer than was seemly.

Yes. He definitely owed James Knight a set-down next he saw him.

Though, shaking the bottle, the contents looked drinkable. With any luck at all, it would be alcoholic in some way.

He twisted the lid in the direction labeled 'Open' and then yelped and jumped back as the contents fizzed out.

Damn—

He leapt for the sink while twisting the cap back on. For all this century's love of labeling, you would think someone could have mentioned something about the contents being under pressure.

Tentatively, he loosened the cap again. This time the fizzling settled enough for him to screw off the lid entirely. Giving a tentative whiff of the bottle and not getting much, he took a sip.

Pondered for a moment.

Took another sip.

It was not . . . unacceptable.

Though definitely not alcoholic.

He recapped the bottle, wiped it down and set it on the counter next to the Pringles and Haribo.

A further perusal of the fridge found two unnaturally-shiny apples, a container labeled 'yogurt' and a can of something called Cheez Whiz. Bacon-flavored.

It would do.

His eye throbbed. The pounding in his head had increased. He paused. Swallowed past the tight clenching of his chest.

Breathe in. Breathe out.

Make that four attacks in the last hour.

Controlling the spasming of his lungs, he strolled over to the large fireplace, situated his . . . feast . . . on the small table beside the sofa and contemplated the black panel sitting on a table next to the fireplace. It was the size of a large painting. He knew it to be a television, as Miss Fleury turned it on occasionally.

After two weeks of reading the newspaper and brooding over his inability to return home, he was tired of fighting. He just wanted to pass an hour without panicking.

He reached for the rectangular thing Miss Fleury had called a remote. By now, he knew that any button labeled 'Power' turned on an apparatus.

A moment later, Timothy was listening to two men and a woman discuss a terrible tragedy that involved an airbus colliding with a mountain peak in the Alps.

Interesting.

Tragic. But interesting nonetheless.

If this 'black box' would survive the crash, why not manufacture the entire airplane of the substance? Surely some twenty-first century engineer should have thought of that.

The Pringles weren't too vile. Salty and crisp. They went nicely with the Pepsi.

Pressing a few buttons on the remote taught him that the 'channel' buttons would change the scene.

Again. Interesting.

Working his way through the Pringles, he spent nearly half an hour listening to a disembodied female voice talk about a crisis within the fostering system.

If nothing else, the television helped take his mind off the body aches. And kept the anger and anxiety at bay . . .

He changed the channel when he hit the end of the Pringles and Pepsi.

Two men fighting. Click. A woman singing in front of a large audience. Click. A man and a woman embracing and— Click!

*That* image would be burned into his memory for a while.

Shaking his head, Timothy realized he was now watching moving . . . drawings. They most certainly weren't actual people.

Two little girls dressed like girls *should* be dressed. In, well, proper dresses.

But one was able to make it snow inside.

*. . . wanna build a snow-man . . .*

The music wasn't horrid. He continued watching.

The Pringles and Pepsi must have helped. The throbbing in his head had lessened a little. He felt a little more energetic. Timothy shrugged and reached for the bag labeled Haribo.

He coughed as the sour taste hit his tongue. Who would voluntarily eat something like this? Though . . . wait. It turned sweet after a moment. Too sweet. He set the bag aside.

Picking the candy out of his teeth, he moved on to the Cheez Whiz. It was a little more complex to dispense, but the can fortunately had helpful instructions. Tilt and press. He could do that.

He tilted and pressed until a stream of something orange and brown-flecked ended up on his finger.

Mmmmm. It didn't taste too bad. He studied the can. Quite good actually. With a nod, he sat back and reached for one of the apples.

Ah, how tragic. The girls' parents had died.

But the Cheez Whiz with the apple was amazing.

Squeeze a nice dollop on. Take a bite. Crunchy, salty, sweet, creamy. The bacon added a nice tang.

It wasn't bad at all.

And Miss Fleury accused him of being unable to feed himself.

*Hah.*

He settled further into the sofa, propping his feet up on an ottoman as he had seen Miss Fleury do. Highly unorthodox, but as she had said . . . when in Rome . . .

Besides, doing so allowed him to rest his head against the sofa back, further easing the pounding pain. And he could still see the television clearly out of his un-swollen eye.

This story was strangely compelling. The older sister, Elsa was her name, had magical powers. She was the heir to the throne but had to be isolated, kept away from everyone else for their own good.

Clearly a metaphor for the heavy responsibilities which fell on anyone who had to govern . . . one did have to sacrifice personal happiness for the greater good.

Excellent moral there.

*. . . You know the rules. Conceal. Don't feel . . .*

He would have to consider adding that to his list.

*Rule #314: A gentleman conceals all and never feels . . .*

Absently, he finished both apples and the entire can of Cheez Whiz. Delicious. He would have to ask Miss Fleury to procure more of it.

And then it happened.

Elsa began to sing that song. The one he had heard playing on Miss Fleury's phone to alert her someone was calling.

*. . . Let it go. Let it go . . . I don't care what they're going to say . . .*

Timothy stilled. The pulsing pain in his head and body receding. Everything focusing on the moving figure in the screen in front of him.

Elsa was . . . turning her back on her past. Accepting who she was and refusing to follow everything she had been told to do.

He shook his head. So selfish.

Look what happened when she 'let it go.' The entire kingdom fell into a frozen winter. Yes, she was happier in her ice castle but at a terrible cost to everyone else. She needed to return, tuck her gifts back away and accept the responsibility to which she had been born.

It was the only way.

He swallowed and, without taking his eyes off the screen, reached for the container of yogurt.

What a fascinating story. The figures moving and singing. The snow-man decidedly humorous. Intellectually engaging.

He had no memory of eating the yogurt. He stared into the empty container for a moment before shrugging and reaching for the bag of Haribo.

After the fifth one, they really weren't too bad. The sour and then sweet worked together . . .

Elsa had been captured. Anna was dying.

*Ah, see.* Elsa was being punished for her selfishness. By embracing that part of her which should remain hidden, she had doomed her sister and her entire kingdom.

Such a powerful lesson in that. One needed to curb personal tendencies which would be deleterious to the better good. That's why there were rules which governed behavior.

A lesson he had, fortunately, learned early.

This was clearly going to end in tragedy. Anna would die, killed by Elsa's selfish behavior . . .

An excellent cautionary tale but a pity the ending was so obvious.

And then . . .

Anna sacrificed herself for her sister and . . .

*. . . . an act of true love will thaw a frozen heart . . .*

Well . . .

That was a surprise.

He had *not* seen that coming . . .

Elsa opened her heart. Instead of being punished for her audacity—for daring to allow her inner desires to override her duty—she was . . . rewarded.

She embraced her full self and merged the two together to rule, loving everyone.

His breathing sped up. But instead of that familiar lung-crushing vise, his chest felt lighter. Expanding.

As if this idea had . . . merit.

The story ended and names scrolled across the screen. He sat still, unable to move. Numbly, he reached over and pressed the 'power' button. Instant silence hung in the room.

*No.* He refused to accept it. The idea was wrong.

Love changed everything? Just . . . be yourself and love others and everything will be all right?

Surely *that* was not the proper moral here. The lesson to be learned.

What kind of a rule was that?!

His heart continued to pound in his chest. He found himself swallowing over and over.

What a crock of nonsense. The world did *not* function like that.

Order. Control. Unyielding command. A sacrifice of personal desires for the greater good.

And, even then, everything could come to naught. You might find that a generation or two later, everything you had sacrificed and eschewed and forfeited and *let go* had been for nothing . . .

Ah, yes. *There* was his friend panic . . . becoming quite good mates, weren't they?

He pinched the bridge of his nose.

Breathe in. Breathe out.

Why? Why, why, WHY was he here?!

Jasmine was utterly defeated.

She had made it as far as Abbey Dore. Which was still like thirteen thousand miles from Caerleon . . . or something like that.

It had taken her twice as long to return home. Mostly because she had to keep pulling off the road to give herself pep talks.

*You can do this. You are an intelligent, courageous person.*

She wasn't sure the talking had helped. And it had seemingly frightened several people, including one elderly woman who had crossed herself while hurrying past the BMW.

But what other choice did she have?

After chatting with Cobra, Jasmine didn't have the courage . . . ehr, heart . . . to continue on.

*No one missed you.*

She didn't know what to make of her confusing memories. In the car, had her sister tried to hold her back? Why had her memory changed? The vision of a dark-haired sister urging her to run had haunted her for as long as she could remember. Which memory, if either, was the truth?

Granted, she might have had the gumption to make it to Caerleon, if Rita hadn't texted two minutes after Jasmine hung up with Cobra.

*Have you made a decision yet about those pillowcases?*

And then two minutes later . . .

*Oh, and what about the necklace? That one you always wear? I'm pretty sure it's an heirloom too. Breanne definitely needs that. No reason for you to keep something that rightfully belongs to us.*

Jasmine grasped the pendant hanging from its chain. The china, the pillowcases . . . whatever.

But the pendant?!

Something visceral awakened at the thought of parting with it. It was *hers*. Not just a gift from Marmi, but a vital part of her soul.

She lifted the gold charm in her hand. A beloved friend.

In life, objects rarely mattered. They were just ephemera.

But this pendant *mattered*. It was a symbol not only of the love she and Marmi had for each other, but their shared mysticism.

Jasmine knew the meaning behind the pendant too well. A dara knot twining inside a quatrefoil shield design. Strength and endurance wrapped in protection. Ancient symbols, that for her, still thrummed with power.

They even showed up in her dreams, for goodness' sake. No *way* she was giving the pendant to Rita.

*rita I'm happy to send along some of the pillowcases with the china which means breanne will have all sorts of stuff from her ancestors*

*but marmi gave the pendant to me and I intend to keep it as a memory of the woman who raised me*

Rita's response came quickly.

*I really don't think it's yours to keep, Jas. It belongs to the family and a decent person would return it.*

Sheesh. Manipulative much?

Rita had continued to text and Jasmine had continued to ignore her.

Avoidance was *such* a useful personality trait sometimes.

If the woman wanted the necklace that badly, she could fly to Herefordshire and rip it from Jasmine's neck. Or at least try.

Tired and defeated, she parked the car (still scratch-free, hallelujah) in the old stables behind Duir Cottage, gathering her things. Jasmine unlocked the back door and kicked it shut, dumping her sketching supplies and bag of groceries on the counter.

"Honey, I'm home!" she yelled. Mostly because she wanted to be annoying.

A figure stirred over on the couch.

Jasmine turned on the entire bank of kitchen can lights and swiveled toward the sound just as Timothy stood up and turned around.

"How was your da—"

She stopped, staring at his face.

"Good grief! What happened?"

Eye swollen shut, hair poking out in gravity-defying ways, shirt untucked and wrinkled, a towel wrapped around his hand. And, wait, was that blood on his pants?

She walked over and grabbed his arm, pulling his enormous body into the kitchen.

He flinched and ground his teeth together, clearly not appreciating her touching his person.

Total win.

"Please tell me you walked down to the pub and got into a fight with some guy named Malcolm because he insisted Chelsea was going to win the cup this year, but you still have this lingering man-crush on David Beckham, so you were all like, 'No, man, it's Manchester U all the way,' and four beers later, you tried to crack Malcolm's jaw, but he has a wicked left-hook and leveled you—"

*Wait.* Was she speaking out loud here?

"A pub, Miss Fleury?"

"Ya know, like a tavern."

"And I could get drunk there?"

"As a skunk."

"An excellent piece of information."

"And your eye?"

He gave her The Look with his (one, open, seeing) eye. Which, quite frankly, reduced its effectiveness. It was less than a half-Look. Like The

Look was the exponential sum total of every muscle in his face being able to communicate disdain simultaneously and with a portion of it out of commission—

"Are you quite through, Miss Fleury?"

*Right.*

"So, your eye—"

"I see no point in discussing it."

"Hahahaha . . . good one, 'I *see* no point' . . ."

The Look ratcheted up to at least two-thirds effectiveness.

No talking or joking about the eye. Eye puns not funny.

Got it.

"So how *did* you spend your day?" she asked instead. "Harassing villagers? Despoiling innocents? Pillaging? I mean, you nineteenth century lords do have a reputation to maintain—"

"Pillaging? I do believe you are off by—at a minimum—six hundred years, Miss Fleury."

"Well, I'm sure we could find you something to maraud then, if you'd like. Or at least talk haughtily to. Denigrate with a few pithy insults—"

He was pinching the bridge of his nose now. Both eyes closed.

Breathing slowly, as if wrestling for control.

He looked . . . defeated.

And why did that pull at her heartstrings?

The man did Not. Need. A. Mother.

And maybe if she reminded herself of that fact every other second it would finally sink in.

Though he might need a bodyguard, given the state of his eye—

She chewed on her cheek, using the pain to focus her attention away from her bleeding heart.

"Miss Fleury. I am standing here, trying to decide if I was sent here to learn something—"

"You were sent here to learn something, alright. To learn how to actually be a human being, as opposed to a robot—

"Robot?"

"A human-like machine without a heart."

His head reared back, his good eye going wide.

"And you are of the opinion that I resemble this . . . *robot?*

"If the shoe fits . . ."

His breaths came in heavy puffs, chest heaving. He swallowed. Silence.

"Are you sure that is what I need to learn? Or am I merely being punished by having to endure your presence?"

*Oh!* Well, if that didn't just knock the air right out of her—

"You are the most arrogant, conceited excuse for a man—"

"How dare you! I am a peer of the realm, respected and sought after for my opinions—"

"Pah-lease! The only thing you are is *despised*—"

"I would not expect one such as you to understand."

"Do you even have a real friend? Like someone who would come to your aid if you needed it?"

Another swallow. More of The Look from his seeing eye.

"A Linwood does not need aid—"

"That's a solid *No* then."

"My life has a purpose, Miss Fleury." His voice low and so very cool. "At least my disappearance in 1815 will be noted—"

"Huzzah for you!"

"Could you say the same thing about you? If you disappeared, would someone come looking for you?"

Jasmine gasped. Her vision instantly dimmed, her eyes filling.

Of all the things to say—

He locked eyes (well, eye) with her, surely noting her tears.

She gave herself about thirty seconds before a solid ugly cry set in.

Make that twenty-five seconds.

With a sniff, she lifted her chin. And with a curt nod of her head, she brushed past him, intent on the stairs.

Then, realizing she was going to need reinforcements, she strode back into the kitchen, swiping at her wet cheeks.

She grabbed a carton of banana chocolate brownie Haagen-Daz from the freezer, a spoon and, at the last second, one of her sticky notes from the fridge door.

"I bid you good night, *Lord* Linwood." She slapped the sticky note onto his (broad, muscled) haughty chest and, with a flip of her head, retrieved her dignity.

And then she went upstairs, stomping and sniffling the whole way.

Timothy stood rooted in the kitchen. Head pounding. Eye throbbing. Cut hand stinging.

His body feeling as beaten and down-trodden as his soul.

Breathe in. Breathe out.

With a snarl, he grabbed the sticky note from his chest.

And froze.

*You know my name, not my story.*

He closed his eyes as an unfamiliar emotion swamped him.

It felt suspiciously like shame.

He could hear Miss Fleury crying.

*Rule #192: A gentleman should never make a lady cry.*

Gah! Had he ever made a woman cry before? He thought not, though his mind was not exactly in tiptop form. Granted, no woman had ever gotten under his skin like Miss Jasmine Fleury.

*A human-like machine without a heart.*

Is that really what she thought of him?

He braced his hands on the marble counter, trying to swallow past . . . whatever emotion was currently choking him.

Frustration. Anger. Panic. Fear. Regret.

Loneliness.

There. He had admitted it to himself.

He was alone. Utterly isolated . . . but, then, he had spent his life alone, hadn't he? Why should it bother him now?

It wasn't a Rule—*a gentleman should be alone.* Nope. That had never been codified.

And he had never felt . . . *lonely.* Until recently.

He had the viscountcy to focus on. His place in the world to maintain. The Rules to follow.

But without those things . . .

Nothingness stretched around him. Like a void. Everything feeling . . . frozen.

His eyes drifted to another one of Miss Fleury's notes on a cabinet door. It had somehow migrated downstairs.

*Sometimes good things fall apart, so better things can fall together.*

Was that true? Or did things sometimes just fall apart?

Why *was* he here? To make Miss Fleury cry? To ruin others' lives? What did the universe want of him? What did he need to do?

A sign. A message. Anything. If he received something, he promised he would do it. Something more specific than the pithy sayings plastered on the walls of Duir Cottage.

Pain swamped him, dragging him to his knees. How could there be no air in the room? And why did panic have to literally hurt?

*Bing-bing.*

A sound came from near the sofa. His new phone.

Heaving, he staggered to his feet and picked it up.

*Message from James Knight.*

The words blinked at him. He touched the screen and a note appeared.

> *Timothy. Stop being an ass. You made Jasmine cry yet again. Apologize. For once, stop protecting your precious pride and this antiquated idea of how you should behave. Let. It. Go.*

He stared at the words for a good five minutes.

Well, he *had* asked what he needed to do.

*Let it go.*

And as he did, his breathing calmed.

A sense of rightness drifted through him, that James' words were important.

*Let it go.*

Fine. He would let things go.

And maybe, if he did so, the portal would let *him* go home.

# Chapter 15

DUIR COTTAGE
APRIL 5, 2015

*So how, exactly, does one 'let it go'?*

Timothy pondered this as he dressed the next morning.

What did 'let it go' mean precisely?

Wear a wrinkled shirt?

Stop fretting about Kinningsley?

And wasn't the thought of it all supposed to be freeing? Like a weight lifted?

Instead, all he felt was . . . overwhelmed.

Drained. Empty.

He had spent the better part of the previous evening learning his new phone. The book James had sent was particularly useful. As was Google. He had also discovered a thing called Wikipedia, which was a fountain of information.

But repeated searches of 'Viscounts Linwood' or 'Kinningsley' had pulled up all sorts of error pages. Clearly, his future (past future?) was to remain hidden.

Despite everything, he still considered it his duty to ensure Helm Enterprises never found footing within his lands. Even if he had to write it into his last will and testament.

All of this assuming he could return to 1815 in time to woo Miss Heartstone. He would see her in May, which was thankfully still a good six weeks off. If *letting it go* would convince the portal to allow him to return, then he would do it.

Sighing, he drew on a pair of those blue trousers everyone wore—jeans, Miss Fleury called them. He had resisted wearing them, as they seemed less elegant than was strictly proper. But as he was determined to let things go . . .

The jeans sat low on his hips but otherwise were remarkably comfortable. Next, he donned a silver-gray form-fitting shirt which buttoned up the front and had a subtle texture woven into the fabric. He tucked it into the jeans and then pulled on a weathered black belt. The entire effect felt casual and yet . . . good.

The swelling around his eye had also gone down. It wasn't too bruised. In another day or two, it would be good as new. Which was fortunate, as he intended to best the punching bag the next chance that he got. Pocketing his talisman gear, he left his bedroom.

Then he tried the portal for the first of probably fifty times for the day. But to no avail. The stone pulsed with energy, but nothing happened. Merely deciding to 'let it go' was clearly not sufficient.

Miss Fleury was in the kitchen, leaning back against the marble countertop, staring at her phone. The morning light poured in behind, rimming her dark head in golden light.

She really was remarkably lovely. Her hair was down and curly, though a section of it across the front had been woven into a subtle braid, keeping hair off her face. She was dressed in tight jeans and another of those stretchy shirts—called t-shirts. (Google had clarified that for him.) Over it all, she was wearing what could only be described as a frock coat. It was a dusky green color, tight across the bodice and then flaring into a skirt which reached almost to her knees. A pair of boots completed her ensemble, laced up her calves. Interestingly, the boots had a significant heel, giving her several more inches of much-needed height.

He had to admit, if the universe insisted on trapping him in this century, he was grateful to have landed with her. She was a fiery sprite. A fey princess tumbled to earth to tempt poor mortal men like himself.

Not that he would say as much to her.

But James was right. He did owe her an apology.

When was the last time he had apologized? For anything?

He paused, thinking.

Nothing came to mind.

*Rule #80: A gentleman should never do anything for which he must apologize.*

One had to actually *be* in the wrong before an apology became necessary. And adherence to The Rules ensured he never was. Wrong, that is.

She raised her head as he walked farther into the kitchen. Raked him up and down with her eyes, cocked an eyebrow. Then turned away to face the window, shoulders rigid.

The cut direct.

He deserved that. His behavior *had* been rude over the past two weeks, particularly the previous evening.

Apologize. He could apologize. He *needed* to apologize.

He could do this. Say he was sorry. Let it go.

And hopefully, by doing so, be allowed to return home.

He cleared his throat.

No reaction. She didn't turn around.

Though the slight stiffening of her shoulders indicated she had heard him.

Silence.

"Miss Fleury, I—"

The words clogged his throat.

He could do this. He could. Deep breath. Surely, if nothing else, she could hear his pounding heart.

"Miss Fleury, I . . . I-I must apologize for my behavior last night." He cleared his throat. Almost there. "I was unbearably rude and hurt you. It was . . . I-I was wrong."

There. He had admitted it.

Well, what did you know. It felt . . . good. Like a small weight lifted. Huh.

Miss Fleury turned around with excruciating precision.

"Excuse me?" Her eyes so very round. "Wh-What did you just say?"

The maddening woman was going to make him repeat himself, wasn't she?

It figured he would not be let off the hook so easily.


Jasmine felt the shock jolt through her again.

There was no way she had heard him right. He seriously had *not* just apologized.

She had come downstairs determined to avoid saying a single word to him all day. How like him to take all the wind out of her sails.

"Excuse me?" she repeated.

He stood across the room, just inside the doorway. Staring. Dressed in designer jeans and a tight-fitted button down which hugged his shoulders.

Yep. She wasn't gonna lie. Jeans were a good look on him. Now if he just weren't so stiff and snooty.

As if hearing her thoughts, his body noticeably relaxed. Shoulders went down, hips sagged. Everything moving from 'stalker' to more 'professional executive.'

Then he hooked his thumbs into the front pockets of the jeans and shifted his weight to one leg, taking the transformation all the way to 'international playboy.'

"I-I am sorry." He looked at a spot about four inches to the left of her head as he spoke, as if the words were painful. "I apologize for my behavior."

Silence.

"What?"

His eyes snapped down to hers. "Surely you heard me correctly, Miss Fleury. Or are you just going to make me repeat myself a third time as a sort of penance?"

Surprised, Jasmine smiled. "Mmmm, that *is* tempting."

He blinked, as if something startled him.

"What?" she asked again, cocking her head.

"Nothing."

She added a questioning eyebrow to her head tilt.

"You have a beautiful smile," he said after a moment. And then swallowed, as if uncomfortable. "It quite illuminates the room."

She sucked in a gasp. *Oh!*

"Wh-what a lovely thing to say." Jasmine turned her gaze away. "Apology accepted. Thank you."

A pause.

"I am sorry for the things I said too." She brought her eyes back to his. "It wasn't kind of me. I know this situation has been hard for you."

He nodded. "James told me I need to . . . 'let it go.'"

"Let it go?"

"Yes."

"Okay."

"I . . . I am not entirely sure what that means."

"Okay?"

"Let it go."

"Oh—right. It means to stop worrying. *Hakuna matata* and all that."

"Pardon?" He shot her a quizzical look.

"Never mind." She shook her head. "Instead of focusing on your pride or worrying about things you can't control, focus on becoming a more . . . open person."

"More open?"

"Yes.

A pause.

He shuffled his feet. And then rubbed a hand against the back of his neck.

Both motions quite endearing. Looking so much like a little boy.

Aaaaaaand there went her mothering instincts again. She probably needed therapy.

Correction. *More* therapy.

He shrugged. "I anticipate that if I can learn how to 'let it go,' the portal will allow me to return home."

*Ah.* She allowed herself another wide smile. "I'm glad this day has come."

"Pardon?"

"Bargaining."

"You do realize this entire conversation does not make much sense, correct?" He frowned.

Jasmine smiled wider. "I think you need to just . . . *let it go.* Stop trying to force everything to make sense."

He opened his mouth, as if to speak. And then closed it again. Clearly at a loss.

"My mind does not work well with abstracts, Miss Fleury."

She cocked her head.

"You say, 'Be more open,' but I do not understand what behaviors that entails." He gestured toward her. "I require specificity."

"Specificity?"

"Yes. What specifically are the steps for 'letting it go'? What are the rules?"

"Rules?"

"My life as a nineteenth century gentleman is governed by rules, handed down by generations of my forebears. What would be similar rules for a man in this century?"

She paused.

"Your life has rules?"

"Yes, yes, Miss Fleury, but what would the twenty-first century rules—"

"Like what kind of rules?"

"Pardon?"

"What kind of rules do you have in the nineteenth century? Are these like written rules or just suggestions? Do you check them off or something?"

"There is no need to write them down. My father insisted I memorize them entirely by the time I was twelve or so—"

185

"So there is an actual list?"

"Yes, yes. Are you not hearing a word I say?"

"So what are some of these rules?"

He shrugged. "They are merely the rules for a gentleman. Though many are specific to being a viscount and a bearer of the Linwood name—"

"Tell you what, Timothy. Why don't I get you pen and paper and you can write down some of these rules. Just a couple, so I can get an idea of what you're talking about. How does that sound?"

Three hours later, Jasmine looked up from her seat at the kitchen table as Timothy walked back into the kitchen, a stack of paper in hand.

"Here you are. One list." He set the pile in front of her.

She sat back. Stared in awed silence. Her mouth formed into a permanent surprised 'O.'

There were, like, fifteen pages of rules.

She reached for the stack, counting.

Make that eighteen.

"Impressive." She lifted an eyebrow.

She had thought to call his bluff. No way had he memorized all these.

"My father was nothing if not thorough in my education. Linwood men have been memorizing and adding to these rules for several hundred years." Timothy pulled out a chair and sat across from her.

Wow. Talk about an interesting (though highly dysfunctional) family legacy—

"And you recalled all of this from memory?"

He nodded.

She flipped through the papers. So many rules. One per line.

"So what's rule . . . nineteen, for example?"

"Rule number nineteen?" He tilted his head, thinking. "A gentleman never loses his temper."

She turned back to the second page.

Why, yes. He was correct.

She went forward a handful of pages.

"Rule number . . . one hundred and thirty-two?"

"A gentleman should never refer to another person by their first name in public."

Yep. Right again.

Drat.

She lifted her head. They stared at each other for a moment.

"I am afraid to ask exactly how many rules we're dealing with here—"
She flipped to the end.

"Three hundred and thirteen."

"Three hundred and thirteen?!"

She blinked. Yep. Mouth definitely going to be an 'O' for quite a while.

"Thorough. As I said. There were originally only three hundred. One rule for each of the three hundred Spartans who held off the Persian army during the Battle of Thermopylae. A rule for each warrior who preserved the noble Greek way of life. A fitting metaphor, I suppose, as The Rules are meant to be warriors preserving the Linwood heritage. But then my father was forced to tack on the other thirteen to combat my recalcitrance."

Recalcitrance? Was that even a word?

He took pity on her. "My unruly behavior."

She studied the man sitting across from her. So isolated and contained. Not a hair out of place.

The idea of him loosening up enough to misbehave seemed . . . unlikely.

Though, ya know, strangely attractive . . .

She shook her head.

And then turned to the last page:

*Rule #303: A gentleman does not engage in trade.*

*Rule #304: Mathematics should remain in a theoretical sphere.*

*Rule #305: A gentleman does not toil with his hands like a common laborer.*

*Rule #306: A gentleman does not indulge in the vulgarity of practical mathematics.*

*Rule #307: A gentleman does not manufacture machines, either with his own hands or with the help of others.*

*Rule #308: A gentleman does not design or use machines to bring a good to market.*

Machines? Mathematics?

Timothy shifted. "I think he deliberately left the number at three hundred and thirteen, just to emphasize his point."

She looked up, questioning.

He gestured toward the papers. "It is a prime number—three hundred and thirteen. Not to mention all the negative luck associated with the number thirteen. My father could have a rather odd sense of humor."

Jasmine struggled to form a response.

Just . . . no words.

The list said it all, didn't it?

Well, it quite literally did . . . say it all, that is.

It described his world. Every move and emotion proscribed for him from the cradle.

She continued to browse the pages.

He had insisted on using one of the fancy fountain calligraphy pens that James preferred. Obviously, both men were used to writing with slanted goose quills.

His handwriting was beautiful.

"That would be number one fifty-three." He tapped the paper.

Ah, yes. Indeed it was.

*Rule #153: A gentleman will have elegant penmanship.*

She continued to look through the pages.

Bowing required—she did a quick accounting—nearly a full page. Apparently the differences between greeting a royal duke, a regular duke and a marquis were excruciatingly precise.

Seventeen different rules for how to use the eyes, glance, make eye contact, how to show disdain or give 'the cut direct.'

A page on how to stand, how to sit, how to walk.

Nine rules for hats, when to remove them, how to use them in greeting. Seven rules for walking sticks.

Twelve different rules for gloves—

"Why specifically gray gloves when on a picnic? That seems improbably specific." She pointed at rule number two hundred and four.

"But gray gloves make perfect sense." He looked at her as if she were daft. "Black is too formal and white shows stains. You clearly have never picnicked during an English spring."

Clearly.

She flipped through more pages. Rules for education. Latin, Greek, French, Italian, German, Spanish, all the ancient texts—

"Yes." He glanced at her. "Rules two hundred and twenty through two seventy-five formed most of the basis for my childhood learning."

Everything was outlined. A gentleman would know how to ride, to shoot, to fence, to box, to swim, to row and to dance . . .

And then one . . .

"Rule number two hundred and forty-three?" she asked.

He didn't hesitate. "A gentleman never engages in undignified hilarity, specifically puns."

How could she ever resist that one?

"Puns aren't punny. Got it." She smiled. Waiting expectantly. Hopefully.

He left her hanging.

All she got was a raised eyebrow.

"Do you ever smile?" she asked.

He didn't answer. But merely flipped back several pages and tapped the paper.

*Rule #29: A gentleman will refrain from all displays of levity.*

Well, there you go.

Jasmine sat back, shuffling the papers together.

Man, Marmi would have had a field day with this. Talk about needing therapy.

He nodded toward her. "So, you have before you the list for a nineteenth century gentleman. I feel that I should 'let go' of this list and learn to adhere to the standards of a twenty-first century gentleman. Surely, if I did so, the portal would allow me to return."

Bargaining at its best, right there.

"I'm not sure it's that simple, Timothy."

His look turned quizzical. He rolled his hand. *Go on.*

"First of all, I can't even imagine that a twenty-first gentleman would have such a list in the first place. Seems kinda antithetical to the entire concept. I would argue that a gentleman is more an internal state of being than an external list of rules, but I digress. I highly doubt you will be able to bargain your way out of this."

"Bargain? You used that word earlier, Miss Fleury. I am not trying to negotiate a treaty here."

"Actually, you are, in a way. Look. There's a thing called psychology—"

"The study of the mind. I am not entirely unfamiliar with the term."

"Excellent. Based on studies of psychology, when someone experiences a tremendous loss, like a death or some enormous change—like, say, finding themselves two hundred years in the future—they go through five stages of grief. Mourning that which was lost. The phases are denial, anger, bargaining, depression and, finally, acceptance."

He sat very still. Or, somehow, even stiller than usual.

Was *stiller* a word?

Where was she?

That's right. Bargaining.

"The phases don't have to happen in a complete linear fashion, but it's a bit of a progression. So, you have already dabbled a bit in denial. And the anger phase, though fun with all the yelling and insults and stuff, was a bit of a pain. So now we're on to bargaining. Or, you're at least to the point where you're willing to talk about things. Which is an improvement, I have to say."

Timothy sat rigidly across from her. Face utterly impassive. Hands pressed flat against the tabletop. Nothing moving.

Just so completely . . . contained.

Every natural, normal impulse so thoroughly restrained, there almost wasn't a human being inside.

She met his eyes. The swelling had gone down on his injured eye, allowing her to see the deadness in his gaze. He looked . . . weary. Like he was just so tired of fighting.

"And judging by your . . . fatigue, I'm going to guess that there is some depression mixed in with everything too."

His jaw twitched. But that was all.

"By depression, you mean melancholy?"

She nodded.

"I have never suffered from melancholy." He moved to flick a bit of fluff off his sleeve.

"I get that. I do. But feeling melancholy from time to time over events isn't abnormal. And it will pass."

He was still focused on picking at imperceptible bits of lint on his sleeve. His flicking became a little more pronounced. Like he was trying to contain himself.

That needed to stop.

The containment. Not the picking.

He drew in several prolonged streams of air. Like a yoga student centering his breathing.

His hands stilled and he turned back to her.

*Wow.* Such amazing self-control. So determined to never break a rule. Never let anything show. Remembering three hundred and thirteen rules and adhering to them at all times must be a strain of almost unimaginable proportions.

In that moment, he seemed . . . too old. His soul weighed down through years of tireless self-vigilance, adhering to an enormous set of rules designed to protect his family and preserve an archaic way of life . . .

It was no wonder he was pissy all the time. How else could one manage under so much stress?

Who worried about *him*? Who looked after *his* welfare?

His eyes instantly flashed to hers. A sharp hiss echoing.

"Pardon? What did you just say?"

She swallowed. And then reached across the table, placing a hand on his.

"Who looks after *your* welfare? And I'm not talking physical here. We've established the whole cook slash valet thing. No. Who looks after your emotional state? Who cares if you are happy?"

He blinked. And then looked down to her smaller hand resting on top of his, head shaking back and forth so subtly she almost missed it.

"I cannot . . . remember a time when anyone even asked me such a question. Is happiness in this life even . . . attainable? Is it even something that should be sought?"

*Oh!*

"Timothy, look at me. Happiness *is* possible. In fact, I would argue it is *imperative*. We *live* to find peace and happiness, to help others to do the same. It's probably the only rule we, as human beings, should have."

He made a harrumphing sound and sat back, pulling his hand out of her grasp, folded his arms across his chest and then focused on a point beyond her head, reeling all emotion back inside.

Utterly retreating back into that empty, hollow place he went.

Yeah. The whole I-am-an-island shtick needed to stop. Talk about unhealthy.

"This information is intellectually interesting, Miss Fleury. But as I said several hours ago, I require specificity. How precisely does my behavior need to change? What are the rules? What do I need to change in order to return and resume my responsibilities?"

And there it was.

In a blinding flash, Jasmine saw him so clearly.

He seemed impossibly selfish on the surface. Demanding. Condescending. Arrogant.

But underneath it all, he was actually . . . selfless. He had sacrificed everything for his family, forcing himself to become the ideal gentleman, the perfect aristocrat. Behaving as he had been coached to behave. Squeezing himself into a box of his forefathers' creation, all in the name of the greater good.

But who was he really? Deep down? He had no understanding of how to live for himself. How to be the person he was inside, rather than the person he had been trained to become.

What if all that selflessness could be channeled into behavior that was more . . . warm? More . . . overt?

How terribly ironic.

Here was a man who knew his place in the world down to the smallest fraction of an inch. He knew his family, his people. Where he came from. What was expected of him. What life held for him.

And yet . . . Timothy Linwood was utterly lost. Not knowing himself. Compare that to her.

She didn't even know her own name. Where she was born. Who her family really was. She had no idea where her place was in the world. What life expected of her.

Even before finding out she wasn't related to her family, she had always felt on the outside. Not belonging. Lacking a home.

But in a certain sense, not having a clearly defined place had freed her. It had allowed her to just be herself. She knew what she liked and what she didn't. She was comfortable in her own skin.

But Timothy had never had that.

He didn't need more rules. Or even a replacement set.

He needed freedom. Freedom from expectation. From societal mores. From outside judgment.

He needed room to just . . . be.

A safe space in which to be a little selfish. Explore who he was and what he wanted.

Wait. Had she said any of this out loud?

"Is my question that difficult to answer then, Miss Fleury?"

*Whew.* Internal monologue that stayed internal. Nice for a change.

He was still leaning back in his chair, arms crossed, face an absolute blank.

"Is that mask of yours a rule too?" It had to be.

An elegant eyebrow went up. "Pardon?"

"The way your face never shows emotion. Is that a rule?"

He reached for the stack of papers, flipped through several pages and then tapped.

*Rule #23: A gentleman suppresses undue emotion, whether of disappointment, of mortification, of laughter, of anger, etc.*

Yep. She officially hated Rule #23.

"Rules, Miss Fleury. I need twenty-first century rules."

She shook her head, slowly pushing the pile of papers away, as if it were diseased.

Though if he wanted a rule or two . . .

"Okay. How about you start by calling me Jasmine?"

He shifted. Rubbed his neck. "I-I quite like 'Miss Fleury.' It describes you."

She shot him a quizzical look.

More subtle shuffling. Wait? Was he embarrassed? "I find you are kind of like a flower. So I enjoy calling you Miss Fleury."

Her eyebrows furrowed further. Surely she was missing something here?

"My first name is *Jasmine*. You can't get much more flowery than that."

He pondered that for a moment, something flashing across his cheeks. There and then gone.

"True. . ."

"Just try it."

Another pause. A stuttering breath on his part.

"Jasmine," he finally said, his deep voice rumbling her name.

The sound *really* shouldn't have sent a thrill chasing down her spine. And yet . . .

"Jasmine." He tried her name again, nodding as if pleased with the sound.

"There. Not too hard, right."

He nodded. "Well then, Jasmine—" Another breath. "What are the rest of the rules?"

She sighed. If she had to tell him every little thing . . . really, there was only one rule in the end.

"No. No rules. Or, well, maybe just this. Be yourself. Accept others as they are. Acknowledge your innermost self. Stop hiding."

His head reared back. A slight crease appeared between his brows.

"What kind of a rule is that? That makes no sense whatsoever. I already am myself."

"Yes . . . but are you? Your truest, most recalcitrant self? Or are you just the automaton your father created?"


Her words punched all the air from Timothy's lungs. Everything leaving in a violent rush.

An automaton? Is that what she thought he was?

An unthinking—what was the word she had used? Robot?

A machine?

"There's a reason your father felt the need to add thirteen more rules, all seemingly aimed at mechanical engineering and mathematics. Are those things you like?"

A long pause. He felt as if the very molecules themselves froze, awaiting his answer.

He had never confessed his passion for machines to anyone. Rarely even admitted it to himself.

*Be yourself. Acknowledge everything that you are.*

That endless war within him fractured.

The side his father had always tried to suppress roared to life. Smashing a lifetime of barriers. Surging through him, hungry, demanding to be heard.

Finally, he nodded his head.

"Yes."

He sprang to his feet. Pacing. The room suddenly too close.

His admission too big.

A hand in his hair, another on his hip.

Chest-heaving. Like he was going to be pulled apart.

His hand itching to grab hold of his talisman cog and never let go. Wanting to reel everything back inside.

But he didn't. He resisted retreating into his learned behavior.

"Those aren't bad traits. Being mechanically inclined. It's nothing to hide or be ashamed of. They're good things—"

"Not when you are destined to be a viscount and must maintain an aristocratic way of life—"

"Who cares. You're letting go, remember? The idea that an aristocrat doesn't engage in manual tasks or trade or whatever is ludicrous. And horrifically outdated. Work is good. Work is healthy—"

"Work is common."

"*Pfffft.* Hardly. Everyone does it. Queen Elizabeth and Prince Charles have their charities. Prince William flies helicopters for a living. That's like the nineteenth century equivalent of piloting a boat or something.

If he had a brain for inventing, he would be running his own business instead. And everyone would think the better of him for it. His wife, Kate Middleton, comes from trade. Not a drop of genteel blood anywhere. Her parents run a party business. They're the servants who show up and organize a social event for others. And everyone loves her. Why? Because she's herself. And she appears, on the surface at least, to accept others the way they are. She's not a snob."

"A snob?" Miss Fleury—correction, Jasmine—really needed to stop using words that made no sense to him.

"A person who behaves as if they are better than someone else."

*Oh.*

"If this Kate Middleton is married to the heir to the British throne, then she *is* better than everyone else—"

Jasmine made a *tsking* sound. "No, you're not getting it. Welcome to a democratized society. No one is inherently better or more valuable or more necessary than anyone else—"

"But—"

"No. I'm not going to argue this point. You need to find a way to accept it."

He faced the kitchen and planted his hands on the cool marble counter, trying to breathe.

The concept of such equality was not horrid. The Americans and the French had fought bloody revolutions based on the same thought.

But if he gave up all his rules, then where was his place in society? Who did he become?

As if reading his thoughts, Jasmine came up behind him, placing a comforting hand on his back.

Her touch scalded. The warmth welcome.

"I know that this entire concept is probably scary to you."

Was that what he was feeling? Fear?

He assessed his emotions. Yes. It *was* fear.

She rubbed his back. Like he was a small child in need of soothing. He should have been angry at her audacity. But . . . the motion was consoling. His breathing slowed.

"Timothy, you don't know who you are. You've never been given the space to explore your own inner wants and interests. I think *that* is what the universe has given you here. A period of refinement, as it were. A time apart to find yourself. To define and accept who you intrinsically are. Learn to accept others as *they* are. The universe has set you on this path. Now you just need to trust the process." She gestured toward the note attached to the fridge.

He closed his eyes, her words letting loose a flood of emotions. He sorted through them.

Fear, yes. But also worry, confusion, anger, pain, agitation . . .

Heartache.

He had always had rules. He just couldn't—

Her hand remained on his back, stroking, calming. Helping him move through the swarming panic.

He drew in a deep, stuttering breath. "I intellectually understand your words, but I cannot see a way to put them into practice. As I have repeatedly said, I require *specificity*."

He lifted his head. Stared at the note before him.

*Trust the process.*

What kind of logic was that? All processes involved rules. What did he need to do?

Her hand stopped. She moved to his side, leaning an elbow on the counter, though she kept a hand on his back.

"Okay, I can appreciate that concern. Why don't you start by making a list? Spend some time. Think about it. And then make a list of things that you personally like and dislike. Not what you *think* you should like or dislike. But, casting aside anyone else's opinion about what a viscount should or shouldn't be, what does Timothy Linwood like? Let's start with that."

# Chapter 16

*What do I like?*

How could such a seemingly simple question be so hard?

Timothy had spent the better part of the previous day pondering the problem, without making much headway. Well, outside of the obvious things he had already admitted to . . . machines and mathematics . . .

So in a bid to 'let it go' and just 'be himself,' he had indulged his baser side. Asking Google over and over about every single mechanical thing around him.

The entire time feeling like a naughty child stealing biscuits from the kitchen.

He started with the broken alarm clock.

It had sat forgotten in the corner of his bedroom, its case shattered. Google helpfully suggested something called duct tape to fix the housing. Which after a small search, he found in a drawer in the kitchen, along with a box of tools.

The clock posed a unique challenge, as it wasn't precisely mechanical in nature. It was digital, as Google helpfully explained. So instead of using gears and springs, the machine used electricity and circuitry.

Timothy had spent most of the day reading and studying. After several hours of trying to read on the small phone screen, Timothy texted James. Who kindly guided Timothy through powering and 'logging on' to the large computer in the downstairs study.

The enormous screen was a decided improvement. As were the engineering books James walked him through purchasing and downloading from a place called Amazon. Which Timothy had always assumed was a river in Brazil but, apparently, he was mistaken.

With the tools, books and a larger screen in hand, he had been able to repair the clock. Fortunately, the problems had been assembly related, rather than any problem with the clock's circuitry. The clock was now covered in shiny metal tape, but it functioned, red numbers glowing.

He felt ridiculously proud.

*Gah!* Why? Why should repairing an inconsequential little machine cause so much pleasure?

It made no sense.

Was this the 'value of work' that Miss Fleury . . . Jasmine spoke of? Or just the natural result of indulging his selfish desires?

If the latter, it certainly explained why so many people did so. It felt wonderful. Would finding other things he liked bring a similar result?

Which all brought him to this morning and the list in front of him. Under *Likes* he had listed:

*Marianne*
*Isabel*
*Machines*
*Mathematics*
*Pugilism*

He pondered the list a little more. And then added one more word:

*Rain*

He did like rain. It was soothing and cleansing. It brought life.

But did he really truly like rain, or did he feel that way merely because he had spent the last hour watching it pitter-patter against the windows in his bedroom?

He was undecided.

Surely he liked more than five or six things. What grown man couldn't create a simple list of the things he liked? Had Jasmine set him to this task just to be vexing?

Though, she would probably counter, what grown man couldn't shave himself?

Google had been helpful on that particular topic. After watching several tutorials, he realized that the necessary components (namely, shaving cream and a razor) had been in the cabinet in his bathroom all along. He just hadn't recognized them for what they were.

Which just went to show what Jasmine knew. She knew no more about twenty-first century men's shaving apparatus than he did. Hah!

It was a relief to have a smooth chin again.

An angry voice broke the silence. Wafting up the stairs.

"What do you mean we need space? I've always come to Thanksgiving dinner—"

Jasmine. Judging by the clamor of cupboards being slammed, she was not doing well. She probably could use some assistance.

Which meant his list could wait.

Unbidden, Rule #85 scurried through his mind:

*A gentleman never puts off until tomorrow that which can be done today.*

Good thing he was not abiding by The Rules anymore, right?

Jasmine was pacing in front of that marble counter in the kitchen. An island, it was called. The entire room was still impossibly disordered. Dirty dishes, empty cartons, papers, books, clothing . . . the woman obviously tolerated a lot of physical disorder.

For herself, Jasmine was dressed in those loose trousers and a tight t-shirt, long hair pulled over one shoulder. A hodgepodge of necklaces dangling.

She was also crying. Not making any noise. Just wiping her cheeks with a towel.

"Rita, the pendant matters to me, okay? You are trying to strip me of everything that Marmi left me, and I have to put my foot down. Besides, it's barely freaking April. You can't un-invite me to Thanksgiving six months in advance. Who does that?"

Another swipe of her cheeks.

A sharp stab of . . . *something* shot through Timothy.

Who was this on the phone? Who had upset her so?

And why did the sight of Jasmine crying make his fists clench and his breathing short?

She turned and froze, seeing him.

"I gotta go, Rita."

She wiped her eyes as she set down her phone. And then rested a hip against the counter, chewing on her still trembling bottom lip.

Timothy didn't know what to do, what to say.

Rule #188 governed situations like these: *A gentleman should pretend ignorance of another's display of emotions, so as to spare the other person embarrassment.*

Based on that, Rule-Abiding Timothy Linwood would have kept his mouth shut and pretended not to notice anything amiss.

But he wasn't supposed to follow The Rules anymore. He had been given only one rule:

*Be yourself.*

Which, as a rule, was fairly ludicrous. It was far too brief and unspecific.

No-Rules Timothy Linwood had no idea what to do.

Rules. He needed rules.

Or, at the very least, a few discreet hints.

Not just faith in some unknown, unseen, unstructured *process.*

Why was that concept so hard for Jasmine to understand?

Tears still tumbled down her cheeks. Her blue eyes watery pools.

What to do?

He *wanted* to pummel the idiot who had made her cry. But that clearly wasn't possible.

His next instinct was to comfort her. Preferably by scooping her up in his arms and kissing her.

That also seemed ill-advised.

"Pardon me, Jasmine." He spread his arms wide, indicating his confusion. "It is plainly obvious you are upset. But I am unsure—"

That was as far as he got.

Jasmine obviously interpreted his open arms differently. She flung herself across the room, wrapped her own arms around his waist and buried her face in his chest.

Weeping as if her heart would break.

*Well.*

That was . . . unexpected.

Without consulting him, his arms reciprocated, gathering her tight against him. Sobs shook her body.

The urge to bloody the person who had upset her seethed. But other emotions roiled through him as well.

Per Rule #23, he had rarely in the past tried to distinguish between emotions. He had merely suppressed them all as a general principle.

So he struggled to identify them.

Anger. That one he knew.

Worry and frustration. Yes, also familiar.

But there were others.

A feeling of fierce protectiveness. A desire to comfort her, to soothe her.

A longing to never let her go.

She continued to weep, soaking his collared shirt, her palms pressed against his spine. In the moment, she seemed too small, so frail. Her head stopping midway up his chest, his arms so large around her back.

After a few minutes, her tears abated. But she continued to hold him, bringing one hand around and resting it on his sternum, next to her head. Relaxing her body into his. Trusting.

Something sharp swelled in his chest. An emotion different from his previous ones . . . something he couldn't remember feeling before.

Warm and sweet. Possessive in its strength.

*Mine.*

Without thinking, he dipped his head down and brushed his lips across her hair. Breathed her in. Peppermint and clean soap.

Of their own volition, his hands rubbed her back. The motion natural and intuitive. One even migrating up to stroke her hair. As if his hands had been created for the sole purpose of comforting Jasmine Fleury.

Her body relaxed further. Her breathing slowed. He stared into the kitchen as he held her, noting a paper she had stuck to the fridge.

*Don't confuse your path with your destination. Just because it's stormy now, doesn't mean you aren't headed for sunshine.*

Did that not define Jasmine? She was storm and sunshine, energy . . . and color. Vivid and bright. Eternal optimism. Even in the midst of a storm.

And how had he treated her over the past weeks? With disdain, even cruelty. Heedless of her emotions. She should have abandoned him, tossed him out on his arse. True, she had stood her ground and refused to allow him to trample her but, at the same time, she had cared for him, fed him, clothed him. Even when he had least deserved it.

He *was* an ass.

Regret filled him. But, right on its heels, came resolve.

He could not change how he had *been*. But, by hell, he could certainly change how he would *be*.

Starting with his treatment of Miss Jasmine Fleury.

The moment lingered, spreading warmth through him that pushed away all the anxiety and panic. Washing him with peace.

He could have held her all day. Wanted to hold her all day, in fact.

But after a few minutes, she pulled back. Gave one final sniffle. "Thank you. For the hug." Her small smile turned wobbly. "I really needed that today. Things are just . . . hard, and it's nice to feel like someone . . . anyone cares."

She popped up on her toes and pulled his head down, planting a friendly kiss on his cheek.

*Ah.* His eyes closed of their own accord. That felt nice. Her soft lips on his skin. Her small hand clutching the side of his head.

He opened his eyes to see her frowning, head tilted. She brushed a hand over his smooth chin.

"Drat," she said, rubbing her thumb across his jawline. "You found a razor. I liked the scruff."

With a final pat of his face, she moved all the way out of his arms and turned to the fridge, rummaging for something.

He had yet to say much at all, but gauging from her reaction, his behavior hadn't been incorrect—

"You eaten breakfast yet?" she asked.

At last. A question he knew the answer to.

"No. Not yet." He cleared his throat. "So what is Thanksgiving?" he asked. And then winced. That might not have been a good topic to bring up. But someone appeared to not want her to attend this Thanksgiving.

She froze. And then carefully pushed back a stack of loose papers to place two cartons of yogurt and a bottle of orange juice on the counter.

Though, he realized, he didn't want to know *only* about Thanksgiving. He wanted to know everything about her. Her history. The life that had made her . . . *her.*

He cleared his throat. Tried again. "What is your tale, Jasmine? Your story?"

She leaned into the marble. Let out a sigh and then gave a wry grin. "It's a looooooong saga, full of mystery and woe . . . You sure you want to hear?"

He nodded his head.

"Fine." She pushed off the counter. "I'll tell you over breakfast."

She gathered their breakfast together. He managed to find two clean bowls.

Sitting at the cluttered table, he listened as she told her story. Voice low and musical, peppered with that throaty laugh of hers. A few blinked back tears. Two hours of talking passed in mere minutes.

"So scientists can run tests to see if you are related to a specific family, but they cannot do the reverse? Take a family and find all its scattered members? That seems odd."

Jasmine sat back in her chair, her yogurt and juice long gone. "As I said, it's a matter of logistics. In order to do the reverse, you would have to compile the genetic code of every person on the planet, and that is an impossibly large task. So without some sort of break-through in the case, who knows if I'll ever find the family I was born into."

Timothy shook his head. How terrible to know nothing about your own history. Your family. His heart grieved for her.

"And your adoptive family doesn't want you?"

She sighed, looking past him. "It's not that simple. I was always a burden to them and now, knowing I'm a cuckoo in the nest, they want to push me out."

"But this was hardly your fault." Timothy felt that anger rising again. That desire to pummel someone for daring to hurt her.

"Yes, but that doesn't change the way they feel. It doesn't help that Rita keeps asking me to return every single thing Marmi ever gave me."

"The same thing happened when my father died. My uncle insisted on having certain items of my father's as mementos. They were, of course, things that had more monetary than sentimental value." Though, as head of the family, Timothy had been able to deflect his uncle's demands.

"In a certain sense, it's silly. It's just stuff, after all. But, DNA or not, Marmi is still the woman who raised me, and some things are special between us. Like my necklace here." She touched one of the chains she wore. "Rita insists it's a family heirloom and demands I return it. But I feel so connected to the pendant. I've had it for as long as I can remember and it's such a part of me . . ." She swallowed hard, eyes glistening.

Kind Jasmine. Her emotions were always bubbling on the surface.

"May I?" He gestured toward the necklace.

Nodding, she swiped at her cheeks and then pulled the chain over her head, handing it to him. He angled the pendant into the light, studying it.

"Mmmm," he said after a moment. "I can see the faint tell-tale marks of a goldsmith's tools but nothing more. There is no assayer's signature or stamp anywhere to indicate the purity of the gold."

The line between her brows deepened. "Really? Given the way Rita has been going on about it, you would think it was a Tiffany piece." She took it from him, looking at it for a moment. "But you're right. There aren't any marks. I never noticed that before. Maybe it truly is an old family heirloom like Rita claims."

"Yes. But even in my time, gold pieces are stamped and had been for hundreds of years. It could have been made by a skilled jeweler who chose not to include legal hallmarks."

"Maybe it was handmade by one of Marmi's friends then?"

"Perhaps. The workmanship is very fine."

She settled the necklace back around her neck.

"Well, I refuse to give it over to Rita without more proof that it truly *is* an heirloom. Marmi never mentioned anything about it belonging to an ancestor, which would be unlike her. She was always one to go on and on about the historical significance of objects she had."

She sighed and wiped her cheeks again before continuing.

"Regardless of all the stuff, Marmi loved me, that much I *do* know." She tapped one of the photographs in front of him. She had pulled them out as they talked about her past. Her memories of the night her family—or adopted family—had been killed.

It was amazing to see the images. Pictures of Jasmine as a small child. So tiny and lost.

He picked up the one where she looked the youngest. She was standing in front of an older woman with graying hair. The woman had a protective hand on her shoulder. Little Jasmine looked at the camera with those same wide blue eyes, hair wild and hanging down to her waist. She clutched what appeared to be a fluffy toy in her arms.

"Rita took that picture the day we returned from Florida. You can see the airport terminal behind us." Jasmine leaned over the table. "Man, I loved that bear to pieces."

Timothy looked up at Jasmine. Noted something. And then looked at the photo again. Then back at Jasmine.

"What?" she asked.

"It's the same." He tapped the photo. "Your necklace."

She snatched the photo from him, studied it for a moment. Eyebrows dipping in puzzlement. "It *is* the same. I never noticed I was wearing it in this photo." Her eyes flared. "I always thought the pendant was a gift from Marmi but—"

"Are you certain it was Marmi who gave it to you?" Timothy had to ask it.

Jasmine froze. She lifted her gaze to his.

"No." A whisper of sound. "I have always just assumed, but I have no specific memory. Certainly not around the time of the accident—"

"Is there a way to know if you were wearing it that night?"

She drew in a hissing breath. "That is a very good question. Let me ask Cobra."

"Cobra?"

"The man James hired to investigate this for me."

"His name is Cobra?"

"I know, right? Who goes by Cobra anyway? But let me ask him."

She brought her eyes up to his, sparkling with hope.

"If the necklace doesn't come from Marmi, then I get to keep it. It *is* mine and no one can take it from me."

"True. But, moreover, it means the necklace belongs to your old life."

She gasped. "You're right." Awe in her eyes. "It would belong to me. The real me."

A smile spread bright and wondrous across her face. Timothy felt that same warm, possessive feeling pound in his chest in response.

Heavens but she was lovely—

She paused, looking at him. Cocked her head.

"We've been chatting too much about me, but what about you? What did you write on your list? Is there something specific you like that you want to explore?"

Timothy pondered it for a moment, remembering the clock from that morning. Would it be too gauche to show his handiwork to Jasmine? Was he now like a little boy, desperate for her approval?

*Be yourself.*

With so many mechanical devices around him, it was hard to know where to start. And then it hit him.

"I would like to continue to indulge my fascination with machines, and possibly save both our nerves from your driving. I want to learn how to operate a car."

# Chapter 17

This was decidedly *not* what he had in mind.

Timothy held the car in his hands, the words *Cyclone RC Racing* blazed on the side. The toy had arrived with the morning mail, courtesy of James.

He was going to have to call Knight out next he saw him. Bloody him in a duel—

But why wait?

Text messages were much quicker.

Timothy:  I should have been more specific in my request.

*James:*  *Please tell me you chuckled at least a tiny bit on the inside? C'mon. It's funny.*

Timothy:  I am overcome with hilarity.

James:      *Remember, you agreed to loosen your cravat.*

Timothy:  No, I believe you told me to do so. I did not agree one
            way or another.

James:      *You're splitting hairs.*

Timothy:  If I must.

James:      *I think you'll actually enjoy the toy truck. And thank you for
            apologizing to Jas. How's the whole change thing going?*

Timothy:  Slowly. I must say, it would go considerably better if I
            could drive an actual car.

James:      *Hah! I'm liking this sense of humor coming through.*

Timothy shook his head, staring at his phone.

The past several days had not been easy. Attempting to change a lifetime of rules and behaviors was no simple task. Frustration still roiled in
his chest at times. Tight and hot.

Trusting the process was difficult. Particularly for someone used to
facing problems head-on and solving them.

He still ached to return home, to the life and language and customs
which were familiar. But the portal remained firmly closed, despite trying
it at least twenty times a day.

He *had* been making changes, however. Letting go of the rules which
had governed him—not caring about the proprieties and endless social
minutiae which had hitherto regulated his life.

Case in point.

The toy car rested on a blindingly clean counter. He surveyed the
large combined kitchen/dining/sitting room with profound satisfaction.

Every surface gleamed.

Turns out there was a machine to clean *everything*.

A dishwasher which washed the dishes automatically. A disposal
which ground up food waste. A machine which emitted a powerful jet
of steam to vaporize grime. Another which instantly sucked up dirt.
Cleaners and scrubbers for every surface type and rubber gloves to
ensure his hands did not get dirty. The *coup de grace* was the small round
robot which—can you imagine it?—swept and mopped the wood floor,

whirring and humming as it went. He had spent an hour that morning printing labels (Printed labels! Such heaven!) for the refrigerator shelves.

Who needed a maid with such machines everywhere? Why had Jasmine not mentioned all these wonders on the first day? He would have launched into a cleaning frenzy within minutes.

The best part, however, was the fridge door. Jasmine had reinstated his *Cleanliness Is Next to Godliness* sticky notes and then added her own underneath—

*Thank You.*

Done in her swirling handwriting and decorated with cute mice bowing in gratitude.

He liked it so much he hadn't rearranged the notes to fix their crooked alignment.

He didn't want to mar the Jasmine-ness of them.

Yes. Looking about the glistening room, he had thoroughly indulged his love of machines by this point.

But it was obviously not far enough. What more did he need to do? Jasmine told him to stop thinking about the changes in terms of bargaining, but he couldn't help it.

Less than five weeks remained until Miss Heartstone and her mother visited his estate. If he were not there when they arrived, he could most assuredly assume she would have nothing more to do with him, which would destroy any hope of resuscitating Kinningsley's finances.

But every time he thought about Miss Heartstone, Jasmine's lovely face floated in his vision.

So alive. So free. And why did the thought of returning to 1815 without her cause that possessive burning to flare in his chest?

They had spent so much time talking together over the last few days. When had he ever spoken at such length with anyone? Much less a woman?

James: *I've chatted with Jasmine, and we've come up with a plan to teach you to drive. In the meantime, I was hoping you would do me a favor?*

Timothy:   Of course.

James:   *You agree? Just like that? Man, you are changing!*

Timothy:   It is the least I can do in exchange for your hospitality. I am a gentleman, Knight.

James:   *True. Which is precisely why I need you. I have a fine gelding stabled in Marfield, but I am desperately in need of    a true horseman to exercise him.*

Timothy:   Say no more. Riding would be my pleasure.

Two hours later, Timothy stood beside Jasmine in the stable yard, waiting for a groom to bring out the horse. Jasmine had insisted on driving him over. She had a sketchpad in hand, eager to draw the horse for her mural.

After nearly three disorienting weeks, being in a stable offered such familiar comfort. The smell of hay and manure wafting through the yard, a forceful reminder of home.

*This* world he knew. *This* he understood. Finally, something which required no explanation.

Well, not too much, at least.

James had clarified that Timothy could not ride the animal cross-country, pounding through farmer's fields. He would, however, be allowed to run the steeplechase course and explore the large pastures.

Though Timothy refused to wear one of those ridiculous looking helmets. As a lord, expertise with horses had been a rigorous part of his upbringing. A gentleman was required to have a perfect seat and carriage when riding. If he was thrown from his horse, he deserved the injury to his head.

Jasmine shifted next to him. She was wearing that frock coat again with tight jeans and knee-high boots. She shot him a look. "Those shades look good on you. They match the dark coat."

It took him a second to catch up to her meaning. By shades, she meant the smoked-glass spectacles he wore, cleverly called *sunglasses*. A brilliant invention, as it allowed him to see without squinting in the bright spring light.

Though the rest of his outfit felt decidedly more familiar. Tight caramel-colored breeches tucked into riding boots, topped with an open-collar white shirt and fitted riding jacket.

"Seriously," she continued, "have you thought about a future in the Secret Service? All you need is an ear piece and shoulder holster to pack heat." She placed a finger against her ear and then spoke into her hand. "The suspect has left the perimeter. I repeat, the suspect has left the perimeter."

She smiled brightly, looking at him expectantly.

Was there a joke in there? Another one of her terrible puns?

She was speaking English, of that he was sure. But it came out almost like gibberish. How could the English language have changed so much over the intervening two hundred years?

It left him floundering.

And he had come to really dislike the feeling. Not understanding. Not knowing.

She pursed her mouth. "Yeah, you probably need to watch an unfortunate amount of television to get all of that. Sorry. As you were." She gestured toward the stable, a wry grin tugging at her lips.

That panicky sensation tried to ease in. But he breathed through it.

It didn't matter that he didn't understand. It was *okay*, to use one of Jasmine's favorite words.

She patted his arm, giving him one of her glowing smiles. Encouraging.

*Trust the process.*

A groom led a sleek chestnut horse out of the stables, bringing the animal toward them. The gelding was a prime goer, tall and muscled, moving with a fluid grace, ears alert. He didn't skitter when a loud truck rumbled past the car park, showing his excellent training. Basically, everything a gentleman's horse needed to be.

"Wow. He's big," Jasmine said at his elbow, easing away.

Timothy pulled off the sunglasses and tucked them into his jacket pocket. Taking the reins from the groom, he brushed a hand down the horse's neck, patting the animal, making soothing noises. Letting the gelding learn his scent and voice. The horse whickered in reply, nudging Timothy's shoulder.

Ah, he was a good animal.

Not that Timothy would have expected anything less of James' cattle. Knight had always had a first-rate eye for horseflesh.

Just feeling the well-worn leather reins in one hand, the soothing warmth of a muscled horse under the other . . . it washed the tension from him. He had desperately needed this small piece of *home*.

Lost in the everyday motions of coaxing a horse, Timothy turned to see Jasmine staring at him, eyes wide.

"You're really good at that," she said.

"Pardon?"

"The horse. You've already made friends of him." She cocked her head. "You're a horse whisperer, aren't you?"

That made no sense.

Timothy shrugged the concern away. "You grew up around cars. I grew up around horses. It is merely a matter of what is familiar."

His own words sank deep.

It *was* only a matter of familiarity. Once this way of life—of letting go, of allowing his internal self to be external—became more familiar, the fear would ease too.

He could do this.

"I guess." She pursed her lips, as if unsure. "Driving a car seems a lot simpler. I've never ridden a horse."

He paused, resting a hand on the horse's neck. "How is that possible? You are afraid of this sweet boy?"

"Uh, *yes*. Hello? He's huge. He could trample and eat me in two bites."

"You do know that horses, as a general rule, are not carnivorous?"

She edged back. "I'm not 100% sure on that one—"

"Well, that decides *that* then."

Timothy swung himself into the saddle, the horse prancing sideways, adjusting to his weight. Jasmine's eyes went even wider, as she backed away, clutching her sketchpad to her chest.

She looked adorable. Unsure. Faintly worried.

Timothy nudged the horse over to her and leaned down a hand.

"Put down your pad and join me."

"What?!"

"You have taught me much about your era. Give me the pleasure of reciprocating in some small measure."

She looked at his outstretched hand, wariness evident.

"I shall keep you safe. Trust me, Jasmine."

She locked eyes with him, pools of summer blue, and pulled her bottom lip into her mouth, worrying it with her teeth.

The entire process drawing his eyes down to her mouth, which really was the *last* thing this situation needed.

Not noticing his noticing, thank goodness, Jasmine nodded her head and set her drawing stuff on a nearby concrete ledge. With a determined lift of her chin, she placed her hand in his, bracing a foot against the stirrup.

That was his spunky girl.

Timothy refused to consider why he tended to use possessive pronouns when thinking about her. This entire episode of his life would seem like an extraordinary dream once he returned home. Miss Jasmine Fleury relegated to nothing more than a bittersweet memory.

But for now . . .

Effortlessly, Timothy pulled her up to straddle the horse before him, her back to his chest. Seated in front of him, she was so short her head fit neatly into his shoulder.

She let out a breathless giggle, clutching the pommel tightly.

"I have you." Timothy wrapped his arms tightly around her, tucking her back against his body. Breathing in the heady scent of her.

Horseback riding with a woman. It was the oldest romantic situation in the book. A way to cuddle and hold your lady-love without risking impropriety.

Well . . . not too much. He was holding her scandalously, *deliciously* close.

He closed his eyes and leaned into her, around her, relishing the soothing familiarity of being seated on a horse, of holding a beautiful woman in his arms.

*Ah.*

Tension flowed from his body. She clearly felt it too, as she relaxed back into him. Head nestled into his shoulder, angling her body and face toward his.

"Helping me adjust to being up this high?" she murmured.

Yes. *That's* what this was.

"Of course. I promised you could trust me. I know what I am about."

She chuckled. "Of that, Lord Linwood, I have no doubt." Her blue eyes caught the sunlight, quickening his breathing. She did that thing with her bottom lip again, pulling it between her teeth.

Did she not realize the motion practically begged him to kiss her?

Soft. So soft.

All of her.

His arms flexed, determined to gather her another fraction of an inch closer. She just felt so . . . alive in his arms. So right.

The contact between them went from warm to electric in the space of a heartbeat.

His heart pounded in his chest. Surely she could hear it.

Did she understand she was about two seconds away from being kissed senseless? All she had to do was raise her face just a fraction of an inch in invitation . . .

And then she *did* just that. Lifted her head.

*Hallelujah!*

He bent down—

Only to have her twist further toward him and place a hand against his chest.

"Are you sure you want to go there?" she asked, her breath a gentle puff against lips.

He was a man holding a beautiful woman. *Of course* he wanted to go there.

Did the woman understand men at all?

It was only natural.

And he wasn't precisely betrothed to anyone. Yet. So he could indulge himself. If she thought gazing at him with those soulful eyes so wide and open was a deterrent—

His head dipped again.

Her hand stayed him. "Because I know you're under a lot of stress right now, and I want you to really think about what you want. Not to mention you're going to have to see me every other minute for the foreseeable future. So if this gets awkward . . ."

He paused.

*Blast.*

She did have an excellent point.

Clever, kind, vibrant *and* intelligent.

Usually a good combination . . .

She patted his chest and turned fully forward, hands back on the pommel.

"Tell you what, Timothy. You think about it and, if you still want to kiss and cuddle, let me know. We can talk about it."

He froze.

*Talk about it?* What man ever wanted to *talk* about it?

Is this how kissing worked in the twenty-first century? A couple politely discussed the ramifications of the kiss before embarking on it?

And where was the fun in that?

He hated feeling like he was fumbling in the dark for a flint and steel, scrambling to strike a spark so he could see—

"C'mon, big guy." She patted his knee. "Let's just ride."


Jasmine's knees were shaking by the time Timothy dropped her back in front of the large barn. He hadn't done anything more than just walk her around the stable yard, but it had been enough.

She was still trying to decide if the knee shaking was the result of merely riding the horse or the lingering shock of being held against Timothy's chest *while* riding said horse.

Timothy's decidedly muscled, broad, *warm* chest.

Yep. The whole thing was definitely going into her Most Swoon-Worthy moments. Assuming she would ever swoon. Or actually maintained such a list.

Though with one Timothy, Lord Linwood around, she probably should start.

Without his rules and snooty demeanor, the man was now proving dangerous to her peace of mind for an entirely different reason.

She leaned against the fence, balancing her sketch pad against the rails, content to watch Timothy move through the steeplechase course.

What was it about the sight of a handsome man in tight breeches effortlessly riding a thoroughbred horse that made a woman's heart skip a beat?

Granted, the description sort of provided the answer, didn't it?

Timothy sat the horse like it was an extension of himself. Which, to his purview, it probably was. An activity as common to his everyday life as eating and breathing. Even to her untrained eye, she could clearly see the difference between his seat and those of the other riders.

He easily jumped his mount over higher and higher railed fences, testing the animal's agility and strength, smoothly maintaining his own balance and center of gravity.

Confident. Graceful.

So utterly in his element, oozing this masculine power. The strong English lord who commanded men, who bore responsibilities she could only begin to fathom. He just looked like Someone Important.

It was that charisma of his. That sense of power. Of authority.

That was how things were with Timothy.

Like him. Hate him. Whatever.

But you couldn't *ignore* him. He demanded attention. As if the force of his personality held its own gravity, sucking everyone and everything into his orbit.

Heaven knew, *she* couldn't take her eyes off him.

And judging from the glances and outright stares he received, she wasn't the only one. Wait? Was that woman over there videoing him?

*Sheesh.*

A tiny thread of pride filtered through her.

*This* was the man who had come within an inch of kissing her barely an hour ago. For the *second* time.

Not that she was counting or anything.

(Who was she kidding? She was *totally* counting. C'mon, a girl *had* to count stuff like this. He was a gorgeous, dynamic lord who rode a horse like a centaur . . . Hello? Romantic fantasy much? Who *wouldn't* want to kiss that?)

A huge part of her regretted that she'd stopped him. Man, she had been seated in front of him on a *horse*, for heaven's sake. Like a damsel in distress.

*Gah.* She totally should have just gone for it.

But the Concerned Mother part of her recognized he was emotionally vulnerable right now and that kissing would probably just exacerbate the situation. (Which, by the way, should she really use the word *mother* in conjunction with *kissing*? It seemed wrong . . .)

So she had made the *right* choice.

But obviously not the funnest. Or the most memorable.

She should totally get a medal for taking one for the team like this.

*Remember that one time when I could have made out with a nineteenth century lord—on horseback, mind you—but I didn't because his entire world view had collapsed? He was trying to rebuild his internal sense of self, and I didn't want to mess with his head, so I said,* No. *Cause I'm just noble like that . . .*

Granted, if he gave it some thought and decided he wanted to take her up on the offer . . .

She most certainly didn't have it in her to say *No* a third time. A smart girl knew her limits.

He rode closer to where she stood, allowing her to study him. His profile taciturn as ever, but she now knew his eyes went soft and gentle when he was concerned. Twinkled a little more when he was amused. Narrowed when he thought hard about something.

Nothing about him was monolithic, she realized. His hair, though dark, had glints of red in the sun, turning it more dark brown than black. And even though it was barely past noon, he already had hints of a five o'clock shadow creeping in.

So maybe he never fully smiled or frowned. But he still clearly felt all those emotions. You just had to know how to read him.

He nodded to her as he rode past, breaking into a gallop, body moving effortlessly with his mount.

*Bing-bing.*

Her phone. She pulled it out from her pocket.

Text from Cobra. At last!

*Necklace definitely on you at scene of accident. Noted in the police report.*

She gasped. A hand instantly at her mouth, feet hopping in joy.

*hurrah that's fantastic*

Unconsciously, her hand drifted from her mouth to the necklace around her neck. It was hers. Truly and definitely belonged to *her.*

So odd to think the pendant with its knot-work design was actually something from her past. Surely it would lead her to her real parents.

"Whatever is the matter?" Timothy's voice cut in. He rode up, leaning toward her, sounding almost . . . concerned. "I noticed you jumping from across the field."

She wanted to wrap her arms around his neck and hug the stuffing out of him.

"The necklace *was* found on me at the accident. It's something from my past life. And Rita can't have it now no matter what!"

He blinked and then nodded. "That is most excellent news."

That's it? That's all she got?

She pursed her lips. "Please tell me you're jumping for joy on the inside?"

A pause.

"I am ecstatic." Total deadpan.

The sad part? He probably was.

Figured.

A couple seconds, and then Cobra's reply:

*Discovering you were wearing a small trinket the night of the accident is hardly a break-through, Miss Fleury.*

She deflated.

"Dude. He's such a kill-joy."

*it's better than nothing*, she texted in reply.

*We'll see. For now, I have no other leads. Could you send me detailed photos of the pendant? Manufacturers' marks, that sort of thing.*

*sure but I can tell you right now there are none*
*just some faint tool marks nothing else*

A pause and then—

*You said it was gold?*

*it is gold been wearing it enough years to know that*

That was true. Anything fake would have rubbed off by now, but the knot-work still shone bright and new.

*All gold would have at minimum a stamp indicating what kind of gold it is, 14k, 24k, etc.*

*nope nothing like that*

*Well, send me photos anyway. As detailed as you can make them. There's gotta be something there.*

Jasmine tucked her phone back into her pocket.

"I take it Cobra did not have anything useful to say." Timothy's tone was kind as he leaned toward her.

"No. Not really. He just confirmed that I was wearing the necklace when I was found. There are no other hints."

But at least she had something she knew belonged to *her*—as much as she could know anything.

"I have faith more information will surface." He nodded his head toward the pendant. "Someone somewhere at some time gave you a valuable gold charm. That is not the act of an uncaring individual."

The thought caught in her throat. "Thank you. That is a very . . . kind observation."

Yes. There had to be a person who had missed the little girl with the expensive pendant.

He studied her for a moment, hands resting across his pommel. "What is that saying you like? *Don't confuse your path with your destination. Just because it's stormy now, doesn't mean you aren't headed for sunshine?* Remember that."

"Right back at you, big guy."

With a cocky raised eyebrow, he saluted her and whirled his horse, riding off at a gallop.

The view just as excellent going as coming.

# Chapter 18

A BYROAD OFF THE A465
HEREFORDSHIRE
APRIL 14, 2015

Y ou're driving too fast"—pause—"again."

"Madam, I most certainly am not."

"Are too."

"I have completed adequate student driving hours and, need I remind you, this vehicle is a precision piece of German engineering. Besides which, it is equipped with Drive Assist Plus. An alarm will sound if I get too close—"

"You spend waaaaay too much time on BMW's website—"

"The car wishes to go fast. I am merely being politely compliant."

Jasmine tucked her right foot under her bottom, forcefully sitting on it. It reeeeeally wanted to brake, but seeing as Timothy was driving . . .

Well, Timothy driving *was* the problem.

Though she now had definitive proof that an obsession for powerful cars and offensive driving was somehow hardwired into men's DNA.

He had learned far too quickly. The whole clutching and shifting thing should have thrown him for longer than ninety minutes. In the interest of public safety, James had made him study and pass an online test covering driving rules. After which, Timothy spent several days as a student driver with her on empty back roads.

None of which had phased Lord Linwood. He had passed it all with flying colors. A complete natural.

But, she was starting to realize, he was a genius when it came to mechanical things, in general.

Like bona fide, freakishly, how-the-hell-did-you-do-that smart.

The garbage disposal had jammed and *bam*. Timothy was there with his phone and tool box. An hour later, she heard the thing purring like a kitten.

He had pulled the entire mechanism apart, diagnosed the problem. (His explanation: A kernel of popcorn caught between the shredder and motor gasket housing . . . she had just nodded and taken his word for it.) He had the entire thing reassembled in less time than it took for her to shower and get dressed.

And like riding a horse or writing in that fancy calligraphy of his, he made it all look so easy.

Though, he had made no more mention of their second almost-kiss. Clearly he had thought about it and decided it was . . . *ill-advised*, as he would say.

Which was . . . good. It was good. It was a good choice for them both. She had to agree.

Smart. Careful. No need to make things more complicated than they already were—

And if she kept telling herself that, maybe one day she would believe it.

Why hadn't she kissed him when she had the chance?

It was just . . . he was actually sorta okay company, now that he no longer had all those rules to fixate on.

Scratch that. Fantastic company.

Intelligent. Observant. Nerdy. Dry-witted and sarcastic, but then, who wasn't?

They spent hours chatting every evening, her laughing so hard she had snorted a toxic amount of Pepsi at one point. Him . . . surely laughing super-duper hard on the inside—though she never got more than an extra-sparkly eye twinkle on the outside. Not that she minded really.

Why did he have to do the whole sexy, aristocratic brooding thing so well?

Each morning, he would spend a couple hours in the stables-turned-garage behind Duir Cottage working out aggression with Marc's punching bag. Or he would head over to the stables and go for a bruising ride. The exercise seemingly calmed him, made him ready to tackle the day.

And then he would clean, bless his sweet little heart. The kitchen, the bathrooms, all her incessant messes. He had even discovered the washing machine. She had come downstairs that morning to find all the kitchen linens neatly laundered and folded according to color, the pantry meticulously organized, every can label turned outward, arranged from chicken noodle to vegemite. He had already alphabetized all her sticky note sayings and organized them on the wall opposite the kitchen island.

If he ever decided to give up lording, he could *totally* have a career as a domestic HGTV maven. Martha Stewart-esque. Still dripping condescension but with the addition of a posh accent and chiseled abs. Guaranteed must-see-TV.

For her part, Jasmine continued to sketch the mural. The figures were coming together nicely, but she needed something more specific for the background. Hence today's excursion down to Wales, trying again for Caerleon.

No more word from Cobra about the pendant, but it had continued to show up in her dreams.

*Trees. Fog rolling in.*

*Hurry. She needed to hurry. They were waiting for her.*

*She sprinted forward. A golden tendril curved around her ankles in greeting and then spooled off into the fog. Pleading, urging her on.*

*In the distance, she could hear a fountain, water chiming. The giddy laughter of a young girl.*

*Oh, if only they would wait for her! She needed to reach the courtyard.*

*The shimmery ribbons swirled. Whirling, spinning. Twining into a dara knot, criss-crossed.*

*Pulsing, waiting.*

Jasmine shook her head. Why did the tendrils keep forming a dara knot in her dreams? Why the sense of urgency? Was it a message of some kind? Or just her poor, overworked brain wanting so desperately for the pendant to be the link to her family?

It was hard to say.

The hedgerows of the narrow country road passed at a blur. A light rain had started, spotting the windshield. Timothy accelerated around a turn, throwing her against the passenger door.

"I should have made you do more student driver hours. You are hopelessly illegal. And probably going to get us both killed."

He sniffed, shifted down into second gear and peeled around a Fiat. "I assure you, Miss Fleury, after driving a high-spirited pair of thoroughbreds pulling my high-perch phaeton at top speed through the chaos that is nineteenth century London traffic, sitting comfortably behind the wheel of a non-sentient, un-opinionated machine on a quiet country road is child's play."

The car growled aggressively as it moved back into its lane, obviously not agreeing with his lordship's assessment of *un-opinionated*.

"Wait. So you don't shave or dress yourself, but you *do* drive your own carriage? That makes no sense."

"Would a modern prince permit a servant to drive one of his expensive sports cars?"

"*Touché.*"

"No sporting gentleman alive would allow a mere groom to handle his prime cattle. 'Tis a matter of pride and honor, Miss Fleury."

"Both of which we know you have in spades."

He merely shrugged in acknowledgment.

She shook her head as Timothy effortlessly steered the car around a double-parked delivery van (with only inches to spare) and clamped harder on her I-need-to-brake-right-now right foot. Sitting in the passenger seat, the side where she normally drove a car, didn't help. The rain took up a steady patter against the windows.

"I thought you were going to call me Jasmine from now on."

"I told you. I like Miss Fleury. Using the names interchangeably does not bother me. And seeing how I was told to just *be myself* . . ."

He had *not* just said that.

She stared at his profile. His face utterly impassive. As usual.

"You're teasing me. Like actually, full-on *teasing*. Admit it."

Something flashed across his cheek. That same something she had noticed off and on for weeks now.

Surely she wasn't seeing—

No. It couldn't be—

"Stop the car! Stop it right now!"

With a glance of alarm, he veered off the road, lurching to a halt in front of a farmer's gate.

"Whatever is the matter?" He looked around and then fixed her with a wide-eyed gaze.

Jasmine was frozen in her seat. Staring at him.

"Do this," she said, stretching her lips wide, baring her teeth.

He sat back, alarm deepening.

"Why should I wish to look like a rabid dog?"

"Just do it."

"Is this some sort of odd twenty-first century driving game? Where you see an animal and then act out—"

"Please." She batted her eyelashes.

With a long-suffering sigh, he gritted his teeth, pulling his mouth wide.

No. Freaking. Way.

She gasped, hand to her mouth.

"You. Have. Dimples."

He flinched. Causing said dimples to disappear.

"Oh my word! Dimplesdimplesdimplesdimplesdimpl—"

"Jasmine!" He looked about, as an adorable flush crept up his face. Refusing to meet her eyes.

She was so beyond caring.

"You have dimples." She clasped her hands under her chin. "Like deep, pinch-your-cheeks-they're-so-cute dimples!"

He took in a deep breath. "I fail to see how the presence of dimples—"

"Do it again. I want to see them again."

Yep. There was The Look, full-force. Did he not know she was beyond caring?

"Miss Fleury—"

"C'mon. Pleeeease." She tilted her head and fluttered her eyelashes enough to make a southern belle proud. "Pretty, pretty, pretty pleeeeeeeease."

He sighed, closed his eyes and then bared his teeth again. And there they were, one in each cheek. Deep and perfectly round.

Dimples.

"Oh, they're just so cute." She cooed and touched her right hand to his face, rubbing her thumb over said dimples.

They instantly vanished.

Stubborn man. Denying her the soul-satisfying pleasure of dimples.

He merely stared at her, gray eyes pensive. And then slowly lifted his own hand, retrieving hers from his face. Wrapping her hand in his broad palm and ever-so-carefully dragging her fingers downward. Brushing them across his lips in the process, before settling their hands on the center console.

Never once breaking eye contact with her.

The entire motion thoroughly goosebump-inducing.

He didn't let go of her hand.

Which was actually the nicest part, in the end. The simple act of having his warm strong fingers engulfing hers should *not* have sent tingles chasing her spine . . . but there she was.

Sheesh. Talk about swoon-worthy.

She felt like fanning herself and doing her best Scarlett O'Hara impression:

*I do declare, my lord, but you have set my poor little heart aflutter . . .*

"You need to smile." She gave him a textbook example. "Then we could all enjoy your dimples more often. It's a tragedy to keep them hidden from the world."

"I was raised to obey rule number twenty-three and its corollary, rule number twenty-nine," was all he said.

*A gentleman suppresses undue emotion, whether of disappointment, of mortification, of laughter, of anger, etc.*

*A gentleman will refrain from all displays of levity.*

"I hate all those rules that forced you to not show emotion . . . it's the most unhealthy, emotionally-stunted, unnatural way—"

She stopped herself mid-rant. Logic. The man needed logic, not raving. Emotional logic.

Which should have been a complete oxymoron, really, but it just wasn't when talking with Timothy Linwood.

She tried again. "Showing your emotions is normal. I admit, you have made exceptional progress with accepting certain aspects of this century, like machines. But now it's time to move on to emotions."

"I am perfectly capable of expressing emotions."

She sat back, waiting expectantly.

He remained impassive before her. Doing his normal I-am-a-statue impression.

"Soooooo, is this you expressing emotions? Because, if so, I'm not getting much of a read on them . . ."

Still nothing. Man, it was uncanny how still he could sit. If he ever needed a career change, he could hire out as one of those palace guard guys who couldn't move a muscle while tourists did all sorts of things to distract them—

"A palace guard?"

She closed her eyes, giving her head a shake. "Timothy, expressing emotions is normal. It's healthy. Laughter is the best medicine and all that."

Now it was his turn to raise a questioning eyebrow.

"Laughter is the best medicine? That is an unexpected phrase."

"It means that if you want to stay healthy, you need to laugh. You don't want to be sick, do you?"

He shrugged, face back to its normal impassive mask.

"I have stayed well up until now. My bodily humors rarely fall out of balance."

Okaaaay. That was odd.

But she lost whatever else she was going to say. His thumb started rubbing across the back of her hand, causing her stomach to do this fluttery-gooey thing.

He was still trying to distract her. And it was *working*, drat him, slowly dissolving her girly insides to mush. She gave herself a mental shake.

"Seriously. Let's practice." She settled into her soft leather seat. Looked at him. Expectantly.

"I can hardly be expected to smile when there is nothing humorous to induce me."

Mmmmmm. Now he was just being difficult.

"Fine. Allow me to help you." She pursed her lips. His thumb was still going in lazy circles. And he had upped the ante by moving up to the sensitive inside of her wrist. The man had no mercy. "Did you hear about the guy whose whole left side was cut off? He's all right now."

She winked at him. Waggled her eyebrows.

He stilled, thumb pausing. Raised an eyebrow.

And then resumed his gentle exploration of her hand.

Nothing. She got nothing.

"C'mon. That was hilarious."

He shook his head. Every line of his body communicating disappointment.

"As I said, rule number two hundred and forty-three specifies—"

"I know, I know. Puns aren't punny. But where's the fun in that?"

"Anyone who would consider puns a source of amusement clearly has a penchant toward self-torture—"

"Not even. Puns can totally be hilarious. I'll prove it."

He shook his head at her and then lifted her hand to his lips. Planting a gentle kiss on her knuckles. Lips so very soft, his breath warm and lingering.

*Oh dear.*

Cue heart-fluttering and hand-fanning again.

He was clearly trying to change the subject. She narrowed her eyes, letting him know that she was on to his game.

A dimple flashed and his eyes smile-twinkled.

It was a start.

He brushed her fingers with his thumb, letting her know he was on to her too, and then slowly released her hand. Sliding his hand away inch by inch, skimming his fingers from her wrist to her fingertips.

Wow. Was this one of those gentleman things too? How to seduce a lady by only touching her hand?

Her right hand certainly thought so. It instantly felt cold and lonely. Traitorous appendage. She was totally disowning it. Going all left from now on.

Timothy shifted the car back into gear and, with a confident glance into his rear view mirror, pulled onto the road. Face back to his standard cut-marble-impassive.

He was going to be a tough customer.

"What is the difference between ignorance and apathy?" She tried again.

He shifted the car and said, "I do not know, and I do not care."

Drat. He was good.

And still nothing.

She would crack him.

She sat silent, trying to think of more bad pun jokes. Rain drummed against the car. How did that one go about a frayed knot in a bar?

No. She needed to think of puns that were more his *milieu*. Though she would probably need help from Google.

She thought for a moment. Snapped her fingers.

"My tailor is happy to make a pair of pants for me, or at least . . . *sew it seams.*" She hit him with her brightest smile.

The dratted man didn't so much as flinch.

Just a glance out of the corner of his eye and that raised eyebrow. Though it was a decidedly *challenging* eyebrow.

This was *so* on.

"So what is your plan once we reach Caerleon?" his smooth voice asked.

"You're trying to change the topic."

"Not at all. Merely making polite conversation."

"You're running scared. Afraid I will make you—*gasp*—smile."

"Not in the slightest—"

"*Brock.*" She tucked her hands into her ribs and flapped her elbows. "*Brockbrockbrockbrock-bacock!*"

The eyebrow went a fraction of an inch higher.

"Is this more of your driving game? I do not, as a general rule, find chicken impressions humorous—"

If Timothy thought *that* was going to be enough to change the topic—

"Is that one of the rules too?" she asked. "A gentleman of distinction will never laugh at impersonations of poultry." She mimicked his haughty aristocratic drawl.

Again. Nothing.

"You're killing me here. Do you find *anything* funny?"

He took a too-fast corner.

"I naturally find certain events humorous."

A long pause as she listened to the rain *swish* on the road, waiting for him to finish his thought.

He didn't.

Letting the silence imply that he had yet to find *her* humorous.

Oh, yeah. This was soooooo on.

She would crack him. Like . . . like a coconut with a machete.

Like a firecracker in a tin can—

No, wait. That just made a cracking noise . . . the can didn't necessarily bust apart. Though if you put enough firecrackers in and lit them with a long fuse, it might—

Where was she?

"You were going to crack me. How about like an egg? It would be a more straight forward simile—"

*Grrrrr.*

She pointed a finger at him. "This is *so* not over, mister."

His glanced at her, that dimple flashing again. Eyes dancing. But no smile.

He was definitely toying with her. Teasing.

This was so going to be a smack-down—

She was totally going to scour the internet for the funniest puns *ever*. The man wouldn't know what hit him.

Timothy came to a t-stop and turned right. The BMW's navigation noted they were seven miles from Caerleon.

"Again, what do you hope to find at Caerleon?" He nudged his chin toward the GPS panel in the dash. "I think your mural is coming along spendidly."

She shot him her best I-know-you're-just-trying-to-distract me look.

He returned with a signature I-could-care-less flick of his eyes.

Fine. She could bide her time. She would go along and then take him down when he least expected it.

"It is one of the rumored sites of Camelot. I'm just hoping to get some sketching done. Backgrounds for my King Arthur mural," she said.

He nodded and drove in silence for a few moments, rain drumming hypnotically.

And then he leaned toward her, as if imparting something profound and secretive.

"Did you know that the roundest knight in King Arthur's court was Sir Cumference?"

Jasmine blinked. All the air leaving her in a startled laughing gasp. Embarrassingly loud and far too giggly.

Timothy did not. Laugh, that is.

But his eyes definitely twinkled again. And those dimples flashed.

And she spent the rest of the afternoon wondering if there hadn't been a wink in the mix too.

# Chapter 19

Jasmine liked his dimples.

If talking about something was an indication of personal preference. Which the scientist in Timothy was inclined to believe it was.

She had mentioned them seventeen times over the last few days. Three references occurring just this morning.

It was . . . interesting.

Others rarely realized he had dimples. His father had abhorred them, considered them a flaw in his breeding. Yet another reason his sire had disliked seeing Timothy smile.

Their jaunt to Caerleon had not been particularly successful. Rain had set in with a vengeance by the time they reached their destination, greatly reducing visibility. Jasmine had not been able to sketch anything helpful. Her words.

Though the trip had allowed Timothy to expand his list of likes:

*Driving in the rain with Jasmine.*
*Holding Jasmine's hand.*
*Teasing Jasmine.*

There was definitely a theme.

Jasmine was creeping her way into more than just his lists. She had taken up residence in his brain, crowding his other worries about the viscountcy's finances, about Miss Heartstone, about returning to his own century, about the disturbing reality of his estate becoming a merchant conglomerate.

Granted, between his obsessive study of mechanical engineering, delight in cleaning and organization, and rejection of The Rules, his frantic desperation to return home had faded.

Or maybe, all of that was just Jasmine too. Spending time with her, hearing her giggly laugh, her crazy ideas. Whatever the cause, he checked the portal only twice a day, morning and night.

He wasn't sure if that was progress.

After several days of rain, they were driving once more. The weather forecast called for overcast skies with only a twenty percent chance of rain, so Jasmine wanted to try Wales again. Specifically, Caerphilly Castle.

Modern technology astounded him. How could scientists know what the weather would be hours and days into the future? And yet, the forecasts were remarkably accurate.

Timothy shifted down and steered the car onto a connecting byway. The machine was another absolute marvel. Turning what would have been a journey of several days over rough country into a pleasant two-hour drive, listening to Jasmine chatter along the way. The woman did like to talk. Which was just fine by Timothy, as he adored the sound of her voice.

"Like you've mentioned before, the real King Arthur was probably a ruler of the Britons who lived around the beginning of the 6th century, right after the collapse of the Roman Empire," she said from the seat beside him.

She was currently staring at her phone. She had been peppering him with information about the various Arthurian legends for the last hour while eating candy from a bag labeled *Gummy Teeth and Lips*.

"So there is no definitive evidence that Arthur was an actual historical figure. He was probably an amalgam of several different men. Prime candidates for Arthur are a Roman-British leader named Aurelius Ambrosius who shows up in later records. There is another ruler named Riothamus from the same era. He is one of the few people they have actual contemporary evidence for. He is mentioned in a couple of Roman letters."

She paused, reading. Popped more candy into her mouth.

"Interesting," she continued. "There is some speculation that this Ambrosius guy and Riothamus could be one and the same person as they lived at the same time. I guess Riothamus is more a title than a name and could be translated as something like 'supreme ruler of the Britons.' This area of southern Wales was actually a center of their power, though the kingdom may have stretched through western Britain and even into Brittany in northern France."

*Ah.* At last something with which he was vaguely familiar. "The languages are all similar—Welsh, Cornish, Breton. They are thought to all derive from the same original ancient source."

"The original mother tongue of the ancient Britons?"

"Yes. The ancient Kingdom of the Britons is said to encompass all areas west of Bath. The last stand of Celtic peoples against the invading Saxons and Angles who swarmed the island once the Roman battalions left."

"Mmmmm, so interesting." She still studied her phone. "I wonder if I could include some of this in my mural somehow. Capture something of the real people behind the myth."

"As I have said, Arthur would have been dressed more like a Roman general than a medieval knight."

"True. But there is something to be said for meeting people's expectations. Having King Arthur as a Roman would involve too much explanation for little Arthur. But I'm going to try to think of something."

She paused and then tapped his arm. "Hey hot stuff. You come here often?"

He glanced at her. And then shook his head.

She had stuffed several candy teeth into her mouth, layering them on top of her own teeth. Giving her a crazed, bucktoothed expression.

"You know you want to smile. Admit it." She nudged him again. "Or is it that you can't handle the *tooth*?" She wiggled her eyebrows, the motion dislodging one of the fake sets of teeth. She caught it before it fell into her lap.

She had been doing this for at least a week now. Trying to goad him into smiling.

"Of all the humorous possibilities in the universe, you opt for candy teeth?" he asked.

"It's not as low-hanging a fruit as you might think."

"My non-candy lips are calling you out for your falsehood."

"Well! My *candy* lips are smiling at you in mockery." She pulled a pair of lips from her bag, sticking them to her mouth. "You aren't fooling me. I saw that flash of dimple. You're roaring with laughter on the inside."

She did look decidedly ridiculous with the bright red sugared lips clinging to her own. Blue eyes dancing. Dark hair loose and curled around her face. She sucked the lips into her mouth.

"Mark my words, mister. You *will* smile and laugh before I'm through—"

"What in heaven's name?!"

Timothy swerved off the road, stopping with a lurch on the shoulder. Eyes staring in astonishment.

A wonder of curved steel rose before him. It was a track of sorts, like the kind a mine cart would roll along. Only elevated and twisting and turning. A series of carriages flew along it, whipping the hair of those sitting inside. It seemed to defy gravity. Another machine rose next to it, a sort of capsule spinning and twirling. Again, he could see people inside, clutching on to the sides and laughing.

"Timothy? Hello?" A hand waved in front of his face.

He shook his head, eyes still far-too-wide and riveted at the sight.

"It is wondrous. What is this place?" Surely his amazement was palpable.

Jasmine looked at the spectacle and then back at him. "It's just a kiddie carnival—"

"Carnival? It's not Carnival. We're in April now—"

"No. It's *a* carnival, like a fair or a circus."

*Oh.* More words which had shifted meaning on him.

"Is that series of carts supposed to represent a dragon?" His eyes were still focused on the wagons flying along the track.

"Something like that—"

"Can anyone ride it?"

"Well . . . sure. It's meant more for little kids though—"

"Why would an adult not wish to indulge too? It looks enjoyable. I should like to ride it." He was out of the car and halfway to the festooned entrance before Jasmine caught up to him.

"You're seriously going to ride the kiddie dragon roller coaster?"

"Is that what the machine is called? A roller coaster?"

She just shook her head. And then danced ahead to face him.

"Will it make you smile?"

He paused, staring into her upturned grinning face. And then glanced at the shining metal machine behind her. "Very possibly."

"Sweet. I'm so taking a picture of this for James."

"I should think you would like to ride too."

"Oh, I do. Don't worry. But it's not going to stop me from documenting this."

Five minutes later, Timothy was seated in a too small cart, knees into his chest, eagerly leaning over the sticky metal side, trying to see how exactly the carriage was attached to the rail.

"Hah. The cart is affixed to a chain which rotates around the track, pulling the cart with it."

Jasmine, sitting in the cart behind him, shook her head. Though the mechanism seemed quite straight-forward to Timothy.

"You are like a kid in a candy store. Anyone ever told you that?"

He paused, lifting his head to fully look at her. "No. No one has ever described me thus."

"Why am I not surprised?" She lifted her phone. "Smile for James—"

"We have already discussed smiling."

"—or not. It's whatever. Though I would like to point out that the dragon on this roller coaster *is* smiling."

He craned his neck forward to see the front car. Sure enough. The dragon *was* smiling.

"The dragon may be smiling, Miss Fleury, but it seems to be more maniacal than humorous."

"You know, even a maniacal smile would be okay by me—"

The cart lurched forward, cutting off her response. Timothy grabbed the side, the twisting motions of the small train requiring him to hold on tightly. He could hear Jasmine behind him calling 'Weeeeeeee' as the train moved around the track. Though she didn't seem to have her heart in it. If he didn't know better, he would think she was being sarcastic. But what was sarcastic about this experience? It was an utter delight.

The ride ended all too soon.

Which meant that they would just have to ride it again.

And again and again.

Nearly an hour later, Jasmine practically dragged him away.

"Enough! If we're doing the kiddie carnival, we need to have the whole experience. I see a sparkly pink unicorn over there that has my name on it. I'm going to assume being a crack shot with a rifle was one of your rules."

It was indeed.

———————

Two hours later, Timothy's stomach felt woozy.

It was probably the last carnival ride spinning him upside down combined with the fluffy, sugary candy Jasmine was still eating.

Though the glittery pink unicorn tucked into the crook of his arm could also have been a factor.

Granted, he took pride in having won the unicorn. He had won so quickly, the game attendant had politely asked him *not* to play again. Apparently, twenty-first century marksmen were unaccustomed to compensating for weapons which consistently pulled hard to the right.

"You sure you don't want any more cotton candy?" Jasmine asked, tucking another mound of the blue mass into her mouth.

Despite the eighty percent chance of no rain, the weather had decided to side with the remaining twenty percent. A few raindrops fell. Music played in the distance.

"Quite sure."

"I think Mr. Sparkles disagrees with you. Don't you, Mr. Sparkles?" She leaned in and touched her nose to the stuffed unicorn.

She had been talking to Mr. Sparkles for the last hour. He apparently had opinions about everything—the number of times each spinny ride needed to be ridden (four), what color shirt (bright pink) that large, bearded man should *not* have been wearing, how much sugar Timothy should eat . . .

Jasmine darted ahead of him and walked backwards a few steps, heedless of the rain.

"Personally, I think a sugar high and then the resulting sugar-crash are kinda requisite when doing the whole carnival thing. You're not getting the full experience here."

"My stomach informs me the experience has been sufficient. Thank you." He shifted the unicorn in his arm.

"Mmmmm, there was another flash of dimple there. Mr. Sparkles is smiling." She shrugged and peeled off the last of the cotton candy from its paper cone. "I think you should consider it a sign. He's setting a good example for you."

She ate the bite, licking the blue residue off her fingers and then tossed the empty cone into a nearby rubbish receptacle.

The music became louder. They walked around a tent to see a stage set up in an open area. A man and woman stood on the stage, singing and strumming what appeared to be guitars. The tune they played was one he recognized, a traditional song considered old even in his time. A crowd had gathered in front of the stage, some people dancing.

At which point, the rain decided to get more serious. It wasn't a heavy rain. Just the typical drizzle of spring that had enough warmth to hint toward summer. He stopped under the awning of a tent, sheltered.

With an exuberant laugh, Jasmine walked into the open, spreading her arms wide, face tilted toward the sky. Her long hair hung free, curling and thick nearly to her waist, swinging back and forth with her movements. She was wearing that same outfit, the one with the frock coat, tight jeans and knee-high laced boots.

He had become inordinately fond of it, quite frankly.

Standing in the grass, rain speckling her face, arms outstretched, eyes closed . . . she seemed more fey than human. A forest sprite bubbling with laughter and mischief. A bit of constant sunshine in an otherwise dreary world.

*Just because it's stormy now, doesn't mean you aren't headed for sunshine.*

With Jasmine, one could have both simultaneously.

That yearning sensation pounded in his chest.

She opened her eyes and turned back to him. Grinned widely. Skipped to his side.

"You clearly have never danced in the rain, have you?" she asked. "I bet it's one of the rules. A gentleman shall never spontaneously dance in the rain."

"Mmmmm, I daresay if my forebears had ever considered it a danger, it *would* be a rule."

"Well, in that case . . ." She took the stuffed unicorn from his hand, setting it down on the ground next to the tent. "As attractive a couple as you and Mr. Sparkles are, I think he can take a rest while I claim you for a dance or two."

She grabbed his hand and tugged, trying to bring him out into the soft rain, her fingers cold in his.

"Ah. But it *is* a rule that only a gentleman can ask a lady to dance. Not the other way around."

He leaned back, forcing her to put her whole weight into moving him. Not that it helped. She was far too small to budge him. Though her lips pursed adorably as she tried.

With a sigh, she stopped pulling on his arm and took two steps forward, placing herself right in front of him. Still holding his hand. Almost of its own accord, his thumb sought the softness of the skin inside her wrist.

"You're going to be a tough customer, I see. Though I am catching glimpses of a dimple and your eyes are definitely cheery, so I know you're teasing me. Very well then. Let's play out this drama."

She angled her body and dug a toe of her boot into the grass, twisting her ankle back and forth, all the while casting a longing look back at the crowd milling and dancing.

"Oh, woe is me." Her sigh was convincingly forlorn. She cast her free hand over her eyes. "All this lovely dancing going on and here I am. A lady bereft of a dashing partner to sweep me onto the dance floor." She peeped at him and then swung her eyes back to the stage. Gave his hand a little shake. "*Pssst.* Now it's your turn to say a line."

How could a red-blooded man from *any* century resist such a thing?

He tugged on her hand, pulling her into him, wrapping her arm behind her back as he gathered her close. Bending his head, he whispered in her ear.

"Dance with me, my lady?"

She mock-gasped and placed her free hand over her heart. Eyes so very wide. "My stars! I thought you'd never ask."

Breathing in the scent of her—clean soap and peppermint—he clasped her other hand and swung her into a loose waltz which matched the one-two-three count of the music. He barely registered the rain dripping against his face. Every sensation was caught up in the miracle of the woman in his arms.

She was just so . . . vibrant. Free and unfettered by worldly expectations. Radiantly buoyant, even though he knew exactly how much of her world had crumbled around her.

He was a moth drawn to her flame. Helpless to keep away from the potentially scalding brightness. The reward worth any danger.

He drew her closer, tucking her body tight against his. So close it would send every matron in 1815 into a collective scandalized swoon.

She responded by nestling her head into his chest, leaning into him. Trusting. Giving.

A feeling swept through him. Something he could not remember feeling in . . . forever.

He contemplated it for a moment. And then labeled it.

Peace. Calm.

Happiness.

How long had it been since he felt . . . happy?

The sensation bubbled in his chest. Burst through his veins until he felt he should float away from the effervescence.

She stirred in his arms, pulling back to smile dreamily at him.

And then she froze.

Pulled them to a stop.

All the air leaving her lungs in a *whoosh*. Eyes going instantly wide.

"Whatever is the matter—"

She brought a soft palm up to his cheek, her thumb brushing over his dimple. Tears welled in her eyes.

"You were *smiling*." Her voice not more than a wondrous whisper.

"I was?"

She nodded, full of awe. "It was . . . beautiful."

She brought up her other hand, cupping his face. Her little hands pressing softly into his cheeks.

"I know guys don't like to be called beautiful, but that's what it was. It was like your entire face just, *poof*, came to life. Your eyes crinkled and all those hard edges softened and your *dimples*"—here she actually bounced on her toes—"oh, they were just adorable—again, I know, I know, adorable isn't the word that a man would choose either—but they were. Deep and charming. Totally swoon-inducing. Did you know that in Norwegian, dimples are called smile holes? *Smilehuller.* I had a Norwegian roommate for a semester, and she taught me all these interesting words . . . Anyway, it is a *travesty* to deny the world the awesomeness of your smile holes, Mr. Linwood. You need to smile more. Like all the time. Just so the rest of us can enjoy the sight—"

"Like this?"

That bubbly euphoria broke through again. He could feel his face stretching, unused muscles moving. The entire feeling utterly marvelous. Why had he ever resisted this?

Scrunching her shoulders, she giggled. "Yes! Exactly like that!

She launched herself into his shoulders, wrapping her arms tightly around his neck, burying her cold nose into his throat.

Timothy continued to smile as he swept her into his arms, her feet dangling. It just felt so damned good. Like lifting a world of weight off his shoulders.

After a moment, he set Jasmine back down. She continued to laugh, wrapping her arms around his waist.

"What finally did the trick?" She craned her neck back to look at him.

He leaned down. "You." Whispered in her ear.

"*Me?*" A small blissful smile. "I *knew* those puns would get to you eventually."

He merely smiled larger and gathered her close.

The music changed to a tune he didn't know. But the words arrowed through him.

*You are my sunshine. My only sunshine. You make me happy when skies are gray . . .*

He spun Jasmine out and then brought her back close, her laughter golden bright.

*How* he wanted more of her. More of her smiles. More of her cheer. Her endless patience. Her kind soul.

Would that he could keep this perfect moment forever . . .

He wanted to blast away all those logical, viscount-ish thoughts that marched inside his head (orderly, in a line), determined to sully his mood.

There was no future for them. Not together, at least.

Mentally, he took aim. Fired. The thoughts evaporated.

But it wasn't enough. The thoughts continued to crowd in, soldiers of a long war, brutal in their cool reasoning.

Jasmine could never be *his*. The very idea was . . . impossible. The gulf between them two hundred years in the making. His nineteenth century life was too structured to allow her in. Too many others relied on him to make responsible, unemotional decisions.

No. She would be an ephemeral burst of light . . . A comet scouring his skies, leaving a brilliant memory in its wake. She had been wise not to allow their relationship to progress any further.

Some other man would be blessed to go through life with her at his side.

He nearly closed his eyes at the wave of pain which shot through him.

Breathe. Just breathe.

*Please don't take my sunshine away . . .*

They didn't make it to Wales in the end. When they finally returned home, damp but content, Timothy added one more item—slowly, wistfully—to his list before going to bed:

*Dancing in the rain with Jasmine.*

# Chapter 20

You have been giggling fairly maniacally for the last thirty minutes, Miss Fleury. Would you care to tell me where we are going?"

Jasmine just grinned and smiled, stuffing her laughter behind a hand. She had spent all of yesterday planning this.

It was going to be awesome. Huge.

Epic.

Yep. There was no stopping the giggling. It just bubbled free no matter what she did.

They both deserved a break. Things with Rita had been so strained lately. She was *still* texting demanding Jasmine return every random thing she could think of. The woman was completely mental.

Worse, Cobra had no more leads. He had scoured all U.S. missing children reports for five years before and after the accident, coming up empty-handed. No child named Minna anywhere. Granted, who knew if that was her name, a nickname or just a poor memory playing tricks on her.

Her pendant hit a dead end too. It was indeed gold with no hall-marks. Beyond that, they knew little. The leading theory was that it had been handmade by someone close to her and, because the item had never been intended for resale, the maker didn't think to add the required hallmarks. There had been some talk between Cobra and James about possibly contacting goldsmiths in Florida, but after thirty years, no one held out much hope.

Basically, aside from her repeated odd dreams featuring the dara knot, her search was at a standstill.

The portal remained stubbornly closed to Timothy. Which was bad . . . right? She was afraid to examine *that* particular little emotion too much . . .

Basically, they needed a fun holiday. And after seeing Timothy smile the other day . . .

*Gah!* Her stomach still did this gymnastic twirling tumbling thingy every time she thought about it.

He had just looked so . . . relaxed. So carefree. So . . . un-Linwood-ish.

And now she was greedy. She wanted more, more, more of that smile. More of his happiness. More of his contentment.

And if her luck held, she would get him to *laugh* too.

Timothy Linwood . . . *laughing.*

She had been awake half the night contemplating what his laugh would look like, sound like.

Was he a Crinkle-Eye Laugher? The type whose eyes disappeared?

Or was he a Throw-Back Laugher, chin lifted, teeth bared toward the sky?

Or a Shy-Duck Laugher, with his head tilted forward, fist raised to his mouth?

Was the sound of his laugh quiet? Or more rumbly? Guffaw-ish?

She bounced in her seat. She wanted to know *now!*

But she could wait until the end of the day. It was going to happen, one way or another.

She had a very good plan.

"Just follow the GPS. It will get us there."

And then she succumbed to another fit of giggles.

Forty-five minutes later, Timothy stood outside the car park gate, staring upwards. Mouth unfashionably agape.

"Bloody hell. That is *not* what I think it is, right?"

Dumbfounded felt like too weak a word to describe the depths of his astonishment.

He shook his head. "How is such a thing possible? That cannot possibly be safe. I'm quite sure it defies every one of Newton's laws."

Jasmine clung to his arm, still giggling like an escaped patient from Bedlam.

He smiled at the sound. He couldn't help it. She was utterly contagious.

"I know. I know." She jumped up and down. "It's going to be sooooooo awesome. It's one of the biggest roller coasters in all of Europe—"

"You are impossibly incorrigible—"

"You would be too if you were about to initiate the inexperienced into the mind-blowing g-forces of a world-class roller coaster. No more kiddie coasters for you, buster."

"Are those people hanging upside-down?"

"Yes."

"And going in circles?"

"It's called a loop-de-loop. And the tighter one over there is called a corkscrew."

"Good heavens! The cars just plummeted! Like going over the edge of a cliff—"

"I know, right? Your stomach practically comes out your nose—"

"You can hear their screams all the way over here."

Her face lit, eyes shining, she slid her hand down his arm and threaded her small fingers through his. And then danced forward, turning to pull him along.

She gave another crazed giggle. More jumping. "Let's go! Letsgoletsgoletsgo—"

So impossibly adorable. Infectious delight.

Timothy laughed.

Soft and low, but a *laugh* nonetheless.

A giddy breath of pure joy.

Though quiet, the sound didn't escape Jasmine. She whirled on him, eyes wide with surprise.

"You laughed!" she crowed in triumph, jumping into his arms, wrapping herself around him.

Naturally, he reciprocated by gathering her close. Burying his nose in her hair, giving another chuckle.

*Ahhhh.* The joy of holding her, of being near her. The sheer dizzying brilliance that was her soul. How could a man *not* laugh when hugging her?

She pulled back, taking his head in her hands, running her thumbs over his dimples.

"And you're a Buttery Laugher, no less," she said. "The kind who chuckles under his breath, and it's all low, rumbly, sexy, smooth like butteh."

If she said so.

"You made that too easy for me." She planted a solid kiss on his cheek. "I thought it would take at least a hundred foot drop to get a laugh out of you."

But before he could follow-up and, hopefully, get her to move that kiss about three inches to the right, she had her feet on the ground and was tugging him toward the roller coaster.

———

"Wait! That isn't the last of *my* extreme sour zombie gummies, is it?" Jasmine studied the plastic package Timothy held and then pushed her loop-de-loop-mussed hair out of her face to get a better look.

Wild hair was totally an acceptable price to pay for the most *awesome, uh-mazing, ridonculous roller coaster ride EVER*. All said in a sing-song voice while doing sparkly jazz fingers. That had earned her an extra-deep dimpled smile and soft Buttery Laugh.

The walk around the paddle boat pond and sugar rush from the zombie gummies was helping settle her stomach.

"*Your* extreme sour zombies?" Timothy fixed her with those silver eyes of his. Lifted his eyebrows.

Jasmine narrowed her gaze, staring at the bag, brushed her hair back again.

Yep. There was only one left. And it was a pink one, no less. Her favorite.

"I'm pretty sure it's one of the rules. A gentleman will always give the last extreme sour zombie gummy to his lady."

Timothy shook his head, all mock-mournfulness. "No. I cannot say I recall such a rule. And even if it did exist, someone made me give up *all* my rules. Soooooooo . . ."

With a wicked glint in his eye, he reached into the bag and drew out the last gummy zombie with a flourish. It sparkled in the sunlight, all glittery with extra-sour, pucker-inducing sweetness.

Without breaking eye contact with her, he lifted it to his mouth, preparing to drop it in.

*Oh!*

The man was an utter cad.

"Don't you dare." She shook her head, eyes menacing. "You need to share. Sharing is definitely one of your rules."

He paused, cocking his head in thought. "Actually, I cannot say that it is. Viscounts, as a general principle, are not taught to share."

"Well they should be! Sharing is good for the soul."

"Only someone who has spent her life being compelled to share things would say that. Those of us who have never had to apportion our possessions—"

"Share!"

"Make me!" He held the candy above his head, well out of her reach.

She glared.

And then he smiled. That slow-spreading one that started somewhat lop-sided on the right side and then traveled left until *bam*, at the very last second his dimples popped and his eyes crinkled.

Be still her poor little heart.

Now she had to start it beating again.

It was *lethal*, that smile.

How could this teasing, darling man be the same dour, pompous lord who stomped through the portal over a month ago?

A man she was coming to thoroughly adore.

*After* she killed him for eating her last extreme sour zombie gummy.

He dangled the candy from his raised fingers. Taunting.

Stupid tall man.

She grabbed on to his shirt and jumped for it. But in the process, her hand touched his ribs. He twitched.

She paused.

No. Way.

She danced her fingers across his ribs again. He jerked back.

"Jasmine . . ." he said warningly.

"You're ticklish!" She darted in, getting a few fingers into his ribs.

He chuckled, batting away her hands with his free arm.

With little success.

"I would advise you—"

"You didn't realize I'm, like, a champion tickler, did you?"

She did a little testing. Ribs. Ticklish. Side. Ticklish. Knees. Ticklish.

With each touch, he squirmed and twisted, chuckling helplessly. Soft, warm, buttery goodness.

It was totally awesome.

He danced away from her fingers, held out a staying hand, gasping. "I am a peer of the realm and, as such, have a certain dignity to maintain—"

"Dignity shmignity. If you wanted to remain proper, you shouldn't have taken my favorite pink gummie!"

She feinted for his ribs again, and he made the fatal mistake of trying to block her with both hands.

Practically offering her the candy in the process.

She claimed the gummy zombie with a gleeful chuckle.

"Wow! I'm remembering why I don't like these things." Jasmine buried her face in Timothy's coat sleeve as they rose into the sky. Refusing to look down.

"The view is exquisite. This is the perfect place to watch the sunset."

"Yes. But I always forget how *high* ferris wheels are. So carelessly open to the elements. So easy to rock and tip me out—"

An errant gust of wind tugged at her coat, causing the car to sway. She clutched Timothy's arm tighter.

Fought the panic rising in her throat.

She and heights had never gotten along. Maybe it was because the ground was so very far away and so ruthlessly hard. Or, more likely, the fact that she was so very breakable and *wingless*.

Timothy tucked an arm around her, pulling her tight against his side. She turned her face into his chest.

"You are shaking. Are you cold?"

"If you mean cold with *terror*, then yes." Her voice was muffled. Talking to someone's right pectoral had a way of doing that. Though it was a wonderfully solid pectoral.

Scrunching his brow, Timothy pulled away and leaned waaaaaay too far forward, causing the chair to tip. Giving Jasmine a clear view of *exactly* how far away that hard, hard ground really was—

"*Timothy!*" She clutched his jacket lapels, shrieking in terror.

He sat back, nodding his head thoughtfully.

"Indeed, I am not entirely sure I trust this apparatus either." He looked at her, tightened his grip around her shoulders. Face totally deadpan. "It is most definitely *up* to something."

It was up to something? *Oh no!*

Panicking, she sneaked a peek over the edge, trying to understand—

Annnnnnnd then it sank in.

With a choked laugh, she whirled back to him just in time to watch the naughtiest little-boy smile dimple his cheeks.

"There is no need for embarrassment, Miss Fleury." Still grinning, he gestured toward the edge with his chin. "Personally, I suffered from a fear of hurdles as a child, but I got over it. I have faith you will *rise* to the occasion."

*Oh. My. Word.*

She gasped. And then collapsed into a ball of laughter against his chest. He rubbed her back, brushed one of those kisses against her hair.

"That's better," he murmured. "I much prefer your laugh."

Jasmine wiped her eyes, still chuckling, nestling back against his chest. Impossible, punny, punny man! Just when she thought she couldn't like him any more . . .

But how sweet to distract her fears. Who knew once all that Lord Linwood ice melted, there would be this warm, funny, excessively nerdy but totally goofy guy inside?

Though what he was going to do when he returned home and had to obey that stupid pun rule again—

"Home?" He stiffened.

Drat. Was she *still* doing that non-filtered talking thing?

"Yes, you are," was his soft reply.

Dang. She needed to stop—

"Please, do not stop on my account. I quite enjoy always knowing your thoughts."

Shaking her head, Jasmine sat up.

"So, what about home? About 1815? I'm not sure you even checked the portal this morning. You're slipping, Lord Linwood." Her tone all teasing affection.

The question won her another dimple-touched smile. Though she could feel his urgency to return home had abated. He was less frantic about it.

Would he be allowed to return to his own time? She knew that, for others, the portal had acted a bit like a matchmaker, uniting them to their soul mate.

And here she and Timothy were. Forced together by the portal's machinations.

Up until two weeks ago, she would have said, 'Thanks, but no thanks,' to the idea of there ever being anything more than air between them.

But now . . . given how much her feelings had changed. The idea didn't seem so . . . impossible.

He relaxed, though he kept a warm hand pressed against the small of her back, his thumb running in lazy circles, effectively sending her heart into pumping overdrive.

He had made so many changes, but he still remained in her century. Would he ever be allowed to return home? And was it terrible that she kinda sorta didn't mind him being stuck with her?

He hadn't answered her question.

"Hoping your villages will become self-pillaging?" She gave her most gentle, hey-I'm-just-teasing smile.

A beat.

"It is actually a possibility. If I do not return soon, my tenants might find themselves without a home or livelihood."

Her eyebrows flew up in alarm. "What? Timothy, what's wrong?"

He looked away. And then drew in a deep breath. Shifted his shoulders, as if . . . embarrassed?

"My former man of affairs embezzled from my estate, paupering me. Daniel Ashton found the problem—"

"No! So all this time, you haven't just worried about Kinningsley becoming merchant holdings in the future. You have been stressed about solving this crisis in the past. Are you bankrupt?"

"Not yet. Though it is a decided possibility. If my land is sold off to pay creditors, it is likely my people will be tossed out of their homes. Homes they have had for centuries."

"Oh no!" Her heart fell with a sickening thud.

"So you can understand why I have been so desperate to return home."

"Yes! Why didn't you tell me?" Could she have been any meaner about it? "And here I have been cruelly teasing you about pillaging. I am so sorry—"

"There is nothing you could do about it. And until I return, there is nothing I can do about it either."

"True, but I'd like to think I'm a friend. And friends *tell* each other things like this. You haven't been able to help me find my family in the U.S., but it's still nice to have a listening ear. What will you do?"

Another huge gust of air left him. He looked away, eyes pensive.

And she *knew*.

Knew what the solution was. C'mon, she wasn't an idiot. She had watched enough BBC costume dramas to understand how his world worked.

"You have to marry an heiress, don't you?"

He sighed. Shrugged. "That is one solution—"

"Are you betrothed?"

Just asking the question made her stomach sink.

*Of course*, he would be betrothed. How could she not have seen that one coming?

"No! I am decidedly *not* betrothed." *Very* emphatic. "I learned of my financial situation mere days before coming to this century."

The relief which swept through her was astonishingly powerful.

"But surely marrying a wealthy heiress would solve—"

"Jasmine, I refuse to talk about other women when I am with you. It feels . . . wrong."

He emphasized his words with a spine-tingling pass of his thumb across her lower back.

Right. Her cue to just let it go.

Move on. Drop the topic.

A brief war raged within her. Her mothering impulse determined to solve his problems fighting an intense battle with her decidedly *non*-motherly attraction to him.

Mothering won out. Stupid maternal instinct.

"I wish there were some way I could help." Jasmine leaned forward, resting her hand on his chest, but arching her neck so she could still look at him. Sneaky attraction trying to get a hold. "I have some money. Marmi left me an inheritance of sorts."

A pause.

"I would never ask that of you."

"I'm not much of an heiress, anyway. Maybe enough for two high-perch phaetons and four horses. But it's yours if you need it."

"Thank you for the offer. My financial needs extend far beyond a coach and four, unfortunately. But I shall never forget your kindness." He raised a hand, brushing hair from her cheek. Fingertips lingering oh-so-softly. Scalding.

Jasmine swallowed.

"You will find a solution. I know you will. You are too intelligent and capable to not rise above this set-back—"

"Have I told you yet what a remarkable woman you are?"

"Me?"

"Yes. You." His eyes glowed. "I have just confessed the deepest shame of my life. Told you I might need to marry for money. And instead of judgment, I receive immediate offers of help. I cannot remember ever feeling this free with anyone. So accepted for who I am."

*Oh!*

"Thank you. What a lovely thing to say."

She felt her throat tighten. She blinked hard. Now was *so* not the time to cry.

Talk about sending a guy running for the hills.

"I cannot be scared off that easily." He shook his head, eyes still fixed intently on her.

At that moment, the wheel lurched to a stop, sending them swaying. Jasmine grabbed on to his shirt, fisting it in her hands, gasping, trying not to look down, down, down—

Why did stupid ferris wheels *always* have to stop when she was at the very top? It was a total conspiracy.

Timothy flexed the arm wrapped around her, pressing her closer to him. Totally working the situation to his advantage.

Well, two could play at that game.

She snuggled fully into him, leaning her head against one pectoral and sliding a hand inside his jacket to rest on his other.

Strictly for comfort purposes, of course.

His heart thumped under her ear, fast and swooshing. Surely it wasn't beating this fast just because of the rocking ferris wheel.

Was he still thinking that kissing was a bad idea? Because she had sooooooo changed her mind on that one.

Though Emme would freak out and be all judgy and, like, *ehww, how could you?* Which was understandable given that whole *situation* in the past. But Emme hadn't met No Rules Timothy. No Rules Timothy who smiled (!) and laughed (!!) and told punny jokes and fixed her broken things and held her with such tenderness . . .

She really liked *that* Timothy. *Anyone* would like that Timothy—

"Does Emme still dislike me that much then?" His deep bass voice vibrated straight from his chest.

*Oy vey.*

"Uh . . . let's say an apology wouldn't be a bad idea."

Silence. They were still stationary. Heaven knew why. Totally at the mercy of the ferris wheel gods.

"So what happened with that anyway? With Emme?" She *had* to ask it.

He shrugged. "I made a regrettable choice. One I never intend to make again." The resolve in his tone said it all. "And you are correct. I do owe her an apology."

Good enough. She'd take that explanation.

Another lengthy pause. The sounds of the amusement park drifted up. Screams as a roller coaster plunged. The *ding ding ding* of the prize booths. Children laughing and crying.

He brought his other arm around, skimming his fingers from her shoulder to her elbow and back again. Leaving tingling goosebumps with each pass.

"Mmmmmm." His voice rumbled under her ear. "And what was this about kissing me?"

Jasmine smiled against his chest. Pressed her face into him.

"Jasmine?" He jostled her shoulder. She could hear the teasing laughter in his tone.

"You're terrible. A gentleman would pretend not to have heard me say that."

"True. But a *man* would be a fool to let that comment pass."

The ferris wheel lurched to a start. Gasping (again), she grabbed another handful of his shirt.

"Miss Fleury." A finger pressed her chin upward.

She lifted her head and stared into his pale eyes. They faced into the setting sun, the warm light raking his face, turning his irises into shades of molten gold.

"I have you." He ran a thumb over her bottom lip. She was quite sure every hair on her neck and arms instantly came to attention. "And I will not allow anything to harm you."

That thumb did its brushy-thing again. Her lips joined in the tingling. He slid his fingers along her jaw. Soft. Tender. Another thumb-swoop.

Uhmmm . . . *wow*.

His eyes drifted down to her mouth. And then . . . he grinned.

Not the smile she had been seeing. The one that spoke of a lost childhood and joy re-found.

No. This smile was *all* male.

Possessive. Anticipatory. Decidedly wicked.

A thrill snaked down her spine.

"I know that smile, Lord Linwood."

Said smile grew larger.

"You do?" His eyes stayed firmly focused on her mouth.

"Mmm-hmm. It's the I'm-thinking-about-kissing-you smile."

His eyes flicked up to hers, eyebrow raised. "There, you are wrong."

"Not even—"

"This is the I-am-*going*-to-kiss-you smile."

*Oh!* Well, in that case . . .

His hand left her face and spanned her waist and ribcage all at once, pulling her that final inch into him.

Her eyes fluttered closed. She felt the gentle puff of his breath against her lips.

Sweet. Warm.

Testing but not touching.

Teasing man.

She arched up. Closing her mouth over his.

That first touch of his lips . . .

*Oh my!*

Every cell in her body focused on the sensation.

Soft. Exploring. Agonizingly tender.

Jasmine had kissed more than her fair share of men over the years. But not one had made her feel like this.

Alive. Whole. Enthralled.

As if she were something to be revered. Treasured. A gift.

The man could *kiss!*

She responded in kind. Moving her body up to meet his, snaking her fingers into his hair. Reveling in his strength. In the way his huge body engulfed her.

His hands tangled in her hair and then angled her head to the side, allowing him to capture more of her mouth.

She lost all sense of time. The world condensing down to just him. To the rightness of his arms around her. The delicious rush of his lips on hers.

"Jasmine. You undo me." His voice a raw whisper.


Timothy tried to think past the noise of blood rushing through his ears. But nothing came.

His lips left hers, nibbled along her jaw, nipped at her earlobe and then came back to her mouth.

So lush. So accepting. Sweetness which hinted at her untamed soul.

How could *this* woman turn him inside out? Flay him bare and then have him revel in the sensation of finally being *seen?*

A thousand thoughts burned through him. Kinningsley. His troubles. Miss Heartstone. The approaching deadline. His uncertain future.

And, yet, when he was in Jasmine's arms, it all seemed small. Insignificant. As if he could conquer anything with her at his side.

Pulling her mouth back to his, he sipped her lips. Let his world narrow down to just him and her. This moment.

Where he guarded every emotion, she bared everything. Where he was stoic and cool, she was warm and effervescent. Sunshine to his midnight.

She seemed his opposite in nearly every way.

But therein lay the deception.

She wasn't so much his opposite, as his *completion*. Bright where he was dark. Free where he was tethered. Round where he was concave. Reaching outward to fill his hollow surfaces.

The other half that made him whole.

That flooding sense of *rightness* filled him. She was right. *They* were right.

He pulled back, resting his forehead against hers. Eyes closed. Face at peace.

The last gasp of sunlight touching his cheeks.

And knowing she was so right for him, how could he ever let her go?

# Chapter 21

CAERPHILLY CASTLE
CAERPHILLY, WALES
APRIL 30, 2015

The wind whipped across the stone ramparts, tugging at Timothy's coat.

They had *finally* made it to Caerphilly Castle in Wales and were standing atop the enormous gatehouse, looking toward the inner keep. Jasmine leaned against the cold rock wall, fingers effortlessly sketching the view. It was fascinating to watch the world come alive under her pencil.

He had recognized the ruined castle with its massive walls and distinctive leaning tower as they pulled up. In his day, it belonged to the Marquess of Bute. Timothy had actually visited the ruin once while staying at a nearby estate. At that time, it had been overgrown and covered with trees and vining plants.

Though still a ruin, now it was scrubbed clean and, though collapsed into rubble in many places, it stood proud. Wind snapped the banners rising above the inner towers and rippled the extensive moats surrounding the walls. Even now, the castle would be a formidable structure.

"This is perfect," Jasmine murmured at his side. "Just perfect. Exactly what the mural needs. You can practically see the knights riding out in their armor."

Truth.

He could nearly hear the horns calling warriors to battle. Smell the campfires and hay and refuse of everyday living. See ladies in their jewels and velvets waving silken handkerchiefs from the ramparts.

Did those who built this castle foresee a future where the castle would sit abandoned in the midst of a modern world, cars whizzing around its perimeter? Surely not.

They thought their castle would stand tall and proud for millennia. A beacon for the ages of their might and honor.

But it had only stood for maybe two hundred years before becoming obsolete. No longer relevant. Stone carted off and the entire site left to fall into ruin. Changing technologies and social mores making castles and the barbarism that drove them unnecessary. Everything that had been sacrificed to build this place coming to naught.

It was a familiar feeling for him.

He waited for the inevitable panic to set in. But nothing came.

Just birds chirping, cars rumbling. The distant laughter of school children running through the keep.

Heavens but Jasmine had changed him, hadn't she?

Since telling her of his troubles, a gentle sense of peace had grown on him.

Some might label it *futility*, he supposed.

He had changed. He laughed now. Teased and joked. Indulged in machinery and regularly kissed an American-born woman with no known family connections or inheritance.

A woman he had no intention of ever being without.

He had never gone looking for love. Had considered himself incapable of the emotion.

Most Linwood men seemed to avoid it.

But now it stared at him out of two lovely blue eyes.

Basically, just as Kinningsley had become everything his forebears despised. He, Timothy Linwood, had turned away from his heritage.

And yet, what else was to be done?

The portal would not allow him to return. He had taken to checking it just once a day. The longer the portal remained closed, the more an idea had taken hold.

Perhaps . . .

Perhaps he wasn't meant to return to 1815.

He wasn't sure he wanted to spend the rest of his life in this century. The thought of never seeing Marianne or Isabel again flooded him with grief.

And as returning to his own time most likely meant leaving Jasmine behind in 2015, he was torn on the entire idea anyway. Would she be permitted to return with him? And, if so, keeping her in his life in 1815 would be . . . difficult.

But it wasn't like he was being given a choice about it either. He could live constantly waiting for the portal to let him through. Or he could just move on. Establish a life for himself here.

He had even chatted with James about it the night before. He had started the conversation with a much needed apology, expressing his regret over his behavior with Emme.

It had lifted a weight he hadn't even realized he carried.

From there, he and James had discussed options. Investments. Things Timothy could do if he were not allowed to return to 1815. It had been nice to chat with James over the last several weeks. They laughed over memories of their time together at Eton, all the common experiences of growing up in the same small village. He recognized it as a gift. To have an old friend he could talk to anytime, someone of his own milieu who had experienced both centuries as well.

And it wasn't as if this century were all that bad. He enjoyed watching more of those animated films with Jasmine. Disney movies, she called them. Laughing and talking with her, telling stories about their child-hoods. He read voraciously, his mind often overloaded with information about circuits and electrical currents and motors. He tinkered and cleaned. He still rode and boxed regularly.

But the thought of giving up his heritage was profoundly painful.

Partially, it was the knowledge that, without him, the viscountcy would struggle. Though his heir, Uncle Linwood had a wife and no sons. Without an available family member to marry, Miss Heartstone's money would be lost. Uncle Linwood would never stoop to any other measure to recoup the family fortunes.

However, Timothy realized the pain was more than inbred duty and honor.

The simple fact was this:

He *liked* being a viscount.

And how long had it taken him to realize it?

He had never questioned his life before. Never asked if he would actually choose to do what he did.

But now, thanks to Jasmine and her insistence he explore his own emotions and feelings, he *knew*.

He liked making decisions and serving in the House of Lords. He liked caring for his family and tenants. Liked being the *paterfamilias*.

It was more than mere duty and adherence to a set of rules for him. There was tremendous satisfaction in the work of it all.

And it had all been taken from him. Without his permission.

He continued to carry his talisman gear. The one he made so long ago. It reminded him of where he had come from. Of the responsibilities he just couldn't seem to reconcile with leaving behind.

Could he ever rebuild such a life for himself here? But for the sake of remaining with Jasmine, how could he not?

"You're quiet today." Jasmine nudged him with her elbow. "Well, quieter than usual . . . which is pretty darn mum."

He shrugged. "Just thinking."

"I have been wondering about you," she continued. "It's not normal to skip straight from bargaining into acceptance. I would expect some depression along the way. Just a sense of sadness. A lack of will to do anything."

"That fairly sums up the emotion, I suppose."

A knowing smile. "It should pass. Just give it time."

How did she do this? Drag personal thoughts and emotions from him so easily? It was her gift.

The breeze grabbed at the edge of her sketching pad, threatening to tear the paper. Without thinking, he set his hand on the paper, stilling it so she could continue drawing.

"Thank you." She flashed him an impish smile from underneath the knitted sailor's hat she wore. It pulled down over her ears and kept her hair out of her face, making her look more like a page boy than a grown woman.

He studied her profile as she drew, committing the beauty of her to memory. Tracing the line from her forehead, over the bump of her button nose, across her plump lips and around the curve of her sharp chin—

"You keep staring at me like that, my lord, and you're liable to get kissed."

As if *that* would deter him.

He continued to stare, a wry grin tugging at his lips.

She had done this to him. Turned him into a man who craved tenderness.

Without even lifting her pencil from the paper, she popped up on her toes and softly brushed his lips with hers.

"You know I can never resist your dimples," she whispered against his mouth, giving him another peck.

Her easy affection always caught him off guard. She was like a silken summer breeze—warm, tender, seeping effortlessly into every crevice of his soul.

Jasmine, who just made everything more . . . bearable. It wasn't her almost incessant cheerfulness or quirkiness. It was that combination of gentleness and steel that was the core of her. That she would not allow him to trample her, but at the same time, used kindness and humor to bring him out of himself.

He liked the person he was around her. Liked hearing her voice, her crazy thoughts, her soft laugh.

He leaned back against the rampart, shoulders to the castle, all his attention focused on her. She finished her drawing and he took the pencil and pad from her hand, setting them down.

"Come here." He pulled her to stand between his legs, wrapping his arms around her waist.

She came willingly, tucking her hands against his chest, craning her neck to look at him. Deep blue eyes dancing, fingers curling into his coat.

How could a man resist her?

He dipped his head, just as she arched in his arms, reaching for him. Their lips met gently in the middle.

Her mouth cool from the spring breeze. She smelled of sunshine and fresh air. Tasted of freedom and happiness.

Something unfurled within him. He could spend a lifetime like this and never get enough.

He pulled back, resting his forehead against hers.

"Care to share your gloomy thoughts?" Her words a puff of air against his nose. "You have certainly heard enough about my woes."

"Rita still texting?"

"Every chance she gets. Relatives!"

"Amen."

"Cobra says there's nothing more to be done. I'll probably just never know who I am. And I need to come to terms with that."

A pause.

"Yes. Sometimes that is the only answer."

"Perhaps." She popped on her toes, brushing her lips over his one more time. "But sometimes just talking makes it easier to bear."

He closed his eyes. Soaked in the luxury of holding her.

"No. There is truthfully nothing to be done. I cannot return home," he finally said.

"Really?" She feigned surprise. "I would *never* have guessed."

He gathered her close. "Holding you helps," he whispered in her ear.

They stood in silence, wrapped around each other. A car alarm beeped in the distance. Wind ruffled his hair.

He finally voiced his thought.

"What if I never return?"

A beat.

"I have wondered the same thing."

"Would you mind? If I remained here?"

"No." A shrug. "It's been nice having you around."

"You like No Rules Timothy?"

She chuckled against his chest.

"Something like that."

"Good. Because I like bright, beautiful Jasmine."

She froze. Pulled back.

"Really?" Eyes so very wide and breathless.

"Of course. How could a man not?"

She rolled her eyes a little. "Seriously? Do you want to hear all the stories?"

Her tone wrested a small grin from him.

"Dimple-touched. That's what I'm calling that particular smile from now on. I've decided to start categorizing them. Make a study of it."

That comment earned her a subtle chuckle.

"Ah. I see you agree with my research. I'm calling that your Reluctant Laugh. The one unwittingly coaxed from you."

"And this smile?"

"Mmmmmm, *that* smile, Mr. Linwood, is titled Hungry Wolf."

Which about summed it up. He kept the smile on his face as he bent to claim another kiss.

And another.

And another.

Ten minutes later he raised his head again. "So, what are these stories about other men? Anyone you need me to challenge to a duel?"

Her face brightened noticeably. "You offering?"

He brushed his thumb across her petal-soft cheek. "I think I should always enjoy being a knight-in-shining-armor to your damsel-in-distress."

She laughed. A joyous, unfettered sound. "You have *no* idea how long I've waited for a guy to say that to me! You're stuck in this century while your entire life falls apart two hundred years in the past, possibly rendering your estate insolvent and turning it into the very thing your ancestors despised. I have a mental pseudo-aunt harassing me, no legitimate family and little hope of ever finding them, but hey—"

"At least we have each other?"

An enormous smile. "Exactly."

"You have created a marvel here."

Jasmine turned to see Timothy standing in the doorway to baby Arthur's bedroom.

She straightened and took a step back, studying her nearly finished mural. After the visit to Caerphilly, the images had practically flown from her brush. The castle acted as a backdrop, set against the rounded hills of Wales.

Knights and ladies stretched across the foreground. A couple flirting here. Two armored men clashing swords there. King Arthur riding out to survey his land, a gentle nod to Roman armor in his otherwise medieval clothing. And if he looked a little like Timothy, well, that was just coincidence, wasn't it?

She was still working on the more minute details, but it was close to completion. She hoped Emme and James would like it.

"Are you pleased with your work?" Timothy asked from behind her.

She turned to him. He still lounged in the doorway, a shoulder leaned into the door jamb. Thumbs hooked into the pockets of his dark jeans. A deep gray fisherman's sweater pulled over a nubby blue button down, both open at the throat with sleeves pushed up. Hair tousled, still wet from his morning shower. Pale eyes unnervingly clear in the light streaming through the window in front of him.

Basically, he looked delectable, and she wanted to do nothing more than to arch into him like a cat. Purr into his chest while he wrapped his arms around her and sent a hand into her hair.

Mmmm, *why* was she still standing here?

She strolled over and hooked her fingers into the belt loop at his waist, tugging him into her. He didn't disappoint, instantly gathering her into his arms.

The second her head hit his chest, every stress and worry slipped from her body. The man was Prozac. Calming her, narrowing the world down to just him and her and the warmth of being held. Cherished. She sensed more than felt his lips brush the top of her head.

He did that a lot. It was incredibly cute.

"I like how it has come together," she said, finally answering his question. "How are you doing this morning?"

"Good. Checked the portal. No change."

She sighed, snuggling a little closer.

Why *was* he here? She had asked herself that question over and over.

Obviously, he needed to learn to let go of The Rules, laugh, relax, become a more whole person. And they had needed to meet.

Even with that though, he seemed more resigned than happy about staying in this century. He would do it, but he wasn't thrilled. Which didn't make a lot of sense to her. Him being stuck in 2015, that is. The resignation she could understand.

The portal had always seemingly allowed others a choice. Though she adored Timothy and wanted to see where this incredible attraction between them led, she wanted him to *choose* her. Not just be trapped with her by default.

Kinda stupid, when she thought about it. She should just grab him with both hands and never let go. But her mothering always got the better of her. She cared more about his intrinsic happiness than her own heart.

And if the portal opened, he would return. *That* she knew.

He had told her more about his problems in the past. The wealthy heiress everyone wanted him to marry, Miss Heartstone. His domineering uncle with four daughters to marry off—one daughter, Emilia, on the verge of betrothal to a duke's son. Widowed aunts and cousins who relied on his generosity to live. The thousands of tenants on his properties who looked to him to help maintain their livelihoods. The sheer scope of his responsibilities was staggering. No wonder the prospect of bankruptcy weighed upon him.

Which all begged another question:

If the portal opened, would she go with him? Could she return? Would he even want her with him?

She wouldn't mind seeing 1815, hanging out with Timothy in his milieu. She had always been drawn to old ways. Marmi had nurtured that.

But she wasn't naive. Given everything Timothy had told her, she assumed it would be nearly impossible for him to retain a relationship with her if they were in 1815. Most likely, he would need to marry someone like this Miss Heartstone for her dowry. Too many people depended on him. His sense of honor was too deeply ingrained to place personal happiness aboe the misery of so many others.

Granted with the portal firmly closed, the entire discussion was thankfully moot. For now, she was content to cuddle a former nineteenth century viscount and consider herself lucky.

"I came up to see if you wanted breakfast," he murmured against her hair. "You've been up since first light. You have to be hungry."

She nodded and let him lead her downstairs.

He had set two place settings on the table complete with folded napkins and cups for coffee, juice and milk. Toast cooled on a rack.

Timothy slid back a chair. "Your seat, madam." He gestured with a subtle bow.

The man was determined to make her fall madly in love with him, wasn't he?

Giving him her widest smile and a sloppy peck on the cheek—because, quite frankly, you could never be too over-the-top when a man made you breakfast, positive reinforcement and all that—she sank into the chair. With a flourish, he strode back into the kitchen and pulled a pan from the oven, bringing it back over to the table. She could see eggs neatly cracked into small cups.

"May I present coddled eggs?" He set the pan down. The eggs

looked delicious, bits of pepper and herbs floating on top of their gooey yellow centers.

She clapped with suitable feeling, laughing. "You've been holding back hidden talents, Lord Linwood."

"No. Google is truly the master of everything. It took me two dozen eggs and seven YouTube tutorials to get it right."

He smiled, flashing her some dimple-sugar, then went over to the fridge, pulling out a carton of orange juice and another of milk.

In the meantime, Jasmine set about helping herself to the eggs. They did look wonderful. No wonder he preferred them cooked like this instead of scrambled. She slipped one out of its ramekin and onto her plate, licking a drop of golden yolk from her finger.

"Now you're going to have to teach me how to make these," she said. "Do you grease the sides first—"

She raised her head to him. And stopped mid-sentence.

Timothy was frozen in front of the island. Eyes wide. Staring at the back of the milk carton. She could see the rapid rise of his chest from across the room.

His very stillness freaked her.

"What is it?" She dashed over to him, touching his arm. He started and looked down at her.

And then slowly turned the milk carton around so she could see it.

Every last breath left her body in a loud hiss.

She actually had to tighten her grasp on his arm to keep her balance.

She sent out a hand, tracing the color image on the milk carton. And then swiped at her cheeks when tears blurred the photo.

A little girl stared at the camera. Enormous blue eyes set in a heart-shaped face with a stubborn pointed chin, all framed by wild dark hair. She clutched the arm of someone out of frame with both hands.

And hanging from her neck on a leather cord . . . a gold pendant formed into intricate strands.

The word 'Missing' blared above her head, followed by 'Do you know where I am?'

Next to it, a computer age-progression image that did a reasonable job capturing her.

With shaking hands, Jasmine took the carton from Timothy and walked back to the table, sinking down. Studying the images.

*Please help the fostering system find its lost children. If you have any information about this child, we would love to hear from you.*

It had to be her. The resemblance, the pendant, the age progression . . . she was so little though. Probably not more than five or six.

A sense of destiny flooded her. An emphatic swirl of energy. As if Fate had drawn her, relentlessly, to this moment.

But Jasmine was in Britain, looking at a *British* milk carton.

How?

Though if she were British in origin, it would explain why Cobra had been so stumped looking for her in the U.S. At every step, they had assumed she was American.

Staring at the photo, she had vague memories of a nice man. That was his arm she was clinging to. He had a soft voice.

Was he her true father?

Just . . . so many feelings roiled through her.

Relief that she might (finally) get some answers about her family. Sadness that someone had probably been missing her all these years. Grief for the memories she had missed out on.

She swiped her tears away and reached for her phone.

"Do you remember?" Timothy's voice murmured from behind her.

"No. Not really." She swiveled to look up at him with a wobbly smile. "But I hope Cobra can find me some answers."

She snapped a photo of the carton and texted it to Cobra.

*please tell me you can do something with this*

His response came less than a minute later.

*Shaking my head. I never thought to look abroad. Forgive me. It's fortunate Britain still does the milk-carton campaign. Weren't you a cute little thing? I'm on it.*

# Chapter 22

The next hours passed in agonizing slowness.

The first hour she spent pacing in front of the sofa, phone in hand, Timothy sitting patiently, watching her, telling her that answers, any answers, were good.

Basically talking her off the ledge.

Bless him.

He was her rock in the storm. The one who anchored her despite the stormy seas swirling around. Pale eyes tracking her calmly as she restlessly walked the room. Finally, he caught her hand as she swept past him.

"Enough. Come sit. Relax and focus on remembering what you can." He tugged her down onto the sofa with him, taking her phone and placing it on the sofa arm.

Smart man.

She cuddled into his chest, which predictably, instantly calmed her. The steady thump of his heart under her ear. The gentle swoosh of his breathing.

She brought up the new photo before her eyes. Concentrated. Slowly bits and pieces came back to her.

But for some reason, everything was all tied up in memories of the car accident.

Fear. Cold. Hunger. Loss.

A woman's screams. That girl's face, framed in dark hair, so like her own.

*"Minna, open the door and then run. Think safe thoughts. You must be saved."*

*Hands pushing her, falling, getting up and then running. Fire and fog, branches scratching her legs, cutting her bare feet.*

*Away, away . . . she had to get away . . .*

And then right on its heels, the same memory. But twisted.

*The terror of knowing what lay ahead. Fire. Danger.*

*The girl's scream. "Mummy, she opened the door!"*

In a blinding flash, she realized.

Two memories.

They were two *different* memories.

Two different little girls.

In the first memory, her dark-haired sister told her, Minna, to open the door and run.

In the second, a girl screamed, pleading with her to *not* open the door.

No wonder she had found the memories so confusing.

The second one felt like it was her memory of the car accident.

But what about the first with her sister? It had always been the more powerful scene. Was that one a real memory? Or just another one of her vivid dreams?

The *bing* of her phone forced her back to the present.

She scrambled, reaching across Timothy for her phone.

Cobra. Email.

At last!

She sat up and reached for her laptop on the side table, the better to check her email. Timothy moved with her, a comforting hand on her waist.

The email was short with an attached document.

*So . . . I guess this is our answer*, was all Cobra had written in the body of the email.

The attachment spun as it downloaded. And then she read the documents. The history of her life.

Snippets jumped out at her.

> *. . . Jane Doe, found wandering near Leominster . . .*

> *. . . Small female child, approximately six years old based on dental assessment. Partially naked. Feet bare and scratched . . .*

> *. . . Gold pendant on a leather cord around her neck. No other identifying information. Child non-verbal . . .*

> *. . . After months of searching and media attention, no parent or identifying person came forward. Child was registered as a ward of the state . . .*

> *. . . Given into the fostering care of Mr. Michael Crick, a solicitor from Gloucester helping with the case . . .*

Here Cobra had made a note:

> *Mr. Crick and his wife and daughter were killed in the car crash in Florida just a few months after you were placed with them. They had traveled to Florida on vacation to Disney World. You must have been with them on the trip but were thrown from the car. But because you were not their child and the U.S. didn't have computerized records of visiting tourists at the time, no one realized you were there. The U.K. fostering system assumed they had lost track of you.*

And then his final comments. The devastating blow:

> *You were a foundling. In chatting with a British case worker, they have never figured out where you came from. It appears to have been quite the media story in 1989 when you were found. Like we did, they tried to use the pendant to track you by contacting goldsmiths across the country but hit a dead end. Despite all the press, no one ever came forward with a legitimate claim.*

*The common consensus is your parents were unable to care for you, and you either wandered off or were dropped off somewhere in the vicinity of Leominster. Most likely the latter. You were found digging through a trash can by a sanitation worker, cold, bruised and hungry. Michael Crick, the public solicitor assigned your case, was your legal guardian. In chatting with a few people, he and his wife were quite taken with you. You clearly were with them on the family trip to Florida and somehow escaped the inferno that killed them. Unfortunately, the fostering system didn't know where you had gone, hence your inclusion in the milk carton campaign.*

Jasmine stared at the words in disbelief. And then turned to the photos attached. Not many. But enough.

She touched the screen as they loaded.

A balding man with kind eyes crouched beside her tiny self.

Michael Crick.

*Him kneeling down before her. "C'mon, little Jane. You can be our girl for a while."*

Jasmine standing in front of a vintage Peugeot, holding hands with a small girl on one side, a woman on the other.

Of course. His wife. His child . . . the blond daughter about her age.

*Mr. Crick tickling the blond girl, both laughing. Loneliness tugging at her heart.*

The photos released memories, images flooding her.

That fateful night on a freeway in Florida crystallized.

*She leaned to the left and raised her head, peering at the road ahead from the backseat. The fog creeping in, whitely dense. An enormous sense of unease rattled through her.*

*A revelation flashed before her eyes.*

*Up ahead. A ball of fire. Horror. Death.*

*But the fog . . . no one could see . . .*

*So close. They were going to die if they didn't stop.*

*She was so little. She didn't know the words to tell them.*

*Get out. Get out. She had to be saved.*

*She unsnapped her seatbelt and then fumbled for the door handle. Hearing the noise, the nice Mr. Crick turned around, eyes drawn in confusion, slowing the car.*

*"Jane, put your seatbelt on."*

*No, no, no . . . she had to get away. Terror stopped her throat.*

*"No, love. Don't open the door. You have to stay here."*

*She pulled on the door handle.*

*"Mike, stop her. She'll kill herself," the woman cried in front of Jasmine, twisting around. "Jane, stop! You've got to stop!"*

*A child screamed. "Mummy, she opened the door!"*

*And then a smaller hand grabbed at her, trying to hold her in the car. But Jasmine pushed the hand away, desperate to escape.*

*And then she was falling. Rolling. Safe from the danger ahead.*

*A second later, an enormous blast of fire and heat pierced the fog.*

*And she knew. She knew. Her second family was gone.*

Breathing hard, Jasmine absorbed the memory.

She had *known*. She had seen the accident in vision before it happened. And unable to warn the kind Crick family, she had opened the car door to save herself.

Just so . . . awful. Those sweet, kind people.

But she clearly remembered thinking the Cricks were her *second* family.

But where was her *first*? Where had she come from?

Were her other memories even real? The dark-haired girl telling Minna to run for the door? That same dark-haired girl playing in the fountained courtyard and the man with close-cropped hair? And why a fountain at all if she were British? Such things were hardly common in the U.K.

Why did her memories have to be so fragmented and ephemeral?

And after all this time, *this* was to be her answer? Confirmation that she had *never* been wanted? How could a child not be wanted? That happened, like, never.

Until that moment, she hadn't realized how much hope she had held. That somewhere out there, someone had missed her. Longed for her. Would shed tears of joy to know she was alive.

This was supposed to be a Hallmark moment, cheesy and sappy and full of weepy happiness.

Instead, it felt like a bad melodrama. A story that twisted in the wrong direction.

Timothy rubbed her back, reading over her shoulder with her. Surely he understood the implications of everything Cobra listed.

She really was no one. Without family or history.

Nobody.

She sniffled.

Timothy pressed a tissue into her palm.

She bit back her hiccupping sobs. But it was no use.

This was going to be a sloppy, ugly cry.

Chest heaving, she buried her face in her hands. Letting everything loose.

Anger, pain, hopelessness. Never knowing her origins.

Realizing she was utterly alone. Without family or kin.

She felt arms slide underneath her knees and around her back, scooping her up into strong arms. She melted boneless into Timothy's strength. He lifted her onto his lap, keeping her cuddled against his chest.

He didn't say anything. Didn't murmur platitudes or try to silence her display of emotion. Didn't talk needlessly to fill the awkwardness of witnessing her breakdown.

He just held her, becoming once more her rock in the storm. The solid, recalcitrant mass which refused to let her go under.

Allowing her to just . . . *be.*

He rubbed her back with his hands, dropping the occasional kiss on her hair or her forehead. Once her crying had subsided from howling sobs to hiccuppy gasps, he wrapped his arms all the way around her and held her tight.


Timothy kept her snugged against him, her face buried in his neck. Let all the grief and sorrow swamp her.

He held her for what seemed like hours, until her crying subsided to heaving and then to silent dripping tears.

Held her until the shadows lengthened and she finally fell asleep. He carried her up to her bed, gently tucking the blankets around her before trudging off to his own room.

Her pain cut him. He wanted to take it all away, give her every tiny thing she wished to be happy.

Promise to be her family. Beg to be all she needed.

Yet something held him back. Timing, obviously.

But also the thought that, beside himself, he had nothing to offer her. No house. No lands. No money.

No place in the world.

For the first time in weeks, that panicky feeling returned, pounding through him.

How could he build a life here? It was one thing to chat with James about it, toss around ideas. It was something else to face it head on. But what other choice did he have?

He slept fitfully, jagged dreams of Jasmine and Kinningsley haunting him.

He woke the next morning to find Jasmine plastered to her computer screen. Hair tumbled and pulled over one shoulder. Dressed in more of those baggy trousers and a tight t-shirt.

She didn't look at him as he wandered into the kitchen. She just started talking.

"I was this total mystery sensation. A little girl found wandering in the middle of a suburban neighborhood. They figured I had been on my own for a couple days, given the state of my clothing and feet. It was huge national news with all this media coverage. They realized pretty quickly that no one was going to come forward. So it turned into a criminal case . . . child abandonment . . . but they never identified a single subject.

"Funny thing is, I remember being lost. I always thought it was the accident I was remembering, but maybe it wasn't. I have distinct memories of the car accident too, of a child screaming and hands trying to keep me in the car. But those images are different. They feel . . . less. The emotions not as powerful."

She paused, shaking her head. Half turning to him, but eyes turned inward, as if searching for something.

"But my other memory . . . it aches." She rubbed the heel of her hand against her sternum. "Even after so many years. Like it's the point where my life shattered. I remember a woman screaming, the girl with dark hair calling me Minna. I've wondered if that was my name. The Cricks, my fostering family, called me Jane because that was my legal name . . . Jane Doe. Anyway, this dark-haired girl, the one who called me Minna, told me to run. That I needed to run in order to be safe."

Her voice broke and gave a choking gasp. With a shake of her head, she bit back her sobs.

"I just remember fire and being extremely afraid. And then running. What does that mean? Were my mom or my sister being threatened, and so my sister told me to run out of a house and then someone set it on fire, killing her and my mom, and they assumed I was dead too? Or maybe they were killed and the person didn't want to come forward to claim me because it would link them to my dead mother and sister?

"I asked Cobra about it, but he says there is no record of a house fire in the area in the days before I was found. No record at all of a woman or child being murdered or hurt. No one named Minna. Just . . . nothing."

She turned her tear-stained face to him. Eyes puffy and bloodshot. Pleading for understanding.

Timothy stood helplessly. He opened his arms, offering comfort that she had taken in the past. Sniffling, she slipped off the chair and wrapped herself around him.

"I wish I were better with words." He stroked her hair. "Please know that I am so sorry."

He gathered her into his chest, a tight warmth seizing his lungs. Possessive. Fierce. *Mine.*

She came to *him* for comfort. She needed *his* strength.

"Thank you." She sniffed. "It's nice to have a lead, but this feels so unsolved and unsolvable. The authorities couldn't find anything out even at the time. The intervening space of twenty-five years hasn't helped. The case is totally cold."

A thought had been rolling around in his head. An idea which would shed so much light on the situation. He finally voiced it. "Leominster isn't far from here. Only about a twenty minute drive. Even shorter cross-country."

She lifted her head, looking up at him. "You think we should visit? It's been so long, Timothy. I can't imagine we would find anything—"

He shook his head. Her confusion was adorable. "I am merely pointing out that the distance between Duir Cottage and the town of Leominster isn't so large. A small child wandering for several days could make the journey."

"What are you saying?" Her eyes widened.

"Have you considered there might be some connection?" He motioned his head toward the hallway, indicating the doorway down to the portal.

She leaned farther back in his arms. "Do you mean, could I have come through the portal?"

He nodded. "It would explain this situation."

"Wow. That is . . . interesting." Her brow furrowed for a moment and then she shook her head. "It's impossible. The portal was blocked by that old oak tree until 1812. It wasn't accessible in the nineteenth century because it had an enormous oak tree growing over the top of it. The old tree was destroyed in 1812, but before that . . . no one had been able to go through it until Emme did. It's a lovely thought though."

She buried her face in his shirt, exhausted of tears. Weak with sadness and loss.

She always did this. Utterly melted into him. As if his touch soothed her. Just as she did for him.

"I don't even know how old I am exactly. Or when my birthday is. I've been robbed of even those most basic facts." Her voice broke. "I'm sorry. But everyone should be allowed to know their exact age. It's like I just lost everything. Everything that has ever grounded me." Her voice muffled.

He rubbed a hand up her back. "Marmi loved you, did she not?"

"Yes, but she also thought I was her grandchild, so—"

"Would she have cared had she known you were actually a foundling? Would she have turned you out or handed you over to the government?"

Silence. And then a watery sniffle.

"No." More of a gasp than sound. "She would have kept and loved me regardless. Marmi was just like that. We were such peas in a pod. Complete kindred spirits. That is why this has been so hard from the very beginning. Every last part of me feels like Marmi *was* my mother. The woman who breathed as I breathe. Who thought as I think. I just see so much of her in me and to know that I was an impostor in her midst—" Voice breaking.

"You have told me over and over to trust the process, Jasmine. Perhaps this was the path for you. Maybe everyone else abandoned you, but the universe *knew* there was a lonely woman in Marmi who would welcome you with open arms and raise you to your fullest potential."

She stilled in his arms, giving one last hiccuppy sniff. And then pulled back to stare at him with her limpid blue eyes.

"Th-that's the n-nicest thing anyone has ever s-said to me." She placed a hand on his cheek. "Who says you aren't good with words?"

He ran a thumb over her quivering bottom lip. And then kissed her. Soft. Gentle.

And, given the way she sighed into him, he must have done something right.

# Chapter 23

*So, are you going to return the money? It was John Fleury's inheritance. It had nothing to do with you. The money belongs to the family.*

Rita's incessant texts hurt. Jasmine leaned into the marble countertop, staring at her phone.

In hindsight, Jasmine realized she should have stood firm with the china. But be a nice person . . . give an inch—

And this was the result.

Rita wanted Jasmine's small inheritance back. She was threatening legal action.

*Trust the process.*

Jasmine wasn't sure why she had to go through all of this. What did the universe have in store for her?

Timothy had made a good point. The years she had with her grandmother (she would never think of her as anything else) had been magical. Quite literally at times, given Marmi's love of mystical things. But that's why it had been so good. Marmi had taught her so much. About the interconnectedness of things, the vast love of the universe for its creations.

Everything making her the person she was right now, at this moment. Jasmine felt deeply blessed to know she had loved and been so loved in return, even if she never found her real family.

The front door opened and Timothy came in, newspaper under one arm, riding crop under the other. He had already been riding this morning, dressed in worn close-fitted jeans, riding boots, white button down, loose tie and a heathered gray-blue wool vest.

She could see him in her mind's eye galloping through the stable pasture, effortlessly guiding his horse . . . it was endearing how he clung to old-fashioned things. Her look turned dreamy. He smiled warmly in greeting and tossed the newspaper and riding crop onto an entryway table.

He started toward her and then paused in front of the cellar door in the main hallway. "Forgive me while I test this."

He still checked the portal once a day. With James' help, he had been trying to make a life for himself here, but she knew it hurt. His heart would always belong in the past.

She crossed the kitchen and followed him down the steep wooden steps. The single light bulb cast the small space in stark shadows.

As usual, the portal thrummed under her feet, the small space vibrating with electricity. Timothy pressed both palms against the granite slab, standing in the dark depression.

They stood in silence for moment.

And then, his shoulders sagged. His entire body leaning forward, pressing his forehead against the stone.

The sense of his loss in that moment . . .

Her heart physically hurt. Who knew the organ could do that?

*Why won't you let him through?* she mentally whispered. *Why trap him here without a choice? What needs to happen in order for him to go home?*

Nothing.

The poor man.

Sighing, she reached out to grab his elbow. Intent on dragging him upstairs and offering him comfort. Preferably of the making out variety.

And then it happened.

The seemingly impossible.

As soon as her hand got within a couple inches of him, she felt a sharp tug. As if something wanted her to step into the depression next to him.

Into the portal.

Energy swirled around her, wrapping like a cocoon. Golden ribbons of power, grabbing her, tangling in her arms and legs. Nearly dragging her forward.

Startled, she snatched her hand back. And then stood staring at Timothy's bowed shoulders, his hands still pressed against the stone in front of him. The gold tendrils circling him but not making the connection.

They only *touched* her.

And with aching clarity, she knew.

She *knew.*

She had to return *with* him.

If she touched him, the tendrils would unite, drawing them both through the portal.

*She* was the missing component. The last piece of the puzzle.

The knowledge was . . . huge.

Before Timothy could turn and see her wide, wide, wide eyes, she darted up the stairs and into the kitchen.

Mind churning. Heart pounding.

Why? Why her? Why did she need to return with him?

She paced back and forth in front of the kitchen island.

Surely, there would be no permanent place for her in his 1815 life. His responsibilities were too huge.

In 2015, they could be together. She liked having him here with her. Hers and hers alone. No need to share him. She was *terrible* at sharing.

It made sense. She had thought (hoped, wished) the portal drew him here for them to be together. But what if, after all this time, it was the opposite? He was here to bring her back with him to 1815.

Would she go? There really wasn't much holding her to this century.

The mural was done. She just needed to apply one last coat of varnish. After that, what was there for her here? More painting? She could do that in 1815 just as easily.

Her 2015 friends were moving on with their personal lives. Her adopted family had kicked her out of the fold, and things were spiraling downward at a dizzying pace.

The thought of escaping two hundred years into the past was definitely attractive.

But in 1815, Timothy was a powerful lord. *Gah!* She wouldn't even be able to *call* him Timothy anymore. He would be 'my lord this' and 'my lord that.' A mighty viscount who could have nothing to do with her. The selfish part of her heart didn't like that. Not one bit.

Even worse, what if he returned and reverted back to Rule-Bound Timothy? Would she have to stand at the sidelines and watch him retreat back into a mask of duty and responsibility, losing her friend forever?

*Ugh.*

What to do?

But . . . Timothy?

He was resigned to staying here, but she knew he wanted nothing more than to return home. His family, his lands and people needed him. If he were to remain in 2015, it needed to be his choice. His decision.

Maybe *that* was the sticking point.

He needed to choose.

And if he chose the past? Well, she would take him through the portal—

"*Pardon?!?*"

Jasmine whirled to see Timothy standing in the doorway to the hall, expression utterly wild.

"You can take me through the portal?!"

She froze.

Not *quite* how she wanted all of this to come out . . .

"I th-think so," she stuttered. "Just now, when I was down there. The portal . . . it pulled me forward. Both of us . . . together."

Within the space of a heartbeat, he had her bracketed between his arms, hands on the counter behind her, body leaning over her.

The most astonished, dimpled, wondrous smile lighting his face.

Pure Joy, she labeled that one.

"You would come back with me?"

"I think that might be why you haven't been able to return. I'm supposed to come with you."

Somehow Pure Joy stretched even wider.

A cacophony of emotions assaulted her.

She didn't have to ask to know Timothy's choice. He would return to 1815.

Warmth spread through her. The knowledge that he obviously *wanted* her to be with him. Maybe there would be a way . . .

"The nineteenth century has its charms." His voice excited. "I think you would enjoy it. Certainly, you will love Marianne. I am sure she will adore you. Isabel will be delighted to have an aunt. You could paint and sketch to your heart's content. Wear pretty dresses and dance the night away at balls."

Was he actually . . . babbling? Jasmine smiled, his animation infectious.

"That sounds lovely." She wrapped her arms around his neck. "But can we have a frank conversation first?"

"Who is this Frank?" He winked at her.

Laughing, she swatted his shoulder. "You're such a nerd."

"Only for you, my lady." He dipped his head, intent on that soft spot between her cheek and ear.

She *loved* that spot.

"No distracting me." She pushed on his shoulders. He lifted his head, pressed his forehead against hers.

Waiting.

"So let's say that I do return with you to 1815. What happens then?"

He frowned. "What do you mean?"

"You mentioned that you needed to marry an heiress. Probably this Miss Heartstone person you have mentioned. But I'm terribly selfish and liable to get murderish if I have to watch you woo someone else."

"Murderish? Isn't *homicidal* the word you wanted there?"

"That too. It's definitely a stabby sort of emotion. It won't be pretty. I cannot be held responsible, Mr. Linwood."

A flash of Reluctant Smile. He lifted his head, pale eyes drilling into hers.

"There have been expectations that I would marry Miss Heartstone. But now . . ."

Silence.

"But now?"

He closed his eyes. Sighed. A breath pulling from deep within. "I cannot be without you. I have spent an enormous amount of time pondering the issue. I did not expect that you would be permitted to return with me. But now . . . the thought of not having you, dearest, sweetest . . . I-I never expected to love. But you, my darling . . ."

He kissed her forehead. Her cheek. His lips hovered over hers.

"I love you, Miss Jasmine Fleury."

And then he kissed her. Sweet. Longing. Full of hope. Of promise.

Her heart crumbled under the onslaught. Poor thing. It could only handle so much.

She could taste her tears on his lips.

"I love you too," she murmured.

She felt his answering smile. Surely more Pure Joy.

Happiness swamped her. To hold the love of such a man . . .

"Return with me. Live in my century. I cannot bear the thought of giving you up."

Which just made her cry harder.

"Please tell me these are good tears?" His breath a whisper against her mouth.

"Yes." She nodded. "Oh, my love, yes!"

About five thousand hours later (okay, so maybe it was only fifteen minutes), they managed to pull their mouths apart. Timothy scrubbed her wet cheeks with his thumbs.

"But what about your people? Your family and estates? Miss Heartstone and her buckets of viscount-saving money?"

She could see his mind churning, gaze distant. "I will find a way. Somehow."

"I do have my small trust fund from Marmi. It's not much, but it might help. We could convert it into jewels or gold and take it with us."

A pause. "I would never ask that of you. That inheritance was your gift from Marmi. Besides, it cannot be a simple task to retrieve the money."

*Drat.* "You're right. It's all tied up in investments and stuff. It would definitely take time. And with Rita threatening legal action . . ."

"Do not worry. Though I would have been too proud before, now I have no compunction asking Arthur for financial help. Being in this century has given me ideas—"

She gave a shocked mock-gasp. "Lord Linwood! You are not contemplating going into *trade*, are you?"

He gave a wry chuckle. "Not precisely. I will need to discuss options with Daniel, but I think there might be a way to invest in trade without damaging the family prospects too much. It will be tricky, but if Arthur has some loose capital, I think I could find a solution. I have faith we will find a path. The portal brought me to you and now wishes us to return together. Good things fall apart—"

"—so better things can fall together. If anyone can find a solution, it will be you, my love."

He closed his eyes, a puff of air bursting from him, face almost pained. "I will never tire of hearing you call me *my love*."

"So, I guess I'm headed for 1815. But, hold on, someone once told me there are, like, lots and lots of rules to follow. Something about gray gloves and spring picnics . . . I know, I know, it sounded *crazy* to me too."

Timothy gave her his softest Buttery Laugh. "There will be many rules to learn . . . basic decorum, how to greet people, elocution and posture, fan etiquette—"

"*Whoa* . . . fan etiquette? You're joking, right?"

He cocked an eyebrow.

Not joking. Got it. Fan etiquette. Who knew?

"But do not fear, my darling. It is nothing you will have to master immediately. You will have all the time you need to adapt. As soon as we return to Kinningsley, I will recall Marianne from London. She can teach you what you need to learn to be a lady. Though I do not think you will find it too challenging. Your huge heart and charming affections will win over any who would doubt you."

"That sounds . . . perfect." She pressed her palms into his chest. She needed to know one thing. "What about you? Will you go back to being as you were?"

"As I was?"

"Yes. The Rules, remember? Will you go back to following them when you return to 1815?"

He pulled back slightly, gaze suddenly wary. Not a good sign.

"No offense, but Rule-Bound Timothy is a bit of a downer," she said.

"Truly? You did call me a nerd earlier."

"Nerd is a good thing."

He let out a long sigh. "There are certain strictures of society that must be adhered to in the nineteenth century. As I said, you will need to learn certain rules yourself. It is only common courtesy—"

"Okay, I'll grant you that. All the rules about gloves and ballroom etiquette and greeting people, blah, blah. I know I need to obey those rules too." She gave a dismissive gesture with her hand. "But the weird rules about not laughing or showing emotions? Those have to go. I can't watch you withdraw back into yourself. It's not healthy. I need a pledge, Lord Linwood. A guarantee I won't lose the man I love."

He leaned back into her. "Mmmm, the man you love . . ."

"No distracting me. Do we have a deal?"

A decisive nod. "I will abstain from following rules that restrict my range of emotions."

"Pinky swear." She pulled back and held out her hand, smallest finger extended. Eyes determined and serious.

"Pinky swear?"

"You wrap your pinky finger around mine."

He did so. Her hand so small next to his.

"Now repeat after me, 'I, Timothy Linwood, do solemnly swear that I will relinquish all rules which govern emotions and their display, or the lack thereof, for now and forever more. And I also grant Jasmine Fleury the authority to police my adherence to said oath.'"

He raised an eyebrow, but repeated the words. A smile tugging at his lips.

Then he pulled her tighter into his chest. She went willingly, loving his arms around her.

"I do believe that pinky-sworn oaths have to be sealed with a kiss." He dipped his head.

She wrapped her hands around his neck, arching up on her tiptoes. "I do think you are completely correct in the matter, Lord Linwood."

# Chapter 24

H ow are you feeling?" Jasmine had to ask it. Again.

"You mean have I changed in the last five minutes?" Timothy replied.

"Yes."

A soft Buttery Laugh. Man, she loved that sound. "As you would say, I'm good. You will be able to see the front facade of Kinningsley once we top this hill." He gestured up the narrow lane.

She tucked her hand tighter around his elbow. And then used her free hand to lift her skirts.

Her skirts!

Emme had an impressive stash of Regency era attire. When Jasmine had called to give her the low-down on everything Timothy-related,

Emme had been surprisingly supportive—both about No Rules Timothy and Jasmine returning with him to 1815—saying she would miss Jasmine. As a parting gift, Emme had insisted Jasmine help herself to the clothes too.

So Jasmine was now wearing a sprigged muslin high-waisted dress covered with a blue velvet pelisse, which was like a tight overdress-thingy. The ensemble hung straight to her ankles with only a single thin petticoat underneath, the entire effect meant to mimic the flowing dresses of ancient Greece and Rome.

A matching blue silk bonnet perched on top of her hair which was pulled back and curled. She had watched an awesome YouTube video on how to do perfect Regency hairstyles. Though she had no idea how to recreate the look without a curling iron and hair spray.

She found the thought of Marianne's impending tutoring comforting. There would be a lot to learn, but she could do it. Just like going to college or something. Another skill set.

Timothy had already helped her learn a few basics. Mostly just how to curtsy and greet someone. He had called her a natural.

She could do this. She would spend her days with Marianne learning to be a nineteenth century lady, while Timothy spent time with Arthur and Daniel, resolving his financial woes. Timothy figured it would take around six months to a year for both of them but, in the end, all would be well.

Interestingly, the entire process had been tinged with a sense of *rightness*, for lack of a better word. As if she were putting together the self she had always been.

When she strolled into the kitchen of Duir Cottage in her 1815 clothes, Timothy had stared at her for a full minute before letting a slow, wicked smile dimple his cheeks. Classic Hungry Wolf.

She took that as approval.

Timothy was back to looking every inch the nineteenth century aristocrat. His coat brushed, cravat perfectly tied, boots gleaming. Top hat and gloves back in place.

The trip through the portal had been . . . simple. Almost uneventful.

Ironic, really, given all the trouble it had caused.

Walking downstairs, hand-in-hand, the portal had pulsed strong, those golden tendrils of energy swirling around her. As if welcoming them, tugging her forward. Eager.

All she had to do was hold hands with Timothy, wrapping him in the gold ribbons as well.

She had smiled, thinking of Timothy and how happy he would be to see his family, his home. The second their hands touched the stone, the world had turned black, vertigo rushing over her.

And then they were in 1815. Just like that.

All the hustle and bustle of modernity gone. Instead, the world became fields and clean air and quiet.

Without any transportation and Haldon Manor still a building site, they had opted to walk the few miles cross-country to Kinningsley.

"There." Timothy pointed up the lane and across the fields. A stately mansion rose in the distance.

She froze, all the air swooshing from her lungs.

The word *impressive* was an understatement. She knew he was wealthy. Knew he was a lord and a viscount.

But . . . *wow!*

The house gleamed in the sunlight, golden stone shaped into regal columns and pedimented friezes. Imposing in its grandeur. The entire building an homage to classical architecture.

"I take it meets with your approval?"

"It'll do," she replied archly.

He flashed her those darling smile holes of his.

She suddenly felt overwhelmed. It was more than just having to learn the social mores of this time period. Timothy had promised he would find a way for them to be together. Obviously, that meant marriage.

Not that they had talked about it *specifically* or anything. A woman had to be superdy-duperdy careful how the ol' M-word dropped into a conversation.

But the *implication* was definitely there. And she knew they loved each other.

Which meant she would be a viscountess and mistress of this house, these people. Everything.

Again. *Wow.*

A breath of panicky nervousness tried to wreck her excited mood. Could she do this? It would be a huge task . . .

Pep talk. Baby steps. With Timothy and Marianne's help and some time, she could do this. Learn what she needed to learn. She had at least a year. No need to be worried. Though maybe she should have brought a copy of Timothy's rules, just in case.

"Will your absence have been missed, do you think?" she asked as they continued to walk.

"Given that both Arthur and Daniel know about the portal, I hope they put the puzzle pieces together and concocted some story to explain my absence."

"So no vultures swarming, eager to take over the estate?"

Another Dimple-Kissed smile. "I doubt my Uncle Linwood would make an appearance. We shall see what has happened soon enough."

As they walked up the lane, approaching the house, heads swung in their direction. Farmers doffed their hats, maids curtsied, gardeners bowed. But no one waved hello. No one smiled in greeting. In fact, no one said anything beyond a murmured, 'My lord.'

All very careful. Measured. Cautious.

This was his life, Jasmine realized. This was how people always treated him. A title more than a human being. As if he were placed onto a shelf labeled *Other* and not allowed to play with the rest of the toys.

She knew this distinction was partially of his own creation—that he had deliberately placed himself apart. But she couldn't help the surge of protectiveness that tore through her.

He was so much more than just a title. He was a fiercely brilliant man with passions and dreams and a caring heart. Who also happened to be amazingly talented at dish cleaning, pantry organization and, let's face it, kissing.

Things, she realized, others rarely saw in him.

Did anyone, besides herself, know the real Timothy Linwood?

As they drew near the curved front steps, a female figure burst out of the front door, dark hair bouncing as she took the steps at a half run.

"Timothy! At last!" she cried, throwing herself into his arms, planting a decidedly warm kiss on his cheek.

Marianne. The woman could only be his younger sister, Arthur Knight's wife. How perfect she was already here! Jasmine could start her lady-training immediately.

For his part, Timothy gathered his sister close, sweeping her into a tight hug that pulled her off her feet.

*This* was more like it.

Someone else who saw the real Timothy inside.

Petite like Jasmine with dark hair and her brother's gray eyes, Marianne exuded a gentleness of spirit that her brother did not. She clung to him, her voice muffled against his chest. "We were so terribly worried. You have been gone for so long and without a word."

"Hush, Marianne. I have returned. But why are you here? I thought you and Arthur were in London?"

"How could I remain in London when you had disappeared?" She shook her dark head. "You did not return from Kinningsley. Then word reached us you had never arrived here, though your horse was found wandering near Haldon Manor. Arthur thought you had estate issues to resolve. But then Daniel said you had been called away on Parliamentary business. And, in the end, they both admitted they did not know where you had gone." She pulled back and looked up at him, her bottom lip quivering. "I was so afraid you had been robbed and murdered, and they would return your lifeless body to me." She buried her face in his neck-cloth again.

His face crumpled as he held her. "I am safe and whole, sister—"

"And then Uncle Linwood showed up on the doorstep—"

"Uncle Linwood is here?"

Marianne spoke *sotto voce*, but Jasmine leaned in, hearing her clearly. "Yes, and he has been *horrid*. Well, more horrid than usual, saying you have mismanaged the estate and all is lost, that the viscountcy is bankrupt. Is that where you went, to find a solution? Arthur is beside himself, as all our capital is tied up in rebuilding Haldon Manor at the moment, and we haven't a farthing to advance you to help weather this crisis. What is to be done, Timothy?"

*Oh no!* Jasmine swallowed.

Arthur had no liquid money. That was . . . bad.

Timothy stilled and then lifted his eyes. His gaze troubled but his jaw determined.

It was okay. They would be okay. There were other options, weren't there?

Marianne hiccupped. "I am just so very relieved you have returned, brother. But why did you act so rashly? Why not tell me of the betrothal yourself?"

On the heels of Marianne's other comments, that didn't make much sense. Had Timothy's cousin, Emilia, finally become engaged to that second son of a duke? Timothy had mentioned the possibility often enough.

Marianne pulled back and dabbed at her eyes with a handkerchief, shooting Jasmine a questioning glance.

"We most certainly did not expect you to arrive with a female guest. It will be quite scandalous—"

"What betrothal, Marianne? Did Uncle finally solidify the betrothal with the Duke?"

Marianne looked surprised. "Yes, that too. But I was referring to—"

"Nephew, welcome. We have been most concerned about your welfare." A cool aristocratic voice cut through the air. Jasmine swiveled to see an older gentleman coming down the front steps.

Silver-haired and haughty with the same pale gray eyes as his niece and nephew.

It was like seeing Timothy thirty years in the future. Cold, withdrawn Timothy, that is. Rule-Bound Timothy.

The man stopped at the base of the stairs, face impassive. Every emotion sucked inside a chilly exterior. This could only be Timothy's uncle and heir, Mr. John Linwood.

"Really, Marianne, such an emotional display is a disgrac—"

"Uncle." Timothy silenced his uncle's rebuke, keeping a firm arm around Marianne. "What an unexpected surprise. How odd for you to suddenly decide to take a trip to Herefordshire."

"Not odd at all, Nephew, given the circumstances. The family name and honor must be maintained, despite others' seeming disregard for them."

Jasmine watched Timothy literally stiffen at his uncle's words. His face retreating back into that well-worn mask.

*Drat.* This was so not good.

Worry tugged at her heart. First, the news that Arthur might not be able to help financially and now Timothy's uncle was here, railing on him about propriety. Ingrained habits were hard to break. And being back in the same environment that bred them would be a challenge.

Trust. She needed to trust him. Timothy could do this. *She* could do this. They would find a way. The portal and Fate had brought them this far . . .

"Will you present your guest, Nephew?" Mr. Linwood gave Jasmine a scathing look, up and down. Eyes narrowing.

Gesturing for Jasmine to join him at his side, Timothy said, "Marianne, Uncle Linwood, may I present Miss Jasmine Fleury?" Jasmine curtsied. It may have been somewhat wobbly, but she was a work in progress, right? "Miss Fleury, my sister, Mrs. Arthur Knight and my uncle, Mr. John Linwood."

Marianne returned the curtsy, smooth and elegant. Not a wobble in sight. How did she do that?

Mr. Linwood merely gave a haughty nod.

And then he turned, utterly dismissing her.

*Not* the most auspicious of beginnings.

*It's okay,* she told herself. She was in this to win the war, not every little skirmish.

With a sweep of his hand, Timothy indicated they were to go up the stairs and into the house. He turned and offered Jasmine his arm, his face still tucked behind that old mask.

She gave him her most encouraging smile. He visibly relaxed at seeing her, flashing her his dimples. But his body remained stiff as he led her up the stairs. She knew him well enough to recognize the tense set of his shoulders as worry and nervousness.

Marianne kept shooting her looks. Distressed, concerned, *speculative* kinds of looks.

What was going on here?

Inside, Kinningsley was expansively impressive. The large front door opened into an enormous central hall. Though *hall* seemed too tame a description. It was more like a ballroom, with a coffered, barrel-vaulted ceiling and freestanding columns lining both sides. Niches with marble statues were carved into the walls at regular intervals. Everything glittered with gold and veined marble. The room was lit through skylights in the ceiling, surely a modern invention for the time period.

It was utterly breathtaking.

All of this was Timothy's? And, by extension, possibly to be hers? The scope was staggering.

Obviously, plenty of buildings in the twenty-first century were similarly grand. But she had never been in one that was someone's *private* home, with the possibility of it becoming *her* private home.

Somehow the reality of it all far outstripped her expectations. And her expectations had already been of the extra-big variety.

A footman approached her, waiting patiently. Timothy calmly pulled off his overcoat, hat and gloves. He caught her eye and shot a glance at her own pelisse. Understanding, Jasmine unbuttoned her pelisse and handed it along with her bonnet and gloves to the waiting footman.

Yes. This way of life would take some getting used to. The air hung heavy with etiquette and prestige.

Marianne stood near her elbow, almost wringing her hands. She kept shooting glances down the long entrance hall. As if she expected someone to come around the corner at any moment.

Turning to his uncle, Timothy tugged down his coat sleeve.

"Uncle, I understand congratulations are in order. Emilia is formally betrothed to the Duke's son?"

Mr. Linwood nodded his head, curt and sharp. "Yes. The Duke and a small party will arrive in three days' time to finalize the contracts."

"Excellent. Is Emilia already here then?"

"Yes. She arrived with Aunt Linwood and Mary yesterday."

"I see I turned up home to a full house." Jasmine didn't miss the bite in Timothy's tone. "Any other invitations you extended on my behalf, Uncle?"

Uncle Linwood cast a glance down the enormous entry hall too, shot a quelling look at Jasmine and then flicked his eyes to Marianne.

What? What was the man trying to communicate here? Was eye-signing part of The Rules too? *Gah!* She had so much to learn.

Marianne seemingly understood the message. "Come, Miss Fleury. Let us leave the gentleman to their talking." She tucked a hand through Jasmine's elbow, intent on leading her through a side door.

"Yes, Nephew." Uncle Linwood motioned for Timothy to follow him in the opposite direction. "Let us talk."

A clatter of voices erupted from the end of the hall.

A group of women stepped into the enormous vaulted entry. Two older women and three younger. All prettily dressed in soft pastel colors, wearing bonnets and gloves.

Was *this* who Uncle Linwood wanted them to avoid? Why?

"Cousin Linwood!" A tall chestnut beauty strode toward them, her gray eyes proclaiming her family. "You have finally arrived."

"Emilia." Timothy clasped her hands and bestowed a polite kiss on his cousin's cheek. "Aunt Linwood. Mary."

He greeted one of the older women, who must be his aunt, and her other daughter. Like her husband, Aunt Linwood oozed hauteur and censure. Timothy held himself stiff. Formal. Reserved.

Not good.

Emilia smiled prettily, clasping his arm. "Miss Heartstone had nearly despaired of you." She gestured toward the other young lady who had stopped in front of him. A young, very . . . nondescript sort of girl. Miss Heartstone? The older woman at her side clearly being her mother.

*Ahhhh.* Was this why everyone was acting so weird? But why?

Timothy bowed to the women, who politely curtsied in return.

"And who is . . . *this*, Nephew?" Aunt Linwood turned her gaze to Jasmine, eyes penetrating and vaguely beady. Her hawk-like nose completed the bird-of-prey comparison. She looked like the type of person who would enjoy swooping and squawking, pecking out the eyes of rivals—

Timothy stepped to Jasmine's side, slipping his cool mask for a brief second to give her a this-is-going-to-be-okay sort of look. He made the necessary introductions. Yep, the other two women were Mrs. Heartstone and her daughter.

The ladies all curtsied, smooth and precise. Like boards moving up and down. How did they do that? Her own curtsy was decidedly bobbly still. More wet noodle.

An uncomfortable little silence ensued once everyone stopped curtsying. The kind of silence that was all catty-contemptuous and dagger-laced.

Or, at least, that was the message Jasmine got from the looks Aunt Linwood shot her way.

Emilia sighed, clearly oblivious to the tense undercurrents in the room. Or possibly just uncaring.

"Heavens, Cousin Linwood! You are so stiff. You can at least kiss Miss Heartstone's hand. You are the soul of propriety—"

"Emilia—" Uncle Linwood shot her a warning glance.

"Whatever is the matter, Father? Certainly there is nothing wrong with Cousin Linwood kissing the hand of his betrothed?"

Say whaaaa??!!

No!

Just . . . no, no, no!!!

Jasmine bit her lips together.

What the hell?! Had Timothy lied to her?

No. She rejected the idea immediately.

She knew him well enough to understand that telltale signs of shock. He was just as surprised as she was.

Timothy froze. And ever so slowly, turned to look at his uncle. Who merely tilted his head the tiniest fraction of an inch. Eyes telling all.

This wasn't happening. Arthur and no money, etiquette, rules and now this?

"If you will forgive us gentlemen, ladies, my nephew and I have much to discuss." Uncle Linwood gestured for Timothy to accompany him into a side room.

Silence.

And then Timothy nodded. "Ladies." He bowed. So proper. So reserved. Face an impassive mask.

Marianne patted her arm. "Let us see you settled, Miss Fleury."

Jasmine shot Timothy one last look as Marianne led her away.

His eyes said it all.

He was a man drowning, pounded under by heavy surf and not a life preserver in sight.

———

"Are you daft boy? Parading a woman like Miss Fleury in front of your guests? And at this time? Have you no sense at all?" The second the study door closed, Uncle Linwood launched into Timothy. Haughty. Arrogant. "Heaven knows how we shall explain this horrid impropriety to Mrs. Heartstone. I just hope the debacle can be smoothed over."

Something hot and livid burned in Timothy's chest at hearing that scathing 'Miss Fleury' on his uncle's lips.

Damn the man!

His uncle strolled to a sideboard and reached for a decanter of Timothy's best brandy.

"What the *bloody hell* have you done?!" Timothy hissed, crossing the carpet. He was a hair's breadth away from beating the man senseless. Finding out Arthur was short on capital was bad enough, but a betrothal?!

Uncle Linwood turned toward him and then took a step backward, obviously reading the blatant anger on Timothy's face.

"You will control yourself, boy. What has gotten into you?"

Anger surged through Timothy. Wild and hot. The kind of fury that turned the world red and got men killed.

"Me?!" He barely resisted shouting. "I am the one who has returned home to find I have been promised in marriage Without. My. Consent!"

"Rule number nineteen."

*A gentleman never loses his temper.*

"Do not quote those damn rules to me, Uncle."

"Well, you seem to need reminding. You disappear for nearly two months and then show up with some doxy making doe-eyes at you—"

"You will not speak of Miss Fleury in such tones. She is a lady—"

"You cannot be serious about her, boy." It was not a question. "I could not imagine anyone more unsuitable. She is *American*. Though it is irrelevant, as you are now promised elsewhere."

And just like that. He was going to have to kill his uncle. Pistols at dawn. Jasmine would probably find it thrilling. He could see her holding on to his arm, bouncing up and down, giggling because she was going to witness a real live *duel*.

The thought robbed his breath.

Timothy paused, pinching the bridge of his nose. This could not be happening. He had plans. He had seen a possible path. This was a disaster of such magnitude—

Ah, *there* came the panic again. His dear old friend. The bitter, terrible irony of it.

His uncle merely sipped his brandy, clearly unconcerned.

The man was cut from the very same cloth as Timothy's father. Funny. He had not disliked his Uncle Linwood this much *before* his jaunt into the twenty-first century.

"How?" Timothy ground out between clenched teeth.

"As I told you when I saw you last at Lady Cartwright's ball, I am well acquainted with Miss Heartstone's guardian—"

"Uncle, we live in 1815. Not 1315. You cannot go around promising family members in marriage without their express, written, cognizant, present, vocal *consent!*"

Yes. Shallow breathing. Heart thumping. Palms sweating. Would that he could find a century where such things did not happen on a regular basis.

"I thought I *had* your consent, Nephew." The loud clink of the glass hitting Timothy's desk was the only indication of his uncle's agitation. "You instructed Daniel to open a dialogue with her guardian. I was merely following up on your inquiry. Her dowry is necessary for the survival of our family fortunes and, given the ferocity of gentlemen scrambling for her hand, I was concerned she would not last on the marriage mart until your return. So I took steps to secure her for you. Mrs. Heartstone liked you best of all the candidates presented and convinced her daughter to accept your suit. I had thought you would be pleased. There is no other dowry as large or as accessible. Does your Miss Fleury come with sixty thousand pounds?"

Timothy's silence spoke volumes.

*No.* He wanted to rage. *She comes with so much more than mere money.*

Jasmine was light. Sunshine to his dreary rain. Joy. Happiness. His every hope and need.

"Who are this Miss Fleury's family? What are her connections?"

It was lowering to realize that several months ago, Timothy would have asked the same question. But now . . .

"Emilia is finally on the verge of a formal betrothal. Your betrothal to Miss Heartstone was a key factor in the Duke's decision."

"So this is about Emilia and your family?"

"Do not be a fool, boy. You have always known this is how your marriage would come about. Keep your Miss Fleury. Set her up as the most vaunted mistress in London. But you will do your family duty and *marry* Miss Heartstone."

Timothy closed his eyes against the pain of the thought, bile rising in his throat.

Mistress?! As if he would *ever* denigrate Jasmine in such a way. She deserved nothing less than his name, his protection . . . every last worldly possession he could offer.

His internal struggle did not go unnoticed.

"You are altered. Your emotions hover at the surface." Uncle Linwood walked to stand in front of the fireplace.

Timothy didn't trust himself to respond to the baiting.

"You were always weak." His uncle flicked a speck of lint off his sleeve. "Your father knew it and tried his hardest to stamp out your mother's insipid blood—"

"Are you quite through insulting my honor and my family, Uncle?" Timothy pitched his voice to be suitably scathing.

Uncle Linwood lifted his eyes, raising an appraising eyebrow. "That is better, Nephew. 'Tis a small comfort to realize you might yet have something of a gentleman in you."

Timothy kept every muscle of his body still. Refusing to allow his uncle the satisfaction of a reaction.

He had promised not to retreat back into his rules, but The Rules were *made* to deal with men like Mr. John Linwood. How could his uncle do this to him? Promise him into marriage without his consent?

"Who knows about the betrothal?" He had to ask.

A pause.

"It was quite thoroughly announced in London. I needed all Miss Heartstone's other suitors to understand she had been claimed."

*Of course.* Timothy closed his eyes for a moment, feeling the noose tighten around his neck.

His uncle pointed out the obvious. "You cannot renege at this point, Timothy. The deal is done. Miss Heartstone will be ruined if you bow out. Not even you are so cruel as to do that to an innocent young woman."

"I will ask her to release me. If she breaks the engagement, she will suffer no harm—"

"Are you daft, Timothy? The viscountcy needs funds. Now." Uncle Linwood stirred the fire to life, emphasizing his point with jabs of the fire poker. "How will your tenants eat if you default and have to sell their lands? Who will care for those family members who cannot care for themselves? Will you relegate them to the poor house? Will you thrust us all into scandal and infamy over a flighty, American *nobody*? No matter your current anger, the deed is done. You have no choice."

Timothy stared straight ahead, chest heaving.

Well, he *had* a choice. He could do as James had done. Pass money into the future (if he could find any money to pass forward, that is). Fake his death. And return with Jasmine to 2015. Make a life for himself there.

But at what cost?

The estate would still be in shambles, unlike the healthy estate James had left to his capable brother. Not to mention, the pain of leaving Marianne and Isabel behind.

And Uncle Linwood, as his heir, was no Arthur Knight. The man would never stoop to trade to restore the family coffers, and without Timothy, Miss Heartstone would be lost. Uncle Linwood would struggle to find husbands for his daughters and most family members would find themselves socially shunned. All unentailed property would have to be sold off. The contents of the entailed properties gutted. Servants let go. Tenants pushed off the land, forced to work in factories or worse. Family members could possibly end up in the poor house.

So many people reliant on one man's decision.

His eyes flicked to the corner of his study. Sir Robert Linwood's armor and chain mail stood there, proud and gleaming. As if the man himself sat in judgment over Timothy and his decisions.

A relic of everything his family held dear. Of everything that honor and heritage required.

Timothy's hand sought the gear in his pocket. He had thought to forget about the cog. About the strangling constraints of his title.

How could he have been so naive?

He wrapped his fist around the metal gear, clenching his jaw, riding the tide of anger swelling through him. Desperately pulling himself further and further inward to avoid hurling an inkwell at his uncle's smug head.

"The honor of all of those who bear the Linwood name rests upon you." His uncle whirled on him. The sudden action betraying his agitation. "Do not be deluded, boy. Do not let Miss Fleury's American notions of equality and romantic love cloud your judgment. You have a duty to us all. Never forget it."

# Chapter 25

Timothy!" Jasmine's hand reached out and snagged him. Dragging him into the shrubbery.

Timothy stumbled in surprise and then righted himself. For someone so small, she could be ferociously strong. He darted a gaze behind him, making sure no one saw them. The social pressures of 1815 life heavier than they had ever been.

Fortunately, the path was deserted, branches rustling in the morning breeze. She tugged him deeper into the trees, understanding the disaster if they were seen together.

When she finally whirled around, he could only stare. She was impossibly lovely in a vivid blue pelisse which matched her eyes, dark curls bouncing around her face.

"Jasmine," he murmured, reaching for her. "How can it possibly be only two days since I last talked to you alone? Held you? It feels like a lifetime."

"Oh, Timothy." She buried her face in his great coat, wrapping her arms around his waist.

He gathered her close, throat tight. Just the simple pleasure of hugging her nearly brought him to his knees. Seeing her occasionally over the past two days—at dinner, over cards, chatting with Marianne—had not been nearly enough.

"How did you ever manage to slip away like this?" he asked. "I have been trying to speak privately with you—"

"Your aunt and cousins have been doing an effective job of keeping us apart. It's seriously a lost art form." She pulled back and reached up, placing a small, cold palm on either cheek. "I felt like I was plotting a prison break just to get a chance to see you. It was all cloak-and-dagger, tiptoeing-down-hallways stuff. I think I owe a footman a kiss." She furrowed her brow. "I totally understand, now, all the sneaking that goes on in historical romances. How else are you supposed to find true love? It would be excessively thrilling if there wasn't this sexist, women-are-chattel vibe to the whole thing—"

Timothy kissed her. Long and hard and fierce.

Bloody *hell* but he loved her.

"Ah, Jasmine . . . *my love*." Surely she could hear the agony in his words . . .

How could he *not* have her? How could they be apart?

*Mine. Mine. Mine.*

Something throbbed and burned in his chest, making his breathing short. He drew her even closer, clutching her to him, kissing her again. Adoring the feeling of her small hands threading through his hair. The way she angled her mouth to capture even more of his.

He tasted tears and pulled back, staring into her swimming eyes.

"Oh, darling . . ." He brushed a hand over her wet cheeks.

"I-I'm okay," she hiccupped. "It's just been a hard couple of days, and you know I cry super easily. There are just so many *r-rules* to remember!" She gave a breathless, surprised laugh.

He smiled. Only Jasmine.

"There's the Reluctant Smile I adore." She dug out a handkerchief and dabbed at her eyes. "Give me a second to get my act together. I naively expected the nineteenth century to be less *Macbeth* and more *Downton Abbey.*"

"I am so deeply sorry, my love. You were supposed to have months before being confronted with a situation like this. Do not think that life here is usually this complex. My uncle is a cad."

"Yes. I quickly gathered you knew nothing about this betrothal. How can he even do that? It's totally medieval."

Timothy sighed. "Precisely. But as a friend of Miss Heartstone's uncle and guardian, he pledged my name in good faith, thinking I would readily agree to the scheme. We had discussed it before I disappeared."

"Soooooooo, what are you going to do? Marianne says you can't break the engagement to Miss Heartstone yourself."

"That is true. It would ruin her, and she is as much a victim of her uncle's machinations as I am of Uncle Linwood's. I cannot be that callous."

"But Marianne said that Miss Heartstone *can* break the betrothal without a problem. Where's the fairness in that?"

"*Nothing* about this situation is fair. But, yes, Miss Heartstone can break our engagement."

"Which, if she did, leaves us where we started. You still need to make up a shortfall of sixty thousand pounds. And with Arthur not having any capital to advance you . . ."

"Yes, I know. I have been discussing options with Daniel."

"And?"

"It is . . . fraught. Without instant capital, the ideas I have will not work. Other ventures will require more time and will be more damaging to the Linwood name and honor. There would be repercussions for family members."

The weight of his title had never been so heavy. Much as his uncle's presence chafed, his words were true. The fact that he had backhandedly betrothed Timothy did not negate the reality of the situation. The viscountcy needed cash. And, as Linwood, it was his duty to see it done in an honorable way. His actions *did* taint the family as a whole.

Returning had been . . . difficult. So much more difficult than he had ever anticipated. Not the actuality of leaving the twenty-first century. But trying to fit all these new parts of himself into his old life.

Viscount Linwood, the name and title, needed a strong dynastic marriage to a lady of his own social class and a large influx of capital in order to remain afloat, providing for tenants and meeting his familial obligations.

On the other hand, Timothy Linwood, the man, wanted nothing more than to snub conventions, marry Miss Jasmine Fleury and live out the rest of his life in peace and happiness with her cheery spirit at his side.

No. Scratch that.

He *yearned* to marry her. Wanted her in his life with a fierceness that bordered on agony. Society be damned.

He rested his forehead against hers. Took a determined breath. "Give me time, my love. Just a little more time. I am trying to find an answer. There has to be one somewhere. I will not give up on us."

"The Duke and his entourage arrive tomorrow."

"I know. Prepare yourself for a couple of horrid days. But after he leaves, we can explore other options. Have faith in me."

Now he just needed to have faith in himself. Was there a solution? He felt like he was hoping and praying for a miracle at this point. There *had* to be a way.

The conflict between Viscount Linwood and Timothy Linwood was tearing him apart. The torment between duty and happiness.

She nodded. "Of course. I'm not going down without a fight."

Which was why he loved her, right?

Despite the storm clouds which threatened, he would find a safe harbor. A way forward through the storm.

"Heavens but you bring the world to life under your brush, Miss Fleury." Marianne stood behind Jasmine's canvas, studying the scene Jasmine was painting.

"It is tolerable, I suppose, if one has a taste for lowbrow melodrama."

*That* snooty voice belonged to Aunt Linwood. A woman Jasmine was coming to actually despise nearly more than her own Aunt Rita. Forget wicked stepmothers. Aunts were the new fairytale bad kids.

Aunt Linwood sniffed and shot Jasmine's painting another scathing glance.

Why did the nineteenth century have to be all *Mean Girls*? It was like junior high drama in petticoats and satin. Though, it would make for *uh*-mazing reality TV . . .

Marianne gave Jasmine an apologetic smile. But that was as much support as Jasmine could expect.

She was tossed to the wolves here.

They were all gathered together for a spring picnic under the large rotunda which stood at the top of the highest hill on the estate, offering a spectacular view of the surrounding countryside.

And by *all*, she meant Timothy's menagerie of house guests.

Marianne and Arthur, of course.

Mrs. Heartstone and poor Miss Heartstone.

Uncle and Aunt Linwood and two of their daughters, the radiantly betrothed Emilia and the more dour Mary, their two younger daughters not being 'out' yet.

The chilly Duke and Duchess, as well as their equally haughty son.

The only bright spot was Sir Henry Stylles, Timothy's neighbor and Mrs. Heartstone's cousin. He, at least, had spared Jasmine a kind look and jovial, whiskered smile.

They were picnicking. A casual affair, Timothy had called it. *Casual* apparently meant fine china, silver and cut crystal for each guest, not to mention a fleet of footmen to wait on them. Everyone wearing gray gloves, of course. They were having a spring picnic after all.

Though the view made for perfect painting. Perched on a hilltop overlooking the entire Kinningsley estate, Jasmine had allowed her imagination free reign. She was rendering the view as dramatic clouds loomed, a solitary beam of light hitting the house while the violent storm raged around.

It was a fitting metaphor.

A week. Jasmine had been in the past for one long, discouraging, frustrating, soul-crushing week.

And she had formed a decisive list of likes and dislikes.

She glanced over at the person who headed her list of dislikes, one Mr. John Linwood and his family. And his incessant obsession with rules and propriety and family honor. The man himself stood apart from the picnicking group, chatting with the Duke, leaning on his walking stick, refusing to even acknowledge her presence. They had all made it blatantly obvious that Jasmine was an 'upstart mushroom who needed to go' (Aunt Linwood's words).

On the like side, Timothy (obviously), Marianne, Arthur, baby Isabel, the calm rhythms of nineteenth century life. The slowness of it.

Those parts felt . . . good. When she was alone or even just spending time with Marianne, she could see herself living here. Taking time to learn everything she needed to learn, being accepted for who she was. *That* idea of the nineteenth century was a soothing balm. It felt like getting acquainted with a new friend. That one you hadn't known you needed until you met them and then you realized you could never live without them.

Much like Timothy himself, she supposed.

She glanced at him, seated on a blanket beside the rotunda, resting his weight on one hand. He chatted calmly with Miss Heartstone and her mother. A slight breeze ruffled his hair and perfectly tied cravat. Though she knew her Timothy was inside that immaculate veneer, he had been adopting his Lord Linwood mask more and more.

The whole thing with Miss Heartstone was ridiculously melodramatic, but Jasmine understood the reality behind it. The weight of his concerns were valid. A lot of people depended on him to make the right decision. Not the easy decision or the best decision for himself.

But the *right* decision for all those involved.

Every time they managed a few stolen moments together, he would reiterate his promise, that he would find a way. But she could see his resolve slipping. There just wasn't enough money and the stakes too high.

How long could she sit on the sidelines, helpless, and watch him enact this drama? And how could she stay with him, if the only solution involved tenants—innocent men, women and children—being cast into the street? She had met some of those people over the past week. It was one thing to know abstractly that people would be harmed. It was something else entirely to put faces and names to the tragedy. Something, she realized, Timothy had known all along.

She and Timothy could secure happiness but at what expense? Such a heavy price would certainly weigh on their relationship.

A hundred times a day, she wondered why was she here. Why had the portal practically *insisted* she return with Timothy? To be a friend to him? Get him through this adjustment back into his old life without completely reverting to his old ways? And then what? Would there be a way for them to be together?

Her dreams had been particularly vivid since coming to 1815. Maybe it was the eerie dead quiet of night. The pitch-blackness of it.

*She was wandering in mist, golden tendrils begging her forward.*

*Marmi's voice haunting through the air.*

*"Come, my dear. You must come."*

*The mist parted and she saw Duir Cottage, sitting alone in a forest clearing.*

*She stumbled inside, the space cluttered with merely the shape of things. The scent of lavender in the air.*

*The portal hummed, bursting with energy. She needed to do something . . .*

*The tendrils flashed down the cellar stairs, dragging her after them.*

*She staggered down the steps, staring as the ribbons coalesced, pulsing into the shape on her pendant.*

*A dara knot surrounded by a quatrefoil shield.*

*Blazing bright in front of the portal. Begging her to return home . . .*

She had woken with a start, tears streaming down her cheeks. The dream haunted her. Was she to return to 2015 after all?

Why, why, *why* couldn't her dreams come with an instruction manual? Why could she never sense the path of her own life? If this were Emme or some other friend, she would totally know what needed to happen. But for herself . . . everything was dark.

Hence her painting. The threatening clouds kinda said it all.

Jasmine added another brush stroke, a swipe of red and then orange, creating a fiery sunset breaking through the storm. Kinningsley gleamed in golden white against all the dark blues of the sky and slashes of red coming through the clouds. The entire composition focusing on the regal house.

"I think your paintings are remarkable," Marianne said. "They have the look of an old master to them. I have never seen their like."

"Yes, well, on that point we may agree, Marianne." Aunt Linwood gave another disgusted sniff. "I, too, have never seen anything quite so vulgar. It quite reminds me of those horrid paintings that young Mr. Turner regularly shows at the Royal Academy—"

"Aunt." Marianne's quiet voice strained with censure.

Jasmine raised an eyebrow. Turner? Seriously? As in Joseph Mallord William Turner, the uber-famous nineteenth century landscape painter?

She would take that back-handed compliment and run with it.

Jasmine moved on to the finer details, highlighting the brightness of the house, the menace of the storm swirling around.

It captured Timothy's life as she sensed it.

Losing herself in her work, she slapped on the oil paint, creating raised impasto in quick Impressionistic strokes, feeling avant-garde for the time period. She was adding highlights of the lightest yellow-green to the clouds when a voice cut through the murmur.

"Miss Fleury, we have been discussing the Americas and trying to pinpoint your origins exactly. Who, again, are your family?" Aunt Linwood, of course. Who else would ask such a challenging question? "We were merely trying to remember if we had acquaintance with a family of American-born Fleurys."

Jasmine raised her head, regarding the woman. Aunt Linwood had moved to sit on a blanket with the Duchess. Both Uncle Linwood and the Duke turned at the question.

Timothy glanced up from his seat next to Miss Heartstone. Knowing him as she did, she could see the alarm in his eyes. Clearly his aunt was up to something with her questioning.

"I do believe I had a French maid once who went by the last name of Fleury," the Duchess said, tone dripping with I'm-a-backstabbing-wench condescension.

Aunt Linwood and the Duchess were clearly soul mates.

"What do you wish to know, madam?" was Jasmine's cool reply.

Aunt Linwood gave an elegantly dismissive shrug. "Your last name is French, but your accent proclaims you an American. I am merely curious about your history. Who are your parents?"

And wasn't *that* the question of the day?

Now *every* head swiveled in Jasmine's direction.

Pleased to have an audience, Aunt Linwood continued, "And did your mother intend to condemn you to a career as an opera dancer when she named you Jasmine Fleury? Or did you adopt the name yourself, thinking it sounded . . . sophisticated?"

A low chuckle spread through the assembled guests. With the exception of Marianne and Timothy himself, of course.

Jasmine caught his eye. His brow a thunder cloud. He was rising to his feet, obviously intent on giving a quelling set-down.

"*Aunt.*" His voice low and laced with all sorts of spine-tingling threats, The Look making a grand appearance.

"Heavens, Timothy, do not censure *me.*" Aunt Linwood shot him an appalled look. "You are the one who has insisted on thrusting this unknown . . . *quantity* . . . into our midst—"

"Aunt, you walk on thin ice. Miss Fleury is my guest, and as such, will be treated with the courtesy—"

"Courtesy? Those of the lower classes do not deserve my courtesy. I am merely confirming that she is, indeed, a nobody. Is that not correct?" Aunt Linwood flashed Jasmine a smile that would have done Tony Soprano proud.

Timothy took a step forward, but then stopped when his uncle placed a hand on his arm, giving him a sharp glance that clearly said, 'Down boy!' With the Duke and Duchess looking on, now was *not* the time to engage his aunt in a family squabble.

And what was there to say anyway?

Aunt Linwood was right.

Jasmine stabbed at her painting with her paint brush.

She *was* a nobody. Abandoned by a family she never knew. Cast out by the only family she had ever known. And now floundering about in a place so far removed from her home it was practically a separate planet.

And then, the icing on the cake, she had to deal with huffy Aunt Loserwood and her posse of hoity-mactoity harpies.

(*Oh!* Which would make a totally awesome band name, wouldn't it? *Big A Loserwood and the Hoity MacToity Harpies.* They could be all heavy metal with long stringy hair, ripped jeans and over-mascaraed eyes, Aunt Loserwood shredding it on the guitar. Now *that* was a happy image . . .)

Where was she?

That's right. Aunt Linwood and her bullies.

Were they going to go all mafia on her? Send in a one-armed man named Pino who had a penchant for long knives and fish feeding?

Not to mention little Miss Heartless over there stealing a move on *her* man. Did she even *know* that Timothy had dimples? That he preferred his eggs coddled? That he made this darling cute sound in the back of his throat when he kissed—

"Good heavens, Linwood! Can no one silence the girl? Is she mad, as well?"

Jasmine snapped to attention, ripping her gaze from her painting.

To see every single eyeball, in what must have been (approximately) a mile at least, fixed on her. Eyes so very, very, *very* wide.

Timothy's included.

*Oh no!*

*Nononononononono!*

She closed her eyes, pinching her lips firmly together. *Please, if there were a kind, benevolent bit of karma somewhere that could make this situation go away . . .*

Jasmine was surprised her scalding blush didn't start her skirts on fire. Granted, the tears spilling down her cheeks would have put it out just as quickly.

How could she have let Aunt Linwood get to her like that?

Timothy moved quickly through the crowd, eyes concerned, intent on reaching her.

But Marianne beat him to it, shooting her brother a shooing, go-away look in the process.

"Come, Miss Fleury." She took the paint brush from Jasmine's hand and then tugged on Jasmine's arm, urging her toward the house in the distance. "The sun can often play tricks on the mind. Allow me to accompany you back to the house to lay down."

The day was actually quite cloudy, but bless Marianne for her good heart.

Jasmine gave everyone a wobbly smile and an even wobblier curtsy. And shooting a desperate I-am-*so*-sorry look at Timothy, allowed Marianne to lead her away.


Timothy watched Jasmine take Marianne's arm, walking slowly toward Kinningsley in the distance. His heart pounding in his chest. How *dare* Aunt Linwood goad poor Jasmine like that!

He took a few steps away from the rotunda, intending to run after her, wanting to take her in his arms, tell her everything would be okay—

A strong hand wrapped around his elbow, jerking him back, holding him firm.

"Do not even *think* about it, boy." Uncle Linwood hissed in his ear. "You will not undo everything I have worked to build. You must send Miss Fleury away. She will destroy everything. Too much is riding on your behavior right now, and that woman is a threat to your composure. You have had your fun dallying with Miss Fleury. Now be a man. Show us that you can do what is needed to preserve your family."

Send Jasmine away? He would sooner cut off his arm.

But . . .

Voices slipped through his anger, through his resolve. The Duchess saying something about Jasmine's poor manners. Aunt Linwood agreeing, assuring her that Timothy would send Miss Fleury packing by morning. Everything laced with privilege and power and *expectation*.

What was to be done? Why could he not just callously decide *to hell* with everyone and everything, marry Jasmine and bask in happiness?

Why did he have to *care* about the responsibilities of his birth?

Why, why, *why* could he not find a solution to his situation?

His hand sought the gear in his pocket, wanting to crush it into dust.

The painting she had done of Kinningsley was prescient.

He was a cog in the ship Linwood, buffeted by storms on every side. In danger of sinking altogether. Taking all hands down with her.

And the only ray of light keeping him afloat right now was Jasmine.

The sunshine of his soul.

But he could not see a way to keep her.

All he could do was pray.

*Please. Please don't take my sunshine away.*

# Chapter 26

As soon as she entered the house, Jasmine thanked Marianne and then practically dashed up the stairs, down the hall and into her bedroom, throwing herself across the canopied bed.

Face down. Chest heaving. Hands over her head, as if she could undo the last hour.

Timothy's face!

She had read his shock. His horror.

How could she ever have entertained the idea that she, Jasmine Fleury, could become a viscountess? That she could learn to navigate this century?

Forget having to memorize rules.

How about simply learning to keep thoughts firmly as *thoughts*?

Stupid. She was just so, so, so stupid.

Like stupid royalty. They should give her a crown. Let her ride the float in the parade with a Miss Stupid sash across her chest.

The entire afternoon had shown her *exactly* how delusional she had been. How much she had been holding onto hope.

She hated *Hope* sooooooo much.

Why did she always do this? Wish for an outcome that would never be. Wanting the knight in shining armor and the happily ever after ending.

But fairy tales would never be her lot. She would forever be the unwanted, unknown child in the background. The orphaned *nobody* without name or people. Never the princess claiming her chevalier.

How did Jasmine think this was going to end? With hugs all around and a rousing chorus of love triumphs all? Dizzy kisses in the rain after a romantic midnight proposal?

He had never *been* hers. He was never *going* to be hers. Too many lives were riding on his decisions right now.

She couldn't see a path forward.

She pressed her face into her pillow, trying to quiet her gasping sobs. Her poor pillow had been doing that a lot over the past few days. The nineteenth century seemed made for weeping.

Nope. Not going to work.

It was going to be ugliest of ugly crying.

Wounded animal crying.

Which pretty much described how she felt.

How could she ever let Timothy go? But, seeing the enormous height of the barriers between them, was there a ladder tall enough to cross them?

Eventually, her tears subsided into sleep.

And that same dream.

*Golden ribbons pulling her through fog and mist. Urgent.*

*Dragging her to the cottage, down to the portal, dancing in the design of her pendant.*

*"Come home." The scent of lavender. "Come home."*

*The tendrils pushed her toward the portal. She could feel the swirling energy, taste the metallic buzz of electricity.*

*She just needed to go home . . .*

She woke with a start, blinking for a moment in her dark bedroom. Disoriented. The fire burned low in the grate, casting the room in shadows.

That dream . . . so vivid.

*Come home.*

Was this it, then? She knew Timothy felt as trapped as she did.

But, tellingly, he had *not* come after her today.

She heard Marianne and Arthur on the stairs, bidding Uncle Linwood goodnight. *Ah.* It was late. All the house guests were retiring.

Maybe . . . maybe it was time to have a more in-depth talk with Timothy. How did he see this situation playing out? He said he had a plan, but that had been days ago . . .

Waiting until all was quiet, Jasmine slipped from her room, still wearing the pale blue muslin gown she had on earlier. Determined to find Timothy.

She followed candlelight to his study. She pushed open the door to find him sitting behind his desk, head in his hands. She closed the door behind her.

He raised his head at the sound.

He was a mess. Untied. Cravat hanging limp around his neck. His shirt open at the collar. His waistcoat unbuttoned and askew. He had no coat on.

Entirely undone.

And in that instant, she *knew.*

The gutted look in his bloodshot eyes. The hopelessness. The emptiness of his soul.

There was no solution. No *them.*

Never to be.

She fisted her hands into her skirts.

"Will you not fight for me?" Always lead with your strongest material.

He closed his eyes. Knew exactly what she meant.

His voice so quiet when he did speak.

"I cannot find a way—"

"No. You're doing it wrong. You jump straight to the heart of it. Be honest. Do you think to set me up as your mistress? Emme, Part Two?"

Now he flinched. Hard and sharp.

"That was beneath you." He met her eyes.

He was right. It *was* beneath her.

But at least there was some fire in him now.

Good.

She wanted him mad. As hurt and hurt*ing* as she was.

"I have never once considered you as simply my paramour—"

"Then I ask you, again, will you fight for me? For us?"

"I c-cannot find a plan. I am trapped, Jasmine. Too many depend on me, too many lives are at stake—" His voice cracked.

"Then who am I to you?"

The question hung between them. His shoulders slumped.

He touched a finger to the neatly aligned papers in front of him, ensuring they weren't a hair out of line.

That small gesture nearly breaking her heart.

"The woman I love"—voice breaking on a gasp—"the love I cannot have."

It was her turn to flinch. Tears instantly stinging.

*The love I cannot have.*

She folded her arms across her chest, as if she could stop the words from reaching her heart.

He stood up from the desk, coming to her. Grasped her upper arms.

"But you must know, Jasmine Fleury, you are the woman I will *always* want."

She refused to lift her head to his eyes, staring at his bare throat instead. "You don't have to be noble like this, Timothy—"

"But I do. It is everything I have been raised to be. I cannot be the kind of man who allows others to suffer . . ."

No . . . selfishness had never been his way.

"Why?" She hiccuped the words. "Why must things be like this? Why must we impose a ridiculous rigid morality on this situation? Station? Honor? Those are things that will be obsolete within fifty years. A hundred years tops. The portal has drawn us together . . ."

He rested his forehead against hers, heavy breaths coming against her lips.

"It is hardly that simple, Jasmine. You are imposing *your* morality on me. This is my world. Like it or not"—he gulped—"the world right here, right now, cares about personal honor and status. Rigid social hierarchy. Unbending cultural rules. When those rules are broken, innocent people suffer. I probably will not be around to see the world fifty years from now, much less a hundred. This is *my* reality, and if I choose to live here, I need to abide by it."

She raised her hands to his chest, feeling the heat of his body underneath her palms. The rapid beat of his heart.

Its frantic thump mimicking her own.

"Timothy." Her voice an agony.

"Jasmine. Darling Jasmine." A husky whisper of sound. He pulled her the last inch to him, tilting her neck with one hand.

Devouring her with his kiss.

A kiss that branded. Seared. Marked her as forever his.

Her knees melted into the floor, but it did not matter. He held her weight easily with one hand around her waist.

She arched into him, clasping his face with her hands. Breaking away to scatter kisses on his cheeks, his dimples, his chin. Back to his mouth.

Soft. Hungry. Desperate.

Each touch of her lips telling him how *right* she was for him. How perfectly they fit together.

How much love she held back in her heart.

She did nothing to stop the tears hitting her cheeks.

"So that's it then?" she finally whispered, pecking his lips. "Us. Done. Gone."

Another harsh breath. "I have yet to find a path, Jasmine. Not without causing harm to my family and abandoning responsibilities that have been mine from birth. That is my reality."

"What happens to me now? Do I just return home without you? Assuming the portal even allows it?"

"Darling . . . darling . . . you destroy me"—an agonized whisper—"At this moment, I am nothing more than a cog. A gear in the gigantic wheel of time. Nothing more. Whatever happens in the future will happen. But here and now, for the people who rely on me this year and the next and the next, I must play my part."

A particularly violent sob escaped her mouth.

The portal had practically *begged* her to return with him.

Why? To break her heart anew? To show her how pointless optimism really was?

What else could be stripped from her? She had lost everything, everyone. Centuries away from friends. The only family who had ever loved her dead or vanished.

And Timothy . . .

To now lose him too . . .

And what was left.

Just herself.

The vast emptiness consumed her.

*Come home.*

She couldn't stay here. She was causing too much trouble for Timothy. And, for herself, she couldn't bear to watch him marry someone he didn't love.

No. That she would not do.

His life was a shipwreck waiting to happen.

And she wasn't strong enough to play witness to it.

Lord Linwood's private study
Kinningsley
May 22, 1815

Jasmine was gone.

Timothy had known she would go. Had nobly all but told her to leave the night before.

Sacrificing everything for duty and honor.

But still . . . the sheer *shock* of it left him breathless.

The starkness of her note, scrawled in pencil on a sheet of her sketching paper, perched on his desk:

> *I cannot bear to watch you go through with this. Forgive me, my love. I care too much, and you know how impossible it is for me to keep my mouth closed. I would turn murderish and stabby, remember? If you are reading this, then the portal has allowed me to return. I sincerely wish you happiness in the path you have chosen. You, of anyone I have ever known, deserve to smile at life. Know that you will always hold my heart.*
>
> *I love you, now and forever. JF*

He clenched and unclenched his fists, sucking in great gulps of air.

He could do this. He could fight his way free. Just as Sir Robert Linwood had at the Battle of Agincourt.

Somehow . . . someway . . .

The bitter irony of it. He stood in his study, facing Sir Robert's armor and chain mail, perched proud and gleaming in the corner. Judging.

That forceful reminder of everything honor required.

He closed his eyes against the sight.

Took another ragged breath.

The air smelled of ash. Of devastation.

Jasmine. Gone.

Never to be seen again.

Never to hear her laughter. See her crazy smile. The taste of her lips.

Allow the blazing sunshine of her soul to burn away his darkness.

Even worse, what was she returning to? A broken family and unknown future?

How he had failed her . . .

Timothy glanced down at his desk. Everything on it neat. Precise.

*Rule #104: Cleanliness is next to Godliness.*

Order. Control.

He was so bloody damn tired of control. Of honor. Of responsibility—

Something snapped. The sound nearly audible.

His arm swept the desk. One strong slice and papers, inkwell, blotter, quills, ledgers . . . everything scattered.

Crashing to the floor.

The candelabra followed, hurled straight at the mirror over the fireplace mantle. Shattered glass exploded into the room, littering the floor.

If anyone heard the noise, they stayed wisely away.

Books were next. Ripped off their shelves, thrown into a corner. A vase of flowers fragmented against the fire irons.

Timothy grabbed a fire poker and turned toward Sir Robert Linwood's armor, intent on reducing that damned symbol of honor to scrap metal.

But he froze before swinging, arm raised. Seeing himself reflected fifty different ways in the bits of mirror carpeting the floor.

Every angle the same.

Broken. Fractured. Feral. Snarling.

*He* was mangled metal.

Like that ship so very, very long ago. Blown to smithereens. Useless. Lifeless.

Everything rushing up and out.

But just as quickly, everything rushed inward. Sucked back into the vacuum of the explosion.

Imploding.

A sound broke through the room. Low and keening. Wounded.

His heart savaged his chest. The pain suffocating.

The poker slumped from his hands.

He stuffed a fist against his mouth, but it was like attempting to stop the ocean with his bare hands.

His knees buckled—he felt himself falling.

Falling, falling, falling.

Down to the floor, back up against the bookcase. Elbows on his knees, head hung between his shoulders. Hands pressing into either side of his head.

The gasping noise continued. Heaving. Choking.

Gone. Gone. Gone.

*Arghhhhhhhh.* The agony threatened to consume him.

He reached for the cog in his pocket. That talisman which had always grounded him.

He clenched it in his fist, feeling it cut into his skin. Harder. Focusing on the pain.

It wasn't enough.

Alone. He was just so utterly . . . alone.

He couldn't breathe. No matter how hard his lungs worked, no matter how fast his heart beat, the air wouldn't go in.

How could he go on—

His future stretched before him. So barren. So pointless.

Why? Whywhywhywhywhy should he live this life?

He was just so tired. So tired of fighting, of trying to be and do and say the perfect thing.

Tired of a mother who had retreated from him. Tired of a father who forced him into a narrow mold.

A life without . . . *her.*

Without his brilliant, vibrant, spunky, caring, buoyant Jasmine . . .

Was such a life even worth living?

He was crying. Sobs cut through him. Wrenching. Squeezing. Tearing.

That shocking moment of clarity.

Grinding . . . refining his soul to the hardest, purest core. Down to the few things that matter above all else.

Until there was only one left.

Jasmine.

She was it.

The one thing he *refused* to give up.

How long did the process take? An hour? Two?

All he knew was that he raised his head and the shadows in the room had changed. But, then, without Jasmine, nothing would ever look the same.

He wasn't alone.

Someone had sat down beside him, resting a head on his shoulder. A warm hand on his arm.

He breathed in her soft scent. Knew it as well as his own beating heart.

Marianne.

She stirred, wrapping a free arm around his shoulders.

He turned his head toward her. Her eyes brimming pearls.

"She is gone." His words a husky rasp.

There was no need to clarify *who* he meant.

Marianne brushed back his hair. "Oh, Timothy. You bear too much and let yourself"—*gasp*—"live too little."

A pause. She traced the path of his tears with her thumb.

"There should be more happiness in your life." She kissed him on the cheek, lips gentle. "I like her—your Miss Fleury. Surely there is a way for you to be together."

*Your Miss Fleury.*

The pain twisted deeper. He swiped under both his eyes with his thumbs.

Marianne didn't quite understand the situation.

"There is no easy way to say this, Marianne. It is something Arthur should have told you years ago. There is a time portal in the basement of Duir Cottage. Miss Fleury is not from our era. The chasm between us is insurmountably large."

Marianne's eyes went so very wide, but she didn't look jaw-droppingly shocked. Timothy told her his tale from meeting Jasmine to seeing James and Emme to driving a car to their decision to return together.

All throughout, Marianne's gaze remained surprised, but understanding.

When Timothy finished, she smiled at him. Soft and forlorn, but a smile nonetheless. "Well, that certainly explains everything. The goings on at Duir Cottage have always puzzled me. I am actually grateful for the explanation. It's much more satisfactory than Arthur running a smuggling ring or keeping a secret paramour."

"Marianne!"

They still sat on the floor, golden sunlight flooding the room.

"You need to go after her." A hushed whisper. "You are more . . . *you* when she is around. More Timothy and less Lord Linwood."

"Timothy." A harsh laugh. "I have never had the *luxury* of being Timothy."

More silence.

"Perhaps. But you *deserve* to be Timothy."

Another brittle laugh. He hung his head. "Sister, too many depend on me. The price is too high—"

"Listen to me, brother mine." Her voice suddenly edged with steel. "I do not give a *damn* about your family responsibilities."

The rawness of her words shocked his head upright. Staring.

"There. I have said it." She sat back, jaw firm and unyielding. "You have allowed yourself to be controlled by Uncle Linwood. And father before him. And peers and supposed friends and needy aunts, uncles, cousins all desperately looking to you with their hands outstretched. You. Are. Not. Their. Salvation.

"*Live*, brother. Please do not become *him*. Father was a bitter, lonely, sad man. Eaten from within by the acid of his soul."

His coarse breaths jangled in the room.

"This is about more than just our family, Marianne." Voice hoarse, cracking. "Even if I speak with Miss Heartstone and convince her to cry off. Even if I am able to slip through the portal to fetch Jasmine, the viscountcy will still be bankrupt. This affects all of those who inhabit Linwood lands. How can I turn my back on them?"

Silence.

He looked at his hand. Cut from the cog he held.

Fitting that there should finally be *literal* blood on the damn thing.

So pointedly symbolic.

Marianne's hand appeared, dabbing at the wounds with a handkerchief. Healing. Cleansing.

More symbolism.

"I remember this piece. It was the flywheel for that boat you made. So many years ago."

He nodded.

"You kept it all these years." Her implied *why?* hung in the air.

"It was"—voice cracking—"it was a talisman. What I needed to become. A gear. A cog in the machinery of our family history."

"*Oh!*" Her soft exclamation anguished. "No, Timothy. Nonononono-ono . . . you have it wrong. That was never your goal. You are not a part of the machine. You *are* the machine."

He jerked his eyes to hers.

"You *are* the boat, brother. You steer it and the rest of us will follow you wherever you go."

He turned back to the flywheel . . . staring as if he had never seen it before.

The original wheel of the mechanical ship. The piece which guided the rest.

"Set your own course." Marianne's voice was insistent in his ear. Soft. Pleading.

He closed his eyes. Allowed the possibility of her words to suck him down.

Everything in him turned inward. Narrowed down to a pinprick of sensation.

To the whoosh of air in his lungs. To the steady beating of his heart. Nothing more.

His heart.

*Ah, Jasmine.*

She *was* his heart.

Without her, he had none.

Just the thought made his pulse beat faster.

A life without Jasmine . . . it wasn't one he wanted any part of living. He faced it plainly.

To have her. To keep her. He would fight to his very last breath. Sell anything. Do anything.

*This* was the emotion which had driven Sir Robert at Agincourt. Not honor.

Love.

Pure, cleansing, perfect love.

And then, it was as if a vision opened up before him.

Jasmine seated beside him in a car, singing along to some terrible song at the top of her lungs. Turning to two small children on the back-seat—dark-haired and gray-eyed—giggling as they tried to keep up with the lyrics.

Jasmine tripping down the main stairs of Kinningsley in a high-waisted dress, scooping a wriggling baby out of a nurse's arms to cover it with kisses before turning back to him, descending behind her. Face radiant with love and devotion.

Jasmine in his arms, dressed in a silk ball gown, hair curled and tumbling about her cheeks, waltzing around the dance floor. Popping up on her tiptoes to whisper something scandalous in his ear.

Jasmine shining brilliant. Vivacious and kind. Taking the *ton* by storm, as he knew she would.

The fire ignited over his heart. But it spread, jolting through him like lightning. Filling his blood. Expanding his soul.

"Timothy?" Marianne clasped his head in her hands, turning his head to her. And then touched his dimples, flashing deep. A tear splashed onto her cheek. "Oh, Timothy," she breathed. "*There* you are. I have wondered when I would see that smiling, happy boy I once knew."

His shoulders sagged, the weight of her words settling on him. But his smile did not waiver. He clenched his jaw in determination.

"You are right, Marianne. A life without her . . . it isn't one I care to live. I will find another solution to Kinningsley's problems, even if I have to fill the long walk with machinery and establish a market in the entrance hall. Uncle Linwood will have an apoplexy."

She gave a soft laugh.

"Will you mind?" He jostled Marianne's shoulder.

"Not at all." She shook her head. "The fire and events of this last year have shown me how ephemeral life can be. Nothing physical remains of Arthur's ancestral home. All that 'heritage' supposedly lost. And yet, I feel it still thrives in the love Arthur and I have for each other. In the joy Isabel brings. Heritage is love. It lives in the stories we tell of those who have passed on."

"Marianne." Timothy gathered her into his arms. Held her for a while. "Thank you."

She cuddled against him, relaxing into his chest with a sigh.

"I love you, brother mine."

"Dearest, dearest sister, I love you too."

"Go to your Miss Fleury. Marry her. The Linwood name will survive. It always has. And you will be happy. And of everyone I have ever known, you *deserve* happiness."

His smile grew wider. The joy bubbling through him more pronounced.

He was the master of his own ship. He would steer his own destiny.

He would win her back. Nothing else mattered now. Without Jasmine, his very life turned to ash. To nothingness. He would go where she wanted to be. Live where she wanted to live.

Because any time and any place would be home to him. So long as Jasmine Fleury was there.

Jasmine loved a knight-in-shining-armor fairytale. And he intended to give her happily-ever-after.

But first, he needed a plan.

Daniel raised his head from the steward's desk as Timothy strode through the door an hour later. Scanned him from head to toe.

"May I help you, my lord?" One couldn't fault the young man's tact.

"I have spoken with Miss Heartstone, and she has released me from our engagement. I intend to offer for Miss Fleury instead." Timothy cut to the chase.

"Ah. She is an excellent choice."

"I agree. But that does leave us with the small problem of being utterly insolvent."

"Indeed it does." Daniel sat back. The beginnings of a wicked grin touching his lips. He nodded toward Timothy. "Nice outfit."

"Thank you."

Daniel's grin widened.

"Miss Fleury does have a small inheritance from 2015 which she would bring into the marriage."

"Can she transition the money into gold or gemstones so it is portable into the past? I imagine modern-cut gemstones could command a respectable price."

"Excellent suggestion. I will also have to sell off family heirlooms and anything that has value, but hopefully we can avoid turning any tenants out into the street. Beyond that, I have an excellent idea for a long term solution. It will take time to build and no doubt will scandalize my family, but given what I know about the future, it will bear generous fruit."

Daniel exhaled a long breath. He shot a gaze toward the ceiling and mouthed what looked like *'Hallelujah.'*

Timothy smiled, broad and a little wicked. "If you have a moment, Daniel, let me tell you my ideas. But be prepared. We are about to become the richest men in all of England. And be damned if it is vulgar or not!"

# Chapter 27

Where was she?

Jasmine slowly spun in a circle, trying to understand.

It just figured her path home wouldn't be straight.

After leaving Timothy the previous night, she had cried approximately two thousand gallons of tears and weathered several hundred panic attacks (or something like that). When dawn kissed the sky, she crept out, leaving a note for Timothy. Her heart dragging against the soles of her feet as she walked the miles to Duir Cottage.

Just so . . . alone. A vast emptiness expanding through her chest.

Timothy.

The arrogant, stuffy lord she had been so eager to send home. And now she couldn't begin to understand how she could live without him.

Ah, the bitter irony. Some god somewhere was having a grand ol' laugh at her expense.

But then her thoughts had devolved into thinking about all of those she had lost.

Her first family. And then her adopted one. Marmi. Boyfriends. Girlfriends marrying and moving on.

And here she was. Still alone.

Like . . . really, creepily, what-the-hell-happened alone.

She had walked down to the portal, ribbons of power swirling in welcome, tugging, pressing her forward. Eager. She had stepped into the dark depression, felt that swooping sensation of falling, falling, falling . . .

And . . . now what?

What happened?

She stood in a . . . meadow. Or was it a walled garden? An orchard?

It was hard to say with any specificity.

She was going to go with orchard. If a grove of oak trees could be called an orchard. Tipping her head to the right, she could see the wall of a wooden palisade which appeared to enclose the area. The oak trees within the space ran the spectrum between ancient giants to young saplings.

Turning around, she could see the portal clearly. A black gaping maw in the ground. A young oak tree stood next to it, its roots starting to encroach on the portal, but not quite covering it.

Okay . . .

Logical deductions were not quite her specialty, but she was going to give it a try anyway.

Obviously, in everyone's interaction with the portal, they had made one very *large* assumption:

The portal only allowed travel to a fixed point two hundred years in the past, moving between 2015 and 1815, for example.

Turns out *that* little expectation was not accurate. Because she was obviously not in 2015 or 1815 currently.

The portal could be used to travel to any time period, provided it was accessible and not buried under a tree or something else equally large.

Right.

So . . . where was she?

Logic. She could do this.

Obviously, she wasn't within a couple hundred years of 2015. Duir Cottage would be here. Modernity would be here. So either she was in a distant non-technological future, which seemed unlikely, or . . .

. . . she was in the far, far past. And that little sapling planted over the portal would eventually become the ancient oak which had guarded the portal until its death in 1812.

How old had that oak tree been? Twelve hundred years? Thirteen?

Which made this time period . . . like really, really old.

She took a couple more steps forward, hesitant to explore, but she couldn't see or sense any danger.

The area seemed to be a sanctuary of sorts. An ancient grove of sacred oak trees.

Why did the portal bring her here? What was she meant to see? And why was her heart pounding out of her chest?

There was a faint path snaking toward the palisade. Walking toward the wooden wall, Jasmine could see a crack in the logs.

A door.

She approached the door, standing in front of it for a moment. The latch was apparent. Wooden. A simple bolt.

Deep breath.

Her hand shook as she gently lifted the bar. Pulled the enormous door open.

A pastoral world lived beyond.

Trees, yes. But so much more.

Uhm . . . *wow*.

A wide ditch surrounded the palisade with a plank bridge extending in front of her.

And then beyond that . . . structures.

Conical huts sat in front of a forest which encroached around. Cattle lowed. A dog barked. Two small children tore past, chasing a runaway chicken which squawked madly.

People stood here and there, dressed in decidedly Roman looking robes, loose and belted at the waist.

It gave every indication of a peaceful village.

A Roman village . . . but still.

Jasmine crossed the bridge, trying to decide if she should continue being awestruck or if she should feel afraid.

But the fear wouldn't come. Something told her this place was safe.

The running children returned, a chicken in the taller boy's sturdy arms. His companion noticed Jasmine. Stopped. Said something to her loudly. Jasmine couldn't quite catch it. It sounded vaguely Latin-ish, she supposed. Had he just said, 'She is come'?

Or was it, 'He vomits'?

Stupid Latin.

Several more people noticed, excitedly coming toward her. She was soon surrounded by villagers talking, poking, stroking the muslin of her gown. They were all small like her, which was just crazy awesome. Jasmine could never remember being in a crowd of people and not feeling tiny. So this was what normal-sized people felt like all the time. Weird.

Hands tugged her forward, taking her along a small path around several huts.

Until there it was.

An achingly well-known house.

Different from its brethren and set apart, the large rectangular house sported a tile roof. Modest in comparison to something like Kinningsley, it still boasted a pedimented facade supported by a columned portico. The house was plastered with pale stucco, but there was a line down the right side, where newer stucco had joined with old. Had that portion of the house been damaged and repaired at some point?

And why was this place so familiar?

The crowd called, words rushing past Jasmine so fast she couldn't decipher them. Men and women darted around her. Others pushed her, urged her.

What was happening? She didn't feel threatened. Just caught up in their excitement.

The front door to the large house opened. More hands clutched Jasmine, urging her forward.

A petite figure emerged from the dark of the doorway.

Female. Dressed in a long, high-waisted blue dress with a red shawl of sorts wrapped around her body and over her head.

Looking like a living Roman statue.

The woman's eyes landed on Jasmine and then blazed with light. As if in . . . recognition.

How was that possible?

The woman clasped a hand over her mouth and ran up the short walk.

Jasmine gasped as she drew near.

It was like looking in a mirror. Seeing her own face staring back at her.

The same dark hair. Creamy skin. Egg-shell blue eyes.

Though there were differences too. The woman looked older than Jasmine. More careworn. And though their faces were similar, they were not exactly the same.

The woman's face was a little longer, her chin not quite as pointed. But still.

The woman was close enough now to touch.

Who was she?

"Minna?" The woman cocked her head, tears spilling over. And then she said it again, "Minna?" followed by a series of words Jasmine didn't quite understand.

"I'm so sorry." Jasmine shook her head. "I don't understand your language—"

The woman let out a quiet gasp. And reached out a trembling hand to touch the pendant hanging around Jasmine's neck.

"Minna," she said again. This time emphatically. Face fierce.

And in that gesture, memory flashed through.

A girl's face, urgent, terrified.

*"You must hurry, Minna. You must come. They mustn't find you. Hurry. Hurry."*

Without thinking, Jasmine repeated the words, staring into the woman's face.

Something snapped within her. Scenes and images shuffled through with startling clarity.

Words. Language.

*Jasmine sitting in an atrium beside a fountain, playing with a wooden doll.*

*Laughing with her sister. Another woman joining them. Same dark hair. Same pointed chin.*

*Their mother.*

*"Come, my beauties. Minna. Gwen. It is time for bed."*

*And then a man. Tall with curling brown hair and a smile full of love.*

*"Good night, Papa. "*

But this time the memory expanded. She could see the house more clearly. The atrium cutting up through two stories, a gallery running around the second floor. A circular oculus cut into the center of the roof overhead, letting in air and light. Bright mosaics on the floor, a dog chasing a hare while deer danced away. And the man. Her father. Dressed in a breast plate and short skirt. Knees bare. Sandals laced up his calves. Looking for all the world like a Roman soldier.

"You remember?" The woman in front of her spoke again.

And this time, Jasmine understood. The language came back to her, filled her. Latin, but not quite. A language long lost in time.

Jasmine nodded.

*Gwen.* Yes, her sister's name was Gwen.

And she was Minna . . . Maelona.

*Divine princess.*

With a sob, Jasmine wrapped her arms around the woman. Gwen crushed Jasmine to her, both of them sinking to the ground in loud tears.

Yep. The past was all about the crying, wasn't it? Was it a hazardous by-product of time travel?

"Minna . . . Minna . . . Minna," Gwen whispered. "How I have missed you. I have prayed for the portal to bring me word of you. I did not expect the gift of seeing you myself."

Jasmine merely hiccupped, her crying going straight from sobbing to gasping right on through to breakdown territory.

She had found her family. *At last.* The portal *had* taken her home.

Gwen rocked her, making shushing noises against her hair. The moment hauntingly familiar.

*Oh!* She had forgotten. Forgotten being held by her older sister. How could she have forgotten this?

"It's okay, little Minna. I have you," Gwen murmured. "You shouldn't be here, but I don't care. My heart has wept to know of you. To know that you are cared for."

Jasmine absorbed the words. Remaining crumpled in her sister's arms for a good while. Letting the emotions wash themselves out.

Finally, she dug a handkerchief out of a pocket in her pelisse and wiped her eyes.

"Gwen." She gave a watery smile. "I had forgotten. But now I remember." The words felt stilted and odd in her mouth, but Gwen's radiant glow let her know she had understood. "Where am I?"

Because that was the most important question. What had happened?

"You are under the care of our father."

"Our father?"

And even as Gwen nodded, a deep part of Jasmine knew the words which would follow.

"Yes, our father. Emrys Wledig in our language. But called Aurelius Ambrosius by others."

Jasmine forgot how to breathe.

"The King of the Britons?" she asked.

Gwen nodded.

King Arthur.

Jasmine was absolutely *literally* the daughter of the man behind the legend of King Arthur.

Making her a princess. For like . . . real.

She closed her eyes. Feeling the threads of Fate coalesce, intertwining, weaving. Pulling her across time and drawing her to those who were her own.

Back to the time period and place she had been born . . . 515 A.D.

The numbing *rightness* of it all stunned her. That all her life had pushed her toward this moment.

"Come, sister." Gwen pulled Jasmine to her feet. "Come. Father is in residence today. He is not often here, but he comes when his duties allow a brief respite. He will be beside himself with joy to see you. He has aged, but still talks of his little Minna."

Gwen led her inside the house, through a columned entrance foyer-ish area . . . and there it was. The fountained atrium of her memory.

Smaller than she remembered. Or rather, she had grown since then. But the mosaic still glinted on the floor. And now she noted the paintings. Birds and garlands chased by rabbits and prancing cats. Charming.

Gwen gestured for Jasmine to follow her across the atrium and up the stairs on the opposite side, climbing to the second floor. She ran her hand over the railing of the balcony which surrounded the atrium as they walked, entering a room over the front pediment of the house. Open shutters looked out to the grove protected within the palisade.

And there, seated at a desk covered in scrolls and quills, was a silver-haired man. Dressed in the white tunic and embroidered purple and gold toga of a Roman king. Though probably in his late fifties, he still exuded the power of a younger man.

He looked up as they entered. Eyes widening as he saw Jasmine. Eyes of startling blue. The same eyes Jasmine saw every day in the mirror.

He went utterly still and then slowly rose to his feet. Darting a glance to Gwen, as if to confirm what he saw.

She nodded. "Yes. 'Tis Minna."

He exhaled, the noise a gentle pop in the room. His face softened, and he moved around the desk.

"Daughter." The word reached Jasmine as he wrapped his arms around her. Gently. Tenderly. As if she were a most precious possession. "Though it is dangerous for you to be here, I am *so* blessed you are come."

Cue crying fit number two.

She melted into him, everything so crushingly familiar. His scent of wool and metal and wine. The strength in his arms.

Her father! She was holding her *father.*

Who happened to be the man behind the King Arthur legend . . .

Would she ever recover from the wonder of this moment?

A good while later, after crying herself nearly sick (cause, ya know, she *still* had that going on) and kissing her father's face and hugging her sister some more, Jasmine sat on a fainting couch, munching on bread and salty cheese with olive oil and wine. Listening to her father and sister.

Her father was only here for a couple of days. His duties as king kept him tethered to his larger fortifications in the south and east.

This compound was a place of worship and rest. A site so sacred not even pilgrims were allowed to visit. Its purpose hidden from the rest of the world.

"We have worried about you so." Her father smiled. "You were so young. So much younger than any of us would have wanted you to be. Usurpers were intent on making a bid for my throne and suspected the power we protect. They attacked in the night . . ." His voice trailed off.

"I remember a fire."

"Yes," Gwen nodded. "They overran us and partially burned the house. Father was away, fighting in Gaul. Mama—" A break. "—Mama was killed in the raid."

*A firm hand shook her awake.*

*"Minna . . . Minna." An indistinct face loomed over her, pulling her from sleep. Gwen. "Wake up, sister. We must get you to safety."*

*A woman screamed. Jagged terror filled with pain.*

*Jasmine lurched awake, the sounds of battle ringing. More screams. Metal clanging. The smell of smoke.*

*"Quickly," Gwen hissed. "Not a sound."*

*Jasmine clutched her sister's hand as they crept down a back stairway, fire crackling through the building. Free of the house, they ran into the night. Fog engulfing them, hiding them. Through the gate and into the sacred grove of oak trees.*

*She sensed the portal ahead, pulsing. Calling.*

*"Open the door and then run." Gwen whispered, breathless, sprinting forward. "The portal will save you. Think safe thoughts, and you will be led to the one who will be your teacher."*

*The portal was suddenly in front of her.*

*"I love you, sister mine." Gwen pushed her.*

*Jasmine stumbled forward, only to touch nothing. Just darkness and falling, falling, falling.*

*And then she was on her hands and knees in a cool, dark place. Terror stricken, she stumbled forward, finding stairs and a door. The cool night air hit her as she exited the building, branches scratching her legs, cutting her bare feet.*

*Away, away . . . she had to get away . . .*

"I remember that night," Jasmine whispered. "Poor Mama."

"She was the Keeper." Her father's eyes were gentle.

"The Keeper?" Jasmine cocked her head.

"The Keeper of the portal, child. Just as you are. Do you not know even that much?"

Jasmine shook her head.

"Your mother was the Keeper before you. But the gift passes to only one in a generation—"

"It skipped me," Gwen said with a soft laugh.

"It was you, child." Her father gave Jasmine a gentle smile. "At your birth, your mother saw signs in the heavens. She saw the power settle on you. Knew that you would be the new Keeper. But in that same instant, she was also given additional knowledge. An understanding that you would only be hers for a short while. That there was another, in a distant time who would raise you in the old ways."

*Marmi.*

"When we were attacked, I knew I had to save you," Gwen said. "The portal was the only way. As Keeper, you control it. No one can pass through unless you decree it—their lives somehow important or part of yours. Of course, it allowed you to pass through. After sending you through, I climbed one of the oak trees, hiding in its limbs until the danger passed. Praying that you would be led to the right person in the future." Gwen's eyes were hopeful.

Jasmine nodded, throat tight. She could almost *feel* Marmi's ghost drifting into the room. That familiar scent of lavender surrounded her. Breathing comfort and *home* with every heartbeat.

"I am glad." Gwen patted Jasmine's hand.

Her father cleared his throat. "The Keepers have a unique place in our world. They protect a powerful force and are more holy than kings or priests. They are always women, the maternal figure of our tribe. The mother of us all, in a sense. Your own mother had a heart big enough to love a thousand children."

Those words reverberated through her. Like a tuning fork, finally finding the right frequency. Truth.

Her mothering instincts weren't just a personality defect she inflicted on friends and the occasional boyfriend. They were the result of her mystical calling as a Keeper. The mother of her tribe.

Jasmine tried to absorb all the information. After a lifetime of living on the tiniest snippets of her past, she felt swamped with information.

She had a mother and a father. An older sister.

And she. Her. Jasmine Fleury . . . ehr, Minna . . . was the Keeper of the portal. How true it was in the end.

She had *known* that Emme and James belonged together. Had wished for Emme to find her way, and she had.

The same went for Georgiana. And then Marc.

Every person who traveled the portal was known to Jasmine. Or integral to her life in some way.

It also explained why the portal had drawn her so strongly. Like visiting an old friend. One that you could trust . . .

Marmi would have loved all of this. Jasmine wiped a tear off her cheek. And then a warmth enveloped her. Lavender. Soft. Comforting.

As if Marmi had heard her.

And then there was another presence beside Marmi.

Gentle. Whispering. Pouring through her.

Her mother.

Both of the women watching over her, guiding her.

*You have never been alone, child.* The words slipped through her mind, fine as silk.

A sense of a hand brushing against her soul.

An overwhelming feeling of love. Bright and cleansing.

Gwen slid over to her and gathered her close again, soothing.

They talked for hours after that. Not that Jasmine knew, as there were no clocks.

She heard stories of her childhood.

Of the pendant with its twining design. The dara knot a symbol of their sacred oak trees, of knowledge, of power. The quatrefoil surrounding it . . . a prayer for protection. The swirling lines mimicking the tendrils of power Keepers could sense in the earth. A gift from her mother at her birth.

Their fears for her safety. Her father and Gwen's happiness that she had been led to Marmi.

Jasmine soaked it all up. Feeling whole in a way she had never imagined.

But even in the midst of it, there was an aching sense of lack.

Something missing.

She had found her family. Had found so many answers.

But they were her past. Not her future.

In short—they weren't Timothy.

The pain of his loss was visceral. Cutting.

How she wanted to share all this with him.

But, maybe, if she could control the portal, they could find some other solution to his problem. Bring something valuable through the ages. Hope bloomed.

"You were never meant to remain in our time, daughter." Their father cleared his throat, bringing her attention back to him. "But now that you are come, I can give you that which has always rightfully been yours."

Gwen beamed at her and motioned for two servants to enter the room, carrying what appeared to be a ridiculously heavy wooden chest between them. They set it at her father's feet. He reached down and opened it with a flourish.

What on earth?!

The chest gleamed with gold coins, gold dishes, goblets and the occasional flash of a gemstone. Everything tumbled together, glinting in the sunlight.

The whole thing looked decidedly pirate-treasure-ish.

Seeing her very wide eyes, her father touched her arm. "This is your dowry, child. The portion that would have been yours had you been raised in this time period. A princess of this realm. I am blessed to be able to give it to you."

What could she possibly say? A dowry?! She had an honest-to-goodness *dowry*.

It was, like, so medieval and here's-some-money-take-my-daughter but, at the same time, so glittery and golden and awesome. And, let's face it, potentially viscount-saving—

She and Timothy . . . they could be together . . . provided Timothy hadn't gone and done something stupid, like married Miss Heartstone or worse . . .

But even *that* profound revelation wasn't the real treasure of her day.

"Thank you so much." She wrapped her arms around her father's neck "But seeing you and Gwen again has been the best gift of all."

She covered his face in kisses. Just as she had as a tiny girl. He pulled her close.

"My sweet Minna. How I wish I could keep you here forever. But my kingdom is a treacherous place and my priests foretell of dark days ahead. Though we love you dearly, you cannot remain here. It is too dangerous—"

"Sire! Mistress!" A servant ran into the room, beckoning wildly. Eyes wide. "You must come! We are being . . . invaded . . . perhaps."

# Chapter 28

Jasmine followed her father and sister out of the house, across the way and into the palisade. The servant darting ahead of them.

Her father and her sister!!! *Gah.* She still couldn't get her head around it.

Entering the grove of oak trees behind her father and Gwen, Jasmine didn't understand what the problem was at first. But then, everyone parted. As if pushed aside by a pair of enormous unseen arms.

*Oh!*

Jasmine stared. Blinked.

Rubbed her eyes.

Yep. He was still there.

Stared some more.

A medieval knight stood in front of the portal.

Like . . . a full-on, knight-in-shining armor.

Gleaming armor. Lots of it. Blazing in the sun. Breastplate thing over chain mail tunic and trousers. Metal greaves buckled to his shins and thighs. Visored helmet on his head.

Sword in hand.

Uhmm . . . a really large sword.

Raised aloft. Ready to fight through the hordes.

Who were, wisely, warily keeping their distance.

And then, the knight's head swung her way. Paused.

Down went the sword, sheathed into the scabbard at his hip.

Gloves pulled off. And then he reached for his helmet.

One tug. Two. And it came free.

Jasmine gasped. And then swiped at her cheeks, bouncing on her toes.

Because he was *here*.

Just *look* at him.

Hair tousled and wind swept. Chin stubbled.

Pale eyes the same metallic gray as his clothing.

Basically, utterly magnificent.

A fairytale.

*Her* fairytale.

Her heart threatened to beat out of her chest.

Because let's face it.

Grown men from the nineteenth century did not dress up in medieval armor, travel fifteen hundred years into the past to chase down a twenty-first century woman to tell her she had forgotten her purse.

At least . . . she hoped not.

Her father turned his head to her, raising a questioning eyebrow. "Please tell me you know this man?"

She nodded her head.

"Is he worthy of you?"

"Yes!" A sob. "Forever worthy!"

Timothy drank in Jasmine. How was it possible it had been less than twenty-four hours since he had seen her last? She stood within the small group of gathered people.

He hadn't been sure what to expect. Initially, the portal had remained rigidly closed. But he had placed his hands on the cool stone, conjuring up images of Jasmine and his love for her. Visualizing their time together in 2015.

And then it had opened.

Taking him *not* to 2015.

But here.

They must be in Roman times, judging by the clothing. When the ancient oak was first planted.

Many things made sense to him at once. Jasmine's resemblance to the woman by her side. Her speaking in a strange language to the older man. It sounded like Latin but not quite.

But he noted it all peripherally. Because there was only one prize for him.

The beautiful woman standing in the midst of them all.

His beloved Jasmine.

That delicate hand over her mouth, bobbing up and down on her tiptoes . . . exactly as he adored her.

She stopped bouncing and walked toward him, eyes pools of blue summer sky, hair curled and framing her jaw. Face incandescent.

Such joy. She *breathed* it. Optimism and happiness.

Every hope of his future.

How had he thought he could live without her for even five minutes? Much less a lifetime?

He was an idiot.

Could she find it in her heart to forgive him for ever doubting—

"Of course, I forgive you my love!" she cried, breaking into a run.

What? Had he said that—

*Oh!*

Dropping his helmet with a crash, he swept her into his arms. Laughing as she covered his face in kisses.

"You came," she whispered over and over. "You came. You came."

"Ah, my dearest love. How could I not? Without sunshine, my life ceased to have meaning."

She smiled, that huge smile which beamed straight from her soul. Like he had said—sunshine.

"And there was the problem with my list of likes."

"Your list? You came all this way because of your list?"

"Of course. It was fundamentally flawed."

She pulled back. Nose adorably wrinkled and confused.

"For example, I like the way you crinkle your nose when you are uncertain."

"Really?"

"Yes. And how you bounce on your tiptoes and giggle when you are excited." A nuzzling kiss against his throat. "I like how you sway against me when dancing in the rain."

"Mmmm, I like that too."

"I like listening to you sing to the radio while I drive. I like the little noises you make when you eat something you love. I adore how you cry over anything and everything. I like the way you kiss me—"

Jasmine obliged with a chuckle, melting her lips against his.

He pulled back after a moment. "Basically, my entire list is comprised solely of Jasmine-based activities. But there was a problem." His voice caught.

"Yes?" She pressed her lips against his temple.

"I did not have Jasmine. My entire list collapses unless you are with me. I stupidly allowed the only important part of my list to slip through my fingers. And that was just unacceptable."

"But Kinningsley. Your estates—"

"Worthless without you. My entire life . . . pointless. Daniel and I will find a way. I was a fool to think I could live without you. That I could even breathe without you." A breath. "I love you more than life. You *are* my life."

She answered him with a sob against his cheek, tangling her fingers in his hair.

His throat burned.

"Darling, promise you will never leave me again?" he choked.

She pulled back, face streaked. Impossibly beautiful.

"Oh, Timothy." She wiped a tear off his cheek. But it was futile, as another one immediately tumbled.

"Please? I will follow you anywhere you wish to go. Live anywhere you wish to live. Any *time* you wish to live. My only requirement is *you*, darling, wonderful, lovely, perfect—"

She silenced him with a kiss. Her mouth soft and yielding. The sweetest honey. He could drown in her, never let her go—

Someone cleared their throat. Loudly.

Jasmine pulled back with a start. Timothy looked past her to the stern man standing behind. The man who looked like he was waffling between tearing Timothy limb from limb and clapping him on the back in congratulations.

Gently, Timothy set Jasmine back on her feet. But she instantly tucked her hand into his.

She extended a hand to the man. "Timothy, this is my father, the real live Aurelius Ambrosius."

Shock jolted through him.

Aurelius Ambrosius?

The ancient King of the Britons. One of the last. With his silver hair and stern eyes, he looked every inch the part.

As Jasmine would say . . . *wow!*

She then turned to the king and said some words, introducing Timothy, he assumed. He bowed, formally and politely.

The king said something.

Jasmine grinned. "He wants to know what your intentions are toward me."

Collapsing to one knee, Timothy placed a fist on his chest. Surely the pose would be self-explanatory for her father. "Beloved Jasmine, would you please do me the honor of accepting my hand in marriage? I cannot offer you much more than myself. But that much I give you freely and eternally. Please say you will be my wife."

Jasmine clasped her hands under her chin. Happiness pouring from her.

"Yes! Yesyesyesyesyesyesyes!"

Timothy jumped to his feet, gathering her into another lingering kiss. Her tears mixing with his own.

"I love you," she whispered against his lips. "I love you so much, and we're never going to be apart again."

"Perfect," he said as she wiped his cheeks.

"Oh! I almost forgot! I have a dowry!" She did that tiptoe-bouncing thing he adored. "Like, a big one with gold coins and jewels and stuff. It's totally awesome and piratey. I bet it attracts dragons who want to steal it, and you'll have to wear your armor and ride out with that huge sword of yours to fight the fire-breathing monster. I'll bring popcorn and watch—"

He laughed, helplessly.

"What?" She looked bewildered. "I'll totally be rooting for you—"

"I love you, Jasmine Fleury—"

"That's Maelona Ambrosius to you, buster." She poked a finger into his chest. "I got a dowry to prove it. I will even consider sharing my pirate horde with some of your people. Though not your awful Uncle Linwood. I'm not *that* nice of a person."

"Agreed. No sharing with arrogant family members."

"I'm guessing that viscountesses don't have to share?"

"They do not."

"Good, because I'm probably going to be terrible at sharing you, too. Fair warning."

"Duly noted."

"And I know exactly where and how I want to live."

"With me, I hope?"

She laughed. "Exactly."

# Epilogue

Miss Jasmine Fleury married The Right Honorable Timothy, Viscount Linwood in the parish church in Marfield on a sunny Monday morning in August.

For the local population, Lord Linwood's wedding even eclipsed the excitement of Napoleon's defeat at Waterloo two months prior.

The couple had posted their banns and attended church together for the requisite three Sundays before the marriage. The bride was a complete unknown to the people in the parish—and American to boot—but Lord Linwood was so taken with his bride-to-be, that everyone counted her a blessing.

The bride was radiant in her gown of gold and white. Looking like a woodland goddess, if the whispered words of one old farmer were to be believed.

Lord Linwood certainly looked pleased. He had *smiled* as his bride walked down the aisle toward him, the first time anyone could remember him doing so. Gaze so full of love, there was hardly a dry eye in the congregation.

Notable guests attended the nuptials, including the Earl of Stratton and his blond wife, the former Miss Georgiana Knight, who was one of their own.

Lady Stratton waxed poetic to one and all about Miss Fleury with whom she had a prior intimate acquaintance. Lady Stratton told wondrous stories about the origins of Miss Fleury's Welsh family, including her connections to ancient Briton royalty. These claims were substantiated when servants began talking about the enormous Roman-Welsh treasure Miss Fleury brought into the marriage. A chest full of gold and jewels . . . said to rival the dowry of even the wealthiest foreign princess.

Mr. John Linwood and family did not attend the wedding. Gossip was rampant that Mr. Linwood was no longer received by Lord Linwood. Miss Emilia Linwood, who had been betrothed to the second son of a duke, came to her senses and eloped with a handsome doctor four days before the nuptials.

Miss Heartstone, who had been previously betrothed to Lord Linwood, took her broken engagement to heart (pun intended), refusing all other offers of marriage and declaring she would wait for her majority, when she would take possession of her enormous fortune herself. Her mother was most displeased.

But all of this drama was eclipsed by the happiness of the newly wed Lord and Lady Linwood.

Mrs. Arthur Knight doted on her sister-in-law and the new Lady Linwood insisted upon Mr. and Mrs. Arthur Knight remaining in residence at Kinningsley until Haldon Manor was rebuilt. It was said that Mrs. Knight helped Lady Linwood to adjust to her role as a viscountess.

In the months after the wedding, London broadsheets raved about the remarkable new Lady Linwood. Her fey beauty. Her clever wit. Her kind heart. She was declared a nonpareil of the first order.

For himself, Lord Linwood spent weeks closeted with Mr. Daniel Ashton, working on a matter of some privacy. On a Tuesday in

September, Mr. Millet, the inn keeper at the Old Boar, was startled to see a large wagon moving down high street, the words *Helm Enterprises* painted onto its wooden sides. The wagon was said to have turned down the lane to Kinningsley.

The wagon was just the start of a larger merchant enterprise. Lord Linwood had invested in steam engines and cargo transportation, which was now booming with the French threat removed. Helm Enterprises, Daniel Ashton said when questioned, described Lord Linwood's feeling about his viscountcy—a ship with his lordship at the helm, guiding them all into the future.

No one much cared what Lord Linwood did in his spare time. As long as his lordship didn't sell their lands out from under them, ensuring they retained a roof over their heads, no one gave the matter a second thought. Though many found comfort in the knowledge that his lordship would provide for them for years to come.

Fall passed peacefully, greens fading to reds and golds, finally giving way to white frost and pillowy snow on Christmas Day.

For the village of Marfield, all was right in the world.

For Jasmine Fleury Linwood, things were a little more unsettled.

She was currently standing in Duir Cottage with guests arriving in less than an hour.

That part was fine.

The problem arose when she had dismissed all the servants to return to Kinningsley . . . and then realized she needed the bread heated.

Which, without a microwave or toaster oven, posed a bit of a problem.

She stood in the front parlor chewing on her cheek, when her husband came through the front door, shaking snow off his greatcoat. Shucking gloves and his hat.

Warm morning sunlight flooded the house, catching the lighter tones in his hair.

She sighed in delight. As she always did when her handsome Lord Linwood walked into a room.

*Mine.*

He lifted his head and smiled. Dimples deep. Eyes crinkling.

He smiled often now. Easily and readily.

And quite scattered every thought from her head each time he did.

Grinning far too widely, Jasmine tripped over to him, wrapping her arms around his waist. Snuggling against his chest.

For his part, Timothy gathered her close, planting one of those kisses on her head.

"Are we ready?" he asked.

"Almost. Just trying to figure out how to warm bread. Are the others here?"

"Yes. Stratton is just tucking the horses into the barn. How are you holding up?"

"Good."

"Were you able to communicate with your father?"

Jasmine pulled back a little, nodding her head. "Yes. He and Gwen are doing well."

Her father—which still freaked her out to say, quite frankly—had made Jasmine promise to never return to their time. It was too danger-ous for her. As the portal's Keeper, she needed to stay in a time and place of peace.

But the 'No Visiting' rule did not outlaw letters. Gwen was an avid correspondent and found so many facets of nineteenth and twenty-first century life fascinating. For her part, Jasmine adored having a sister, someone who saw the world as she did. Their relationship such a pre-cious gift.

As for the rest, it hadn't taken Jasmine more than five minutes to decide to live in the nineteenth century. Though Timothy would have followed her anywhere, she knew he would be happiest here. And if he were happy, she would be happy too.

All traces of Rule-Bound Timothy had disappeared. Though The Look made the occasional appearance. Never at Jasmine herself, but impertinent ladies and boorish gentlemen were on the receiving end of it, particularly if they implied anything rude about his perfect wife. His words.

But at the moment, he was all smiles.

Today was an important day. Hopefully, the first in many such days to come.

The door opened again, admitting Sebastian and Georgiana, followed closely by Arthur and Marianne. Daniel Ashton came in last.

"I'm so excited." Georgiana clung to her husband's arm. "I could hardly sleep last night."

"Me either," Daniel chimed in. "It's been too long."

"Agreed." Jasmine nodded.

They all took places in the parlor. Timothy and Sebastian leaning into the fireplace mantle, talking quietly about a parliamentary bill. Daniel listened in, offering his opinion from time to time. Georgiana and Marianne instantly dove into a discussion of children.

But tense expectation hung in the room.

And then Jasmine heard what she had been straining to hear. Voices. And then footsteps coming up from the cellar.

James popped his head around the corner first, barely seeing a thing before Georgiana squealed "James!" and threw herself into his arms.

Promptly bursting into tears.

Arthur held back for moment. But James would have none of it and pulled his younger brother into his arms, the three siblings huddled together.

Marianne clasped her hands under her chin, tears in her eyes, leaning into Timothy, who wrapped her close to him.

Emme followed right behind James, and Jasmine ran to her, gathering her dearest friend into a tight hug.

Which meant she missed Kit walking into the room and being caught into Daniel's arms.

"I have missed you, sister." He pecked her on the cheek.

Marc and Sebastian had actually never met, so they clasped hands, introducing themselves. James and Emme did the same with Daniel.

It took only five minutes for everyone to start talking over each other. Jasmine's worry about the cold bread swept aside as they gathered for an informal meal.

As they were dishing plum pudding, James paused and said, "I almost forgot. I was finally able to see what was going on with the Linwood family in the twenty-first century. Seems like your gamble with Helm Enterprises will pay off. The twelfth Viscount Linwood currently resides at Kinningsley which has been immaculately maintained over the last two hundred years. It is listed as one of the finest stately homes still in private hands in the entire country. The viscountcy thrives as few other aristocratic titles do in the twenty-first century."

Jasmine caught Timothy's eye as James spoke. Noted the deep satisfaction. The sense of peace radiating from him. He winked, smiling widely.

Before long, the men were talking football. Totally predictable, Jasmine realized. James and Marc taking pains to enlighten those who were uninitiated in the sport.

The women chatted about Isabel and baby Arthur and hopes for future children.

All too soon, it was time for goodbyes.

"I don't like this." Georgiana grumbled against James' shirt.

"Me either," Kit agreed.

Jasmine shrugged. "It's not hard to get together. I think a spring equinox gathering would be fabulous. Who's in?"

A rousing chorus of 'me' met her ears.

Several hours later, Jasmine nestled into her husband's arms on the sofa in front of the fire in their own chambers at Kinningsley.

Snow fell outside, blanketing the world in a quiet hush of twilight. The house eerily still as all the servants had been given the holiday evening off.

"Did you have a good day, darling?" Timothy pressed a kiss into the top of her head.

"Mmmm, yes. One of the best."

A pause. The fire popped.

"Will you ever regret staying in this century with me?" he asked, voice low in the dim light.

Jasmine chuckled, shaking her head. Timothy pulled back with a questioning look.

"Ah, Timothy darling, there will never be any regrets. I am home."

A small smile. Dimple-kissed. "Kinningsley feels like home to you then?"

"No, my darling love, Kinningsley isn't home." She sat up enough to cup his face with her hands. "Home, I've realized, has never been a place for me. It is people. Gwen and my father. Marmi . . . *you*. Wherever you are, wherever you go . . . as long as I am with you"—she touched her nose to his—"I am *home*."

And after a lifetime of wandering, of never knowing her place . . . home was a wondrous place to be.

# Author's Note

A s usual, when writing a story set in the past, I have incorporated select aspects of history and then blatantly made up others. Though, be warned, there are spoilers in here if you haven't finished *Refine* yet.

Some facts that I borrowed from reality and/or history:

Lists of social rules and behaviors, like the one that Timothy Linwood follows, were not unheard of during the era. A generation later, Queen Victoria herself was raised by her mother under what was termed the 'Kensington System'—though, in her case, the system was intended more to ensure Victoria's dependency on her mother and chosen advisers—but it did specify behavior as well. Though I did not uncover an actual set of protocol rules from the era, I did study a number of period etiquette books. My favorite being an author who waxed poetic on the baseness and depravity of puns. How could I resist that?

As for Jasmine's background, modern populations of Celtic descent (Welsh, Irish, Scottish, Cornish, Breton, etc.) are all closely related genetically. Though I took liberties with Jasmine's genealogy, I assume that a child born around 480 A.D. in Wales would have purer genetic markers than those born today. Additionally, there are several modern day examples of foundlings (i.e. children found wandering without parents or history) in Britain in the mid-1980s. Some of the children still haven't found their genetic families. The missing children milk carton campaign—which died many years ago in the U.S.—saw more success and held out much longer in the U.K.

When it comes to finding the man behind the King Arthur legends, there is no shortage of candidates. The information I present on Aurelius Ambrosius and Riothamus is one of several possible explanations. The topic itself is huge and fills books of speculation, which I will spare you here. In the end, it is unlikely that Arthur was one single man, but rather several men who later contributed (with significant embellishment) to the medieval troubadours creation of the King Arthur myth.

That said, I did try to recreate what a high-born Roman-Celtic house would have looked like circa 515 A.D. Late Roman Britain was a unique mix of Celtic and Roman building styles and customs, more cosmopolitan and Mediterranean than the later Dark Ages. A visit to the archaeological site of Herculaneum outside Naples, Italy was enormously helpful in understanding the layout and interior decoration of Roman buildings.

And while we're on the topic of King Arthur, let me say that I arrived at that little plot twist in a rather roundabout way. In *Intertwine*, I had stated that the ancient oak tree had been planted in Roman times, making the tree at least 1300 years old, which is basically as old as an English oak can get. So when I got to *Refine*, I realized that I wanted Jasmine to have a connection with the portal from an earlier time period. Based on what I had said in *Intertwine*, that time period couldn't be any later than about 500 A.D. So if you ask Google what was going on historically along the Welsh/English border circa 500 A.D., you realize that lands you smack in the middle of the origins of the Arthurian legend. How could I *not* incorporate it all into the story?

Also, a small detail I never found a way to incorporate into the storyline. For those who have read the entire series, I had initially intended for the character of Auntie Gray to have a much larger role. But, as happens with a series, that changed over time. For me, Auntie Gray is a descendant of Gwen, which explains her knowledge and understanding of the portal. Though her family are not the Keepers of the portal, they are dedicated to protecting it, as Gwen herself did.

Ancient Celtic druid cultures did revere oak trees and maintained groves of sacred trees which were enclosed within a wooden palisade and encircling ditch, as described here. In fact, the word *druid* itself is derived from the Celtic word *duir*, which means oak. Hence the name Duir Cottage.

Caerphilly Castle is a lovely place to visit and remains one of the largest medieval castles in Britain. And it was, indeed, owned by the Marquess of Bute in the early 1800s.

As usual, I made up a good many things: the town of Marfield and all house names. Also, the crisis within the British fostering system was of my own creation. My apologies to all the hardworking people who take in and help those children.

For each of my books, I create a Pinterest board of all the visual references I used when writing. So if you would like to see a dara or quatrefoil knot, Caerphilly Castle, etc., don't hesitate to look me up over there. Just search NicholeVan. A huge shout-out to Jefra Linn for her awesome pinning skills and creating a style board for Jasmine's wardrobe. Whenever I needed inspiration, I would hop onto Pinterest and see what new lovely things she had pinned for me.

As with all books, this one couldn't have been written without help and support from those around me. I know I am going to leave someone out with all these thanks. So to that person, know that I totally love you and am so deeply grateful for your help!

First of all, thank you to all those who read *Intertwine*, *Divine* and *Clandestine* and sent me excited emails, asking about the next book in the series. Your encouragement and enthusiasm means more than I can say.

To my beta readers—you know who you are—thank you for your helpful ideas and support. And, again, an extra large thank you to Annette Evans and Norma Melzer for their fantastic copy editing skills and insights.

A huge thank you goes to Lois Brown for her always helpful plot suggestions and insights.

And I cannot even begin to thank my brilliant editor, Erin Rodabough. She has the amazing gift of being able to hone in on problems and provide solutions. Not to mention just being an all-out awesome friend and travel buddy. Thank you so very much.

Thanks, again, to Andrew, Austenne and Kian for your patience and being willing to play Minecraft (and Disney Infinity and JustDance 4 and Sonic . . .) for hours on end while I wrote.

And finally, no words can express my love and appreciation for Dave. Thanks for always supporting me and listening as I work through problems, even though you get exasperated when I have to explain that the *droit du seigneur* and serfdom were long gone by Regency times. You will always be my one and only knight in shining armor.

# Reading Group Questions

Oh yes, this book has reading group questions.

Why?

Well, the English professor in me couldn't publish this book without making it vaguely educational. And obviously your reading group would show excellent taste by selecting this book—reading groups don't always have to be about the classics and Oprah's Book Club. Sometimes you just need a shameless don't-judge-me read. And any book that has reading group questions has to have redeeming literary qualities, right? So you're totally justified in assigning it.

You're welcome.

1. One of the strong themes of this book is balancing your personal needs with those of your family. Where do you feel the line should be with this? Has there been a time when you felt like you had to sacrifice something important to you for the greater good of your family? If so, what?

2. This is a classic tale of opposites attract. Do you believe that people who are quite different can find love and happiness together? If so, what do you think makes such relationships work?

3. Timothy changes significantly over the course of this book. Did you find his changes believable? Do you think that it is possible for someone to really change that much? Why or why not?

4. For me, writing is only fun when I can incorporate a lot of voice, meaning there is attitude and personality in the narration—so you get a sense of Jasmine's and Timothy's thoughts throughout the book. Do you find this kind of narration more enjoyable to read or do you prefer the writer's tone to be 'invisible'?

5. When writing historical fiction, you face a conundrum. Do you stay completely true to the language of the period or do you allow it to be more modern (and therefore more accessible to readers)? Some argue that the language of the past would sound colloquial to those of the same time period. For example, a gentleman of 1813 might describe a new carriage as 'bang up to the mark,' whereas my brother would describe his new truck as a 'sweet ride.' Though the phrasing is different, the words would have the same casual meaning in both eras. Considering this, how should language be used in historical fiction? Should authors use completely modern language, instead of trying to recreate the cadence of older English, in order to more perfectly capture the sentiments expressed?

6. As a writer, I feel the look of words on the page can communicate meaning as well. Therefore, I deliberately used line breaks, non-traditional punctuation, italics and visual cues to help convey tone and cadence. Did you find this helped as a reader, making your reading flow more easily? Why or why not?

7. Alright, let's cast the movie of the book. (Cause hey, we can dream big, right?) Who plays Timothy? Jasmine? Etc. In the movie version, what aspects of the book should be thrown out, condensed or altered? Also, what should the theme love song be?

8. The book plays subtly on the word refine and its derivatives: refined, refining, refinement, etc. How do the multiple meanings of the word play throughout the book?

# House of Oak Series

Be sure to check out the rest of the books in the House of Oak series, if you haven't yet. Though the books are related, each can be read as a stand-alone novel:

> *Intertwine* (James and Emme)
> *Divine* (Georgiana and Sebastian)
> *Clandestine* (Marc and Kit)
> *Refine* (Linwood and Jasmine)

If you haven't yet read *Intertwine*, book one of the House of Oak series, turn the page to read the prologue.

# *Intertwine*

## HOUSE OF OAK, BOOK 1

### PROLOGUE

The obsession began on June 12, 2008 around 11:23 a.m.

Though secretly Emme Wilde considered it more of a 'spiritual connection' than an actual full-blown neurosis.

Of course, her brother, Marc, her mother and a series of therapists all begged to disagree.

Thankfully her best friend, Jasmine, regularly validated the connection and considered herself to be Emme's guide through this divinely mystical union of predestined souls (her words, not Emme's). Marc asserted that Jasmine was not so much a guide as an incense-addled enabler (again, his words, not Emme's). Emme was just grateful that anyone considered the whole affair normal—even if it was only Jasmine's loose sense of 'normal.'

Jasmine always insisted Emme come with her to estate sales, and this one outside Portland, Oregon proved no exception. Though Jasmine contended *this* particular estate sale would be significant for Emme, rambling on about circles colliding in the vast cosmic ocean creating necessary links between lives—blah, blah. All typical Jasmine-speak.

Emme brushed it off, assuming that Jasmine really just wanted someone to organize the trip: plan the best route to avoid traffic, find a quirky restaurant for lunch, entertain her on the long drive from Seattle.

At the estate sale, Emme roamed through the stifling tents, touching the cool wood of old furniture, the air heavy with that mix of dust, moth balls and disuse that marks aged things. Jasmine predictably disappeared into a corner piled with antique quilts, hunting yet again for that elusive log cabin design with black centers instead of the traditional red.

But Emme drifted deeper, something pulling her farther and farther into the debris of lives past and spent. To the trace of human passing, like fingerprints left in the paint of a pioneer cupboard door. Stark and clear.

Usually Emme would have stopped to listen to the stories around her, the history grad student in her analyzing each detail. Yet that day she didn't. She just wandered, looking for something. Something specific.

If only she could remember what.

Skirting around a low settee in a back corner, Emme first saw the antique trunk. A typical mid-nineteenth century traveling chest, solid with mellow aged wood. It did not call attention to itself. But it stood apart somehow, almost as if the air were a little lighter around it.

She first opened the lid out of curiosity, expecting the trunk to be empty. Instead, she found it full. Carefully shifting old books and papers, Emme found nothing of real interest.

Until she reached the bottom right corner.

There she found a small object tucked inside a brittle cotton hand-kerchief. Gently unwrapping the aged fabric, she pulled out an oval locket. Untouched and expectant.

Filigree covered the front, its gilt frame still bright and untarnished, as if nearly new.

Emme turned the locket over, feeling its heft in her hand, the metal cool against her palm. It hummed with an almost electric pulse. How long had the locket lain wrapped in the trunk?

Transparent crystal partially covered the back. Under the crystal, two locks of hair were woven into an intricate pattern—one bright and fair, the other a dark chocolate brown. Gilded on top of the crystal, two initials nestled together into a stylized gold symbol.

She touched the initials, trying to make them out. One was clearly an F. But she puzzled over the other for a moment, tracing the design with her eyes. And then she saw it. Emme sucked in a sharp breath. An E. The other initial was an E.

She opened the locket, hearing the small pop of the catch.

A gasp.

Her hands tingled.

A sizzling shock started at the back of her neck and then spread.

*Him.*

There are moments in life that sear into the soul. Brief glimpses of some larger force. When so many threads collapse into one. Coalesce into a single truth.

Seeing *him* for the first time was one of those moments.

He gazed intently out from within the right side of the locket: blond, blue-eyed, chiseled with a mouth hinting at shared laughter. Emme's historian mind quickly dated his blue-green, high collared jacket and crisp, white shirt and neckcloth to the mid-Regency era, probably around 1812, give or take a year.

Emme continued to look at the man—well, stare actually. His golden hair finger-combed and deliciously disheveled. Broad shoulders angled slightly toward the viewer. Perhaps his face a shade too long and his nose a little too sharp for true beauty. But striking. Handsome even.

Looking expectant, as if he had been waiting for her.

Emme would forever remember the jolt of it.

Surprise and recognition.

She knew him. Had known him.

Somehow, somewhere, in some place.

He felt agonizingly familiar. That phantom part of her she had never realized was lost.

The sensation wasn't quite deja vu.

More like memory.

Like suddenly finding that vital thing you didn't realize had been misplaced. Like coming up, gasping for air, after nearly drowning and seeing the world bright and sparkling and new.

She stood mesmerized by *him* until Jasmine joined her.

"Oooh, you found him." The hushed respect in her voice was remarkable. This was Jasmine after all.

Emme nodded mutely.

"Your circles are so closely intertwined. Amazing."

Jasmine turned the locket in Emme's hand.

"What does this inscription say?" she asked.

Emme hadn't noticed the engraved words on the inside left of the locket case. But now she read them. Her sudden sharp inhalation seared, painfully clenching.

Oh. *Oh!*

The words reverberated through her soul, shattering and profound.

Emme didn't recall much more of that day—Jasmine purchasing the locket or even the little restaurant where they ate lunch. Instead, she only remembered the endless blur of passing trees on the drive home, the inscription echoing over and over:

> *To E*
> *throughout all time*
> *heart of my soul*
> *your F*

---

Visit www.NicholeVan.com to buy your copy of *Intertwine* today and continue the story.

# About the Author

Nichole Van is an artist who feels life is too short to only have one obsession. In former lives, she has been a contemporary dancer, pianist, art historian, choreographer, culinary artist and English professor. Though Nichole still prefers the label 'adaptable' more than 'ADD.'

Most notably, however, Nichole is an acclaimed photographer, winning over thirty international accolades for her work, including Portrait of the Year from WPPI in 2007. (Think Oscars for wedding and portrait photographers.) Her unique photography style has been featured in many magazines, including *Rangefinder* and *Professional Photographer*. She is also the creative mind behind the popular websites Flourish Emporium and {life as art} Workshops, which provide resources for photographers.

All that said, Nichole has always been a writer at heart. With an MA in English, she taught technical writing at Brigham Young University for ten years and has written more technical manuals than she can quickly count. She decided in late 2013 to start writing fiction and has loved exploring a new creative process.

Nichole currently lives in Utah with her husband and three crazy children. Though continuing in her career as a photographer, Nichole is also now writing historical romance on the side. She is known as NicholeVan all over the web: Facebook, Instagram, Pinterest, etc. Visit her author website at www.NicholeVan.com to sign up for her newsletter. You can see her photographic work at http://photography.nicholeV.com and http://www.nicholeV.com.

If you enjoyed this book, please leave a short review on Amazon.com. Wonderful reviews are the elixir of life for authors. Even better than dark chocolate.

CPSIA information can be obtained at www.ICGtesting.com
Printed in the USA
LVOW10s2144261115

464289LV00003B/147/P